A SAM ACQUILLO LONG ISLAND MYSTERY

The Last Refuge

Chris Knopf

Ashgrove Publishing
London

ACKNOWLEDGMENTS

Heartfelt thanks to Literary Agent, Mary Jack Wald. Thanks to the following for contributions factual and practical: Randy Costello, Cindy Courtney, Sean Cronin, Mary Farrell, Whit Knopf, Meagan Longcore, Su Strawderman and Rich Orr.

CHAPTER ONE

My father built this cottage at the tip of Oak Point on the Little Peconic Bay in the Town of Southampton, Long Island, in the mid–1940s when there was nobody else around to build anything. They were all still at war, most of the young guys anyway, and the older guys were either too poor or too scared of the future – or too damaged by the Depression – to take a chance. But my dad had vision before people called it that, and he bought this nine-tenths of an acre parcel right at the edge of the bay. Waterfront, they call it now. Then it was called stupid and expensive, even though it only cost about $560 a lot.

The price of this kind of property has gone up a lot since then.

He built the house himself, a little at a time, without a mortgage. The first year he dug the foundation with a pick and shovel, laid up cinder block and put on the first-floor deck. Then he built the rest of the house room by room as he got the money, and the building materials, most of which he scrounged out of local dumps and empty lots and the handful of construction projects that were going up at the time around the city and out on the Island.

He was too old for the war, but he fought plenty at home. My dad wasn't a nice guy. He was a real bastard actually, but he treated me okay, most of the time.

I live in this place now, by myself. I was born about the time my father winterized the cottage, so for all intents and purposes, this is where I grew up. We also had an apartment in the Bronx where he stayed during the week, but my mother and my sister and I lived on the bay year round after he installed the oil furnace. I don't remember ever being in the Bronx, though he used to tell me about the room I had, and how my sister and I played in the backyard around the crabgrass and sumac trees, until 'the Negroes all moved in and scared away the regular people'. That was more or less how he put it, speaking the words with an acid fury. He was an active racist, like all the people of my father's generation I knew growing up.

All I remembered of my childhood was the restless water and neon sunset sky of the bay. The persistent breeze that could suddenly snap into hysteria and the smell of rotting sea life at low tide. I'm breathing it in now, and sometimes it seems like life's only durable reference point.

The cottage is all on one floor, with a corner-to-corner screened-in front porch facing the Little Peconic. It's the best room in the house, and it's where I sleep all year round. Beginning about early April, till a little before Christmas, I leave off the storm windows. That was why I could always hear Regina Broadhurst moaning in the night. She slept with her windows open as well, and since her house was right next door, the only thing to stop the noise was the cicadas, the flip-flip of the little bay waves, and about five hundred feet of windswept Long Island air.

When my mother died, I called a local used furniture guy to come over and take everything out of the house. Occasionally I see one of our things for sale in the window of an antiques store, or the thrift shop on Main Street, depending on its perceived value. I got $2,000 for the whole thing, which included hauling it away. They had to take a lot of stuff they didn't want, but that was part of the deal.

I held on to my dad's '67 Pontiac Grand Prix. I keep it running and drive it around the eastern end of the Island. I try to stick to the back roads during the summer season. The big stupid car has a huge engine. Traffic makes it overheat.

Because it's so big and improbably shaped, people don't realise that the '67 Grand Prix was one of the fastest production cars Detroit ever made. My dad and I retrofitted it with a four-speed from a GTO, which made it even faster. I let the paint fade into the undercoat, but I patch the rust holes as they surface. It's something to do.

My dad never appreciated the car like I did. He really only got a few good years out of it before those guys beat him to death down at the neighbourhood bar in the city where he used to hang out.

After the furniture guy stripped the cottage, I stripped the paint my mother had put over the old varnished knotty pine that covers the walls. She'd done it to get back at my father for getting killed and leaving her alone on a permanent basis, not just during the week. I re-varnished it and bought a new couch and a woodstove for the living room. Also a kitchen table and chairs, and a bed for the screened-in porch. I haven't got around to doing anything else, but the little cottage feels bigger, and even echoes a little, and at least it's wiped clean of the cluttered, congealed misery of my parents' lives.

This all happened about four years ago, after I came out here to stay. The place had been empty for a while – my mother spent her last years imploding into herself at a nursing home in River-head. My sister saw her more often than I did, even though she had to fly in from Wisconsin. I said I was too busy at the company to break away, but actually I couldn't stand to see my mother in that place, surrounded by all those demented, hollowed-out mummies. Or suffer the reproach I always imagined I saw in the contour of my mother's set jaw.

It was also true that the company had stolen a great deal of my time, including the time I should have had for other things, and other people.

My mother didn't like Regina Broadhurst, the woman who lived next door. But she liked everyone else in the neighbourhood. They would seem to be all over the place during the week, then they'd evaporate on the weekends when my father came out East to stand in the front yard, fists on hips, glaring at potential tres-passers.

Regina was tough to like, and even tougher when I moved in full time four years ago. By that time she was pushing eighty and hard as a hickory tree. Ropy, and not much of a smiler. Her white hair sprung chaotically from her head in woolly clumps. Her hands, like her knees, were all knobby and twisted up with arthritis, so she'd point at me with her knuckles when she wanted to emphasize a point. Which was often.

I had trouble escaping her because she was always calling me to come over and fix something. This was a habit she got from my father, who would look after all the mechanical systems in the neighbourhood, being the only local certified mechanic and bound by some strange force of philanthropy. Regina's husband had died so long ago he may as well have never existed at all. The house he built, which expressed the same *ad hoc* attitude as my father's, was always on the verge of general collapse. She would stand at the edge of the scrubby bed of wild flowers that defined our property line and release a single noun the way you'd send forth a carrier pigeon. Something like 'furnace,' and my father would swear at her and go fetch his tools. This was such a routine occurrence that when she did it to me the first time, I complied without hesitation.

Like my father, I swore at her under my breath. Some precedents can only be honoured in whole cloth.

The people who built this neighbourhood were all like my father. They worked at jobs that got their clothes dirty, joined unions, bought cheap furniture, and put statues of the Madonna inside big tractor tyres out on their lawns. Many spoke with accents, or at least their elderly parents did. Their boys played baseball in the street just like in the city. Their daughters were mostly pale and overweight, though a few turned beautiful right before they flew the coop.

The neighbourhood, arrayed randomly on a ragged peninsula made of sand and covered with scrub oak and mountain laurel, was little better than a squalid summertime tenement for the first thirty years it was here. It didn't help that an old brick manufacturing outfit was on an adjacent shore. Their last serious enterprise was making rubberized life rafts for the Navy during World War II. They finally surrendered about thirty years after the Japanese. After that, property values got a little better, as the houses were winterized, and real estate in general out here went supernova. But even now, in the first year of the new century, a neighbourhood like this, in a place like this, is a little like a guy in a cheap suit accidentally invited to a gallery opening.

I said I slept on the porch, but mostly I'd sit at the table and smoke Camels, drink over-priced vodka and look at the bay. I had a bargain going with Nature. She was supposed to let me do this long enough to get my fill, before shutting down all my internal organs, and I was supposed to worship her greater works, like the saltwater taffy hydrangea at the edge of the lawn, the fishy, smelly flavor of the breeze and the gaudy red-purple sky that shattered into a billion shards as it played across the Little Peconic Bay.

Late at night, usually after darkness had completely settled in, I'd hear Regina moaning in her sleep. The sound was from the damned, filled with despair. It either expressed the state of her soul, or the lady just made a lot of noise in her sleep. But it wasn't all that great to listen to, cutting across the black peace of a quiet summer night.

Happily for me, she'd stop after a little while, and I could go back to my agitation without the external soundtrack.

IF YOU spend a lot of time alone you can almost forget how to talk. The language may be forming continuously in your mind, but the mechanics can atrophy. That's why I got a dog, so I could speak out loud without technically talking to myself. The thought of bumping around inside the little cottage talking to God, or inanimate objects, or my dead friends and family, was disturbing. Eddie was a pound dog on the way to getting gassed, so he seemed willing to listen to whatever I wanted to say without complaint, if not entirely devoted attention. Other sentients have cut worse deals.

The strategy worked most of the time. Though it didn't entirely stop God or dead friends and family from crowding onto my screened-in porch to hector me with details from my massive ledger of failings and misapprehensions, usually first thing in the morning – with the vodka crackling around my nervous system, jolting me awake, my stomach in flames and my heart pumping up high around my throat.

Eddie's principal domain was the half-acre of lawn that separated my house from Regina's, and the thin stretch of pebbly beach beside the Little Peconic. These he monitored on a regular timetable, nose scanning the turf and tail spread aloft like a mainsail. Occasionally he'd shag tennis balls I hit for him with the three-quarter-sized baseball bat I kept by the side door. It had Harmon Killebrew's signature branded into the rock-hard oak grain. My father had it stowed in the trunk of the Grand Prix, at the ready for incidents of road rage.

Most of the balls bounced out toward the beach. Some went over the flower bed into Regina's yard. Eddie was mostly indifferent to Regina, though he kept one eye on her whenever she was out there hacking away at her raggedy flowers. She spoke to both of us with about the same degree of warmth. Even so, whenever she caught him retrieving a ball she'd scratch his ears. He'd give her a tentative wag, which I admit I never did.

One afternoon in the fall of 2000, I was out in the drive working on the Grand Prix, which I did whenever the temperature was above freezing and below eighty-five degrees. I was under the car on a wood creeper when I caught a whiff of something. It was strong enough, and strange enough, to stop my work. Then it seemed to disappear, swept away by the clean, dry October air. About twenty minutes later it was there again. Holding the wrench still on the bolt, I stopped turning and took another whiff. There was something primal in the air. It reminded me of a pile of leaves I'd once set on fire that had a dead squirrel hidden inside. Something corrupt, decayed.

I rolled out from under the car and stood up. Eddie stood in the middle of the lawn and twitched his nostrils at the air.

I went inside and washed my hands, then walked back out to the driveway and grabbed a heavy cotton cloth. I told Eddie to stay in the yard and walked over to Regina's house. I rang the doorbell, but she didn't answer. I went around the house and tried to look in the windows, but they were obscured by sheer, lacy blinds. I went to the back door and pounded hard on the casing. Nothing. I yelled for her. Still nothing.

I wrapped my hand in the wipe cloth and punched out a window in the kitchen door. As I reached in to release the lock, I was knocked back by the strange smell, only now it was close by and strong enough to take on mass.

'Goddammit.'

I put the cloth up to my mouth and walked around inside her place. She was in the bathtub. Black and swollen, face down in the water.

JOE SULLIVAN was almost a generic cop. Big in the gut and across the shoulders, liked to wear sunglasses, carried a Smith on his hip and a chip on his shoulder. His hair was blond and cut short. His shirt was perfectly pressed and his shoes polished into porcelain. He was a Town cop. His beat was the North Sea area of Southampton. He'd been doing it too long, I guessed, from his bored, tight-assed look and his fastidious attention to personal detail.

I sat in one of my two Adirondack chairs on the front lawn and waited for him to walk over. There were a half-dozen cars over at Regina's, most of them with bubble gum machines blinking on top. A few people were gathered, whispering at a respectful distance, but events like this are all sort of routine and dismal once you find out it's only an old lady dead in her bathtub.

'Sam Acquillo, is it?' Sullivan asked as he dropped down in the other Adirondack.

'Yup.'

'I knew your folks. Sort of. Your mom, anyway. Played with a kid down the street. Saw you around once in a while.'

I nodded.

He flipped open a little notebook when he saw I wasn't going to chat. Probably relieved.

I gave him the statistical details of time and place. We've learned it all from TV. He wrote it down with deliberate thoroughness.

'I guess you can't live forever,' he said, looking at me.

'Nobody's done it yet.'

Eddie trotted over looking alert and light-footed. All the people milling around and the blinking lights from the cops and EMTs represented high entertainment value. When he wasn't patrolling the yard, Eddie was usually more than content to just hang around under my feet. But was never one to pass up a party. Sullivan made some sort of squeaking sound with his lips and beckoned him to come closer, which he did, and got his ears scratched for the trouble. Sucking up to law enforcement.

'Know if she's got any family?'

'A nephew in Hampton Bays. Haven't seen him for a few years. Kind of a meatball. Mows lawns, or something. Saw him here in a crappy red pickup about the time I started fixing up this house. She didn't like him.'

'How do you know that?'

'She told me.'

'Name?'

'Don't remember.'

'Tha's okay. I'll find him if he's still around. Have to notify somebody.'

I was a little distracted watching them roll Regina out in a bag. That was how my mother wanted to go, in her house, but we couldn't figure out a way to look after her. It was a full-time deal at the end. Her heart and lungs were in perfect shape, but she would take off her clothes and wander around the neighbourhood, complaining about the way Harry Truman was running the country.

My sister brought in a succession of live-in nurses to stay with her, but nobody can watch a demented old lady twenty-four hours a day. It made my sister feel guilty that she couldn't be there herself, but she had a husband and a pair of dopey kids out in Wisconsin. There was never any suggestion about sending my mother out there, ostensibly because she was determined to stay in the house by the Peconic. Of course, by then, she might as well have been living on the third moon of Jupiter for all she knew about it.

'Mind if I get back to work?' I asked the cop.

He wanted to be annoyed by my lack of engagement, but I really wasn't worth the effort. He stood up and adjusted his belt, sagging under the weight of belly and ordnance.

'Whatta'ya do out here all the time?' he asked me, now more curious than friendly.

'Fix that piece of shit car, mostly,' I said, truthfully.

'Early retirement must be nice. I got a lot of time before that.'

'Didn't retire,' I told him, as I went over to the Grand Prix and rolled myself back under to see if I really needed to replace that front universal, or if it had another few years left in its sloppy mechanical soul.

IT'S NOT that easy to find a place to drink in the summer out here, for obvious reasons, but by early October the good places are mostly back to normal. Mine was loosely associated with a workingman's marina on a little cove slightly outside the busier parts of Sag Harbor. The Pequot was such a crummy, hard-bitten little joint that even regular townspeople mostly overlooked it. The inside walls were unfinished studs and wood slats that had aged into a charred, light-absorbing brown. There wasn't even an operable jukebox or Bud sign. There were Slim Jims, and lots of fresh fish year round, since the steady clientele were mostly professional fishermen.

When it got dark the night after I found Regina, I drove over there in the Grand Prix. Already autumn leaves were swirling around the streets in little vortices made by passing cars. The Grand Prix rumbled through the tangled whaling village streets of Sag Harbor like a PT boat, and I watched the leaves swoosh up behind me in its wake. The fall is a good time to be anywhere in the Northeast, but especially good to be out here with the soft-edged light and crystal salt air.

At the Pequot, you were rarely menaced by the threat of unsolicited conversation. It was a place where you could sit by yourself at a little oak table, and a young woman with very pale skin and thin black hair pasted down on her skull would serve you as long as you stayed sober enough to clearly enunciate the name of your drink. You could almost always get a table along the wall over which hung a little brass lamp with a shade made of red glass meant to simulate pleated fabric. Though the place itself was pretty dim, you could read under those lamps, which I always did. It gave me something else to do besides sitting there raising and lowering a glass of vodka and something to look at besides the other patrons or the wonderful ambiance. You could get a lot of reading done before the vodka had a chance to establish a hold.

I don't even know why I went there all the time. I guess it was some ingrained impulse to put on a clean shirt around dinner time, get in the car and drive someplace. To be someplace other than your house, at least for a little while.

'You eating?' the waitress asked, holding back the plastic wrapped menu till I gave her an answer.

'What's the special?'

'Fish.'

'Fish. What kind of fish?'

'I don't know. It's white.'

'In that case.'

'I could ask.'

'That's okay. White goes with everything.'

'You get it with mashed potatoes.'

'And vodka. On the rocks. No fruits, just a swizzle stick.'

'We don't have fruits.'

'Good, then I'm safe.'

'But I can give you a slice of lime.'

'That's okay. Save it for the fish.'

'Fried or baked?'

'Fried.'

'Okay. Fried with a lime.'

'Exactly.'

I'd been trying to read Alexis de Tocqueville, and not getting very far. It was okay, though I always felt with translated prose that I was missing all the inside jokes. But since this guy gets quoted a lot, I figured it was worth slogging through.

'I think he would've shit his pants,' said the waitress, dropping the vodka with a lime in it on the table.

'Who?'

She pointed to my book.

'If he came back he'd really shit his pants about everything that's going on now.'

'You read this?'

'At Columbia. American Studies. My dad wants to ask you about your fish.'

I looked past her and saw the owner of the Pequot coming toward my table. For a brief moment I thought I'd managed to turn a simple little dinner order into cause for a fistfight, but the way he was wiping his hands on his apron looked more solicitous than accusatory. His name was Paul Hodges, and he'd been a fisherman himself at one time, among other things, though he wasn't the kind to talk about what those other things were. He had a face that blended well with the inside of his bar. The skin was dark and all pitted and lumpy, and his eyes bugged out of his head like somebody was squeezing him from the middle. Old Salts don't usually look like the guys from Old Spice commercials, they mostly look like Hodges, kind of beat up and sea crazy. He had very muscular arms for a man his age, old enough, it turned out, to have a daughter old enough to study de Tocqueville at Columbia.

'You wanted to know the fish?'

'Yeah, but only curious. I'm sure whatever you got's gonna be fine.'

'It's blue.'

I smiled at the girl. She rolled her eyes.

'I told him it was white.'

'Yeah. Blue's a white fish, sort of. Maybe a little grey. Caught right out there north end of Jessup's Neck.'

'That's great,' I told him, relieved he wasn't mad at me about anything, since I really wanted to keep coming there and had less than no stomach to fight with anybody about anything at all. Ever again.

'Bring it on.'

He kept standing there wiping his hands on his apron.

'You're Acquillo's boy.'

I looked at him a little more closely, but no deeper recollection emerged.

'Yeah, I guess.'

'Fished with him. You wouldn't remember.'

'That was a long time ago.'

'Yeah, but I seen you around with him before. Weren't that many around here then. You knew who was who.'

'True enough.'

'Now I don't know any of these fucking people.'

I kept trying to fix him in that time, but all I saw was the old man behind the bar at the Pequot. I also couldn't imagine my father fishing. Even though he was always bringing home a bucket of seafood for my mother to clean and overcook for dinner whenever he was out from the city. Even when he wasn't there we lived on fish because that's what people without a lot of money did in those days. It was basically free, and plentiful. You wanted to put on a little style you went out for a steak, or something like pork loin. Something that came from a farm, not the old Peconic Bay that was just outside the door.

Hodges didn't look like he was in much of a hurry to go back to the kitchen. Without asking, he pulled out the other chair at my table and sat down. I suddenly started feeling hungry.

'I heard what happened to him,' said Hodges.

I focused on my vodka, but had to answer.

'That was a while ago.'

'I know. He was a guy with some pretty firmly held convictions, your father.'

'That's true, too.'

'And wasn't all that shy about letting you know what they were.'

'So you knew him.'

'Not well. Just came out on the boat a few times. Crewed for me and my boss. Done his job well. Had to keep him away from the customers.'

Hodges sat back to give his belly a little leeway and rested his elbows on the armrests of the chair.

'Never bothered me, though,' Hodges added.

'No. Me neither.'

Hodges nodded, chewing on something in his head.

'Not that I'd let him. No offence.'

'None taken.'

'How'd you want that fish again?'

'Fried.'

He nodded again.

'Better that way. You bake it you got to deal with the parsley, the custom herb-mix, the special lemony butter sauce. Fried, it's just there kind of contained in its lightly seasoned breaded batter, ready to eat. No muss.'

'Next time I'm going baked, no doubt about it.'

He registered that and finally left me alone with my Absolut and de Tocqueville. I'd almost started to get a little traction with the thing when his daughter showed up with a fresh drink.

'On the house.'

Apparently, once you actually had a conversation with the Hodges family there was no going back.

The fish was pretty good, especially inside the lightly-seasoned breaded batter. I stayed another hour and read, distracted from the packs of malodourous crew coming in off the late arriving charter boats, and a cluster of kids, probably underage, who piled into the only booth in the place, elbowing each other and goofing on the world in urgent *sotto voce*.

I walked the bill over to the girl and asked her if I could bother her father one more time before I left.

'How long you been around here?' I asked him when he came out of the kitchen.

'In Southampton?'

'Yeah.'

He pushed out his bottom lip and thought about it a minute.

''Bout forty-five years, give or take a few. Came out of Brooklyn. Don't actually remember why, or why I stayed. Fish edible?'

'Definitely sustain life.'

'Then we done our work here.'

'I was wondering about an old lady.'

'Old lady like "old," or like, "lady"?'

'No, just an old lady. Next door neighbour, wondered if you knew her.'

Hodges picked a piece of something out of his back teeth, popped it back in his mouth and then swished it down with a mouthful of beer from a glass stowed out of sight under the bar.

'At my age, old's a relative term. Which old lady we talking about?'

'Regina Broadhurst. Lived to the east of me at the tip of Oak Point. Been there as long as my folks were. Maybe longer.'

Hodges smiled at something inside his head before he answered.

'Sure. Seen her around. One of the old bitches down at the Centre.

Never said anything to me that I can recall. I don't think she's all that fond of men.'

'The Centre?'

'The old folks hangout, the Senior Centre down behind the Polish church.'

I was genuinely surprised.

'Senior Centre?'

Hodges looked at me like I'd disappointed him. He ticked off a few points on his fingers.

'First there's the two-dollar breakfasts Monday, Wednesday and Friday. Then there's the three-dollar cold cut and potato salad lunch every day. Then there's the five-dollar Sunday supper. You eat better than anywhere else in the Village and it's practically free. The worst you have to do is say a few prayers and put up with a bunch of fuckin' old bitches like Regina Broadhurst who act like you're the only charity case in the joint. Of course, they're wolfing down the same free shit you are. Subsidized, anyway.'

'I get it.'

'Not exactly. I pay my own way. Work in the kitchen. Once a week, gives me full meal privileges. Can even bring Dotty with me.'

'Dorothy,' said the girl without looking up from the small stack of cheques she was tallying up.

'You're wondering why I'd eat anywhere's but my own place.'

Hodges looked defensive.

'No. I can see it,' I said.

'You can get tired of fish.'

'He hits on the old ladies,' Dotty slid in.

Hodges gave her a little fake backhand and lumbered back through the swinging door into the kitchen. I thanked him as he retreated and asked his daughter to settle up my bill.

'He actually does it for the church,' she said to me quietly. 'For years and years. He's says he hates religion, but he does things for people. He hardly ever eats there.'

'Nothing wrong with a good deed.'

She seemed to be taking her time with my cheque. Stalling.

'Why did you want to know about Mrs Broadhurst?' she asked abruptly as she handed over the slip.

'She's dead. They fished her out of her bathtub today. I found her.'

'Oh my God.'

'Just wondering if your Dad knew her. He's been around here a long time. She didn't seem to have any family or friends.'

'He's going to be sorry he called her a bitch. You should have told him right away.'

'Probably should have. But don't be too sorry. She was a bitch.'

She almost smiled at me despite herself.

'That's very harsh.'

'I know. Speaking ill of the dead. God doesn't like it.'

'God doesn't care. People do.'

'Apologise for me,' I told her as I started to leave.

She stopped me. 'I know Jimmy. Or at least, I used to, sort of.'

'Jimmy?'

'Jimmy Maddox. Her nephew.'

'Really.'

'Wow, like a real asshole. I knew him at school. At Southampton High School. I'm sorry to talk about somebody like that, but some people you just can't like.'

'It's okay. He's not the dead one.'

'I guess he's still alive. I don't know. I haven't seen him for a long time. He got into bulldozers or something.'

'Construction.'

'Big earth machines. Pushing lots of shit around. It would suit him.'

'Lives in Hampton Bays.'

'I didn't know that.'

'That's what his aunt told me. She didn't like him, either.'

'Charming.'

'No other family?'

'That's all I know about. Jimmy's parents died when he was still in high school. I don't know what happened to them, but he was the first kid I knew who lived in his own apartment. But unfortunately he wasn't cool. He was just fucked up and pissed off all the time.'

'Helluva way to live.'

'Dumb way to live, if you ask me.'

'Yeah,' I said to her, finally leaving, 'only an asshole would live like that.'

I'D PRETTY well forgotten about the whole thing with Regina after a few days. A talent for forgetting was something I'd cultivated since moving into the cottage. I also worked on my body, which was less than it was, but good enough for my age, considering. I'd wanted to be a boxer in my twenties – actually fought a little to help pay for night school. The only Franco-Italian boxer in New York was how I billed myself – in my own mind. I was too small and too light to be much of a hitter, so I figured myself a finesse guy, which people expected from me, being white. In those days, white people were supposed to be genetically smarter than dark-skinned people, so everyone figured if I could dance around the ring it was proof of my brilliance. This I knew from the dawn of cognition to be complete horseshit, despite my old man's attitudes. But I was smart enough to know getting beat into pudding by another boxer was a shortsighted operating strategy. Better to get in and out of there quick and do maximum damage to the other guy's self-confidence in the early rounds. Fool him into thinking you were actually somewhat of a contest. You win more fights that way and get to keep most of the face you were born with.

More than anything, boxing had made hanging around gyms a habit with me. Decent conditioning was also prolonging suicide by alcohol, but that couldn't be helped.

Deep in the pine barrens above Westhampton a rummy old ex-cop ran a youth club boxing school and gym for retired military, other cops and people like me who'd rather cut their balls off than walk through the doors of a typical health club. I know that's a kind of reverse elitism, but screw it.

The guy's name was Ronny and his gym was called Sonny's, which made it authentic, at least, in that respect. It was off-white cinder block on the outside with pale green cinder block on the inside. The lighting was a little less dingy than the gyms in the city. The bags, ring and other equipment was tired but solid, and the stink was just within tolerable limits. Most of the kids were Shinnecock Indians and blacks, or a mix thereof, and the 'coaches' were all local municipal thugs. I went there about three times a week to jump rope, do some calisthenics and spar with whoever. Usually one of the kids. I had to avoid the more serious guys so they wouldn't pester me all the time into what they figured would be an easy way to nurture their egos.

They always say you're supposed to pick the toughest guy in Dodge City, hurt him badly and conspicuously, and the other tough guys would leave you alone. Rarely worked, since there was usually a reason why the toughest guys were the toughest. But a bigger problem for me now was being fifty-two years old. So instead I just broadcast a don't-fuck-with-the-crazy-old-man vibe, hoping to plant a seed of doubt with anyone wanting to exercise his dominance instinct. This, in fact, had worked pretty well so far.

I was at Sonny's working on the sand bag. The cop, Joe Sullivan, was there lifting some free weights. He ignored me for a while, then came over and stood next to the bag. I ignored him and kept hitting the bag in the loose pattern I'd been hitting it with for about thirty-five years.

'Found any more dead old ladies?' he asked me when he saw I wasn't going to acknowledge him just standing there.

I kept working on the bag.

'Hey, just a bad joke,' he said after another minute.

I held the bag still with both gloves.

'Not really,' I said, 'I've heard worse.'

Sullivan shifted his top-heavy body weight from right foot to left.

'I haven't dug up any nephew. You sure you don't know the kid's name? I mean, she's not even planted yet, and we gotta do something with the house. Haven't found a will.'

'No will?'

'Not that anybody can find. Not that anybody's really looked, I should say. Usually there's family that just does everything. I'm not really supposed to be involved in this shit, but I hate to hand the whole thing over to the court in Riverhead, where they'll just pay McNally to settle it out, and I hate that dumb fuck of a lawyer. I guess it doesn't matter. I just know what happens when the court has to handle everything itself. I don't know why I give a shit.'

Municipal guys on the eastern end of Long Island would rather sell their souls than concede to other New York agencies. There was often talk of seceding from Suffolk County itself. The spirit of disenfranchisement runs deep out here.

I hit the bag a few more times, trying to reestablish the pattern.

'Jimmy Maddox,' I said to him as he was about to walk away.

'Huh?'

'Jimmy Maddox. That's the name of her nephew. Works construction on heavy equipment. Don't know where, though I'm guessing he's still in the area.'

'I think I remember that guy. Didn't know he was her nephew.'

'I saw him a few times, like I said, hanging around her place. He could be her only living relative.'

'Now that I got a name, I can find him. That house on the bay's gonna be worth something.'

'House is pretty beat up.'

'Nah, they'll just bulldoze it and put up some big honkin' postmodern. Jimmy could handle the dozin' himself. It's the land on the bay that counts. Nobody cares about the little shit boxes that're sitting on it. No offence.'

I stopped working the bag and held it still between my gloves.

'I can help take care of this if you still want,' I said to him.

'What do you mean?'

'Can you get them to make me the executor?'

'You can't be an executor if there ain't a will. You gotta be an administrator.'

'Okay then, can you get them to make me the administrator?'

'Yeah. I think so. Like I said, nobody really wants to fuck around with any intestate shit. Especially with an indigent.'

'Regina wasn't indigent.'

'Sorry. You know what I mean. No family.'

'Just the kid. Make this administrator thing happen and I'll go talk to him. If he wants in, then I'll cut out. But more'n likely he won't know what the hell to do.'

'You're not kidding.'

'I'm used to looking after the old broad's stuff. It's part of my family heritage. Just get me the papers I need. I don't want to have to work at it too hard.'

Sullivan stood there silently until it sunk in that he'd achieved the goal he'd set himself to. Made him a little perky.

'Okay. That's really cool. I'll talk to the town attorney – they know how to deal with Surrogate's Court, get you some kind of administrator papers or something. If you got the time to get on it now. I really can't. That's great. That's a help.'

He lingered a few more minutes like he'd have more to say if I'd made it easier for him. Eventually he drifted away as I built up my pace on the bag, hitting it a little extra hard, hurting my wrists, and getting a little winded in the process. What is it about human interaction that makes me feel so sick and ill at ease? I am going to grow old and die without ever learning how to achieve common discourse, free of implications that extend far beyond the importance of the moment.

A FEW days later I was in the Village to do my monthly banking. It isn't really necessary to do this in person anymore, with ATMs and PCs. But I didn't have a PC, hardly ever used my ATM card, and never got over the old-fashioned habit of checking everything out with some semblance of a human being. Maybe I did it because banks would rather you didn't, even though they had the tellers there for anybody to use. Most of whom were, by training, surly and aloof. Which suited me fine.

The inside of the bank was standard rehab coral and chrome. The tellers were lined up along one wall manning a mahogany palisades you assaulted after passing through a gauntlet of brass poles and velvet rope. Along the other wall were desks that were supposed to seem friendlier, but in fact felt less approachable. That's where Amanda Battiston sat and conducted business with a continuous but graceful rhythm. She was what they called a personal banker, somebody you got to talk to if you had a big account and lots of juicy business with the bank. Which I didn't, but preferred to deal with a personal banker anyway.

Her husband was the branch manager. He sat in the only enclosed office you could see from the floor. That's where he met with local business people and out-of-town customers from New York City and other faraway places. He was younger than me, but he was a local and I remembered him and his family from when I was growing up. When I first opened my chequeing account he tried to engage me, but I preferred his wife. I didn't like the way his midriff filled out the lower half of his shirt or his smooth meaty handshake. Plus, she didn't seem to care that I didn't have a whole lot of money, even though her husband thought I did. Otherwise, he wouldn't have even looked at me.

Amanda was a little shy of forty and well organized. Her hair always looked freshly combed, though obviously un-permed and secretly on the brink of rebellion. Her olivey skin tone saved her from a genuine need for makeup, though she used some anyway. She had a set of green eyes with the hypnotic quality that came from an excess of colour and contrast. I rarely saw her up from her desk, but when she moved it was quick and young. It made me think of tennis shorts. Though I rarely saw them speak to each other, her marriage to Roy seemed to enclose her like a crystalline display case.

'Mr Acquillo, your free-chequeing status is in dire jeopardy,' she said to me without looking up from her computer screen.

'I didn't know I had any status to jeopardize.'

'Yes sir,' she tapped at her keyboard, having pulled up my accounts when she saw me walking across the parking lot, 'maintaining a minimum balance in the ChequePlus account affords you unlimited free chequeing.'

'So the bank covers all my cheques.'

'Just the cheques themselves, at a dime a pop. Not bad if you think about it.' She looked at me out of the tops of her eyes, waiting for me to make her decision official, which I always did.

'I can get it back up to the minimum. I got a cheque here.'

'I'm sure you're getting great service on your investment account, but don't forget we can handle that for you here as well.'

She began to type in the deposit information while I wrote out a cheque against the tattered remains of a money market account left over from my marriage.

My ex-wife used to try to manage my money. She was insulted when I wouldn't let her. She saw it as an affront to her intelligence. It wasn't, I just had a poor kid's fear of losing everything if it drifted too far from my immediate grasp. I stopped feeling that way long after this particular incision had been opened up in our relationship. Nowadays, I'd be more than happy to let her manage anything she wanted – she was naturally better at most of those things than me, even though she never got a chance to exercise her talents – but that's just another of the lamentable ironies that entangle my life.

Roy came out of his office and pretended not to see me so he didn't have to relive my rejection. Amanda looked up at him neutrally as he passed by. She muttered something about picking up extra food for dinner, as if seeing him jarred a guilty conscience. I took Roy to be a guy who would care about the incidentals.

'Everything is as you've requested,' said Amanda as she swiveled the computer screen around so I could see. 'The deposit will take a day to clear, then you'll be okay as long as you don't let things slip past the minimum.'

'I'll be alert.'

'Did you know Regina Broadhurst?' I asked out of the blue, enough to surprise myself as much as her.

She looked at me blankly, but nodded, 'Yes I did, as a matter of fact. She just died.'

'Yeah, I know. I found her myself.'

Her shoulders dropped in sympathy. 'I'm so sorry.'

'That's okay. It's just that I got myself into a situation where I have to talk to her nephew, who's supposed to be her only next of kin. You know if there's anybody else?'

'I know very little about her. I heard of her death from the people at the Senior Centre. She was a friend of my mother's. That is, they knew each other. I don't know if I'd say they were really friends. I think they worked together years ago.'

'Regina was sort of a hard drink.'

'She wasn't very pleasant. Are you handling her affairs?'

'I didn't mean to. I'm just the next-door neighbour. I don't know, I got myself stuck with this, like I said. Just thought you might know about the nephew, Jimmy Maddox, since you've been out here all along.' 'Not really all along. I was away for quite a while. Like you,' she said, and then suddenly looked embarrassed, as if caught with stolen knowledge of my personal life.

'My mother, on the other hand,' she said quickly to cover the moment, 'would have known, I'm sure. Only she's gone, too. They spent time together at the Senior Centre.'

'Sorry. What was her name?'

'It was only about a year ago. Julia. Julia Anselma.'

'*Italiana. Va bene.*'

'Battiston isn't really as pretty, is it?' she said, this time embarrassed that she'd shared a private little bit of her own.

'No,' I admitted, 'it isn't.'

She scanned the room as if awakened to the intimate drift of the conversation. She sat up straight and tapped a few times on the computer keyboard, covering her tracks. I got up to leave.

'If you want to know more about Regina,' she said without looking up, 'you probably should stop over at the Senior Centre. It's quite a tradition with local people. They'll probably know a lot more.'

'I'll do that. Thanks for the information. Regards to Roy.'

She smiled a twisted little smile and nodded, looking a little unbalanced. I didn't want to disturb her, but I seemed to be doing it anyway. So I smiled back, gently I hoped, not wanting her to be afraid of me or regret that we'd talked. It only made her look more intently at her monitor.

The sharper angle of the autumn sun was rinsing away the remainder of summer's colour. Still, it was clear and the air did little to interfere with the light that shot down Main Street, careening off the worn Mercedes and Rolls-Royces of the year-round rich, and the service vans and dented pickups that reclaimed the village off-season. I bought some flavored coffee and a croissant at the coffee place on the corner before driving back up to North Sea – avoiding eye contact with the tradesmen more embarrassed than me to be seen in a Summer People hangout.

In the mailbox was a bundle of death certificates and a letter naming me administrator of Regina Broadhurst's estate, pursuant to a hearing by the Surrogate's Court, which the Town Attorney, Mel Goodfellow, circled in pen and noted was pro forma, so I didn't have to show up. I was surprised and mildly impressed with Sullivan's prompt action. He must have really wanted this thing off his back.

When I opened the door to let Eddie out the phone was ringing. I pushed the receiver into my ear with my shoulder so I could use both hands to dump a tray of ice into the ice bucket. It was Amanda Battiston.

'I'm sorry if I was short with you.'

'You weren't short.'

'Roy gets really annoyed with me when I talk about my mother.'

'We were talking about Regina Broadhurst.'

'I said they were friends, but mother really didn't like her. She called her "That Woman".'

'Regina had that effect on people.'

'I know.'

'I'm sorry if I got you in trouble with Roy.'

'He doesn't know you're not an Aff-1.'

'Aff-1?'

'Top affluent account. Minimum seven figure net worth.'

'Definitely not Aff-1.'

'He doesn't like it when locals do well. But he likes their business.'

'I could ease his mind.'

'No. That's all right. I just didn't want you to think I was rude.'

'Some time maybe we could get a cup of coffee and talk about your mother and Regina. When you're not worried about Roy looking over your shoulder.'

'I couldn't do that.'

'I understand. Anything else you can tell me, just give me a call. You obviously got my number.'

'It's on your account information. I hope you don't mind.'

One of the few things I appreciated about Abby, my ex-wife, was she never felt the need to apologise for anything. She was often wrong, but rarely in doubt. It seemed like a habit with most women to get you to say that something that was clearly all right was, in fact, all right.

'Figure out a time when you can have that cup of coffee and you can make it up to me.'

'I suppose that would only be fair.'

'Okay,' I said, 'Call me when you can.'

'Okay.'

Eddie barked at me from the side door to let him in. I scratched his ears and gave him a large dog biscuit, the consummate joy of his life. He waited while I gathered up the ice bucket, a glass, a bottle of vodka, and a pack of cigarettes, so the two of us could enjoy our favourite consumables out on the porch together. The Little Peconic was calm, a grey mineral mass flecked with scintillations. The far shore, a grey-green hump trimmed with huge sandy cliffs, hid partially in the coming mist. The pink grandiflora hydrangea at the edge of the lawn had finally succumbed to brown, and would stay that way until the spring buds pushed them off like organic litter. I built my first drink of the day and listened to the noisy complaint of seabirds and insect life, hard against an approaching winter and reluctant to pack it in. It felt like more than the season was priming for change. But unlike the life around me, I'd wait for it in silence, void of anticipation, reluctant only to rush the inevitable.

I FIRST made love to Abby on a mouldy pool table in the attic of a half-abandoned fraternity house on the Charles River. It was a time when fraternities were out of political favour, so the declining membership had consolidated down on the lower floors, leaving a large garret to the dust and rats and me. I was on a government scholarship to MIT. Abby was at Boston University. She lived in an apartment next door. At the time, sex was about all we had in common, though we rarely had time to notice. That would come later. We kept at it straight through my college career, which ended the year it started. It took ten years of night school to get my degree. I loved to learn, I just had trouble with authority. And money.

But that first night I wanted to live for a million years. Naked and wet, mostly drunk and seething with sexual insanity, we stood wrapped in the pool table cover and watched the lights of Cambridge fracture and re-form on the surface of the river.

The walls of the attic room were lined with books. It was furnished with cracked and scuffed red leather Chesterfields and a ratty, oversized oriental rug. I felt like a barbarian squatting between the marble pillars of fallen Rome. And incidentally, screwing one of its princesses.

Her full name was Abigail Adams Albright, which accurately reflected her family's tirelessly vigilant social pretence. I think she might have been a brilliant woman if she'd given herself the chance. If she hadn't been born just a few years too early into a family that was already a hundred years out of date. I admit with shame that I was awed by her family's self-prepossession, by the way they slouched comfortably within a social order presumably anointed by God. I married her partly because I thought old family poise and bone structure was something you could suck up through exposure, like sunshine.

Abby was a pretty girl when I met her, in a big skulled, big blond kind of way. As she aged, her skin and overall shape held up remarkably well, but her expression grew tight across her face until it formed a kind of mask that I used to think I could reach over and peel off.

I lived in that attic for two years after dropping out of school. Abby went on to graduate. I've actually forgotten what her degree was in. Maybe I never knew. I worked at whatever I could parlay into a job in industrial design. That's what I wanted to be – an industrial designer. I didn't know what that was, but it seemed to fit. That I succeeded eventually means something, but I can't tell what. I often wonder about it when I'm sitting on the porch looking out on the Peconic, when the bay water begins to look like the murky Charles and the buoys grow into the implacable towers of MIT.

Before I went to bed I woke up Sullivan. It was later than I'd realised. He was unhappy, but tried to hide it. I heard some feminine snarling in the background. Muffled but edgy. Sullivan spoke louder to cover it up.

'No, we didn't do an autopsy on Regina Broadhurst. Old ladies croak. It's standard procedure. They get old, they croak. Boom. I think an autopsy report would say, "one old lady, deader 'n shit". End of story.'

I nodded with understanding, even though he couldn't see me.

'Did you see anything on her head when you pulled her out of the tub? You know, like a bruise or blood where it hit?'

'I don't do the pulling. That's the county coroner. You'll have to ask her. Or the paramedics. I don't even think the coroner got involved.'

'No other bruises or marks that you remember?'

'Jesus, you think I study week-old cadavers? I don't even like to think about it. Yech. I'm sorry. I appreciate your help, but I gotta get some sleep. You oughta go to bed yourself.'

'Sorry. I didn't realise how late it was.'

'That's okay.'

'Just one thing.'

He sighed.

'Where's her body?'

'Coolin' at the coroner's. Which is also standard procedure until some family member tells us what to do with it, or it gets past some statutory time limit. I don't know what happens then.'

'The family could order an autopsy.'

'If the family turns up they get the body. It's up to them from there. This is usually what happens. You want to know more about it, I'll have to ask around.'

'No, I'm sorry. Go to bed. Just call me when you get a fix on Jimmy Maddox.'

It was quiet on the other end of the line for a moment.

'I got a fix. I got a place where he's workin'. From a builder. I forgot about it.'

'Great.'

'It's on my desk. I'll call you with it tomorrow. I gotta go now, my fuckin' wife's gonna kill me.'

After he hung up I put the portable phone on the table and lit a cigarette. The night was thoroughly established. The bugs were buzzing and little bay waves were slapping at the beach. It was totally dark over at Regina's house. And quiet. No moaning.

Eddie jumped up on the bed and spun around a half-dozen times while scratching up the bedspread before finally dropping down. He looked at me like, 'okay, man, time to sleep.' I told him to stay, but he followed me anyway when I left the porch.

I went out to the car and got the heavy Maglite and my tool chest out of the trunk. I dug out a ten-pound persuader and a cat's paw, and stuck them inside my belt. I put a big old Craftsman screwdriver and a pair of vise grips in my back pocket. The neighbourhood was silent as a cathedral. All you could hear was the tiny surf breaking on the off-white, sea-polished pebbles that lined the bay. No wind.

Somebody had put a padlock on Regina's front door. It didn't look like much. I tucked the cat's paw between the padlock bracket and the door jamb and gave it one good thwap with the little sledge. Almost. Another thwap and it was off. I sat down on the front stoop and looked around at the other houses nearby. No lights came on. Sleeping the sleep of the righteous, or just indifferent. Or wary. Skills learned in New York City.

I had a key for the door. Eddie padded silently up the walk and slid past me through the door. As I figured, the power was off. Everything was still basically undisturbed, though someone had neatened up the living room and cleaned out the dishes that had been left in the sink. The broom closet looked like it hadn't been used in a while. There was just a faded cotton robe hanging by a hook on the inside of the door and some beach towels on a shelf. Eddie scanned the baseboards, snorting into the cracks and corners. I warned him not to bark.

I looked in the drawers of the tall hutch in the pantry where I remembered Regina kept her chequebook for those rare moments she paid me back for something I bought her. The papers stuffed in the drawers were carefully organized. This surprised me. I remembered Regina as an indifferent organizer. The house still smelled like death.

I found the basement door and went down to look at the fuse box. I made Eddie wait for me at the top of the stairs. The mildewy smell was sticky sweet and mildly nauseating. The flashlight defined a tight little island of light and threw big black shadows against the walls. Something skittered across the concrete floor. Eddie whined, but held his post. The main switch was off, so I threw it back on. The light above the panel snapped on. That was too much for Eddie. He broke ranks and ran down the stairs.

'Come on back up. Too many critters down here.'

He was reluctant, but followed me upstairs. In the light I could see the place had been professionally cleaned and organized. I went back to give the tall hutch a better look. Newspaper clippings, old travel brochures, some handwritten notes with indecipherable signatures. A stack of tear offs from utility bills bundled up in a rubber band. Two boxes, one with cancelled and one with unused cheques. Harbor Trust. No chequebook. I slipped the used cheques and bill records into my pocket.

The bathroom still held a faint residue of ammonia that almost disguised the angrier smells. I checked out the tub. It was almost polished clean. I pulled Eddie's nose away from the toilet. The bath towels were laundered and folded over the towel bars in a way that suggested a nicer hotel. The medicine cabinet was empty. I looked around for another place Regina might have stored drugs. Nothing but bath linens and boxes of Kleenex.

I was about to move on to another room. I flashed the light around the unlit corners one last time. There was something on a narrow shelf above the spotless bathtub that I hadn't seen initially.

It was a heavy, black neoprene plug. It was tapered like an ordinary plug, but also threaded. It had the usual chrome pull ring, but no chain. Not surprising since there was nowhere in the tub to attach the chain's other end.

Something about the plug reminded me of factories, heavy machinery and guys in orange hardhats. My world.

Most design engineers pull a few years apprenticeship out on a plant floor as part of an assembly team, or serving as some kind of low-level QC grunt with a clipboard and an over-compensating air of importance. Getting a feel for what the applications boys go through to make your designs work in the real world. I liked being there, though I was just as keen on getting out. So I joined the first R&D lab that would have me and stuck my nose directly into a bunch of test stands and lab equipment. We messed around with a lot of nasty chemicals. Even before OSHA there were strict procedures regulating the use of caustics and corrosive acids. Most labs had special sinks that would drain into lined containers for toxic waste disposal. These sinks were usually stainless steel or some kind of exotic ceramic you could clean of residue from the evil shit we'd dump down the drain – which was really just a big round hole, unless for some reason you meant to contain the waste fluids, in which case we'd use a specifically engineered neoprene stopper.

Exactly like the one Regina Broadhurst apparently used to contain the water in her bathtub. It looked brand new.

THE NEXT morning I was up early, and after giving Eddie a chance to take care of things, opened the door for him to jump into the front passenger seat of the Grand Prix where he liked to sit with his head out the window. The air was agitated but clear. The smell was young and fresh, though a mouldy whiff of burned out vegetation recalled the dry hot summer. When its windows were down the Grand Prix sounded like an injured B-52. They didn't care much about aerodynamics and exhaust flow back in 1967. You needed the normally aspirated, 10:1 compression, 385 horse, 426 ft. lb. torque V8s just to drown out all the wind noise.

Every kid I grew up with knew how to maintain and repair heavy V8s, and in-line 6s that powered all the cars in those days. All sloppy American cars, except for the VWs or the occasional MG. Open the hood of any car built today and you'll see what only automotive engineers understand. Modern cars are run, maintained and monitored by microprocessors, so you can't do anything without the diagnostic technology that jacks into interface connectors distributed around the engine compartment. Regular car mechanics have been reduced to computer jocks with a little grease under their nails. It's all for the good, I guess, since it means better cars and less dependence on a class of trade that hadn't exactly earned the Nobel Prize for commercial integrity.

But, say you know your way around that mess of multi-coloured wires and plastic connectors. If you get close to the actual engine you'll notice a number of thin metal tubes arrayed along the top of the block under the air cleaners that used to sit on carburettors. Only now they filter air going to the little conduits of the fuel injection system. Pop off the air filters of ninety-five percent of the cars made in the world today and you'll see a strange little nickel-plated or extruded plastic housing with a vacuum line sticking out of it. Also a three-pin connector with red, white and blue wires trailing off into an untraceable tangle of control wiring. Its purpose is to introduce a minuscule dose of a specialized organic compound. The compound vapourizes at slightly below normal atmospheric pressure and disperses evenly into the air stream flowing through the filter on its way to the cataclysm of internal combustion. Retrofitted through a custom configuration to the throat of the hungry four-barrel in my Grand Prix, this tiny bit of late twentieth-century technology was responsible for about fifteen extra horses. Since I already had almost 400 in the stable, this wasn't such a big deal. It was more important to all the new cars built around the world that shared a need for greater power, better fuel efficiency and cleaner emissions.

When added to the revenue stream of the company that owned and licensed the technology, it was also responsible for about eighty-five million dollars a year.

It was called a SAM-85, which every mechanic assumes is some dumb engineering acronym with a model number, but it's actually a name. My name. And the year the company got the patent. The damn thing was my idea. It's my legacy to mankind. And I'm sure mankind would just about give a rat's ass if it knew.

I lit a Camel and took a sip from yesterday's coffee, stowed in the aftermarket cup holder mounted to the shift console. Still tasted like French Vanilla.

I'd gone to bed thinking about Regina Broadhurst and woke up doing the same thing. It was annoying, but predictable. She'd occupied an unimportant, but irritating little spot on my consciousness for my entire life. I never really knew that much about her. I just knew she moaned in her sleep and pissed off my old man. Had a crummy little cob-job house and a load of arthritis that probably tormented her every waking hour. Probably couldn't bend too well, or pick things up, had trouble digging in her garden or getting in and out of the bathtub.

The twin exhausts from the Grand Prix burbled in my wake like a pair of inboard Mercs. Eddie's head was out the window, ears pinned back and teeth showing in a grim smile. The sun was bright again and everything looked like it was studded with cheap stage jewellery. The air smelled like a clear conscience. The bay was flat but roughed up by the sturdy breeze. The gulls were trying to look regal, heads to the wind, mustered at attention along the narrow piers and breakwaters. I got Imus on the radio and stopped for a huge hot cup of Viennese Supreme to replace the cold French Vanilla. I clutched it between my legs, warming up my nuts.

This time of year the back roads were a little less travelled, especially during the week. I passed a few pickups and midsized American cars that typecast the regular locals. They'd mostly peeled off from Montauk Highway, the area's main two-lane artery now choked every morning with incoming traffic.

It was becoming almost impossible to live as a middle-class wage earner within the weird economics of the Hamptons. The only real industry was serving the wealthy who bought and sold things with a logic that was both outlandish and incomprehensible. Yet siphoning off even a little of that ocean of money was a lot more difficult than you'd think. And even when you did, it cost so much to live out here that holding on to it was even more difficult. You could buy Venezuelan coffee futures and first tier art on Main Street in Southampton Village. But the closest affordable grocery store was twenty miles up island. The locals used to pass houses from father to son before they could reach the open market. But now the prices were so high few could justify not cashing in at a rate ten times the family price. So the native housing inventory was shrinking fast. More and more sons and daughters were traveling in from the west, or giving up and moving permanently to other places.

But some hung in there. They just couldn't give up the air and the light, the canopies of maple leaves that billowed overhead like huge green clouds. The sea-sculpted beaches that stretched to the horizon and the oily fish stink of low tide.

I stopped at the hardware store. Five or six guys were there to look after three or four customers. Personal service was their forte. I showed the first guy I saw the big neoprene plug. He was prematurely grey, but relaxed. The hardware business had been good to him.

'Have something like it. Not exactly.'

He brought me over to the plumbing aisle. We both dug around in the parts bins and eyeballed the shrink-wrapped stuff hanging off display pegs.

'They might have 'em at a plumbing supply. Looks kind of industrial.'

'It is. I just thought I might have bought it here.'

He nodded, but said, 'Nope. All I got's these here. Do the same thing.'

'Not according to OSHA.'

He laughed, not understanding the joke. His pale blue eyes were kind, and eager to engage.

'Guess not, but there's no pleasin' those people.'

I stuffed the plug back in my pocket and went to the place on the corner for some more coffee. I stopped on the way to check up on Eddie. He was sleeping in the cavernous backseat, off duty.

The flavor of the day was chocolate raspberry. The Summer People sitting around the crowded little tables wore their weary city indifference as an accessory to their jogging suits and Oxford cloth shirts with little embroidered polo players. There was a lot of confused milling around the area where you got your coffee and pastries. Summer People rarely obey line protocols, so I just shouldered my way up to the coffee stand and cleared a spot for myself. Only the women looked like they might object. The men had lived long enough to own houses out here by knowing how to pick their fights. I was very polite to the tiny Spanish ladies behind the pastry counter. They kept their distance even though they'd been selling me bagels and flavored coffee on a steady basis for about four years. I had that effect on people.

Amanda was sitting at a table in the corner, almost hidden behind the deli case. I must have felt her looking at me, because our eyes met the moment I saw her.

'Hey. How're you doing?'

'Okay,' she said, looking at my coffee, 'taking out or staying?'

I sat down at the table. She looked like somebody had tightened her all up. Her face was drawn back and her hands were clasped together in a white grip. Only her posture seemed at ease as she leaned in closer to speak.

'I feel so bad about the way I'm behaving. I really wanted to tell you I was sorry.'

'For what? How're you supposed to behave?'

'I don't know. That's not really what I mean.'

'We're just having a cup of coffee. That was the deal, I think.'

She dropped one shoulder as she leaned in a little closer. I could smell her hair.

'I don't usually do anything on my own without telling Roy what I'm doing. I mean, I don't have to ask permission. I just usually tell him if I'm doing something with somebody. But I thought I might catch you here. I see you come in and out of here all the time. It'd be like . . . coincidence.'

She looked up at me and smiled a tight little smile.

I wanted to get her off whatever subject we were on, even if I didn't know exactly what that subject was.

'I guess Joe Sullivan tracked down Regina's nephew, Jimmy Maddox. You know Joe Sullivan? He's a town cop.'

'I don't know him. Roy probably does.'

'He's a local.'

'Then Roy must.'

'You guys must have met here, as kids, huh?'

'Oh, yes. Roy's always been here.'

It was her turn to whisk me off the subject. She pointed out at the street.

'I ran over here when I saw you pull in. That big car must be quite the collectable.'

I snorted, the closest thing I had to a laugh.

'Collects problems. It's a big dumb thing.'

'But you drive it. It must be more fun than your regular car.'

'No, that's my regular car.'

'My.'

'It belonged to my father. Who was also poorly designed and out of place on Main Street.'

The look on her face told me she regretted picking this tack, as innocent as it looked at first.

I tried to recoup for her.

'Is your father still around?' I asked her.

'No. He died when I was little. I never knew him.'

Man, I've got a real skill with casual conversation. An instinct for scratching at nerves, picking off scabs.

'I'm sorry.'

'That's okay. People die. Our parents die. Even my mother, who never had a sick day in her life.'

I pursed my lips and tried to look understanding, afraid I was going to stick my foot in it again. She helped me out.

'Roy and I went over there when we hadn't heard from her and couldn't reach her. She'd been ironing her little doll outfits. She made her own dolls. She was very talented. It was horrible.'

She looked me in the eye when she said that and took a sip of her coffee. It wasn't as if she was trying to test my reaction. She just looked at me. Her hands rotated the coffee cup, occasionally stopping it to draw imaginary lines down the sides with her fingernails. They were strong, thin fingers, with perfect long nails.

'Sorry. We shouldn't talk about all these sad things. It's just, you know, she was in pretty good health, and to just have that happen. And when you told me about Regina, something made me think about my mother. I don't know what I'm saying.'

'So what was it, a heart attack?' I asked, sensitive to the last.

She shook her head, her face down again.

'That's what they thought. I don't know. Roy looked after all that.

I couldn't really deal with it.'

'Roy must be a good looker-after.'

'Too good,' she said, then regretted it. She smiled brightly and switched gears.

'What are you doing in town today? I know it's not bank day.'

'Just chores.'

'I can see everything from my window. I saw you go into the hardware store. I thought you'd come in here next. You usually do after you stop at the bank. I think it's funny. I ambushed you.'

'I'm glad.'

She looked pleased, 'I wanted to honour our bargain.'

'You did.'

She snuck a look out the picture window as she sipped her coffee.

'Something's buggy,' I said.

She looked back at me.

'What do you mean?'

'I don't know. I used to work on big complex systems for a living. Too complex for anyone to ever really understand. Even us engineers. So a lot of the time you just ran on instinct. I don't know. Sometimes things just felt buggy.'

I drank a little more coffee and tried to keep my mouth shut, but it was hard with this woman.

I wanted to talk to her.

'Maybe you just think too much,' she said.

'No, I do everything I possibly can to avoid thinking about anything at all.'

'You said it's a feeling. So maybe you feel too much.'

'I've already had a lifetime of feeling. My allotment's used up.'

Amanda sat back in her chair, looking into the paper coffee cup she was now crumpling with two hands.

'I understand. I shouldn't be bothering you.'

'You're not bothering me. I'm bothering myself. You're just being nice. I'm not worth it. Not at all.'

She dug a thumbnail into the side of the cup.

'I understand. Really. I do. More than you think.'

Then she got up and left. I watched her delicately navigate the crowded little coffee shop. Nice going, Sam, I told myself. Fucking brilliant.

She got hung up in the chaotic line in front of the pastry counter. I saw an opening form along the window and took it, so by the time she reached the door I was already there, without having to climb over tables or trample baby carriages.

I caught her by the elbow. She swiveled her head around and stared at me.

'You don't know this because I've been coming into the bank every month to do my stuff in person, because that's a habit of mine. And somehow you got stuck with me. So it gave you the idea that I'm a normal sociable person, which I'm not. You're actually about the only person I've said anything to for almost four years. You and Regina.'

'And here I am boring you about my mother.'

'I'm sure she'd have been pleased to know she had a daughter who thought about her,' I said, scrambling for something to say. 'I bet the two of you had a lot in common.'

Some people were trying to squeeze past us to get out the door. Amanda held her ground.

'My mother was a very brave woman,' she said, 'not like me.'

As the morning aged, the light out on Main Street had hardened up. But Amanda's skin still looked like it'd been airbrushed on and her auburn hair sparkled with tiny little fireworks. It caught me by surprise and distracted me from coming up with something else to say, so she slipped away and walked back to the bank without looking back. A familiar sight. A beautiful woman in full retreat.

I WAS overconfident when I set the alarm for 5:30 a.m. Sleep clogged my veins and packed gauze in my eyes. The cigarettes had left their usual rat's ass taste in my mouth. My stomach was skittery, unsure how to play the day.

When I left my wife (and by extension my daughter), she predicted I'd last five years on my own. One to go.

That was around the same time the psychiatrist threw me out of his office. He said there was nothing he could do for me. Actually, he said he didn't want to do anything for me, which I guess in retrospect was a breach of ethics. Not that I cared. I hated the self-important little prig. All he wanted was to get me off vodka and on to antidepressants. This was supposed to prepare me for psychoanalysis, so I could dig out deep-rooted causes.

The therapy was part of a deal I had to make with the Stamford district attorney. She hoped it would cover her decision not to prosecute me for a series of things, including gutting my wife's house. Me and a pair of hard cases from the gym had packed all our furniture and household goods in a big semi, tore out the woodwork, ripped up the floors and stripped the walls. We filled up a few dumpsters, then trucked the semi down to one of those mountainous landfills in the Jersey Meadowlands where we buried all my wife's treasured belongings under a hundred tons of Manhattan garbage.

We left the studs and rough plumbing and all the equipment in the basement. Plus a note on the plywood substrate floor, in what used to be the kitchen, telling her I'd cover full replacement costs.

I'd already given up my share of the house and three-quarters of my money. I still had a little left to live on, after I paid off whatever my wife's insurance wouldn't cover. I'm not proud of it, I just did it. I still don't know exactly why, but it can't be for any good reason.

I did, however, like that DA. My wife and her lawyers had a hard time getting her to muster the appropriate prosecutorial outrage. It helped that she'd been putting in twelve-hour days and weekends during the two weeks my wife had been out on the slopes. We talked about overwork and lost time and sacrifice. Her husband had spent most of their married life finding himself. She'd supported him while he earned a pair of Masters degrees and a Ph.D. He'd complain she was too stressed out. That she'd forgotten how to have fun. I just smirked at her and she looked down at her tired hands and said, 'right'.

So I copped the shrink deal and spent three months sparring with this little jerk who couldn't look at a urinal without analyzing the psychosexual impulses underlying the urge to take a piss.

I never understood any of it. It bothered me that people considered lightheartedness and optimism the norm. I wondered how anyone could be more than half awake and not be at least a little bummed by the desperate hopelessness of human existence.

Mornings like this were especially hard. I was so tired and sick to my stomach. It didn't help that I'd risen to this a million times before. The pain was cinched up tight around my heart.

After making up a pot of coffee, I put on a T-shirt and shorts and went out for a run. I usually saved this kind of thing for the gym, but I was afraid the big black dog was going to chomp down hard if I didn't get my cardiovascular fired up.

A study someone did in the eighties concluded the better grip you had on reality, the more likely you were to be depressed, and vice versa. Science has confirmed that ignorance is, indeed, bliss.

My jogging route took me along sandy unpaved roads threaded through the tall oaks and scrub pines tucked up to the bay shore. Every fifty to a hundred feet was a driveway to a house built on the coast. Other houses were stuck in the woods or perched on pressure-treated pilings above swampy bogs that were grandfathered out of the Wetlands Act.

Twenty minutes into the run I started to feel better. Too distracted by the effort of running to bother with anxiety. By that time I was passing the gate to WB Manufacturing, the abandoned plant built on the peninsula immediately to the east of Oak Point. There was a new cyclone fence and gate securing the entrance, but otherwise it looked like it had forever – all concrete, red brick and rust.

When my father was building his house most of our neighbours worked at the plant. Even then jobs at WB were considered tenuous at best. Manufacturing never really took hold out here, which helped save the East End for all the potato farmers and tennis courts. My father put in a little time there himself, but I think they fired him. If it was like any of his other jobs, he'd gotten into a scrape with somebody, or spouted off about something too loudly, or too often. That was why he could only really work for himself. Today you'd say he was a little light on the interpersonal skills.

That's probably what killed him. They never caught the guys who did it, assuming they even tried. Probably a pair of punks stopping off for a quick drink. He'd probably provoked them. The wrong look, the wrong word, a gesture, a snort – that's all you needed to do. Took about five minutes. They left him in the can, already dead as you can get before the door slammed shut on their way out.

I felt better when I got back from the run. Good enough to take a shower, shave, get dressed and take off in the Grand Prix. Good enough to give it another day.

It took me most of the morning driving around Hampton Bays to find Jimmy Maddox. I started with the construction site Sullivan told me about. They didn't know him, but they sent me over to an earth-moving outfit. They'd heard of him, but didn't want to be helpful. I was polite and moved on.

At the third place there was a sandy scar cut into a tall grove of gnarly red pine. A big florid-faced guy in a grey T-shirt two sizes too small for his gut was rolling out of the cab of a huge Cat steam shovel. The machine looked like a giant yellow critter that hadn't had breakfast yet. Diesel and pneumatic fluids blended with the smell of wet sand that stood in defeated heaps around the freshly cut excavation.

He squinted to hear over the engine noise.

'No, I don't know where Maddox is, but I could probably find out,' he yelled to me as we walked away from the Cat toward a battered little office trailer. He seemed glad to be away from his big machine. There was no one else on the site. Maybe he was lonely. 'What's it for?'

'Just some family business I gotta take care of,' I told him, not knowing what else to say.

'You related?'

'No, it's more a thing I have to do for the Town. His aunt died. I'm helping settle her estate,' I dropped my voice when he closed the trailer door behind us, 'he just needs to sign some papers and stuff.'

The Formica table was covered in blueprints and brown burn marks from forgotten cigarettes. The walls were papered with Labor Department propaganda and calendars with topless women wearing tool belts and wielding impact drills. There were two coffeepots in an automatic maker and coffee stains everywhere. He filled a pair of Styrofoam cups.

'No shit. She leave him anything?'

'Probably a little. Not too much. Didn't have that much.'

'Hey, you never know. Sometimes old ladies got bunches of money squirreled away.'

'That's true. You never know,' I said. 'You think you could find him for me?'

'Yeah, that's right. Just a second.'

He pulled out a muddy Verizon Yellow Pages and thumbed through it with his muddy hands. He called from a black wall-mounted phone. 'Yeah, Davy, this is Frank. You got Jimmy Maddox working on your job? Nah, I don't need him. This guy,' he looked over at me and I shook my head to caution him. He turned his head back down before going on, 'This guy wanted to talk to him about some other job. Doesn't need him right away. Nah, I don't know why he wants to talk to Jimmy, he just does. Must of got a recommendation. I don't know, just checking for him. Nah, don't tell Jimmy anything, let this guy talk to him. Yeah, let him work it out. How's it going over there? Yeah, what the fuck. Don't I know it. Yeah, Davy. Okay.'

They volleyed banalities for a few more minutes before hanging up.

He turned to me from the phone.

'So what's the big secret.'

'No big deal. Like you told him, I just want to work it out with Jimmy. You handled that well.'

'He owe you money?'

I drank some of his ubiquitous coffee. It was pretty good, even from a Styrofoam cup. I watched him write something down on the back of a receipt swiped from the in-box on somebody's desk.

'Nothing like that. You can check it out with the Town. Ask a cop named Joe Sullivan. Tell him you talked to Sam Acquillo.'

He gave me the address of the job.

'That name'll be on the sign at the job. Maddox's working the backhoe on the utility trench. Good backhoe guy. Good enough to pick your teeth with it. Too bad.'

I tucked the folded receipt into my shirt pocket.

'What do you mean "too bad"?'

He shrugged.

'He's a nasty asshole. Nobody can stand working with him. He's just one of those guys. Asshole kid. You know what I mean?'

'I guess, sure.'

'You'll see. Real sweetheart.'

I walked him back to his steam shovel.

'Someday,' the big guy told me as he climbed up over the polished steel treads, 'somebody's going to beat the snot out of that little fucker, you know what I mean?'

The day was coming in cloudy, but still clear, with a breeze that swept the Cat's exhaust up into the pines and out toward the ocean. The diesel roared behind me as I lugged the Grand Prix back to Montauk Highway.

'SHIT, FUCK, Christ, you son of a bitch piece of shit. Fucking piece of shit. Fucking goddammit cock-sucking piece of crap SHIT.'

Jimmy Maddox was about twenty-eight years old, but his face looked a lot younger. Soft and round, barely showing a few smudges of orange fuzz on his upper lip and jowls. Freckles and curly red hair bursting out from under a bright green hat with an orange rim. He looked like the demented trade school son of Ronald McDonald. A little of his Aunt Regina haunted his face and poked through his bitter eyes.

I stood just outside the swing of the big shovel and spray of invective. The kid had an interesting style. The trench he was digging was almost sculpted. The action of the shovel was smooth and controlled. It didn't fit with all that yelling and swearing. Dotty Hodges and the big excavator had it right. A young dickhead. But with a little texture.

'Fucking shitbag piece of fucking shit.'

He knew I was standing there watching him. I thought he'd finish the last section of trench in about half an hour. I decided I'd leave before that. Stand in one place too long and your dignity drains out of your feet. Maybe curiosity got the best of him. Idling the backhoe, he curled the shovel between the little front wheels and climbed down from the seat. He walked past without looking at me, but close enough to hear me call out his name.

'Yeah?' he yelled back, 'And you are?'

He had a good start on a blue collar beer belly. It strained the fabric of his muddy white T-shirt. His jeans were bunched down around a pair of expensive Dunhill boots. His lip was actually curled a little.

'Sam Acquillo. I've got some bad news.'

He spit at the ground.

'Fuck. What is it?'

'Your Aunt Regina died.'

He looked at me as if I hadn't said anything yet. I waited. He spit again.

'Died?'

'Yeah. Been about a week. She's still in the morgue. It's time somebody decided how to settle her out.'

'That'd be you?'

'With your help, if you're interested.'

'You the ex-ec-u-tor?'

I'm not good with that kind of approach. But I was trying.

'I might be. That depends on you.'

He crouched down on his haunches and picked up a piece of dirt. It crumbled in his hand, and he tossed the pieces away like a sod farmer on the last legs of foreclosure.

'Just up and died?'

'That's what it looks like.'

He stood up again, wiping his hands on his hips. I'd moved in a little closer so I could get a better look at his face when he talked. He noticed the intrusion and stiffened a little.

'What's your deal in this?'

'Next-door neighbour.'

He looked over my shoulder.

'You got that old Pontiac. I seen it in the driveway.'

I nodded. 'The cops couldn't find any next of kin. I told them I'd help out. Talk to you.'

He crossed his arms over his belly and leaned back a little.

'Cops? Somebody kill her?'

'What do you think?'

'You a cop?'

'Should I be?'

'Is this twenty fucking questions?'

I smiled. The backhoe was still idling next to the trench. A hundred feet away a gang of foundation guys were leaning on their shovels and rakes, watching the mixer back up. The odour of fresh concrete competed with the mud smell and the scent of raw lumber coming from a large stack of two-by-eights. Maddox was slowly rocking back and forth on his heels, acting out his manifold indecisions.

'I'm just trying to help out,' I told him, 'Something bothering you?'

He uncrossed his arms and shoved his hands in his pockets. I saw him as I first saw him. As a kid.

'Aunt Reggie's the only relative I got left. How'd she die?'

'Just did. I found her floating in the bathtub. Frankly, I think they should nail down the exact cause of death. I think you ought to authorize an autopsy. They got her on ice, but time's going by.'

'I gotta do that?'

'You don't have to do the autopsy. Just authorize it. And take a little responsibility for all this. Funeral, estate, all that.'

He wasn't listening.

'My mom always said she had a bunch of money hid away somewheres.'

'You think so, too?'

His face shifted around under the pale, fleshy surface. I wondered how much of his family he'd already buried in his young life. That kind of thing can put uneven wear on a kid. Ruin his balance.

'Nah, she didn't have shit.'

'You checked?'

His soft face filled up with blood.

'You think I'm stupid?'

'Not yet.'

'You think I don't know what you're gettin' at?'

'I'm not getting at anything. But *you're* gettin' edgy.'

'You're gonna shut the fuck up.'

'Not likely.'

The old punch drunks who used to hang around my neighbourhood gym called it a Western Union. That was when a guy did everything but send you a telegram that he was about to take a shot at your nose.

I just waited for him.

'You're a fucking asshole,' he told me.

I let him talk and take my measurements. I kept my hands loose at my sides and my feet in a partial stance.

Then I took a piece of a second to think about the delicacy Jimmy Maddox showed digging a utility trench with a two-ton backhoe. It made me rethink my estimate of his speed, and adjust accordingly. In an even tinier fraction of a second his cowboy swing was launched toward my jaw.

I caught his fist like a baseball with my left hand and held it. He froze in surprise, straining against my grip. It was hard to hold him – he was stronger than he looked. I popped him once in the mouth and sat him down on his butt. I squatted down as he dropped, keeping my grip on his left fist and feeling the resistance drain out of his arm.

'I used to be a boxer, son. No more of that stuff, okay?'

He nodded with his free hand over his mouth. He wasn't ready to say anything, so I did.

'I'm not accusing you of anything. It's just your personality. So what say we start over. More friendly.'

He nodded and I let go of his right hand. He looked at it like an annoying pet that'd been missing for a few days. Blood ran out of the corner of his mouth and spotted his T-shirt. I handed him the paper towel I'd stuffed in my pocket that morning in a moment of prescience. He held it to his face as we walked over to the Grand Prix. The sun was behind some clouds, and the light was diffused and less forgiving. The blood on his shirt was bright red. His face was back to pale.

'Do any work around chemical plants, Jimmy?'

He looked at me with a frown.

'There aren't any chemical plants around here.'

'Up Island? New Jersey?'

'Never been there. What difference does it make?'

'No difference.'

He was too jangled to argue anymore. I let him sit on the passenger seat of the Grand Prix with his legs out the door while I leafed through the papers for a clean sheet to write on.

'I think it's a good idea to do this. There's no harm in it, unless it bothers you, and that's your privilege. The court's already given me what I need to handle things, but she's your aunt.'

He looked at the letter I'd written out while I was talking.

'Says I want an autopsy.'

'Just sign it, Jimmy. I'll take care of everything. I'll let you know when the funeral is.'

His signature was a graceful Palmer method script. Wrote like he dug holes. Only quieter.

'And if you want, you can say it's okay for me to act as administrator of her estate,' I handed him another piece of paper. 'You don't have to agree. You can get your own lawyer. I'm just sayin' I got the time and I'm willing to do it. I just need your address and telephone number. You get whatever she's got, unless some other family pops out of the blue.'

He read the letter I'd written up. Then shrugged and signed it.

'Money's okay. I don't want any of her shit. Too fucking depressing.'

'Except maybe the house. It's worth a lot of money,' I said.

He snorted into the paper towel.

'She don't own that house.'

It was my turn to look like a dope.

'She don't own that house, Einstein,' he said, somewhat buoyed by my confusion, 'She just gets to stay there. Till she dies. Now everything gets passed back to some other fucker.'

'What other fucker?'

'She never said much about it. I only know about it 'cause she didn't want me gettin' ideas about her stupid house.'

A black mass of clouds was clumping up over the rangy oak trees. The breeze was working itself into a northwesterly wind. There was something mildly electric about the air – warning of an incoming storm. The concrete guys had stopped working to look up at the sky. Maddox looked wearily over at his unfinished trench.

'Fucking piece of goddam piece of shit weather.'

CHAPTER TWO

There were thousands of bars in Greater New York City that looked exactly like this one. It'd been there since before the Second World War. All the woodwork was simulated mahogany stained a deep, Victorian brown. It ran like wainscoting three-quarters of the way up the wall. Above that the plaster was painted pale green, and decorated with framed, faded covers of magazines that had ceased circulation about the time MacArthur returned to the Philippines. The carpet was probably red at some point, but had turned a brown dinge. So had the vinyl stool cushions. Around the bar itself the floorboards had worn down to the grain. The footrail was solid brass, shiny on the top. At the corners of the bar were racks of hard candy and Tums. Bottles lined a back wall that was mostly mirror, decorated with false muntins.

It was a few doors down from the entrance to the stairs that led two flights up to my father's Bronx pied-à-terre. One of our family myths was that my sister and I had spent our early years in that apartment, but I never remembered it that way. We'd visit, occasionally, and sit on the scratchy living room sofa and watch TV while my mother cleaned the bathroom and put my father's clothes back in the drawers and closets. The place smelled like grease, gasoline and oil, because that's what my father and all his clothes smelled like.

He wasn't a drinker in the traditional sense. But he preferred sitting in that bar to sitting alone in the apartment. He'd nurse a shot and a beer for hours, alone at a small round table along the wall, discouraging anyone who might want to engage him in conversation. Not that he had to try that hard. Some people have that unapproachable aura about them. Like me. People get close, then veer away, bouncing off the invisible shield.

Thirty years ago I went there to talk to the bartender. I had my gym bag with a change of clothes at my feet. I was also nursing a beer, partly for financial reasons. I was living on a starvation budget, all my money going toward night school. The bartender was about my father's age. He'd inherited the place from his uncles. The standard bartender look was fat and grizzly grey, but this guy was slender and handsome, with a squared-off jaw and black crew cut. A Navy man, with an anchor on his forearm and a portrait of a destroyer above the cash register. He spoke out of the side of his mouth, and rarely put a T at the start of a word when a D would work better, so you knew he belonged in the Bronx.

I didn't know how to go about asking him what I wanted to know, so we'd been talking about the Yankees and the economy. He had a nephew my age who was going to Penn State. For some unaccountable reason I told him I was out of school and working as a carpenter. Maybe I thought going to night school at MIT would put him off. I don't know. I was young.

When the conversation drifted into crime on the streets I had an opening. I looked around, appraisingly.

'This place seems pretty quiet. You must keep it that way, huh?'

'Yeah, I get it done. Don't like any funny stuff.'

'Wasn't there something in here, though, a big fight or something? That's what I heard, is all.'

He was wiping off the bar at the time, which gave him an easy way to move away from me. I sat there with my beer, acting disinterested, until he drifted back into earshot.

'Sorry,' I said. 'I'm just being nosy.'

'Sure. It's nuttin'. Dis guy got his ass beat to shit. Tha's all there is. You ready?' he asked, pointing to the empty glass.

'Sure.' My heart thrilled at the expense.

I tried again.

'D'you know him?' I asked.

'The guy?'

'Yeah.'

'Yeah. He come in here all the time. Ornery bastard. But never gave me no trouble.'

'A regular.'

'Yeah, I guess so. I never knew his name. Mechanic. Always come in cleaned up, but you can tell by the index finger here, see? Mechanics can never get this part along the side completely clean. From holdin' wrenches. Gets in the cracks. You can scrub the shit out of it with Boraxo, but when you're workin' every day, the grease just gets in there.'

'So I guess you didn't see anything.'

He straightened his back and looked at me, still holding his hand so he could show me how to identify car mechanics.

'No. I didn't see anything. Nobody saw nuthin'. What's with this? You know him?'

'No. No, I'm just curious.'

'Well, enough about all that, okay?' he said, and moved on down the bar, adjusting mixers, dropping dirty glasses into the washer, putting fresh fruit slices in the bin.

I was too young to know where to go from there. So I let it drop and spent the next hour looking into the mouth of the beer glass. I didn't know how to think anymore. I couldn't make myself leave, but I wanted to leap off the stool and run the whole way back to Boston. I wanted to find Abby and drag her out of her class and take off all her clothes and lie in bed with her. I wanted to slink back to my dad's old apartment and curl up on the sofa with the TV on. I wanted and I didn't.

The runaway contrapositions must have found their way into my right hand, because when I put the glass up to my lips it shook so hard the beer splattered down the front of my shirt.

'Hey, you okay?'

'Yeah, sorry. Tired is all.'

He tossed me his soggy bar rag.

'Here.'

I thought I'd leave quietly after that. He was down at the other end of the bar working the tap. I put down twice as much money as I needed to, waved to him and got off the stool. When I reached down to pick up my bag, he called to me.

'Hey, kid.'

'Yeah.'

'You live around here?'

'No. Just seein' a buddy.'

I held up the bag as proof. He nodded the way people do when they're unconvinced.

'Hey, don't push it. You don't want to know.'

'Okay.'

'Okay.'

I started to leave.

'Kid.'

'Yeah.'

'There's nuthin' nobody can do.'

'I know that.'

He topped off the glass and set it up in front of a scraggly old woman who probably wasn't all that old. I started to go again and he called me back again.

'Kid. Com'ere.'

I walked back and he met me at the end of the bar where it curved into the wall. He leaned over the bar top and lowered his voice, exaggerating his side-of-the-mouth style of speaking.

'It's not like it sounds. Don't listen to what people tell you. It's always different, what's really going on. You just don't know that yet. Only now you do. So get the fuck outta here.'

The bright daylight outside the bar made me squint. My eyes adjusted by the time I reached the subway back to Grand Central. As I sat on the platform with my gym bag on my lap, a vast emptiness filled my mind. Knowing by not knowing. My first lesson in the Tao of murdered fathers.

THE SENIOR Centre was in a building located behind a Catholic church founded by Polish potato farmers. The roof was Spanish tile. The windows were very tall double-hungs open at the top for ventilation. There were a few shiny old cars in the parking lot and white-haired people going in and out the door. The mood was reflective. It was almost lunch time.

The lobby had a reception desk like a hospital or a nursing home. A woman who was probably in her nineties was at the helm. Her hair was polar white and her skin the colour of fresh dough. Her wet blue eyes had seen it all, but not much of it had stuck.

'Yes?' Her head bobbed when she talked.

'Just looking around.'

'Oh, you're too young,' she said.

'Thank you. I'm looking for a friend.'

'Lots of friends here,' she said in the unanswerable way some old people have.

'It's a specific friend. Paul Hodges. Mind if I go in and see if he's here?'

She waved her hand at the air and looked down, then abruptly looked back up again as if her head was being operated by remote control.

'Oh, I don't know anybody's names. Go on in there and see if he's here.'

I had a thought and tried it out on her.

'Do you have a list of people who normally come in here?'

She looked at me and moved her mouth around, chewing on the idea.

'I don't know.'

I got the feeling she didn't know how to think about the question.

'Do people have to sign up to come here, or do they just come in when they feel like it?'

'Oh, whenever. I don't think there's a list,' she looked around the empty desk area in front of her, searching for explanations. 'Do you think we should?'

'No, I'm just wondering who comes here. Just curious.'

She tried to understand me, but the necessary circuitry had been disconnected. She looked upset.

'I'm sorry to bother you. I'm just curious. This looks like a nice place.'

She lit up, relieved to be back on familiar ground.

'Oh yes, it's very nice. Would you like lunch? Here's our activity schedule for October.' She dug a slim blue pamphlet out of a drawer. She slapped it down on the reception desk and patted it like the head of a grandchild.

'Lots to do. Lots to do.'

I folded it once and stuck it in my back pocket.

'Thanks.'

She nodded and looked back down at her desktop full of nothing. I went inside. It was a big open room with circular tables set up around the periphery. Women who looked as old as the people at the tables were moving around with trays of food. I spotted Hodges at a table by himself with a steaming plate of hot turkey sandwich. His back was to the wall and his eyes fixed on his meal.

'You're right. It looks good.'

He frowned.

'They won't serve you. You gotta have a Senior Card.'

'That's okay, Mr Hodges. Already ate.'

I sat down a few seats away. His frown got a little deeper.

'Go ahead,' I said to him, 'eat.'

'I'm going to. This is my lunch.'

'Go ahead.'

He did, reluctantly. Old manners die hard. At the surrounding tables elderly people lingered over their coffee or tea and were joined by people who looked to be volunteers. I felt like an interloper in an entirely alien place. Tolerated, but not really welcomed.

Hodges got me a cup of coffee to go with his. I told him I'd found Jimmy Maddox. He seemed a little interested. Then we talked about fishing for a while before I asked him if anyone in the room had hung out with Regina Broadhurst. He squinted his big frog eyes and looked around the room, but shook his head.

'Not that I can remember.'

A big woman, late forties, with a huge head of jet black beauty-parlour hair and a blunt hatchet of a nose, strode towards us. She wore some sort of undefinable casual clothes and a red knit sweater that clung to her body like chainmail. Behind her plastic-rimmed glasses her eyes were sharp and on the move. She looked like an overfed predatory bird.

'Hello.'

Her hand thrust forward to shake mine. It reminded me of a karate chop.

'Hello,' I said back, taking her hand.

'I'm Barbara Filmore. The executive director.'

'She runs the place,' said Hodges, helping me out.

'Sam Acquillo. I'm with him.' I nodded towards Hodges. She kept her eyes on me.

'I understand you were trying to get a list of our clients,' she said, neither as a question nor a statement. By then I'd forgotten that I had.

'No ma'am, not exactly. Just trying to look up a few old friends.'

'Like me,' said Hodges.

'We don't keep those sorts of records. Are you connected with the state?'

Only someone from Social Services would call a bunch of old geezers clients.

'No ma'am. I'm just looking for old friends of my mother. She passed away recently.'

'I'm sorry.' She didn't move much, and stood very close to where I was sitting. I got the vague feeling that she'd tackle me if I tried to make a run for it. 'Who are you looking for?'

'Regina Broadhurst and Julia Anselma. Know 'em?'

Her face was immobile.

'They've passed away as well. Very recently, in fact. I'm sorry to have to tell you. What was your name, again?'

'Sam. I guess you should expect it. They weren't kids.'

'They hadn't been well.'

'Really.'

I slid my chair away from the table. Her head turned to follow me, but the rest of her stayed in place. She took off her glasses and stuck the tip of a temple in her mouth. She slid her weight over to her right leg as if to relax her posture, but I noticed her move even closer to where I was sitting. At that distance I could see she'd had some kind of facelift. They wiped off the character lines around her eyes and pulled back the skin at her throat. It helped explain the hawkish mask.

'Anybody here know those two? Julia and Regina?'

'I'll ask.' She didn't look like she would. 'Is there anything else? We're about to rearrange the tables for this evening's activities. We'll be asking everyone to let our volunteers get to work.'

'They're clearin' us out,' said Hodges, still in a helpful mood.

Miss Filmore smiled mechanically but didn't look over at Hodges.

'Okay, I guess we'll let you go,' I said, standing up. 'Just have a question.'

She might have arched an eyebrow if she'd had loose skin left around her eyes to do it. Instead she put her glasses back on and cocked her head.

'Yes?'

'Do you ever ask family, or anybody, about clients who, you know, pass away?'

'We don't like to discuss it. For obvious reasons.'

'They just don't show up for bingo one night,' said Hodges.

'I wouldn't characterize it that way,' said Miss Filmore, without looking at Hodges. 'We simply feel that dwelling on mortality is not a constructive pursuit for people of maturity. We stress life and looking forward.'

I looked over at Hodges and he shrugged. Give a man a square meal once in a while and I guess you can stress anything you want. He stood up to leave with me.

'Why do you ask?' she asked me.

'It's a long story.'

'Certainly.' She said the word the way you'd drop a heavy bag on the floor.

We moved around her and would have left right then, but she wasn't quite ready to have us dismissed.

'You're welcome to visit anytime you'd like. But please check in with us occasionally. My office is just inside the front entrance.'

'Certainly.'

We walked out together, and Miss Filmore escorted us all the way to the front door. She wanted to shake hands again.

'It's wonderful to have people show some interest in the elderly,' she said by way of seeing us off. 'They have so much to offer, but tend to get lost in the shuffle.'

'Yeah, so I've noticed.'

Hodges climbed into a rusty Ford Econoline after looking over the Grand Prix. As I drove off, I looked back at the Senior Centre and saw Barbara Filmore still standing at the door, a trained professional, alert to threats and poised to seize opportunity.

AMANDA'S CAR was in my driveway when I got home. I didn't see it at first because it was raining hard and silver Audis aren't normally parked in front of my house. She was in the driver's seat, her head back on the headrest. I thought she might be asleep, but she jumped out of the car when I pulled up and ran behind me through the rain and up to the back door. Eddie, thoroughly drenched, awaited.

I let us into the kitchen and the cottage filled up with the smell of wet dog. Amanda's hair was all flattened out, which made it more obvious that she had a very pretty face. It was still strained, and there were dark semicircles under her eyes. She clutched her windbreaker close to her throat and shivered. I looked up at her from where I was drying off Eddie with an old beach towel.

'Sorry. I'll turn up the heat.'

'That's okay.'

Eddie sniffed at her knees and wagged his tail. She rumpled the top of his head.

'My, aren't you a handsome boy. What's your name?'

'Eddie Van Halen.'

She kept scratching his face.

'Are you a guitar player?'

'He gave it up. No money in it.'

I switched on the furnace, hoping there was some oil left. I only ran it once in a while to keep it from rusting up, or when I couldn't keep the house above freezing with the woodstove in the living room. The radiators clanged into action.

She stood in the doorway between the kitchen and living room and watched me bunch up newspapers and toss kindling into the stove. I overstocked it with split red oak and opened up the dampers.

'You want some coffee?'

'You drink a lot of coffee.'

'Yeah, too much. Want some?'

'I drink too much coffee, too. Sure.'

I built a five-cup pot of fresh ground Cinnamon Hazelnut. The rain was trying to beat in the windows, but the house started to feel warm. From the kitchen, I could look through the living room and out to the screened-in porch. Beyond the porch the bay was all in a charcoal grey and white-tipped uproar. The nearest buoy, a red nun, was rocking back and forth like a dweeble. The only thing in the room besides the stove was a pull-out couch. I sat on it after Amanda sank down next to the stove and took a sip of her coffee, holding the cup with both hands. Somehow while I was fussing with stove and coffee she'd managed to brush back her hair and smooth out her face. She wore Reeboks, clean, faded Wranglers and a chambray shirt under her cotton windbreaker. The shirt was opened to just below the top curve of her breasts. Her chest had seen a lot of sun – it was very dark with freckles that were almost black.

'So,' I said, for openers.

'I'm sorry I'm bothering you again.'

'You mostly bother me when you say you're sorry.'

Self-effacement can be hard work on the receiving end.

'You like your privacy. I'm making you uncomfortable.'

'I'm just not used to other people sitting in my living room.'

'I understand that. I've lived alone.'

'Where's Roy?'

'He had to go to the city.' She looked up as if unsure I believed her. 'HQ keeps a pretty tight rein, so he has to go in two or three times a month. I took off early. They'll cover for me.'

'Does he know you're here?'

She busied herself petting and cooing at Eddie. He didn't discourage her.

'Of course not. That bothers you?'

'Not really. I'm just not much for company.'

'I'm sorry. I should go.'

'No, I mean, *I'm* not good company. Me. Obviously. You're fine.'

'I still should go. You're probably busy.'

She started to stand up. I waved her back down.

'Nah. Drink your coffee. I got nothing else to do.'

'When we talked about Regina Broadhurst it got me thinking about my mother again. Not that I ever stopped. It's all I've done since she died. They're all dying. Our parents. Yours, mine.'

'It's been five years since my mother went. I don't think about it much.'

Amanda leaned back against the wall and looked at me through frustrated, anxious eyes. Tears rushed up into her voice.

'She was just a sweet, wonderful old woman. She made dolls for charity for chrissakes.'

The impossible tangle of her emotions created an attraction current that drew her legs back against her chest. She pulled them to her and rested her head on her knees.

'I'm an engineer, not a shrink. But it looks to me like it all happened too quick for you and you got what they call unresolved issues.'

A couple sessions of court-ordered therapy and I'm fucking Sigmund Freud.

'I know. They have grief counsellors, but Roy was really unhappy about the idea. Doesn't approve of it.'

'Can't say he's helping out too much here.'

'No, you can't say that.'

Eddie found people down at his level irresistible. He tried to lick her face, from which she gently demurred. I told him to bug off, so he went out to the screened-in porch, a little put out.

'It's none of my business, but since you're here in my living room,

I guess I can say you should talk to somebody about this and to hell with Roy. With all due respect.'

'Maybe I can just talk to you.'

'Now I know you need help.'

She smiled at me. 'You want me to think you're just an old burnout.' It's amazing how pretty women who like you and wear rough chambray shirts and smell like fresh expectations can say anything they want and get away with it.

'Too burned out to think straight, that's for sure.'

Even though I couldn't stop thinking about Regina floating in that bathtub. She had wicked bad arthritis. Could hardly bend down. She had an old tin-lined shower stall off the kitchen that she could just walk into. My old man used the tub in that bathroom to clean fish. In return he'd leave her a few in the freezer. When I went through the house I saw a bathrobe hanging in the broom closet, which was right near the shower stall, along with a bunch of beach towels. I realised, standing there looking down at Amanda, that Regina never sat on the beach. And never had any guests. Those were her bath towels. Thirty-year-old beach towels she was too cheap to replace.

'What are you saying?'

'I don't know, Amanda. Old habits die hard. I spent most of my life solving engineering problems, which are like big, complicated puzzles. You have to noodle 'em out. Only here I can't say there's anything to noodle. I must be growing an imagination in my old age.'

'You're not that old.'

Amanda smoothed the legs of her jeans down toward her ankles, pushing out the wrinkles and reinforcing the crease up her shins and over her knees. I thought of my daughter's cat.

'I wish you could have met my mother. She was very strict, but she had a sense of humour.'

'I probably would've been a bit young for her.'

'That's not what I meant.'

I felt bad when I saw the tears pooling up in her eyes. I find it hard to talk about death without being sarcastic. Grieving relatives usually don't find it too funny. I went into the bathroom next to the kitchen and got a box of Kleenex. I was able to keep my mouth shut long enough for her to blow her nose and mop up her tears.

'I think I would have liked her, too,' I said.

'How come?' she said, with a sniff.

'I can tell. Probably loaded with charm. A lot of it rubbed off on you.'

'Does that mean you like me, too?'

'Yes. It does.'

'That's so amazing.'

'Why?'

'Because I feel so unlikable.'

For a brief moment, her history poured in from some other dimension, flowed around the living room, then drained away through cracks in the floor and special portals in the wall. It caused a lapse.

'So what made you come back to Southampton?'

She looked at me as if concentrating on my face. Evaluating. She scrunched up her mouth and looked away.

'Something bad,' she said.

'Sorry.'

'What about you?'

'Same here. More or less.'

'I thought so,' she said. 'Want to know?'

'Nah. Enough of that stuff, okay?'

'Okay. If you want.'

The grey-black rain clouds outside made it even darker in the knotty pine room. I opened the woodstove and threw in a few more logs. We were washed by firelight and smoky dry heat. She took off her windbreaker and pulled up her sleeves. She hadn't moved out of the way when I was stoking the stove. Her presence was beginning to unbalance the stolid resignation that decorated the inside of my cottage. I looked down at her and caught a glimpse of a tanned breast held softly in a low-cut flowered bra. I went back to the kitchen to exchange my coffee for something stronger. Something with little blocks of ice in it.

The phone rang. It was Sullivan.

'They gave me a note from a guy named Jimmy Maddox. That's her nephew?'

'Yeah. He's letting me handle the funeral and settle the estate. First I want that cause of death.'

'When you get hold of a bone you sure do gnaw on it.'

'A lot of time has gone by. I'm not an expert on morbidity, but it's got to affect an accurate read. Make sure it's the full deal. Blood analysis, tissue trauma, stuff under fingernails.'

'That's not an autopsy. That's forensics.'

Amanda was standing there watching me. Holding the phone to my ear with my left shoulder, I held up the gin bottle and pointed to the tonic. She nodded. I poured and continued to talk to Sullivan.

'Okay. Do whatever.'

While I talked I watched Amanda busy herself around the kitchen. When she refilled the ice cube trays she leaned into the sink, bearing her weight on her right leg with her left tucked behind like a dancer.

'I'll take care of it,' said Sullivan. 'You just worry about gettin' her in the ground. Call me with the name of the funeral home and we'll send her over there when we're done.'

'Okay, chief. By the way, who cleaned up her house?'

'I don't know. Not us. Unless it was the paramedics.'

'Is that usually what they do?'

'No, that's the family's business.'

Amanda leaned into me when she reached across the kitchen table for the tonic. She poured for both of us and handed me the drink. She mouthed the word lime and I jerked my head toward the refrigerator.

'So you didn't turn off the power.'

'I don't think so. I'll call the County Health people. The power's out?'

'I just turned it back on.'

'Don't forget to pay LIPA. You got the authority.'

'The cop,' I told Amanda when I hung up.

'The cop?'

'Joe Sullivan. Not really the meatball I thought he was.'

'He's doing what you want?'

· 64 ·

'I got Jimmy Maddox, Regina's nephew, to sign an autopsy request. Sullivan's going to get the county coroner to do it for me, which probably took a little pull on his part.'

'That poor woman has to be buried.'

'She doesn't care,' I started going down one road, then quickly switched to another. 'I'm just curious. Got a little itch to scratch. Can't hurt anything at this point.'

Amanda smiled instead of apologizing, which was a step in the right direction.

'I'm sure. Cheers.'

She took a healthy pull on the gin and tonic. We looked around the inside of my barren little house for a while without saying anything.

'I'd better go,' she said, finally.

'Probably should.'

'I feel better.'

'It's the proximity of the Little Peconic. Has that effect.'

'Couldn't be the company.'

Eddie and I watched her get back in the windbreaker. He got a pet on the head before she left. I got a complicated little smile.

The rain grew louder and insinuated itself back into the mood of the room. I put on a sweatshirt and went back out to the screened-in porch so I could sit quietly with Eddie, drink my drink, and watch the lousy weather do its best to upset the resolute tranquillity of the Little Peconic Bay. After a time the world collapsed into a space defined solely by what I could see through the screens, and for the next few hours a tired, threadbare kind of peace took the place of the flat black anguish somebody had bolted down over my heart.

A HEAVY grey blanket of fog was lying all over the area when I got up the next morning. The automatic coffeepot was prompt and at the ready. A shower, a shave, a worn pair of jeans and a freshly washed shirt from out of the dryer. Things that make me feel a little less like an animal.

For almost thirty years work would get me out of bed in the

morning. It would wake me up before dawn, with all the imperatives of the coming day rioting in the corridors of my nervous system. Sometimes I'd actually bolt upright in bed with a scream choked off in my throat. Usually the transition was slower and more tortured. I'd open my eyes and check the clock. I'd never go back to sleep. I never noticed what the weather was like outside. There was no outside; it was irrelevant. Abby was a blanketed mound on the right side of the bed. I'd be on my second cup of coffee at my desk about the time her alarm went off.

She'd tried a lot of different jobs. They all made her unhappy. Raising our daughter was her defined purpose, and she did the job very well. Our daughter was exquisite. The world loved her. She hated her father, so I didn't know her very well. I didn't even know why she hated me, though I could've probably figured it out easily enough.

We lived in a large contemporary house in the woods north of Stamford, Connecticut. I drove to work at an engineering centre in White Plains, New York. In the early days I was on my dictation machine before I started the car. Later it was the car phone jacked into voice mail. Except for an hour or two at a boxing gym I found in New Rochelle, I worked all day and into the evening without a break, even for meals. I ate frozen bagels and prepared foods heated in a microwave in my office. I drank coffee until I could hear my heart rate fluttering in my ears. All day long I'd count my responsibilities in my head like an obsessive-compulsive counting his fingers or the days of the week. Agonies and ambitions streamed through my office, afloat on a river of selfishness and sacrifice. From phone to fax to face I'd hurtle in a vertiginous sprint, breathless and jagged. With the help of one or two other people, I held a slender tether on a twisting angry chaos. Like a bull runner of Pamplona, I knew the beast could turn and gore me at any moment. But I saw no other way.

The building we worked in had a square jaw and was charged with purpose. Our ostensible mission was to give worldwide R&D and engineering support to the company's manufacturing operations. For some of the employees the goal was to provide a staging area from which to launch elaborate corporate intrigues and sub-rosa advancement schemes. I was a lot better at managing the engineering than the politics. Some felt this was my downfall, but that wasn't really true. A little more political acumen, however, would have helped.

I steered the Grand Prix cautiously through the fog on the way down to the Village. I felt like I was in a submarine. The mist was cold – a winter harbinger. I flicked on the heater for the first time that season. It smelled like burnt mould. I was glad I was still in a pretty good mood.

The Village municipal offices were on Main Street behind a colonnaded facade that guarded the occupants from the citizenry. The interior smelled like the lobby of an old hotel. The walls were decorated with aerial photos and geographical surveys hung like family portraits over waiting areas and brochure stands. Cops with creaking leather holsters and contractors angling for zoning breaks greeted each other as they passed in the halls. One of them pointed out the stairs that took you down to the Records Department.

A chest-high counter anchored the front of the room. A woman sat at a desk on the other side, looking at a computer screen through the bottom half of her bifocals. Her iron grey hair was chiselled into a helmet that perched on top of her head. Ceiling-high metal racks, filled with oversized leather binders, stood a few feet from her desk and ran to the back of the room, the end point disappearing into darkness. She ignored me. I waited her out.

'Can we help you with something?'

'I need everything you've got on this property in North Sea.'

I slid a slip of paper with Regina Broadhurst's address written on it across the top of the counter.

She hoisted her wide bottom off the chair and used its mass to propel her up to the counter. She wore a cotton print dress and blocky high-heeled shoes. A bead chain was clipped to the temples of her glasses so they could double as a necklace. She looked at the address and handed it back to me.

'North Sea is in the Town. You'll have to ask them.'

'They sent me here.'

She looked at me like I was the agent of a hostile power.

'It's an estate matter. I'm the administrator.' I showed her my credentials.

'All I need is the title, deeds, maps, whatever you've got.'

'That's all you need? It's not in one place. It'll take some time.'

I wondered what purpose she thought all those records had. Saving them for the Second Coming.

'How long?'

'Well, I don't know. I haven't begun to look.'

'Okay. When should I come back?'

'You're not going to wait? What if I have questions?'

I held my ground.

'All you need to know is that I need copies of everything in this building relating to that address.'

She saw an opening.

'You'll have to pay for copies.'

'That's okay.'

'And that will add to the time. You can't just look at the documents here?'

I looked at the sign on the wall over the counter. It said the Village of Southampton was pleased to promptly provide copies of official documents. Word hadn't filtered down to the troops.

'They're not the ones who have to do it,' she said, catching the drift.

'I'll be happy to go through the files myself, if you're too busy.'

'We have to do it for you. Can you imagine if people just came in here and went through everything?'

I saw hordes of Long Islanders rampaging through mouldy real estate records.

'Is there anyone else who can help me?'

She snatched the address back out of my hand. 'I don't know why the Town thought this information would be here. Unless it's in the dated stacks.'

'I don't know what those are, but I bet that's where you'll find what I'm looking for. Let's see.'

She left me standing at the counter and went off into the tall stands of metal racks. She came back a half-hour later to tell me she needed the rest of the day to do all the copies. I said fine, I'll be back in the morning. I left her in the glow of her weary indignation and went to the corner place to caffeinate what was left of my good mood.

The fog had risen above the rooftops. Underneath, the light was shadowless and diffused, deepening the colour of the red municipal mums tucked around the base of an ancient Village shade tree. I sat on a teak park bench to drink my coffee. The bench had been donated in loving memory of Elizabeth McGill. I thought about the flow of property through successive generations of the dead and their donators. Maybe I should get a bench in honour of Regina Broadhurst. Something hard with a lot of sharp edges, too uncomfortable to spend much time on.

Except for the cottage, all my parents left me was fifty thousand dollars in unpaid nursing home expenses. My sister and I split it. She handed me a cheque before boarding her plane back to Wisconsin. She told me she was never coming back again. The relief in her voice was deep enough to float an ocean liner. A week later a quit claim deed to her half of the cottage arrived in the mail – stuck like a bookmark between the pages of a standard King James Bible. I don't remember the exact psalm that it marked, but it was all about forgiveness. Who in my family was supposed to be forgiving whom, and for what, God only knows.

Joe Sullivan glided by in his police cruiser. He saw me on the bench and pulled into one of the parking slots. I slid my ass over to clear him a spot.

'They're doin' it. The coroner,' he said, dropping into the bench.

'The autopsy.'

'That's good.'

'I know a couple people up there. Bunch of ghouls if you ask me.

But we need 'em. Doin' me a favour.'

'That was good of you.'

'No biggie. I'll let you know if there's anything you should know about.'

I looked over at the side of his face. He was looking across the street at Harbor Trust, Roy and Amanda's bank.

'Anything at all is what I'm hoping you'll tell me.'

He looked back at me. Some of the old mix of duty and defiance was sketched across his face. Local guys often have that look. A vague sense of being one of the chosen, born to the South Fork, and yet one of the conquered, bound to the service of a powerful elite – an occupation force who had swept in from the west, taking possession of the land, plundering her gifts.

'We'll keep you informed,' he said to me.

I felt my face warm despite the cloud cover.

'If there's ever any reason to look into somebody's death, you know, if there's any questions that come up, who does it? I mean, who opens up the case, you?'

'Basically. If there's any goddam reason to. I go over the situation with my boss, who'll talk to the Chief, who'll talk to the DA's office. They officially tell us to go look a little more. And the day sergeant and administrative lieutenant usually get involved. Then if there's what you'd call an actual investigation it gets assigned to one of our plainclothesmen.'

'So it's your call provided three-quarters of the local judicial system say it's all right, and your role is to hand everything over to other people to do the actual work.'

His rounded jowls turned the colour of the Village mums. He slapped his thigh with an open hand as if to drain off the urge to turn it into a fist.

'You can really be a dick sometimes, Mr Acquillo.'

Anger rose in my throat, but I choked it off. I shook myself like a wet retriever. Shedding heat. I stared at the ground until I knew my voice was level.

Sullivan was trying not to breathe too hard. His hands were on his hips, pushing down on the holster belt. I noticed for the first time that he was chewing gum. Probably learned that from the Big Tough Cop Instruction Manual.

'I'm a dick most of the time. Don't take it personally. It's this thing with Regina Broadhurst. It's bugging me.'

'Like how?'

'Are you going to take this seriously?'

He shook his head. Reminded me of a bull shaking off flies.

'I'm trying to.'

'Regina didn't take baths. She couldn't get in and out of the bathtub. She always used a walk-in shower.'

'Gettin' dotty. Got confused. Slipped and fell.'

'I knew her. She was clear as a bell. She'd lived with arthritis for a million years. She wouldn't suddenly forget she had it.'

'What are you suggesting?'

'I don't know. Maybe she didn't fall.'

There, I said it. Right in front of God and local law enforcement.

'Oh, come on.'

'I found an industrial strength neoprene plug in the bathroom. It has a series of O-rings to force a tight seal. We had them in the chem lab at work. You'd need something like that to keep the tub full as long as possible. Any fan of long baths will tell you that ordinary bath stoppers are pretty leaky – the water usually runs out in a few hours.'

Sullivan let out a man-sized sigh and sat back on the park bench.

'Doesn't mean shit. Won't mean shit to the DA, much less to the Chief. I go to those people talking about a neighbour of a dead old lady who's worryin' about a bath plug, they throw me out on my can. We deal with enough crazy shit every day from people we actually have to pay attention to.'

It would be a mistake to underestimate the Southampton Town cops. They covered a big area, and not all of it what you'd expect to find out here. There were some tough little spots filled with hard case locals and immigrant labour. And the Summer People themselves weren't all affected fops. Others thought a little money, or the show of money, bought immunity. Especially during the season when the clubs were in full riot. Guys like Sullivan were serious and could handle stuff. But the trouble they knew would tend to come right at them, out in the open where they could see it plain and simple.

'I'm not really asking you to do anything. I'm just talking here.'

He looked relieved.

'Talking's okay.'

'Not accusing anybody.'

'Accusations, not okay.'

'Doesn't mean I can't talk to you once in a while so somebody other than me knows what I'm thinking. Even if it's nuts.'

'Like I said, talking's okay.'

'Like getting an autopsy report. No big deal.'

He made a noise and stood up.

'Okay. Jesus, what a pain in the ass,' he said as he walked away, trying to maintain a little obstinacy, keeping the narrow, ill-fed portions of his mind in reserve. The cloud cover broke at about the same instant, and the sun tossed a few splashes of brilliance on the sidewalk to help light his path back to the cruiser.

I spent the late afternoon and evening at the Pequot. I thought it would help me think. Or, better yet, not think at all.

That'd been my plan, if you could call it that, when I moved into my parents' house. I didn't have anywhere else to go, or anything else to do. Or, rather, I didn't want to do anything else. I was expected to find another job, which I probably could have done. Some type of job. I still had a good name in the industry. Outside the management of my own company. Abby had kept me somewhat involved in professional organizations, and in contact with people who could help my career, in her opinion. But I let those contacts lapse.

The divorce from Abby was a sleepwalk. My terms were so generous her lawyer really had nothing to do until I gutted our house, which got things a little livelier. If I'd tried to get work at that point, it might have been harder, but I still had a few friends around the business. They took it on themselves to try on my behalf, but I kept my head down until they went away. I started to really like wearing blue jeans and sweatshirts every day. And once I got to Southampton, all the old links just evaporated. I calculated how long I could live on whatever money was left after the carnage and figured if I kept down expenses I'd almost make it to early retirement age. Or, with a little luck, I'd be dead by then. Now, four years into it and for the first time I didn't like the mood I was working myself into. I was getting nervy. It was messing up my sleep, nagging at me in the middle of the night.

DOTTY HODGES had the old place under control. She wore a tight T-shirt that rode up above her belly and matched her raven black hair. Her jeans were cut like pedal pushers which accentuated a clunky pair of yellow stitched Doc Martens and blue and white horizontally striped socks.

I ordered the fish of the day without further inquiry and pulled out good old de Tocqueville to give it another try. I had a rule not to quit a book after I started it, no matter how daunting it got.

The fish took a long time, but it was delivered by the chef.

'It's the baked.'

'Great.'

'Bon appetite.'

He let me take a few bites of the fish before interrupting.

'That Miss Filmore's a hard-on, isn't she?'

'I don't think I made her happy.'

'It's like her little empire. Likes to keep things under control.'

'Always been there?'

'Nah, I've been through a bunch of directors. Used to be all volunteer till the widow of a guy who'd cashed out his potato farm left money for a professional staff. It's a good place, though, Sam. Don't take a broad like Filmore too seriously.'

I got in a few more mouthfuls while he talked. Dotty brought him a beer and refilled my glass.

'Didn't learn much,' I said.

'I called a few people I know from over there. They'll ask around.

Never know.'

'Thanks, Mr Hodges,' I told him, pleased.

'Paul.'

'Paul.'

'You spooked her with that thing about recent deaths.'

'Didn't mean to.'

'She thought you were Social Services heat.'

'Nope. Just nosy.'

He took some time out to drink his beer and let me finish my meal. Dotty swept up the plates the moment I put down my fork and recharged our drinks. It struck me she liked seeing her father talk to somebody.

That it was me showed how out of touch with people Hodges probably was. Would've given my own daughter a good laugh.

'I did find out a few things, though' said Hodges. 'I was hoping you'd come in so I could tell you.'

'Really.'

'Regina and Mrs Anselma hated each other's guts. It was like a blood feud, some thought, only way below the surface. You know, act all civil with each other, but the air's filled with little invisible daggers.'

'That fits.'

'It fits with Broadhurst, but Mrs Anselma wasn't that way. A sweet lady, refined. You know, maybe a little higher class, but everybody liked her. Never had a bad word for nobody but Regina, who'd she stick it to whenever she got the chance.'

'Raised a daughter on her own.'

Hodges was warming to his subject.

'Yeah, well, that's the other interesting thing. No dad in the picture. Ever. Back then this wasn't something that went unnoticed. But Mrs Anselma was such a class act nobody'd talk her down, though it sorta hung around her all the time.'

'Amanda. The daughter. Married Roy Battiston.'

'I knew most of the Battistons. Lowlifes.'

'You think?'

He raised his hand.

'Just an opinion. Shouldn't say that kind of thing about people.' He glanced over at Dotty. 'I just never liked them much. Used to be a passel of them livin' year round in an old summer colony in

Noyac. All the houses up on cinderblocks. Shacks is what they were.'

'Roy runs the local Harbor Trust.'

'No shit. Must've got the brains in the family.'

'Must've.'

'So you knew him.'

'Yeah, though mostly his family. I crewed with his uncle and grandfather out of Montauk. They were serious hard cases. Only worked off and on. Construction labour. Pumping gas. Cheating county welfare. Kind of like me, without the style.'

'Amanda said Roy worked his way out of it.'

'Roy didn't talk much. Big fat serious kid. Looked like a bed-wetter to me. But yeah, hard worker. Stuck to himself. Stayed clear of his grandfather's backhand. Grandmother was no better. Big time drunk. Had a huge rosy face – nose full of busted capillaries. Beautiful people.'

'Including his mother?'

'Oh yeah, Judy Battiston. Worked at the Anchorage for years. Another drinker. Anybody that could stand her could take her home. Ended up at the 7-Eleven. Pretty sad.'

'Now they're all dead,' said Hodges.

'Who?'

'The Battistons. The whole clan. Including his mother. Everybody but Roy.'

He had to leave after that to look after the other customers. I was able to concentrate on forgetting about everything but my vodka and Alexis de Tocqueville, who was having a great time boppin' around the old U.S. I guess I could see some relevance to the country that's here now, but a lot of it seemed alien. I wondered if he ever made it to the Hamptons. Would have found a bunch of hard-nosed Yankee farmers and a few beat-up Indians. And the Bonnikers crabbing like they still do over in Springs. Oceanfront was where you grazed cattle.

Hodges came back at the end of the night and settled in at my table like I'd invited him. The old bastard was growing on me a little, I had to admit.

Not that I was looking for a friend. I never had a lot of friends in the first place, and since moving to the cottage I'd kept to myself. Friends were another thing I wasn't very good at. Probably why I got a dog.

When I was a kid my only friend enlisted in the army to avoid going to jail for car theft. He and I used to borrow expensive convertibles from used car lots and bomb around the South Fork like we were rich city kids. I did the hot wiring and he did the driving, so when the cops were chasing us he was the one who slowed down just enough to let me jump out of the car. I landed in a sand bank covered in wild roses and he sped away. They caught him trying to swim across Mecox Bay, the front end of the convertible nearly submerged in the stony bay beach.

The only hitch in the enlistment idea was he had a genuine fear of guns. His father was a hunter and had decided the only way to cure his son's fear was to take him deer hunting in Connecticut. The woods were full of deer, so there was ample opportunity to get the rifle stock up to his shoulder, but he couldn't get his finger to pull the trigger. By the third try, the old man lost his temper. He started to yell. The kid yelled back. The old man yanked the rifle out of the kid's hands and slammed the butt into his face. Inexplicably, the old man's thumb had slipped into the trigger guard, so the cocked rifle went off right at the moment of impact. The recoil knocked the kid out, so he didn't see the heavy deer-shot blow his father's face off. He only saw the results when he woke up a few hours later, half dead himself from a huge gash in his forehead.

The recruitment officer, having literally heard it all, promised the kid he could enlist as a medic, stationed in Germany, and would never have to carry a gun. Half the promise was kept. He was trained as a medic, and up until an hour before he boarded the transport he assumed he was going to get a chance to learn German.

He drank all the way to Saigon and watched a firefight light up the skies as they landed that night. Two days later, he was in the front seat of a jeep in a small convoy winding along a jungle road on the way to a South Vietnamese firebase somewhere near the western border. They were behind a canvas-covered deuce-and-a-half. Another jeep leading the convoy was the only other vehicle, since the road was supposed to be secure. That was why the machine gunner sitting behind the kid had his M-60 stowed at his feet, with the bandoleers safely packed in boxes in the back of the deuce. Not that he could have done anything about the sniper who shot him through the throat.

That night the kid slept with the machine gunner's blood in his hair and an M-16, his regular issue Colt .45 and a half-dozen ammo bags full of clips snuggled up next to his body like a child's stuffed animals.

He got plenty of opportunity to use it all, right up to the moment the Viet Cong ripped him to pieces while he was trying to stuff a Huey full of wounded grunts. That was near the beginning of his second re-up. He was pretty badly strung out on heroin by then and had forgotten that there was a place called Long Island he could come home to.

My mother got me one of the last deferments you could get for having a dead father. I almost enlisted anyway, thinking I could wrangle school money out of the deal. She fought me on it. Said if I went in I'd never get my degree. Her interference bothered me at the time, since she'd never interfered with anything I'd ever done before. I tried to thank her later on, but she'd forgotten about Vietnam by then, along with everything else.

WHEN I got home Eddie was passed out on my bed on the screened-in porch, snoring. I had to wake him up. Fearless watch dog. But he was glad to see me and glad to get outside.

I had a nightcap and watched Eddie under the moonlight, running the yard, securing the perimeter. It was bright and clear enough to light up the bay so you could see all the way across to Southold. Some lights were still lit over on Nassau Point and Hog's Neck, full of guys on porches, staring back into the mysteries of the Little Peconic Bay.

IN THE morning I called my personal banker.

'Amanda Battiston.'

'Hi. It's Sam. On official business.'

'Ready to open that investment account?'

'And plunge Wall Street into chaos?'

'I'm ready when you are.'

'I need everything you got on Regina's account.'

'We have her account?'

'I got the cheques to prove it. I want to cash one to pay her bills. Keep the lights on. I need to know how much she's got. If there're any other accounts. Savings, or one of your aggressively promoted investment accounts. Any account history as detailed as you can give me. I have one box of cancelled cheques, which I'm guessing goes back a few years. I haven't found her chequebook, so current stuff is important. I need to know what obligations she's got, premiums, taxes, that kind of thing. Do you take pictures of cheques from other banks that are deposited?'

'I don't think so. They might record the bank code. I can ask. This could take a little time.' There was a pause. 'I'm trying to write it all down.'

'I appreciate it.'

'I'll need an original death certificate and a copy of whatever says you're the administrator of the estate.'

'I got that.'

'If there's a safe deposit box the Town Attorney might have to be there when we open it up.'

'Okay. Whatever you got.'

'I don't think I ever saw her in here.'

'I think Regina ran everything out of her mailbox. The flag was up all the time. Didn't drive. Cabbed or took the Senior Centre shuttle to the IGA, unless she could nag me into getting her groceries.'

'You'd do that?'

'Occasionally.'

'That's sweet.'

'Nothing relating to Regina was sweet. Least of all me.'

'No safety deposit. No investments, no savings account. Just one chequeing. Originally opened in 1987, which was the year

Harbor Trust bought out East End Savings and Loan, so it could be a much older account.'

'That was fast.'

'We have computers.'

'How much she got?'

'If you're planning to abscond to Mexico you won't get far. Eight thousand, two hundred and sixty-seven.'

'Dollars?'

'Not pesos.'

'Deposits?'

'One thousand, fifty-two dollars and thirty-five cents deposited, let me see,' I heard the keyboard tap, 'every month for the last twelve months, which is all I can pull up on this computer.'

'Social Security.'

'Looks from the balances like she basically washed it all out every month paying bills. Thirty-two, eighty-one, fifty-five. Here's one back in May for two hundred and eighty-three. Nothing bigger than that.'

'What's the number on the last cheque she wrote?'

'Six-two-oh-four.'

I wrote it down.

'Nothing bigger than two hundred and eighty-three dollars?'

'No. I'm looking.'

'Like in January or June?'

'No.'

'No property taxes.'

'Wouldn't tell me that, but I wouldn't say so from the size of the cheques.'

'Lived on about twelve thousand a year.'

'I've done it on less,' she said.

'Yeah, but not with Regina's lavish lifestyle.'

'Which was financed by tax evasion?'

'She didn't pay property taxes.'

'She must have paid it some other way.'

'No. Didn't have to pay because she didn't own the house.'

'A rental?'

'I'm not sure. Can you give me hard copies of all that stuff?'

'If I ask Roy.'

'I appreciate it.'

'He's back in the city tomorrow.'

'Busy boy.'

'I've got the day off.'

'Me, too.'

There was another pause on the other end.

'I'm going to start my day off by walking on the beach. I usually park at Little Plains.'

'Must be pretty in the morning.'

'At nine in the morning the sun's still fresh, but the mist is lifting. My favourite time.'

'I bet it's possible you'll be bringing along a stack of account records belonging to Regina Broadhurst.'

'Not my normal routine, but the chances are good.'

'Well, thanks for your help. Hope you have a good day tomorrow.'

'I'm guessing I will.'

Eddie was looking at me when I hung up the phone.

'What.'

He didn't answer.

'I know. Stupid.'

WHEN I went to bed it was unseasonably warm and humid. At 8:45 the next morning the air had switched back to clean and clear, with a steady offshore breeze blowing in cool dry Canadian air. I was sitting on the petrified remnants of an old wooden breakwater and looking out at the ocean. The wind was knocking the tops off the waves before they broke on shore, sending up a foamy spray that the sun lit into slivers of pale grey glass. The rim of my Yankees cap was pushed down low to keep the hat from blowing off my head. I was wearing clip-on sunglasses over my wire rims and had the collar of my jean jacket pulled up around my neck. The overall effect made me feel undercover. It was working with the seagulls flying overhead – none of them seemed to recognize me.

Behind me were low dunes covered in feathery dune grass that the wind combed into a green pompadour. Behind the dunes were shingle-style mansions spaced every three to four acres – mountainous houses dressed up with terraced balconies, octagonal windows and colonnaded porches. Mostly empty this time of year, they faced the ferocious sea and never blinked.

I watched her walk out on the beach from a path that led between the dunes. She stopped when she saw me and looked surprised, acting out the part. As she started walking again, the dry sand forced her hips to swing outside their normal arc. She wore a beat-up gold barn jacket, white silk blouse, jeans and sunglasses. I sat still and silent as I watched her approach. Still incognito.

She walked right up to me and stood there enriching the beauty of the beach.

'You.'

'Me,' I said back, still stumped for words.

'It's nice, isn't it?' She looked out at the ocean for confirmation.

In profile, lit by the sun's glare off the sea, the lines that defined her cheek and jaw looked crisper than I'd remembered them. I realised those lines were usually hidden behind heavy reddish-brown waves of hair. The wind was now sweeping it back from her face, clearing the decks. I liked the symmetrical proportions. Her skin was even smoother and more richly tinted than I'd noticed under the fluorescent lights of the bank or my dimly lit house. It began to dawn on me that Amanda Battiston was actually a very beautiful woman. I don't know why it took that long. Maybe she'd been shrouded within a translucent veil that prevented me from seeing what she really looked like. And now, under the autumn light, everything was revealed.

'What?'

'Very nice. The ocean.'

'You weren't looking at the ocean.'

'Yes I was. Out of the corner of my eye. You can't tell with my clip-on sunglasses.'

She smirked.

'They're actually kind of cute. Your sunglasses.'

'Fifty-two-year-old ex-prizefighters can't be cute. Puppies are cute.'

She looked sceptical.

'Prizefighter?'

'Well, sort of. Sounds more impressive than it is.'

'That's why your nose is a little off to the side?'

'That's why.'

'Ouch.'

'That's what I said at the time.'

'I was never a prizefighter.'

'And not always a personal banker, I'm guessing.'

She still smiled, a little less firmly.

'No. I did some other things.'

'Me, too. I improved the fuel efficiency of your Audi Quattro and sired the only perfect female to ever trod the earth.'

'Next to me.'

'I'll take that up with your father.'

'Can't now. He's been dead for a while.'

'So you can be the only other perfect female. By default.'

She sat down next to me on the old bulkhead.

'Finally, perfection. And still young enough to enjoy it.'

I felt her shoulder through the various layers of denim, suede and cotton that separated us. All my nerve endings must have travelled over there for the occasion.

'You're right,' she said. 'You're not cute. Cute's a demeaning term to apply to a fifty-two-year-old anything. You are, however, something which has been disturbing my sleep.'

'Medication'll fix that.'

'I haven't been entirely honest with you,' she said abruptly, like I always did when I was having a hard time getting to the point.

'You don't have to be even partially honest with me. You don't owe me anything.'

She was focusing on the soft straight line of the horizon. Probably helped keep her level.

'Look,' I said to her before she could speak again, 'some people think, female people usually, that you can't properly know someone unless you spill your guts all over the place and reveal every goddam thing you ever thought, felt or did.'

'I suppose that's true.'

'Doesn't have to be. Frankly, I think a keen sense of privacy, emotional atrophy and repression, especially as regards personal history, are highly underrated behaviors.'

A bright little laugh popped out of her.

'Where did they make you, anyway?'

'In the Bronx. I think people pile their past up in these big emotional landfills where they decompose and produce nothing but toxic emissions. Personally, I'm working at shooting all that stuff out into space. I don't want it anymore. I don't want mine, I don't want yours.'

She looked toward me and pulled back – maybe to see me better through her sunglasses.

'You can't forget your whole life. Why live it in the first place?'

'No reason I can think of.'

'Maybe you don't want to.'

Now I got to laugh.

'Jesus, this is exactly the kind of shit I'm trying not to talk about.'

'You started it.'

'I did?'

'Because you thought I was going to say something. Maybe I wasn't.'

I loved the way the waves were breaking under the offshore breeze. Tidy, well-organized curls. Good surfing waves, especially for Long Island.

'I like you, Amanda. But I'm really not what you're looking for. Whatever that is. I tend to end in disappointment.'

I felt a subtle increase of pressure at the point where our two shoulders touched. Maybe a millionth of a psi. She was also looking intently at the ocean. The two of us, sitting there side by side. Nobody talked for a while.

'Okay,' she said, finally.

'Okay what?'

'Okay, I understand. Here.'

She stood up, brushed off her butt and pulled an overstuffed, sealed number ten envelope from the inside pocket of her barn jacket. She sort of tapped me on the forehead with it before she put it in my hand.

'Copies of her last twelve statements. That's all I have. Anything older would be buried in old microfiche from the original bank, if it exists at all.'

She started walking back to the path through the dunes. I followed her, feeling a little off-balance walking across the dry sand. Probably what she intended.

When I came up over the slot in the dunes I saw her Audi and the Grand Prix. Along with a big black BMW 740iL sedan parked there looking invincible and overpriced. Apparently it came with a matching guy in a long black leather duster, black peg-legged pants and motorcycle boots. Even his hair was black as an oil slick. Only the half-ton of gold wrapped around a meaty pinkie introduced a touch of colour. Any other beach he'd look out of place, but this was Long Island. He was leaning against his car, staring at Amanda.

She acted like she didn't notice him. I acted like I did, looking him straight in the eye to pull his attention away from her. When he finally looked, it was like eyeballing a black bear. Only less sentient.

I moved a little quicker so I could escort Amanda to her Audi. She probably thought I was being chivalrous holding her door – she had that awkward, shy smile back on her face.

When I went to get into the Grand Prix, the trained bear was leaning up against my driver's side door. I took my hands out of the pockets of my jean jacket and approached him without hesitation. I wondered what kind of traction I'd get from the old Adidas Countries I had on my feet.

I stood there and waited for him to move. I didn't say anything, and neither did he. Amanda was busy backing out of her space, and wasn't noticing anything. After only a few seconds he shrugged, like we'd just wrapped up a long conversation, and moved out of the way. I waited until he was outside cold cock range and climbed into my car. My hand shook a little when I put the key in the ignition. Adrenaline.

I made a wider than necessary arc when I backed out of my space so I could align the rear bumper of the Grand Prix with the BMW's. I looked at the guy when I gave his car just the gentlest little tap, the armoured-car-gauge chrome of the Grand Prix thumping wetly into the polymer composite that tucked around the ass of the BMW. He didn't seem to mind. He just looked at me with a pair of eyes that would have cooled off a ski slope. They were pinched tight to the bridge of his nose, then angled off to the outside of his face. I couldn't tell if they'd grown that way naturally or been mashed into place. Either way, they showed no affect. He just stood there and looked.

By this time, Amanda was long gone. A little red warning light went on somewhere way in the back of my head. But like we usually did with those things back in the plant control rooms, I ignored it, hoping it would shut itself off again.

CHAPTER THREE

I couldn't drive into Southampton Village unarmed, so I bought a cup of Hazelnut at one of the roadside delis. It tasted like burnt oak leaves, but at least it was hot and caffeinated.

I crossed Sunrise Highway and drove into the Village, noticing as I always did the sudden change in foliage, the native scrub oak and pine turning into luxurious shrubs and cultivated hardwoods, sycamore and dense privet hedges that rose like battlements in defence of shingled mansions and social status, however tenuous and dearly bought.

I arrived at the Village offices a day later than I'd planned. The autumn season for building permits and zoning appeals was going full tilt. People with briefcases and rolled-up blueprints were meeting with officials out on the steps between the oversized Doric columns. The smell of negotiation tinged the air. Faces looked sincere and cooperative. It'd be an ordinary scene if it wasn't for the money at stake. There were plenty of people from Manhattan with bank accounts and egos large enough to fill 20,000 sq. ft. houses built on the most expensive sand in the world. More than the East End would ever be able to absorb, which kept constant upward pressure on real estate values. A small group of regular people who lived out here – teachers, carpenters, pediatricians – had the job of controlling the demand, keeping the golden goose from being strangled by overdevelopment. It wasn't easy. Every day Planning and Zoning faced down the kind of venal avarice that used to overrun entire continents.

I passed through the middle of the transactions unseen, like a wraith, and entered the building. There were a lot of cops hanging out in the lobby, buckling holsters, drinking coffee, going on and off shifts. None of them seemed to want to arrest me for anything, so I moved on down the corridor to the Records Department.

She was still at her station behind the tall counter. She didn't look up, even after I cleared my throat. I cleared it again.

'Yes?'

'I'm Sam Acquillo. I was here a few days ago about a property up in North Sea.'

'That's the Town. You'll have to go there.'

'Yes, we talked about that. The Town told me the records for this place were stored over here. You were going to research it for me and make some copies.'

She looked at me through the tops of her bifocals.

'You were going to come in the next day. I made copies for you.'

Now that she had me on a breach of promise her memory flooded back.

'I had it all ready for you.'

'Yeah. Sorry. If I could have it now I'll get out of your hair.'

She tapped a few more times on her keyboard, then hauled her mass up out of the chair. Her glasses, secured by a bead chain, rested on a shelf formed by her uplifted bust. The furrow above the bridge of her nose had formed a permanent crease, casting her irritation into a structural component of her face. She dug a nine-by-twelve-inch brown envelope out from under the counter.

'There's a charge for these copies.'

'A day late, but,' I said to her, plunking down a five dollar bill. She snatched it up and held it stuffed in her fist. She waited for me to go.

'I guess that's all I need,' I said. She nodded once, smiled and went back to her computer. The end of our relationship made her happy.

'Have a nice day,' she said to me, before smacking the ENTER key on the computer.

'Too late for that.'

Everyone had cleared out from the front steps by the time I got back outside. The autumn leaves were thinning out overhead and the October air was beginning to lose the fight. The sun still had enough strength to warm the paving bricks and the teak bench directly outside the Village offices where I sat to slide the contents out of the envelope.

There were about ten pages. Some were clean Xeroxes, others

were slippery old-fashioned Photostats. Some had the fuzzy edges and optical distortion common to microfilm enlargements. On top was a site plan, dated 1939. The lines were neatly drawn and the hand lettering true to the engineering calligraphy of the time. I'd seen the style before on old drawings. I thought it was incomprehensibly beautiful and other worldly. The plan was covered with stamps noting perk tests, septic and well locations. There were separate sheets with revisions overlaid, and dated as recently as 1998. These were certified by the surveyors, Spring & Spring, in Bridgehampton, and signed-off on by the Town building inspector, Claude Osay. Suffolk County had its own stamp, warning all concerned to submit wetlands clearance with any application for a building permit.

The site itself was roughly rectangular, the borders straight and at right angles, matching the one my father bought about six years later. The adjacent lots weren't drawn in, but there were numbers suggesting subdivisions distributed around the map in a neat pattern. Regina was number thirty-three. We were number thirty-two.

It didn't say who owned the property at the time the site plan was drawn. Another hand notation, far cruder than the ones made in 1939, read 'Bay Side Holdings, Inc., Sag Harbor,' with an arrow pointed at Regina's lot. I guessed its vintage to be the same as the recent building inspector stamps. There was nothing at all about a Mr or Mrs Broadhurst.

Bay Side Holdings showed up on another document that looked like a contract with a real estate agent, Arnold Lombard Co., Southampton. The contract was signed in 1977 accompanying another burst of perk testing. Spring & Spring had certified the results, as they had later, in 1998. I flipped back to the site plan to pinpoint where the tests were done and found another rubber stamp impression with the name Bay Side Holdings.

There was an aerial photograph showing all of Oak Point, and the land next door that held the old WB plant. The complex was bigger than it looked from ground level. I counted one main building and at least ten smaller outbuildings. The neighbourhood property lines were drawn in and numbered with white ink.

Regina's number thirty-three was shaded by something. A high-lighter? So was number thirty-five, next door and the lot after that, and several others on the east side of WB's peninsula. So was the whole of the WB complex. Our lot had a check mark, as did number thirty-eight and number thirty-nine.

There was a letter to the Town appeals board from an attorney named Jacqueline Swaitkowski of Bridgehampton representing Bay Side Holdings, Inc. She wanted to record their intentions to approach the board on a number of lot size and setback issues, all of which she described somewhat hopefully as routine. It was dated June 30, 1998.

That was it. There were no comments from the Town and no record of any actual appeals. I stuffed it all back in the envelope and went down to the corner place for a cup of French Vanilla coffee and a croissant.

Properly fortified, I walked the block and a half up Hampton Road to the big Town building. While the incorporated Village was defined by the traditional boundaries of Southampton, the Town covered half the South Fork, from Westhampton Beach to Bridgehampton, including the Village itself. The geopolitical complexities of New York State took some concentration to navigate, but I'm a trained engineer. Complex systems are my forte.

Bonny Martinez was on duty at the Town Tax Collector's office. She wore a wide smile and a print blouse covered with huge tropical flowers.

'What can I help you with?'

'I'm settling an estate,' I said, pulling out my paperwork. 'Here's the death certificate and documentation showing me as administrator. And my driving licence.'

She scooped it all up and scanned the information.

'Okay, what can I help you with?'

I wrote Regina's address on a piece of scratch paper from a stack on the counter.

'She's been living here for many years, but didn't own the house. I need to know who's been paying the taxes so I can notify them.'

'Okay,' she said, cheerily.

It took a few seconds for her to sit down at a terminal, tap in the address, and pop back up again with the information.

'Bay Side Holdings. Number 675 Dutch Wharf Road, Sag Harbor, New York. Attention Milton Hornsby. We had them on bi-annual automatic payment. Harbor Trust, account number 41-53245-41.'

She wrote it all down on another slip of scratch paper and slapped it down on the counter. Just like that.

WHEN I got back to the car Eddie was in the driver's seat looking down at the instrument panel. Planning a getaway.

'Yeah, I could teach you to drive, but who'd pay the insurance?'

He hopped back over to his side and I rolled the window down for him. He stuck his head out and barked at the closest passerby, who jumped back in alarm. I pulled away as briskly as the big car would allow.

'Great. Here I'm trying to get along with people and what do you do?'

He looked over at me happily.

When my daughter was little she had a half-dozen imaginary friends, the most prominent of which was Eddie Van Halen. I have no idea how that happened, but the hard rocker was a constant, if invisible, presence in our household for years. She always made sure I had the seat belt around him in the car. Once we were driving along and 'Runnin' with the Devil' came on the radio. She turned around to address the backseat:

'That's you, Eddie Van Halen!'

I'd often say the same thing to my eponymously named dog, and get about as much back in response.

My daughter had stopped talking to me a few months before the divorce, so I wasn't sure what she was up to. I knew she had an apartment in Manhattan where she went to live after graduating from the Rhode Island School of Design. She was doing something with graphics on the computer, but I didn't know what. I didn't know how to find out without talking to her mother or her mother's family, which wouldn't work out. Abby worked hard to keep her away from my family, so she never got to know my sister. Abby always insisted we rent or stay with friends like Burton Lewis, the lawyer, when we came to visit. Abby said she didn't want our daughter exposed to that environment, whatever that meant. My mother spent a lot of time with my sister's kids, little meatballs though they were, so at least she got to have grandchildren. She never complained about not seeing my daughter, though it clearly wounded her. But I deferred to Abby, to my deep and everlasting sorrow.

Since it was on the way to Dutch Wharf Road, I thought I'd I stop at the Pequot for lunch. The woods became more dense as North Sea Road turned into Noyac Road. It was narrow, with a double yellow line down the middle, and twisty as it followed the jagged bay coast and bumpy contours of Noyac's little hills. The Grand Prix kept its dignity on the curves if you held a firm hand on the wheel.

Eddie finally tired of the wind and jumped into the backseat where he had plenty of room to spread out. I followed the slow arc around Long Beach, the sickle-shaped bay front west of Sag Harbor. The water was rippled and slick, silver-blue like a sharkskin suit. People were walking on the beach, cuffs rolled up to below their knees and hands in their pockets, their clothes pressed against their bodies by the stiffening breeze. It was too far away to divine their thoughts. Gulls circled overhead.

The clouds and mist of the morning had long ago been chased out by a cool hard breeze traveling down from New England. I lowered my window and let the noisy air swirl around inside the passenger compartment. I dropped the Grand Prix down to a crawl when I got to the houses that crowded the antique streets of Sag Harbor. Slow time was woven into the ivy that hung on the gates and fences of Greek Revival mansions built by bold sea captains.

There was always plenty of room to park at the Pequot. I let Eddie take care of business at a little patch of scrub grass, and was about to let him back in the car when I saw Dotty waving to me from the front door of the restaurant.

'Your dog?'

'Eddie.'

'He's cute.'

'Got to be good at something.'

'You can bring him with you if you sit out on the deck.'

'Outdoor seating?'

'The deck. Go around back.'

I didn't know the Pequot had a small, slightly raised deck off the kitchen with a white plastic table where the Hodges family probably sat to eat their meals and watch the fishing boats come and go. Dotty was there to greet me and fuss over the dog, which was something you have to get used to when your dog's got a personality like Eddie's. Eternally bon vivant. 'So you weren't lying,' said Dotty as she wiped off the plastic table.

'I wasn't?'

'About having a dog to let out. I thought it was an excuse.'

The two of us watched Eddie run his nose over the whole of the deck before coming back to my table to sit down at my feet.

'I guess you're all checked out.'

'Absolut?'

'Yup. And a shot of water for the dog.'

'With or without fruit?'

'He'd probably go for a slice of lime.'

While I was waiting for her to bring our drinks, I spread all the papers I'd collected that morning out on the table so I could capture the information I wanted on my yellow legal pad. I numbered each point and drew a little circle around the numbers I thought were the most important. Then I made a list of the things I didn't know, that I wanted to know. These I also put in order of priority, with the most important getting double underlines. The task felt satisfying. I hadn't done anything like that for almost five years.

Hodges came out with two drinks and a bowl of water. I almost covered the pad and was glad I didn't. I didn't want to insult him. He sat down and stuck the bowl in front of Eddie's nose.

'Good-lookin' dog.'

'He wants you to think so.'

'I got a pair of Shih Tzu back at the house. Little ugly fuckin' dogs. They were Dotty's mother's. She gets 'em as puppies, then dies and leaves them with me.'

He covered the moment by concentrating on Eddie. Dogs are really good for that.

'I got Regina's bank accounts and a plot plan for her house,' I said.

He looked over at all the papers spread out on the table.

'She got a million bucks?'

'About eight thousand. Didn't even own the house. Far as I can tell, though, didn't pay rent, either. Didn't pay anything, but,' I placed a series of cancelled cheques on the table, 'oil, LIPA, phone – no long distance – propane for the stove, Sisters of Mercy, twenty bucks a month. Then it's periodic cheques to the IGA, pharmacy, the kid that cut her lawn, occasional cabs.'

'Paid the cab with a cheque?'

'The rest are cheques to cash, mostly at Ray's Liquors. Can't tell if some of that went to a little fortification.'

'Lived pretty lean.'

'Leaner than me, which is saying something.'

'You got Pequot expenses.'

'No rent, no medical, no taxes.'

'Didn't file?'

'Not that I can tell.'

'Lived under the radar.'

'Typical of the neighbourhood.'

'Who owned the house?'

'Some outfit named Bay Side Holdings. Here in Sag Harbor. Going there next.' I dropped the slip of paper with their address down in front of him. He picked it up and frowned.

'Must be in a house, or something.'

I took the slip back from him.

'Dutch Wharf Road?'

'All houses. Except at the end where there's a busted-up old dock building. Used to have a launch ramp, but the water got shoaled over and nobody bothered to dredge. Maybe the Town closed it up. Anyway, nothin' commercial there now.'

I got Hodges to bring me a ham sandwich which I washed down with a Sam Adams. Eddie took half the fries. Something he wouldn't touch if I dropped it in his bowl at the cottage. Probably didn't want to offend Hodges either.

It took a while to find the head of Dutch Wharf Road. It was over on the east side of town where a lot of the roads are narrow and tangled up with the grassy little inlets that ring that part of the bay. Hard to imagine that Sag Harbor was once America's biggest port, filled with square-riggers and awash in whale oil.

It was just like Hodges said. A narrow, leafy street lined with small cottages, all built at different times, but well established and lovingly cared for. I followed the numbers to the end of the street and the abandoned launch ramp. Number 675 was the last house on the right. It fit in with the neighbourhood – fresh white brick and white clapboard, with the gable end facing the street. It had a very steep roof line, which was the fashion for small Tudor houses in the twenties and thirties. Looked like something you'd find in the Cotswolds. Ivy covered part of the lawn and grew up the facade. No name on the mailbox. There was a basic, anonymous-looking Nissan in the driveway. No garage.

No answer at the door. I'd given up ringing the bell and was about to leave when I heard a sound coming from the back of the house. I went around the north side through a thick stand of arborvitae. The backyard was stuffed with trees and shrubs. It looked like they'd been growing there for about 100 years, which was probably about right. On one tiny patch of grass, illuminated by a spot of sunlight, stood a weathered wheelbarrow filled with sticks and uprooted plant life. A few yards away a guy's butt stuck out from under an out-of-control forsythia. The butt wore khakis and belonged on a large man. I shuffled my feet a little and cleared my throat as I approached.

'Excuse me.'

The guy backed out from under the forsythia on his hands and knees and stood up. He was over six-foot-three, reasonably slender, but with a very big head. Thin grey hair circled a bald dome. He looked to be somewhere in his seventies, on the high side, and wore very thick glasses through which he squinted at me painfully.

'Yes.'

'I'm sorry to bother you. I'm looking for Milton Hornsby.'

He held a bunch of pulled-up weeds in his gloved right hand. In the other hand was a small garden trowel. He looked down as if trying to decide which to discard.

'My name is Sam Acquillo. I have something important to discuss with Mr Hornsby.'

He held up both hands as if in surrender.

'That would be me.'

I leafed through the manila folder I had under my arm and pulled out Regina's death certificate which I held out in front of him. As I talked he dropped the weeds and trowel on the ground and pulled off his gloves.

'I'm here to notify you of the death of Regina Broadhurst. Died last week. You can see my name here.' I pointed to a line on the death certificate. 'I'm also the administrator of the estate.'

I held out that piece of paper with my other hand. He took both to look at more closely. His squint got worse, turning his eyes into thin slits.

'What's your relation?' he asked, still looking at the paperwork.

'Neighbour.'

'Attorney?'

'Nope. Just a neighbour. Far as we know there's only one family member, a nephew. That's one of the things I wanted to ask you. If you knew of any others.'

He was big, but not very healthy looking. He had large, prominent cheekbones, but underneath his cheeks were pitted and sunken in. His khakis and flannel shirt were of good quality, but hadn't been washed in a while.

'I wondered when this would happen.'

'She was pretty old.'

He smiled at that, like it triggered a private joke.

He handed the papers back to me. I didn't take them.

'You can keep them. For your records.'

He shook his head.

'I'm not going to talk to you,' he said, flatly, still squinting at me through his bottle-bottom glasses. He dropped the papers on the ground.

'You're not? Why not?'

'I don't have to.' He started to wiggle his hands back into his work gloves.

'I don't know. I think you do. I'm not a lawyer, but . . .'

'That's correct. You're not a lawyer. I don't know what you are. A neighbour? You're on my property, I know that. Uninvited. I'd like you to leave.'

He bent down to retrieve the little pile of weeds, brushed passed me and took it over to the wheelbarrow.

I could feel that familiar surge of blood warming up my face. I tried to look relaxed and reasonable, even though I wasn't very good at that either.

'According to the Town Tax records, Regina's house was owned by Bay Side Holdings, at 675 Dutch Wharf Road,' I looked around, 'which I guess is here, with you listed as the responsible party. I'm just telling you because Regina's dead. You get your house back.'

He seemed to loosen up a little at that. He let go of the wheelbarrow.

'Very well. Consider me notified. You can leave your paperwork in my mailbox. You know the way out.'

Before I could say anything else he walked away from me. Stooped shouldered, he moved off with his wheelbarrow toward some distant corner of his yard, hidden under the dark shade of oak, pine and arborvitae.

As an amateur boxer I lost almost as many fights as I won, and my brief professional career wasn't much better. There were things about the sport that drew me, things like the training and bag work. Some of the old trainers fit the stereotype of the battered old pros with gritty voices, filled with the wisdom of the street. I liked being around a lot of it. The actual boxing part wasn't as appealing. A lot of the kids I fought were really desperate and half crazy with hopes and fears. There were more white kids than you'd think, and I can't say race was any kind of obvious factor at the level we fought. Not that I could see, anyway. Everybody was basically poor, street worn and edgy. Most everybody figured I was Puerto Rican till I opened my mouth. Seemed like there were a lot of bantams and feathers, wiry little guys with vicious quick hands and hard little heads you could pound on all day with no effect. As a middleweight, or light heavyweight, I was one of the bigger ones. The few genuine heavyweights were usually fat guys or big, slow dummies without the heart for the physical conditioning needed to really make it in the ring. Occasionally, some guy would show up who was big, strong, fast and eager. You knew it as soon as they got on the gloves. They had the mental part. They were smart enough to know what you had to do, but also what you got if you pulled it off. Go from having nothing to owning the world.

The fights I was able to win were usually on points. I never knocked anybody out, though I put a few into the canvas hard enough to get the decision. After a fight like that one of the trainers shoved my face into the corner of my open locker hard enough to split my lip. I still had my gloves on, and blood was splashing all over everywhere. I shrunk back and got my gloves up near my head to stop the next blow, which didn't come. He asked me if what he just did pissed me off.

'What the hell was that for?'

'You got to get pissed, you fuckin' greaseball. It's the only way you win. You don't get pissed, you don't win the fight. That's the kind of fighter you are. From now on, I want you pissed off all the time.'

I wanted to kill him. Instead I just nodded. Then I sat down on the bench and watched the blood from my lip pool on the floor and listened to the roar in my head. He wanted me to be pissed. If he only knew.

After talking to Milton Hornsby I sat in the Grand Prix for a few minutes to let that old roar subside. In the past I wouldn't have let him just walk away from me. I don't know what I would've done, but it would have likely gone on a mental list of all the things I wished I could take back.

Eddie was whining at me to open the window. I opened them all and lit a cigarette. I sat back in the old cracked leather bucket seat and closed my eyes. You don't get pissed, you don't win the fight. But what if you don't want the fight in the first place?

'Fuckin' hell, Eddie. I need a lawyer.'

He wasn't listening. His head was already out the window, taking in the autumn air, looking around for the next thing.

YOU GOT to Burton Lewis' house in the estate section of Southampton Village by driving down a 2,800-foot driveway that shot in a straight line between two twelve-foot-high privet hedges. You drove over polished white pebbles contained by steel curbing that drew the outside edges into perfect parallel lines. At the entrance was a white wooden gate that pivoted open on huge cast-iron hinges bolted to a pair of white posts trimmed-out to look like Empire furniture. Fluffy old blue hydrangeas flanked the gate and softened the effect of the rectangular call box, perched on a curved black post, into which you punched a code to open the gate, or pushed a call button to gain entry. The only clue to the identity of the home was a polite four-by-eight-inch white sign on which the number eighty-five was painted with green paint and circumscribed by a thin green line.

After the initial straight shot, the driveway made an abrupt forty-five degree turn, and if you hadn't run out of gas by then, you came out from between the privets into an open area defined by an oval turnaround. The interior of the oval was landscaped to look un-landscaped, as if the mammoth shingle-style mansion looming above you was situated there just to take advantage of some perfect act of nature.

Burton's great-grandfather built the first house on the site before the turn of the century. That was when really wealthy people competed with Versailles and called the results a cottage. In the thirties, taking advantage of a glut of cheap labour, his grandfather tore it down and built an even bigger monstrosity. Burton grew up in that house, and a town house on the Upper East Side and a half-dozen other houses sprinkled around Europe and the Caribbean. His parents delegated Burton's upbringing, and that of his two sisters, to a team of professionals. Austrian nannies, Swiss ski instructors, Parisian epicures. All three kids suffered from severe parental deprivation, with mixed results. One of the girls was obsessed with Sherlock Holmes and ended up heaving herself off the Reichenbach Falls. The other succumbed to hardcore S&M and died of an overdose hanging upside down in some squalid flop down near Times Square.

Burton took up banking and jurisprudence. Looking like he'd been born in a Brooks Brothers, he took part-time jobs and internships on Wall Street and developed a decent command of international finance before he was out of prep school. He graduated from Columbia in three years, and having grown bored with finance, had earned a law degree from Yale three years after that.

The only conversation he could remember having with his father was when the old man brought him into his study to go over the disposition of the family fortune, with instructions on how to manage it should he die or lose his faculties. Which is exactly what happened about a year after that. Burton was about twenty-three; his father lasted another year before dying insane and leaving Burton, the sole heir, insanely rich.

The first thing he did was tear down his grandfather's house and build another one. It was still pretty big, but at least it fit the scale of the other houses in the neighbourhood, if that's what you'd call it. It fit Burton okay. He was well over six feet tall, and thin, with a face made of weathered brown leather. He had a head full of light brown hair that fell over his forehead and a moustache that emboldened a small, thin mouth. His clothes draped over his gaunt frame in the perfect way you see on mannequins. He often wore a look of puzzled amusement, as if struggling to recollect the punch line of an inappropriate joke. I met him through a mutual friend of Abby's. She'd pulled him into the circle of acquaintances she maintained as a simulation of genuine friendship. We were all still young, but making enough to live in Manhattan. Burton was splitting his time between defending vagrants out of a grungy storefront office in the East Village and an active tax practice down on the Street.

His pedigree was all that mattered to Abby, but Burton's stuff ran deeper than that.

When I was growing up, people like Burton Lewis moved through the world inside an invisible protective enclosure. We saw them in the grocery store or stepping between their nice cars and Herb McCarthy's or the Irving Hotel, but we knew they probably didn't see us. They were a type of celestial being that God had marooned on earth as a penalty for their vanity and arrogance. I didn't know enough locals then to know how they felt about the Summer People, but I was never resentful or jealous. Just removed. I kept out of their way and only wondered about their lives when I rode my bike around the estate section and tried to see the big houses hidden by giant stands of hundred-year-old maples and copper beech.

Abby tried to hire Burton to represent her in the divorce, but he demurred. Claimed the lack of a Connecticut bar exam. The truth is, though he was fond of her, he liked me better. We used to do shots and watch the Knicks together on TV while the other swells practiced one-upmanship out in his living room. I liked him, too, and not for the reason Abby liked to insinuate, Burton being homosexual.

When I pushed the call button on the intercom at the gate, a Spanish woman answered. She said Burton was out in the back jacking up a small utility shed to repair the foundation. He was always building or fixing something with his own hands. I noted it was after eight o'clock and already pretty dark out.

'We have lights.'

'Tell him Sam Acquillo dropped by. I'll come back later.'

'No. He'll want to talk to you. I'll ring him on his mobile.'

'Is this Isabella?'

'Yes, Mr Acquillo.'

'Sam.'

'Sam. He hasn't heard from you for a long time.'

Isabella was Burton's housekeeper. If that's the right designation for a woman who ran such a colossal domestic enterprise. Her husband had been a lawyer in Cuba. Burton used him as an investigator until he dropped dead one day in the middle of an interview with a potential witness. Burton let Isabella stay at his flat until she could find other circumstances and she still hadn't left.

'I'm not much of a communicator,' I told her.

'He thought he'd made some offence.'

It wasn't that easy to make out what she was saying over the intercom, especially given the accent.

'No he didn't. I'll just call him tomorrow.'

'No, I get him for you. Come on in.'

The big white gate swung in and I piloted the Grand Prix down the privet canyon.

Burton's yellow and wood-panelled 1978 Ford Country Squire was parked out front. Combine its raw metal content with the Grand Prix's and you could build a small fleet of Honda Civics. Our taste in cars might have looked like the foundation of the relationship. Though the real reason Burton drove the Ford was simple negligence. He'd had it since it was new and as long as it ran well enough to get him around Southampton, hadn't bothered replacing it. People like Burton, who can buy anything, often don't buy anything at all, or only when driven by impulses most of us would find incomprehensible.

As I hauled the Grand Prix around the circle I concentrated on missing the Ford. I'd stopped off at my house after talking to Milton Hornsby, ostensibly to leave Eddie off so he could spend the rest of the day running around the yard.

I also thought a drink would be a good idea before I did anything else. So I sat on the porch and drank about half a bottle of some no name vodka I'd bought on sale. The first sip wasn't too good, but it improved over time.

By dinnertime my nerves were beaten into submission and my appetite was coming back. I had some leftovers that sopped up some of the vodka, so I could convince myself I was fit to drive over to see Burton Lewis, the only lawyer I knew in Southampton. I thought about calling ahead first, but I wasn't sure if he'd want to see me. Anyway, the surprise visit approach had worked so well with Milton Hornsby.

Isabella opened the door. She looked at me sceptically.

'You lose weight.'

'A little. Nice to see you, too, Isabella.'

She backed up to let me in.

'Not that you needed to. A little fat wouldn't hurt a man your age.'

Burton loped into the grand hall and reached out to shake my hand. He looked as I'd remembered him. He wore a blue and white pinstriped shirt, off-white, mud-stained khakis, ragged tan boat shoes and a blue blazer with the sleeves stuffed up over his elbows. When new, each item probably cost a lot of money, but they hadn't been new for a very long time. It occurred to me that when Burton died he should donate his wardrobe to the Museum of Ivy League Coastal Sportswear. His handshake felt dry and bony.

'I heard you were out East,' said Burton, as if I'd just gotten in last night. 'I thought about calling.'

'That's okay, Burt, I didn't expect you to. I'm not such good company anyway. How's everything with you?'

'But I couldn't quite bring myself to do it,' he said, completing the thought. 'I wasn't entirely sure about your disposition.'

'That's okay, Burt. You look good.'

'I imagine you haven't heard much from Abigail.'

'Only her lawyers. Mopping up.'

'Surely that's all behind us.'

'Pretty much.'

'I'm not a fan of protracted litigation.'

He showed me the way through what I guess was a sitting room – it's hard to define what all the rooms are for in a place that big. We went outside through a pair of twelve-foot-high French doors.

'You're good a man, Burt,' I said. 'Which is a rare thing. Speaking of men, how's the love life?'

He smiled at me. 'You haven't become more tactful.'

'But I have lost a little weight.'

The doors led to a wide stone-paved patio. It was furnished with oversized wicker lounge chairs and big market umbrellas. The night was getting blacker as a spongy wet mist crept in from the ocean. I could hear the surf through the dense privets that enclosed the side yard. Auras formed around the lights that lit up the patio. A chorus of bugs and reptiles were out there bitching and chirping away as they did for reasons of their own. Somewhere in the distance a stereo was playing a jazz recording. Ellington, with Johnny Hodges sliding sax notes all over the register. It reminded me of softer times out on Burton's million-acre lawn, under canvas tents, sipping white wine brought in dripping crystal, and bowls of fruit that would leak down your arms when you took a bite. Abby sitting with a long stretch of strong brown leg jutting out from the deep slit of her skirt. Rich old guys in pastel sport coats and white pants trying not to look. Other women, mostly gaunt and affected, and Burton, struggling to act blasé around some vacuous tennis pro or Mexican gardener. Me on frequent trips to the cocktail station, trying to alter my usual state of edgy dismay.

Abby always yearned for a place of her own out here. A real place, in her mind, suitable for entertaining. Ten years before we split she'd campaigned to find the perfect spot, recruiting friends to join the hunt. They had a great time going from house to house, sunning themselves in the obsequious attentions of venal real estate agents. I was putting the last instalments into a fund I'd established for my daughter's education, and was unenthusiastic about a new round of debt. Of course, it was my waning enthusiasm for Abby that was at the heart of the matter. The day she came to me with the chosen property, I told her no. She thought I was kidding. Then I told her no several more times in several different ways. I probably over-embellished. Her mouth hung open an inch or two while I was talking, but then it snapped shut and never opened again to emit a single pleasant word on my behalf.

Burton let us stay with him a few weeks every summer. I remained in Connecticut during the week and worked, or went to see my mother for short, awkward visits at the cottage, or later, at the nursing home. I sat around drinking with Burton on the weekends, often after everyone else had gone to bed. Burton would have worked hard at staying my friend if I'd let him.

Before we settled into the wicker chairs Burton poured us each our regular drink from a cocktail caddy in the corner. His movements were still graceful and fluid, in contrast to his social manner, which could be surprisingly awkward and shy. I wanted to put him at ease.

'I haven't talked to anybody in about four years. Just been keeping my head down. It's nothing personal.'

'I'd have helped.'

'I know, Burt, that's why I couldn't call you. Turning down your help would have been too painful.'

'Very well. I understand.'

He sat back comfortably in his chair and nodded sympathetically. I felt the warmth of Burton's undivided attention.

'I did hear some rather startling things about you,' he said.

'It wasn't the best time.'

'Professionally speaking, you're lucky it wasn't worse.'

'That's how I look at it, Burt. Luckier than hell.'

'Hm.'

I could see he really wanted to ask me a lot of questions we both knew I was hoping he wouldn't ask, so the conversation hung suspended in midair for a few seconds. I owed him more than that. I took a deep breath.

'It got away from me a little bit.'

'Apparently.'

'I'd've done things differently if I'd kept a better grip.'

'How're you now?'

'Better. Got a little project, I guess you'd call it. Gave me an excuse to bother you.'

'Really.'

'You wouldn't remember, but there was this old gal that lived next door to my parents' cottage. My dad used to look after her, and then I did what I could when I was around. When I moved back there I just took up where my dad had left off. Nothing much, just keeping her place going. Driving her places sometimes. Little shit.'

'Regina something.'

'You still got that memory of yours. Regina Broadhurst. Well, she died last week, and I'm the administrator on her estate, and I'm already over my head.'

'Who appointed you administrator?'

'I got this thing from Surrogate's Court that named me administrator pending a hearing. Mel Goodfellow said since she'd died apparently intestate I was appointed as an interested party to handle things until some more interested party showed up. In which case it'd be up to the court, though I'm not contesting anything. I'm not that interested.'

'It's a little unusual, but I think kosher.'

'There's this Town cop, Joe Sullivan, who rigged it. For some reason he thought Regina's affairs needed more attention than she'd get from the government. I think he's a little paternal about the people on his beat.'

Burton nodded, mentally recording everything. I'd forgotten he had such a killer memory. Something I obviously didn't have.

'There's only one relative we know of, a nephew named Jimmy Maddox. I found him, and he approved me as administrator.'

I handed the letter to Burton like it was a piece of evidence. Exhibit A. He looked it over.

'What sort of assets did she leave?'

'Well that's the thing. She's only got about eight grand in the bank. I don't think she had anything else. Nothing I can find, anyway. Not even the house, which is owned by a company called Bay Side Holdings, which is a whole other story in itself.'

I told him about getting the tax records and going to see Milton Hornsby. About the little house in Sag Harbor next to the abandoned launch ramp.

'Curious.'

'Exactly.'

'He's right that he doesn't have to talk to you. But you have to talk to him, as administrator, as it relates to the transition of the property. You have to handle the dispensation of personal belongings.'

'Her stuff.'

'Her stuff. And settle any outstanding obligations. There might be a security deposit.'

'I don't think she paid any rent.'

'Then there may be a substantial obligation.'

'Nobody seemed to care. No dunning letters I can find. Hornsby didn't say anything. Quite the opposite.'

'Well, if it's any consolation, I think your administrator status is probably defensible. Though this letter you made up for Jimmy Maddox, while elegantly worded, wouldn't hold up under challenge.'

'Does it matter if I punched him in the nose right before he signed it?'

'You said you were better.'

'He swung first. And I didn't provoke him. I mean, I wasn't trying to provoke him.'

'So the dispute was settled?'

'Absolutely. Jimmy Maddox is actually a bigger asshole than I am. He was okay once he got it out of his system. And like I said, if him or some lawyer wants in, it's all theirs.'

He let that hang in the air for a moment.

'So, what do you think?' I said.

'If Mr Maddox is agreeable, and there're no other family members, there's no reason you can't continue as you have. I'd only feel better if the language in this agreement was snugged up a bit.'

'I still want to get Hornsby to talk to me.'

'Don't punch him in the nose.'

'You know what's been going on with property values lately. Regina's and mine are the only two buildable subdivisions that sit on the tip of Oak Point. The only legitimate bay front. Her lot's about a third again bigger than mine. And better, since mine borders the street, the other side of which is just swamp – wetlands, by law – till you get to the channel. She's got a breakwater and a beach on two sides. About one and a half acres. It's worth a bundle. Why isn't he happier?'

'More hostile than happy, apparently.'

'Exactly.'

'I have no idea.'

'And why wasn't Regina paying rent? And why didn't he care?'

'We don't know that he didn't care. Or that he hasn't tried to collect. It's easier to build a fusion reactor than evict an old lady in New York State.'

'Of course, I thought of that. But then why didn't I know? That's exactly the kind of thing Regina would've been all over me to figure out. To fix for her.'

'Some things are too embarrassing.'

I'd thought about that, too. Why didn't she tell me she didn't own the house? Would she have told me she was in financial trouble? Either admission might have been too much of an insult to her dignity.

'Could be.'

Isabella came out to the patio. Burton held up his empty glass and pointed at mine. She took care of the refills. She'd done it before. Burton told her we were all set. She left without saying much to me. Still mad at me on Burton's behalf.

'She didn't take baths,' I said, after Isabella had left.

'Pardon?'

'Regina didn't take baths. She had an old tin-lined shower next to the kitchen. Used big old beach towels to dry herself off. The bathtub is where you cleaned fish. At least we used to. What was she doing in the bathtub?'

Burton held his drink by the top of the glass and swished it around to melt some of the ice.

'I see where you're going,' he said.

'I wish I did.'

'What was the cause of death?'

'I'm waiting to find out for sure. Sullivan's arranged for the county coroner to do an autopsy. The death certificate just says accidental drowning. I mean, what is that?'

'Hm.'

'Maybe I've been alone in that cottage too long.'

'You weren't alone. You had Regina.'

'And Eddie. I got a dog.'

'I'll have an associate do a little research on Bay Side Holdings.'

'That's not why I'm telling you this.'

'I know. It's no trouble.'

Burton Lewis owned a forty-eight storey building in lower Manhattan and all two thousand of the lawyers who worked inside. I guess it wouldn't be any trouble.

'All I wanted was to knock things around a little.'

'It would be good for your soul to allow me to help.'

That might be true, but it was going to wreak havoc with the rest of me. But that was my fault. I knew I needed the help. Every form of refuge has its price.

'I could use the help. I appreciate it.'

'I know you do. While you're at it, give me Regina's Social Security number and I'll see if we can uncover other assets.'

After that we caught up on the state of professional basketball, discussed plans for adding a library as a separate building on the property, the mechanical status of my Grand Prix and his Country Squire, and a case he'd recently helped bring before the Supreme Court. He kept the conversation focused on himself, which I appreciated.

It was late when I got back to the cottage. There was a note from Amanda pinned to my door.

'I'm going on a girl's night out tomorrow night. The Playhouse in Bridgehampton. From nine till whenever. If somebody I know just happens to be there too I can apologise again and this time he has to accept!' Signed 'A.'

It was too late to untangle any more confused impulses or reaffirm secret pledges I'd made to myself. It was time to go to sleep so I could dream about bathtubs and flying fists, and being too late to pick up my daughter at school, or losing her in a crowded shopping mall, having been too distracted to realise I'd let go of her tiny hand.

THE NEXT morning I made a bucket of coffee and smoked my first cigarette before calling Sullivan. I was sitting on the screened-in porch so I could watch Eddie run around in the yard.

Somehow he knew how to stay within my property lines, out of the street and away from Regina's. Even when he jumped off the breakwater down to the pebble beach he stayed within the boundaries. He didn't like to swim, but he loved to run through the water at about belly height, looking for plastic bottles or dead fish, which he'd put in a pile on shore. It's hard to say if he achieved anything of lasting value, his air of determined purpose notwithstanding.

I got Sullivan on his cell phone like he told me to.

'Yeah, well, it's interesting,' said Sullivan, his voice rising just enough above the car noise.

'How so.'

'The cause of death was a traumatic blow to the posterior region of the head – don't you love that, "traumatic"? I guess it was fucking traumatic if it killed her.'

'And?'

'And, it could have been caused by hitting the tub, or it could've been somethin' else. "The actual size and concentration of the contusion is not inconsistent with the subject's head impacting the porcelain surface of the bathtub as the result of a fall, though this does not rule out the possibility of the cause being the striking surface of a broad, blunt object." There was no water in her lungs, which isn't unusual, either. Or other injuries. Nothing under her nails that didn't belong there, no sign of struggle at all. So, basically, they think she just fell backwards and hit her head.' 'I found her face down. How did she get face down if she cracked the back of her head?'

'The report says you could still be conscious after a blow like this. You get disoriented, you might try to stand up, you pass out, you fall face down.'

'Why not just conclude that it wasn't from falling in the tub.'

'They aren't looking for anything else. They're looking for an explanation for her being face down after falling in the tub and hitting the back of her head.'

'What do you think?'

'I think they're full of crap.'

I never liked talking on the phone. You can't see the other guy's face, can't judge what he's really thinking. I took a gulp of the coffee that was cooling down in my mug.

'You think somebody hit her.'

'I didn't say that. I'm just not happy about the disposition of the body. Just like I never bought that crap about Kennedy lurching forward after getting hit straight on with a bullet. I'm sorry, if I shoot you in the forehead, you're going backwards. If you smack your head after falling over backwards in the bathtub, you float on your back, not on your stomach.'

'Was there anything else?'

'That's all I know. That she could've been killed by some flat, heavy object.'

'Like a two-by-four.'

'Nah, I asked that. Wood leaves a different kind of imprint. They've seen lots of those.'

'So you asked.'

'I did. I figured a cast-iron fry pan.'

'You did? How come?'

'I've seen it before. Women like 'em. About the only thing heavy with a handle they're used to picking up. Always within reach.'

'You asked them if she could've been hit with a frying pan?' I was impressed.

'Yeah, and they said yeah. That'd fit the bill perfect. Heavy, flat, except it wouldn't leave nothing behind.'

'Too bad.'

'Except maybe a little carbon from her gas stove.'

'Really.'

'Which would wash off in the bathtub.'

'Right.'

'Except they found a tiny residue in her hair.'

'Really?' I said, even more impressed.

'The lab guys can do some amazing shit these days.'

'So what does it mean?'

'Nothing, just curious.'

'You can't match it with one of her fry pans?'

'Nah. Carbon's carbon. She could've washed a pan, then scratched her head and left a trace. It's really tiny.'

'So you're satisfied.'

'I didn't say that either.'

'You're suspicious.'

'I am a little, yeah. But that don't mean shit around here. I start talking like you and Chief Semple would have my ass.'

'I guess I don't understand cops.'

'Don't start bustin' on cops. Nobody likes to go back over something they figured was a done deal.'

'I didn't mean that. I just don't get the process.'

'For now, the process is you get the old lady planted. I'll get you a copy of the autopsy report.'

'Okay. I appreciate it.'

'I'll get her shipped over to Pappanasta's, if that's okay with you.'

'Sure. Good as any.'

'We can keep talking. Like I said, talking's okay.'

After I got off the phone with Sullivan I went running to work out the accretion of vodka, good and bad, from the day before. I needed to clear my head. I took Eddie with me, even though he hadn't touched a drop. When I got back I felt better, even if my head wasn't any clearer. I had a manila folder with all the papers I'd been collecting on Regina. I spent the rest of the day sitting on the porch with the file on the table where I could take a look at it from time to time. I wrote a few thoughts and 'things to do' on the legal pad. As it started to get dark, I thought about Amanda Battiston and her note. I still hadn't figured out what to do. So I wrote 'fry pan' on the outside of the manila folder and went to take a shower.

THE PLAYHOUSE was on the main route between Bridgehampton and Sag Harbor. It stood in the centre of a huge swarm of parked cars that caught and threw back light from big security spots mounted in the trees. It was a nice house at one time, though decades of hard use had rounded off the edges. During the season you waited in line with the Summer People, but this time of year you could get right in after paying the huge bearded guy at the door. A vintage oak bar anchored the back of an open area where you could dance or sit and listen to the band. The cocktail waitresses navigated the crowd with trays held overhead and faces set in neutral. Smoke formed cirrus clouds around the house lamps, from which warm yellow light painted the plain beautiful and the beautiful divine. The music was loud enough to vibrate your internal organs, but I liked it well enough. A joint wasn't a joint without distorted electric guitars. God made rock-and-roll so people would have something to dance to and guys could pick up girls without having to say anything, a huge advantage for most of them.

I shoved my way through a pack of meatballs in baggy jeans, flannel shirts and baseball caps and caught one of the waitresses by the elbow. She cocked her head at me so I could yell vodka on the rocks in her ear. She nodded and moved off again. A dark-haired woman in a scoop-neck leotard top and scarf was looking at me, making flagrant eye contact. She was sitting on a man's lap, sipping from a shot glass. I broke her heart by looking away and lighting a cigarette. A chubby, wiry-haired guy about my age was twirling a young woman around the dance floor. They moved with the perfect synchronicity you see in dance contests. They looked happy doing what they were doing.

The waitress gave me the vodka. I took my cigarette and drink over to a slippery wet table in a dark corner. People instinctively moved away from me. Couldn't stand to be near all that charm. Music crashed through the crowd and rolled like foamy surf over the tables and bar stools. All the women on the dance floor seemed lighter than air, moving instinctively, languidly to the crunching rhythms. The men lumbered, or mimicked their partner's movements with little or no awareness of their own.

A woman with short blond hair the colour of freshly polished brass sat down in the chair next to me. She was thick around the waist, and looked stuffed into her jeans and flannel shirt. Her lipstick and nail polish were too red, even in the low light. Each hand was laden with heavy moulded-rings and hoop-like bracelets. I guessed her to be on the top side of her thirties.

'Hey,' she yelled to me over the din.

I nodded noncommittally.

'Wanna dance?'

I tried to give her a friendly smile.

'No thanks. Just watching.'

She smiled back.

'Oh, I think you do.'

'Sorry, really don't. Really can't, actually, but I appreciate the offer.'

'I think you do,' she said, nodding at me and winking her left eye. 'If you thought about it, you would really like to dance. This dance.' She made a play for my hand. I drew deeper into the corner.

'Sorry, just isn't my thing.'

'Ha,' she said, strangely undeterred, jerking her head toward the dance floor.

I looked past her shoulder and caught a flash of thick auburn hair as it passed through a smoky column of light from one of the ceiling spots.

'So,' I said to the big blond, who was watching me watch Amanda shoulder her way though the crowd. 'You really think I'd like to do this.'

'Just a feeling,' she yelled back.

I downed the drink, crushed the butt and stepped out on the dance floor. It was important not to think about it much more, since I had no idea what I was going to do when I got there. I'd dedicated a sizable percentage of my life to sitting in all kinds of bars, lounges and nightclubs, but thus far had escaped all attempts to get me to dance, if that's what those people out there were actually doing. This was something I knew nothing about.

I did, however, know how to box. And all boxers since Muhammad Ali knew you had to float like a butterfly. So this is what I sort of did, in approximate time with the music. My partner was unimpressed.

'What are you doing?'

'The butterfly.'

She thought about it. I concentrated on my moves, trying to blend into the general mayhem. I was momentarily sorry I'd never tried to do this before, but the thought passed when Amanda slid into view and took both my hands, pulling me as she danced deeper into the writhing tangle of humanity. My blond partner smiled at Amanda, waved at me and made a graceful withdrawal from the dance floor. Mission complete.

'What the heck are you doing here, Mr Acquillo?' she said in mock surprise.

'Don't rightly know – driven by little voices in my head.'

'What are they saying?'

'That I look like an asshole.'

She laughed.

'Not entirely. You're getting it.'

'Yeah, right.'

When she settled us into a small pocket of air up next to the band, I moved in and got her into a standard dance grip. Right away I felt safer.

'I have never in my life danced to this kind of music,' I yelled in her ear.

'Could have fooled me. What kind of dance can you do?'

'Waltz. I thought you couldn't get laid in college if you didn't know how to waltz.'

I spun her around a little to demonstrate my waltzing skills. The lack of relevance to the actual rhythm didn't seem to trouble her.

'I hope waltzing talent wasn't the deciding factor.'

Our waltz turned into a type of slow dance that might have looked out of place, but felt a lot nicer than that other stuff. It didn't deter the crowd on the dance floor. In fact, some big kid in a baggy sweater and his girlfriend were getting more frenzied by the minute. Everyone else sort of cleared out of their way, but I liked it where we were. They bashed into us a few times, forcing me to close in on Amanda, which was okay with me. I tried to look more nonchalant than I was feeling.

Amanda danced with her eyes cast slightly downward, and every once in a while would look up at me and smile shyly through those thick Italian lashes.

'Don't do that,' I said to her.

'What?'

'That thing you're doing with your eyes. It's making me lose my balance.'

I spun her around again, right into the dopey kid. It seemed to annoy him, and she winced when he dug his heel into her foot. I spun her back again.

'Sorry,' I said to her.

'Gee, some people.'

I waited until I felt him push into me again. Then as I twirled Amanda I hooked my foot around his ankle and pulled hard, and without missing a beat sent the kid face down into the dance floor. His date rushed over and helped him up. We had our little space back to ourselves. I caught the bass player grinning at me.

'What happened to him?' Amanda asked me.

'Must've lost his balance.'

I distracted her with another spin. When she closed back in I added a half spin and caught her around the waist. Her head fell back on my shoulder and her eyes were closed. I was close enough to smell her perfume and the wine on her breath.

The dancing kid's date was helping him to the bathroom. He was holding a bloody nose, though he was able to say 'fuck you, man' clearly enough as he went by. Not a half-hour in the first club I'd been to in years and already I'd drawn blood. I was glad Amanda hadn't realised what happened. Abby always wanted me to defend her from the dangers of the world, and always got mad at me when I did.

The band ended the song and immediately took up another, this one nice and slow, matching our tempo. The bass player was still grinning at me. I'd made a friend.

'Isn't that nice,' said Amanda.

'They'll do anything to keep you on the dance floor.'

Amanda moved in closer and I pulled her tight. Now my face

was all the way buried in that dense mass of auburn hair. I could feel the perfect contours of her body fit into mine, the slim, muscular smoothness beneath her dark blue blouse, open at the neck and collar pulled up, fresh to the touch. The air was thick with pheromones and amplified music, filling up all the space inside the Playhouse, leaving no room for time or fears or regrets to intrude or interfere.

I didn't know what was really going on with her, but right then I didn't much care.

EVENTUALLY THE band took a break and all the clocks started up again and we went over to say hi to her friends.

The brassy blond looked pleased. The other woman was her morphological opposite – tall and thin and dark-haired. She looked a lot smarter, but less fun. She wore a white hand-knit sweater and tiny pieces of jewellery around her neck and fingers. Her hair was spun into large, highlighted ringlets. Her complexion was rough, but cared for. I liked her eyes, but not her pinched little mouth – it was too well designed for disapproval.

I had the feeling the two of them had spent much of their adult years together, locked in continuous, unsuccessful quests for romantic involvement. Holding on to each other through shared heartaches and unrequited obsessions.

'Robin and Laura. Sam, my favourite customer.'

'Robin,' said Robin, the one with the blond hair.

'Laura,' said Laura.

'Hello.'

'Out for the weekend?' Robin asked. 'People are doing that a lot now – coming out in the fall.'

'Here full time. I live on Oak Point.'

'Used to come on weekends, right?' said Amanda.

'It was my parents' place. I inherited it.'

'Some nice rentals up in North Sea. We do well up there,' said Laura.

'We do well up there,' Robin repeated.

Laura picked up her glass with two hands and sucked on the

straw. I noticed she had a pack of cigarettes and a pretty white porcelain lighter. I dug out the Camels and offered them around. Laura took me up on it.

'Walk a mile.'

'If you don't run out of breath first,' said Robin. Laura swatted her.

We lit up anyway. Robin had her eyes on me, flagrantly assessing. I hoped my grooming was up to it. She seemed like one of those wide open women who liked to guess something about you to prove her powers of perception. She was drinking red wine – it went well with her hair. Laura luxuriated over the Camel and looked out at the crowded room, counting the house.

'You're in real estate?' I asked them.

'Yup. Partners for over ten years. House Hunters of the Hamptons.

The old triple H. You've seen our signs.'

I had.

'You do a lot of rentals?'

'Half and half,' said Robin, 'There's plenty of both. Do you ever rent your place?'

'No. My mother lived there until a few years ago, then I moved in. Never had the chance.'

'You'd be amazed at what you can get. A lot of year-rounders rent and go some place else for the summer. Or rent something cheaper. Can pay the whole year's mortgage. You'd be amazed at what everything is worth out here. Most locals are.'

'Even in North Sea?'

'Especially – tend to have lower mortgages, and in this market, you can still get incredible rentals with lesser properties. No offence or anything.

I love North Sea myself. Last of the real Hamptons, if you ask me.'

'I guess I would be amazed,' I said, truthfully.

'What do you get when there's more demand than supply, and the demanders have more money than God and all His angels put together?'

'Inflated property values?'

'The man's a genius,' Robin said to Amanda.

'Isn't yours on the water?' asked Amanda, with innocent sincerity.

'Oh, well,' said Robin, 'that's a whole n'other kettle of fish. Waterfront, you double or triple.'

'Do you rent a lot on Oak Point?' I asked.

The two real estate women looked at each other and shook their heads.

'I always figured there were mostly year-rounders out on the peninsula. Locals,' said Laura.

'That's what I thought.'

'Hm,' said Robin.

Amanda was sitting next to me, so I couldn't see her very well. I could, however, feel the backs of her fingers brushing lightly across my thigh under the table. I let my hand drop to my lap so I could squeeze her hand.

'Ever heard of Bay Side Holdings?' I asked.

They looked at each other again. Exchanging telepathic messages.

'Weren't they trying for some variances a few years ago?' asked Robin.

Laura nodded. 'Yeah, they wanted to reconfigure some of the lot sizes on stuff they owned over there. They were trying to re-shape preexisting boundaries. We didn't pay much attention to it. I don't think the Appeals Board let them do it. The Town's a bitch on non-conformance. Though I don't remember anybody from what's-its-nose, Bay Side, pushing real hard. The only reason I remember anything is 'cause the lawyer they brought in from the City was so adorable.'

'If you like tall, dark and loaded,' said Robin.

'It just sort of went away,' said Laura, ignoring her. 'I have to admit I was a little curious. I get into that stuff more than Robin – spend enough time in those damned hearings and you turn into a zoning junky.'

'High drama,' said Robin, sarcastically.

'It can be,' Laura shot back, a little insulted.

'I thought their lawyer was a woman,' I said to the pair of them.

Laura examined her drink before taking a sip, 'You sayin' I'm a dyke?' she said, in an awkward way.

'Jacqueline something – Polish name?'

The two of them rolled their eyes in unison.

'Jackie Swaitkowski,' said Robin.

'She's a local. Lawyers from out of the city usually like to have a home town connection. Cutey pants had Jackie fronting the thing.'

'Fronting's a good word for it,' said Robin.

'Robin, really.'

'I'm not saying anything.'

'Jackie's a little flaky. That puts some people off,' Laura explained.

'Some people?' Robin asked, rhetorically.

'She's actually very nice,' said Laura.

'Not a big career planned in rocket science,' said Robin, with a forced smile.

'She's a lawyer, Robin, how dumb can you be?'

'In this case, very.'

I was relieved when Laura decided to drop it. Amanda seemed even more uncomfortable than me with the turn of the conversation. Bickering, especially between adults, always makes me tense. I feel like I'm back in the office, struggling to restrain the human compulsion to rend and eviscerate each other. Or back in the dining room with my father glaring down the long table, trying to bait a reaction out of me so he'd have someone to contend with, someone to put up a little resistance against his relentless fury. It always makes me want to be somewhere else.

'I gotta hit the head,' I said to the group. I gave Amanda's hand a final squeeze and stood up. I wove my way through the mass of club goers, avoiding collisions and eye contact, passing unnoticed through clusters of friends and sexual prospectors.

The window was wide open in the men's room, chilling down the sticky urine smell. A rough queue had formed right outside a separate room for the urinals. There was only room in there for two, so I waited my turn. Once inside the room, you had to step up on a short platform to take a leak, which I was halfway through when I heard the door behind me snap shut. I was about to turn to look when somebody shoved me forward into the wall. Piss sprayed off the back of the porcelain and splattered my pant leg.

It wasn't an accidental shove. It had plenty of real meat on it. I assumed it was the kid I'd sent into the dance floor. My sphincter had already cut me off midstream, so my next thought was to get myself back into my pants. As I zipped, I hunched my shoulders and braced for the kid's sucker punch.

Instead, a hole opened up in the universe and a piece of heavy artillery poked through. It fired off at point blank range into the side of my head.

I'd been hit a lot of times as a regular fighter, but I'd never seen stars. I was a little surprised you actually could. They popped in front of my eyes like a fireworks display. I put my forearms in front of my face to block the next blow, which came from the other direction. It ripped off my head and bounced it against the far wall. Then a fist caught me above the belly button, lifting me right off my feet. I ended up on my knees down on the floor. Red fuzz filled up my eyes but I could just make out a pair of black motorcycle boots. I looked up from there into the eyes of the big trained bear that had been hanging around our cars at the beach.

'You don't know what you're fuckin' with,' he said in his clearest trained bear voice – as dead and hollow as his eyes.

I was trying to think of a way to insult his BMW when one of those black motorcycle boots came up off the floor and caught me under the chin, snapping my mouth shut and sending my head for another spin around the galaxy.

This time the stars were talking. Or maybe it was the voices of the people coming through the door. I didn't care. I was on my hands and knees watching my blood puddle on the floor. The bear squatted down next to me and patted me on the cheek.

He left after that, I think. I heard him bust through a group of guys clogging the doorway. They said things like, 'Hey man, what the fuck?' I didn't care. I was hoping to see some more colourful stars, though all I got were these wiggly red balls, framed in darkness that closed in on the red until that's all there was, and I went down into this gooey black hole wondering if this is how my old man felt – watching his life drip out onto the floor of a piss-soaked bathroom at the back of the bar.

CHAPTER FOUR

My office had a sprawling overgrown schefflera that filled the space in front of two huge sheets of plate glass that formed one corner of the room. Right next to the plant was a steel desk Abby bought me soon after we were married. I used to sit on top of the desk cross-legged, yogi style, and talk on the phone. Of the 35,000 people worldwide in our $10 billion corporation, I was the only one who did this.

I was sitting there looking through the leaves of the schefflera at a resplendent spring day when a call came in from the chairman of a corporate subcommittee. I'd never heard of it before, but this was nothing new. Big corporations are like gas giants – huge swirling balls of toxic, overheated gas held together by gravity, and controlled by a form of planetary tectonics that forces the entire mass into endless cycles of expansion and collapse. The energy unleashed throws off institutional debris that recombines as tiny sub-spheres of frantic activity. They drift free for a while before getting snagged by the gravitational field and sucked back into the body of the organization. But along the way there was always the danger that one of them would call you on the phone. 'We're doing a performance audit on your area,' the voice on the other end of the line said, or something like it.

'Sounds fine. When you're done we'll come over and do one on yours.'

'We're hoping this can be as undisruptive as possible.'

'That's good. Because shit like this plays hell with our performance.' I knew most of the people who ran the company. I'd say hi to them in the halls and occasionally stand in front of the board of directors, priestly looking guys in shiny grey suits and white hair, and tell them how I was looking after our $45 million divisional budget. They never looked all that happy or secure. I guess you can make your own crap to live in even when you earn enough in stock options alone to buy a medium-sized city. I think some of them actually liked me. I was one of the few people in the company who did something tangible, who made things you could touch. I symbolized for them a mythical time when substance was presumably valued over style.

But still, when it all hit, they watched in silence through neutral eyes, their minds preoccupied with portfolio management and grandchildren.

One day two big security guards, black guys I'd greet every morning as I walked through the parking lot, stood and watched me empty out the desk Abby gave me. I left it with the schefflera. It didn't seem right to break up the set.

They helped me throw the stuff from the desk into a dumpster behind the building. We talked about our kids and the sad decline of the normally aspirated big block V-8 engine.

I thought of them when I came to in Southampton Hospital, watching a huge dark brown and white mass take shape as a Jamaican physician.

'Hey dere, you know what I'm saying to you?' I heard him say through all the wet glop stuffed inside my brain.

I think I nodded.

'Dat's a yes? You call dat a yes?'

'Yuff.'

'Oh, so dat's a yes. I get it.'

His hair was cut close to his scalp and he wore neat gold wire-rim glasses. His face would have been more handsome if it was smaller. The white medical coat stretched impossibly across his shoulders and chest, and a pink buttoned-down Oxford cloth shirt showed at the neck. He had about a half-dozen pens and a few evil-looking chrome instruments stuck in his front pocket. He leaned into me and adjusted something attached to the side of my skull. Nausea crept around inside my gut. My head felt like it filled up half the room. There was an I.V. in my arm. I looked down at it.

'Get it out.'

When I spoke my tongue lit up like a firecracker. I felt a big lump on the side when I moved it around my mouth.

'Can' do dat now,' he looked down at my chart, 'Mr A-cquillo. You need what's in dere I'm sure.'

I shook my head.

'No painkillers.'

'You don' know what you're askin'.'

I nodded as furiously as my head would let me. Panic began to bubble up in my throat.

'Rather have the pain.'

Some people are afraid of snakes. Or airplanes. With me it's drugs. Especially painkillers.

'Get it out.' I shook the tube. The Jamaican's powerful hand clamped down on my arm. He studied me carefully. Warmth flowed from his hand.

'Don' do dat, now. You're my responsibility.'

I stared at him. His face softened.

'I go get the attending. But you gotta stay still and not do anyt'ing loony, you know?'

'What time is it?'

He looked at his watch.

''Bout five-tirty.'

'I gotta get out of here.'

A broad smile lit his face as he shook his head.

'Oh no, Mr Acquillo, you don' go anywhere till we say. You got a concussion dere prob'ly.'

'I left a dog in my car.'

He shook his head again.

'No, ladies brung the car wit' the dog. He's at the vet's 'round the corner. Good place. He's all set. We do dis all the time.'

'He's gonna hate that. I got to get outta here.'

'I go talk to attending, he come in here and explain your situation.'

I couldn't seem to keep my head up off the pillow, so I set it back down.

'Okay.'

'Okay, but you gotta not try to take off on me.'

I nodded.

'You promise me, or I'll tie you down,' he said.

I nodded.

'Sorry. Not your fault,' I told him.

He let go of my arm and patted it. I lay there when he left and took stock. I was conscious. I knew I was in a hospital – I assumed it was Southampton. I could move my head and all my limbs and digits. I could see, though the outlines were a little fuzzy. I could open and shut my mouth, despite that wad of something on the side of my tongue. It made it difficult to probe around the inside of my mouth, but it felt like I had all my teeth – both the real and the gold ones I got because of Rene Ruiz.

I was in an area contained by rolling room dividers and white curtains. There was a window open nearby and wind from the Atlantic was busting in and flipping through a newspaper on the table next to my bed. No flowers. No get well cards. No worried-looking relatives.

Aside from a hernia I fixed a long time ago, I wasn't very experienced with hospitals. I don't like them. I don't like giving myself to somebody else to look after. Plus, it's wicked hard to get a vodka on the rocks or a pack of cigarettes out of anybody.

The attending doctor was a skinny little guy with shiny skin and hair like balls of single-ought steel wool. He looked me right in the eyes and shook my hand.

'Hey, welcome to the conscious. How'd you sleep?'

'Hard to say.'

He read the chart and nervously clicked a retractable ballpoint pen.

'Markham tells me you tried to go AWOL.'

'Don't want the I.V. Don't like painkillers.'

'Prefer the pain?'

'Yeah.'

'What the hell for?'

'That stuff makes me dopey.'

'Some consider that a nice side benefit.'

'Please. Get it out.'

He spun the bag around and looked at the label.

'Well, we got a lot of important stuff in here – like an anti-coagulant. Don't want you pulling a stroke on us. You do realise you've had a traumatic blow to the head?'

'Two.'

'Pardon?'

'Two traumatic blows to the head. Plus one to the gut and a kick in the teeth.'

'That reminds me,' said the doctor, pulling open my jaw and looking into my mouth. 'You left a piece of your tongue back there at the Playhouse.'

'Shit.'

'Yeah. Not a big one. Otherwise, you're in pretty good shape. Just a slight concussion and a gash. No bone damage.'

'Hard head.'

He reset his heavy horn-rimmed glasses on his nose and looked at my chart again. I wondered if it recorded my manifold sins and omissions. He looked up at me again as if struck with a new thought.

'These things can be cumulative. Going by your face you've been through this before. You made it this far without brain damage, but I wouldn't push your luck.'

'Wasn't my idea.'

'Okay. None of my business.'

'Guy suckered me. Hit like a bastard.'

Markham came into the room.

'Hey, dat's more like it. Actin' civil with the attending.'

'So it was definitely an assault,' said the doctor. 'The police were curious.'

'Who told them?'

'We told them. We always tell them when there's a fight. They'll want to talk to you.'

'If you call a Town cop named Joe Sullivan you'd be doing me a favour. He knows me.'

'I could do that.'

'After all the trouble you give us we supposed to be doin' you favours?' said Markham.

I looked up at him.

'I could've used you the other night.'

'Yeah? Who say I'm on your side?'

'We put about five stitches in your head,' said the doctor, 'where you probably caught a towel dispenser or stall divider. Your tongue'll just have to grow back on its own. Other than that, we'll keep an eye on you for another four hours, then throw you out of here.'

'The curse of the managed care,' said Markham.

'Don't start,' said the doc.

I wiggled the I.V.

'Do me a favour and unplug this thing. I'll sign whatever you want.'

They were both looking at me. Markham looked bemused.

'He don' want any additives. Give him the heebie-jeebies.'

The doc shrugged.

'Okay. Your body.'

'Yeah. Something like that.'

It took about an hour for a nurse to come and unhook the I.V. After that I fell asleep and dreamed of flying fists and frightening confrontations with slobbering demons and polar bears. Mangled corpses of old, white-haired people stacked up like cordwood. The constant look of disgust on Abby's face, and other nightmarish images. This is why I don't like having clear liquids pumped into my veins from little plastic bags. It never goes well.

THE HEADACHE woke me up. I pushed the button for a nurse and got Markham instead. He looked happy.

'Havin' second thoughts?' he asked me.

'Hurts too much to think.'

'Ha. Don' go blamin' me.'

'You on one of those eighty-hour shifts?'

When he spread his arms they seemed to swallow the entire room.

'Someone got to keep de place in business.'

He checked my pulse out of reflex. He pulled a pen-sized examination light out of his front pocket and clicked it on. His lips pursed when he shot it in my eyes.

'Not too bad, considerin''

'That's a comfort.'

He clicked off the light and stood straight, still frowning with concentration.

'You got any beef with aspirin?' he asked me.

'Works on a hangover.'

'It'll help.'

He scribbled on my chart and yelled to a passing nurse. She went off for the aspirin.

'Say, Doc.'

He looked up from my chart.

'Were you here when they brought me in?'

'Sure. I got you from the ER.'

'How'd I get here?'

'Some nice ladies drive you, I t'ink. Don't really know. Dere were some cops, but we shoo dem away.'

'Two or three ladies?'

He shrugged and shook his massive head.

'I only saw two. Dark-haired skinny one and a blond-haired bigger one. Gave me her card. Couldn't tell if she want to sell me a house or jump down my pants,' he said, cheerfully.

'She's in real estate. It's more or less the same thing.'

'I can ask the folks in the ER, but they don' usually see nothing but the patient. Takes some concentration, that job.'

'That's okay. Just wondering.'

'I could ask.'

'Nah. Just curious.'

He tucked his pen back in his pocket and patted the area around my head bandage. His enormous hands moved with a practiced ease. He seemed content with the job they'd done.

'Headache's not the only noise you got in dere, Mr Acquillo. I can see that.'

'Probably what's keeping me awake.'

'I can fix 'at. Offer's still open.'

'Aspirin's looking pretty good.'

'We'll get the dressing changed in a little while. You want anyt'ing, ask for me.'

'Could be a big order.'

He gave my forearm a quick squeeze, leaving the full strength of his grip in reserve. Enough to crack walnuts.

'That's why you call me. I'm big enough to do it.'

I actually slept again for another hour before Sullivan woke me up. He was in civilian clothes – jeans and cotton shirt, with a nylon jacket. He stood over me and shook his head.

'You should have told me,' he said.

'What?'

'You were out. We didn't know how bad you were hurt. I didn't know who to call or how to find out, so just for the hell of it I checked the priors database. Found a bunch of charges in Stamford and White Plains.'

'No convictions.'

'Reformed, eh?'

'I got suckered. I didn't even see him.'

'That was my other question.'

'Hit me from behind. Twice.'

'People at the club thought it might be some big guy with a pinky ring. Was in the head the same time as you, only nobody saw anything.' 'It was full of people.'

'The door was shut.'

I shook my head. It hurt my tongue to talk.

'Don't remember a big guy, looked Italian, maybe?' Sullivan asked again, 'Black hair? Black clothes?'

'Black boots. That was the view from the floor.'

'Any idea why?'

'No.'

'No conspiracy theory?'

'Just some asshole I must've pissed off without knowing it. I'm good at that.'

'Cop in Stamford said you were a pro fighter.'

'Long time ago. Not much of a career. Trust me.'

'I don't exactly, Mr Acquillo.'

I started to wish I'd taken Markham up on his painkillers. I laid back and closed my eyes.

'I can understand that.'

'You ever find out who did this, you have to tell me. Even if you don't want to press charges. I need to know who around here's capable of assault, for whatever reason.'

'I will. If I figure it out, I'll tell you.'

'Nothing you'd want to be workin' out on your own.'

'Not interested in that. Can't anyway. Doctor's orders. One more shot to the head and I'm a drooler.'

Sullivan left me with a look that was equal parts warning and concern. I didn't think he believed me, which wasn't a surprise. I wouldn't have either. It wasn't that I didn't like the beefy cop. In fact, he was growing on me. I just wanted to keep the bear to myself for a while. He was too important to let go.

A nurse came in to give me the aspirin. She delivered it in a little paper cup. She asked me if I needed anything else.

'A cigarette.'

'You'll be released in about a half-hour,' she said sweetly, patting my arm, 'You want the TV?'

'Talk about a killer.'

'Pick your poison.'

I was signing myself out and getting my car keys at the cashier's near the ER entrance when Amanda showed up. She stood back a few feet and waited for me to finish up, then followed me outside where we sat on the teak benches next to the orderlies catching morning cigarettes. I bummed one and smiled at Amanda.

'See what happens when I try to dance.'

'I'm so sorry.'

She leaned over to get a better look at the bandage stuck to the side of my head. She put her hands up to her mouth.

'It's not that bad. They showed me in the mirror.'

'I was so frightened. What happened?'

'You don't know?'

'They said you were in a fight.'

'Not exactly. All the fighting was done by the other guy. I never saw it coming.'

'Why?'

'I don't know. I guess you didn't hear anything, any buzz around the bar? You didn't hear a name?'

'No, there was just talk about a fight. I don't think anyone saw the other fellow very well. He must have left very quickly. One of the bartenders got you into your car. Robin and Laura drove you here. They said you woke up for a second, then passed out again before you got to the hospital. There was a lot of blood. Eddie was really upset.'

'I don't remember.'

'I'm so sorry I didn't go with you. I'm so ashamed.'

'Don't start apologizing, for Christ's sake.'

She smiled.

'It would have been hard to explain bloody clothes to Roy. But I checked on you this morning. I know a girl on the third floor. She asked around and they said you were fine. You don't look fine.'

'Just a little hole in my head. Match the one on the other side.'

'I was having such a good time.'

'Sorry I messed it up.'

'Now you're apologizing. No fair.'

I looked around at our exposed position in front of the big ER double doors.

'We probably shouldn't be sitting here.'

'I know. I just couldn't stand wondering.'

'I gotta go get Eddie. He'll think he's back in stir.'

Amanda was sitting on the edge of the bench, all clenched up. She looked pale and tired. I frowned at her.

'Amanda.'

'Sam.'

'You do this a lot?'

She looked down at her hands, clasped and held tightly between her knees.

'I don't know what you mean.'

'Yeah you do. You're married.'

'Oh, that.'

'I don't.'

'Don't what?'

'Don't do this. Never did.'

She tightened up even more.

'I see.'

'No you don't.'

'You don't want to see me.'

'That's not what I'm talking about.'

'Then I don't understand.'

I leaned around to catch her eye, but she wouldn't look at me.

'I told Sullivan that I didn't know who slugged me. But I do. At least, I know what he looks like.'

Now she looked at me.

'Then why didn't you say?'

'You remember the day we met at the beach? Do you remember a guy in a long coat, hanging around our cars when we left?'

'I don't know. I suppose not.'

'Roy know any big Italian guys, say about six-two, two hundred plus pounds?'

Her eyes shifted away again. But right before it did her face changed.

It turned into something complicated.

'Impossible.'

'You could make a case.'

'If it was Roy, I'd be the one in the bandages, not you. You, at least, can fight back.'

Then she stood up and did what she was getting good at doing. Walking away from me. I got up and followed her across the street to the parking lot. When she got in the grey Audi, I got in the passenger seat.

'Okay, I'm a dope,' I said.

'No, you're not. I'm a fool.'

It was still early in the morning, but it didn't look like it was going to be much of a day. The sky looked uniformly grey through the red leaves of the maple trees that shaded the hospital parking lot. My head was a little wobbly on my neck and my limbs were fitted with lead weights. I wanted to go home and lay down on the porch, but for some reason I wasn't ready to go.

'Thanks for coming to see me.'

She started the ignition and rested her forehead on the steering wheel. I reached over and pulled her thick auburn hair back off her face. Her eyes were closed. Her cheekbones were flushed red, deepening the copper and olive tones of her skin, filling her face with colour where before she'd been sallow and pale.

I leaned over and kissed her neck right below the little freshwater pearl earring that dangled from her right ear. Her skin was very smooth and her neck strong. It smelled like a blend of hope, dread and calamity. She turned her head, still resting on the steering wheel, her face softening back toward normal.

'Just remember I tried to tell you things and you didn't want to hear,' she said, before leaning across my lap and opening the door.

'About big Italian guys?'

'Things. Just things.'

I got out of the car and watched her drive away. I found the Grand Prix parked up on a grassy mound at the back of the lot. There was blood all over the backseat. I got an old blanket from the trunk to cover it up. I thought I might have to throw up before I could drive away, but after sitting down with my legs out the door for a few minutes, I recovered. Eddie almost pulled me off my feet in his desperation to get out of the vet's and into the Grand Prix. He sniffed at my head, but was good enough not to say I told you so.

No one greeted us at the cottage. No notes, no mail. I pushed my way through the door, sampled the salty, dry wood smells and swam in the deep comfort of familiar surroundings. I banged a big cast-iron fry pan down on the burner, crumbled in some ground meat and filled another huge pot with water. When it started to boil I tossed in a handful of spaghetti and made myself a tall Absolut from out of the freezer. The clear liquid burned the wound on the side of my tongue and warmed up my extremities. The wood stove did the rest once I got it cranked up with choice, bone-dry split red oak. I changed into my oldest blue jeans and a thirty-year-old sweatshirt. I put some early Thelonious Monk on the CD player and slopped some sauce from the Italian place in the Village on the pasta. I could only chew on one side of my mouth, but it was worth it. I went out on the porch to watch the clear skies paint the Little Peconic a metal-flecked, pale grey blue. The angled October sun tipped each little wave with reflective silver that winked at me like the sequins of an evening gown. The pink hydrangea were beginning to brown at the ends of their leggy pale-green stalks. But the lawn still looked like a deep forest pool.

And I wasn't dead.

AFTER WE ate, Eddie and I both slept the rest of the day. Too exhausted to feel any more fear, too hardened to thank whoever might be responsible for yet another reprieve, deserved or not.

Three days later I finally got Regina Broadhurst put in the ground. The funeral home was owned by an oversized Greek guy named Andre Pappanasta. He had thick curly black hair and a beard and a voice that came out of somewhere inside his chest. He smiled and laughed a lot, mostly because he never went near his funeral business, preferring to work the counter at one of the five or six pizza joints he owned around the Island. You only talked to him when you made arrangements, which he'd do between phone orders for large pepperoni pizzas and baked stuffed ziti.

The day was brand new, sunny, and the air reasonably clear. My tongue was still sore and my lower ribs ached, but my head had healed enough to leave off the bandage. With a little work my hair covered the wound. The funeral guys were composed and friendly and the priest was bored, but efficient. Half a dozen old crones from the Senior Centre, Roy and Amanda Battiston, Jimmy Maddox and I made up the congregation. We gathered in a viewing room decorated in the calm civility of thick, peach-coloured carpet and semi-gloss paint.

Amanda was dressed in a plain navy blue suit and light blue blouse. When she and Roy met me in the parking lot she squeezed my hand. Her freshly showered smell engulfed my brain, but I kept a safe distance. Roy was scrubbed pink and sombre in a charcoal grey suit. He carried about fifty pounds more than he needed, but it looked like it had settled there permanently. His receding hair was combed straight back. His handshake was warm and dry. Before letting go he added another hand. That drew us into closer proximity than I would have chosen on my own. I could smell the same soap as Amanda's.

'We want to thank you for letting us know about this,' he said to me. 'Regina was a good friend of Amanda's mother.'

She nodded in agreement.

'She didn't know too many people.'

'We lost Amanda's mother last year. It's very difficult,' he said, looking at her gravely.

'Sorry about the short notice.'

He waved off the comment.

'Not at all. We completely understand.'

One of the ushers herded us out of the waiting room and into another room that looked about the same except for the coffin and some funereal flower arrangements. Jimmy Maddox was hanging back, like he'd rather stay in the waiting room, but I gripped him by the shoulder and said, 'Come on, man.'

I had trouble concentrating on what the priest was saying. They always had that effect on me. As soon as I see vestments and big silver candelabras my mind starts roaming all over the place. I got that from my mother. She hated organized religion, even though every Sunday she'd drag me and my sister to the Polish church in the Village. When I was about ten, she just stopped, never saying why. I never asked, afraid a show of interest would start her up again. So I was left with the memory of singsong Latin monotones and my mother fidgeting and snorting away in the pew. Great job of indoctrination.

The priest said something about the mortal remains of the dead, giving me an unwanted image of old Regina carved up on the autopsy table.

A rumble of low voices came from the back of the room. It was

Barbara Filmore. She was wearing a suit made of car upholstery, accented by a black feather thing wrapped around her throat. A veiled hat sat on the top of her hairdo and her glasses low on her nose. The bulge of her midriff drew attention to her thin legs, conjuring the image of an overdressed waterfowl.

She had a baldheaded, roundish guy with a salt and pepper moustache for an escort. He looked bored but attentive. He had those pale beige patent leather shoes and matching belt sets you see in Florida, but rarely around this part of the East End. He wore a light blue guayabera and wrinkle-free beige pants made of some long-chain polymer. I guessed him to be about ten years older than me.

They disturbed the calm of the room for a few minutes before settling down. The priest sent up a few more requests for the Almighty to look after Regina in the hereafter. I prayed for the whole thing to be over.

A pair of Pappanasta's boys came in and hauled her out of there after the priest finally wrapped up his bit. They looked well-dressed and professional, like IRS agents or the guys I used to work with from Accounting & Finance. They seemed to be old pals of the priest's – probably got together a lot after a gig.

Nobody in the room was crying, which I deeply appreciated. Sunlight did nice things with all the flowers I'd ordered up for the occasion. They looked fresh and expensive, which didn't surprise me. Andy always used quality toppings on his pizzas. A matter of principle.

The congregation was forced to talk to each other after the priest said hello, handed out a few banalities, then made a run for it. Probably had a seat warming up for him somewhere. Roy and Jimmy Maddox were stuck with the old folks. I was with Amanda, Barbara Filmore and her date.

'We've had quite the schedule at the Centre lately, Mr Acquillo,' said Barbara. 'I expected a visit.'

'Been pretty tied up.'

'Oh,' she said, as if suddenly remembering there was a guy standing next to her, 'this is Bob Sobol. This is Sam Acquillo.'

'How're you doin'?' he said, absently, looking past my shoulder at the sun and fresh air blowing in from an open door. His grip hurt, which surprised me a little.

'Bob is thinking about buying property out here. He's staying with me. Maybe you could tell him what you know about the area, investmentwise – you've owned out here for some time, haven't you?'

'I inherited.'

Bob didn't seem to care either way.

'Bob also has retirement to consider, so it has to be livable,' said Barbara, leadingly. She looked at Bob for a little help.

'I like the area,' said Bob, finally relenting. There was a touch of the Bronx in his accent, the one I knew as a kid.

'I know some good real estate people I can refer you to,' said Amanda.

The two of them stared at her till she put out her hand.

'I'm Amanda Battiston. Regina was a friend of my mother's.'

'Is that *Mrs* Battiston?' Bob asked her, looking at her left hand.

'It is,' she said brightly.

On cue, Roy came up behind her and stuck his out as well.

'Roy Battiston,' he said.

'My mother was Julia Anselma,' said Amanda.

Barbara perked up.

'Of course, I'm very sorry.' She turned toward Bob, 'Amanda's mother was a regular at the Centre. She also passed away recently.'

Barbara placed a blocking shoulder in front of Bob so he couldn't move closer to Amanda. He didn't seem to notice, or care.

'That'd be nice of you, Mrs Battiston. I haven't found an agent I like.'

'These folks are very likable. At least to me.'

'Long's they're good,' said Bob.

'Yes, they're good, too. Good and likable.'

Bob pursed his mouth and acted convinced.

'Maybe you could show me where some of the better areas are, Mrs Battiston. You must know your way around pretty good, being a native.'

'Most people out here aren't natives.'

'But I guessed maybe you were.'

'I didn't know it showed.'

He shrugged as a type of sympathy for her shortcomings.

'How about financing?' he asked. 'I could use some tips there, too.' Roy dove right in,

'Absolutely, Bob. Come see me at Harbor Trust. Always there to help.'

I started looking around for Jimmy Maddox. Maybe the two of us could go find a piece of heavy equipment to play with.

'But surely you could help me find a place, Mrs Battiston,' said Bob.

'Amanda. I can point you in the right direction,' she said, sprightly.

'Should I get a pencil?'

Barbara Filmore's smile stayed put as her mood took a right turn.

'I'm sure Amanda has plenty to do already.'

'Actually, I do, but I promise to keep my eyes and ears open.'

Bob gave a curt little nod that reminded me of Claude Raines. I thought he was going to click his heals together.

'You must be so busy looking after your mother's things,' said Barbara, putting a little meat on Amanda's excuse. 'I've been through it myself, so I know.' She hooked her oversized pocket-book on her shoulder and slid the other hand through Bob's arm. He didn't put up much of a fight when she tugged him gently toward the door.

'I'm so sorry about your mother. And Regina, of course. Two friends, so close together.'

'They weren't all that close,' said Amanda, spoiling the mannerly mood.

'Well, it's all part of life,' said the other woman, backing the two of them through the door. I was happy to let them go.

When the ushers finally cleared the room, I followed Amanda and Roy out to the parking lot. I let them get a little ahead of me. Amanda walked with her back straight and her shoulders level, with a fluid, feminine roll to her hips. It made me want to follow her out to Montauk and back. But she stopped and turned around, held Roy's arm and waited for me to catch up.

'Thanks again, Sam,' said Roy.

Amanda pulled off a pair of old-fashioned black kid leather gloves a fingertip at a time. When they were off, she opened and shut her fists as if restoring circulation.

'I think Bob wants a native guide,' I said to both of them.

'Ick,' said Amanda.

'He seemed all right,' said Roy, looking at me for confirmation.

'Could be some business for you.'

'That's what we're here for.'

Amanda looked around the parking lot, presumably for her car.

'We're going to get a little breakfast,' she said. 'Care to join us?'

'Yeah,' said Roy before I could answer, 'Sip and Soda. Best waffles in town.'

He looked genuinely excited.

'Sorry,' I told them, 'got to wrap up here. Some other time.'

'You sure?' asked Roy, face bright and eager as a Midwestern regional sales manager. 'I always order Amanda the blueberry Belgian waffle with a side of bacon. Don't I? It's her favourite.'

Amanda cocked her head at me, her face neutral.

'That's a lot of trust to put in a person. Ordering your breakfast,' I said to her.

'Some people you just trust with certain things,' she said.

Roy looked at her.

'Some people you trust with everything,' he said, then looked at me. 'I keep telling her that.'

He smiled with the sort of self-effacing beneficence you like to see in priests. I smiled back.

'I'll take a rain check. You guys go ahead.'

They drove away in Roy's Audi – bigger and darker than Amanda's – leaving me alone with the hard light of autumn trying to bust out from the cloud cover, and the rest of the afternoon to torture myself with conflicting urges and pointless self-analysis.

•

THE LITTLE Aztec lady at the coffee place on the corner didn't know Arnold Lombard Co. Neither did the tough woman from Brooklyn with the pretty skin and chipped tooth who ran the cash register. Luckily, a gang of gnarly old regulars, who hung around in the afternoon doing crosswords and lying about their investment portfolios did.

'Used to be across the street there where what's-his-name opened his real estate office.'

'Sinitar.'

'Yeah. Joey Sinitar and his brother. Builder's kids. Don't know if they actually *sell* any real estate.'

All the guys smiled as if they had the inside scoop on the Sinitar boys.

'Lombard's dead.'

One of the guys shook his head.

'Ain't dead.'

'Somebody told me he was dead.'

'Come as a big surprise to Arnie.'

'You know him?' I asked him.

The old man had dry silvery eyes and the complexion of rough stucco.

'More or less. Kind of a stiff. Sold real estate and life insurance. Mostly to locals. Drove a Lincoln Continental, 'bout the size'a the Queen Mary.'

'Had a daughter.'

'Yeah. Looked like him. All nose. No sense of humour.'

'Know where he lives?' I asked.

They all looked at each other, seeing who wanted to field the question.

'Florida,' one of them finally said.

The guy in the know shook his head again. I waited.

'Ain't in Florida.'

'What're you, his biographer?' said one of his buddies.

'Well?' I asked.

'Lives with his daughter. Nobody'd marry the poor thing.'

'Nose like a masthead.'

'More like a banana.'

'In town?'

'Village. Over near the hospital.'

'Got a place in Florida, but never goes there.'

'Hah.'

'But he's definitely not dead.'

'How do you know?'

The guy in the know let it all sit there for a few seconds to build suspense.

'I saw him yesterday at the pharmacy.'

'What're you doing in there, Charlie? Buyin' Ex-lax?'

'Trojans.'

They all grinned into their coffees. I thanked Charlie and paid for their next round of Hazelnut. The Brooklyn woman thought the largesse ridiculous, but she wasn't a sensitive girl.

I pulled the street address to Arnold Lombard's house out of a disheveled phone book shoved under the payphone at the back of the coffee shop. It was an easy walk over toward the hospital, so I walked. It was a single storey, asbestos-shingle bungalow painted white with black trim and leggy, dejected-looking shrubbery. In front of a tiny single-car garage was a boxy, early sixties Lincoln Continental covered with a tan canvas tarp.

Green algae was growing up from the bottom of the wooden storm door. There was no doorbell, so I knocked. I picked the blue plastic-wrapped *New York Times* up off the driveway so I could give it to whomever opened the door.

It was a woman with a hatchet-shaped nose thrust forward like an angry remark. On either side were gentle, watery blue eyes. Her dark brown hair hung in a loose perm past her thin neck and tumbled down around wiry shoulders. She wore a ragged baby blue tank top, braless, baggy, dark blue sweat pants, and dancing slippers. I guessed her to be around forty-five. The smell of too much time spent indoors spilled out around her, warming up the autumn air.

She looked at me in a tired, kind way.

'Yes?'

I stuck out my hand. She took it without hesitation.

'I'm Sam Acquillo. Here's your *Times*.'

'How nice,' she said.

'Is this where Arnold Lombard lives?'

'What can I help you with?'

'It's kind of a long story. Is he in?'

She stood a little straighter.

'Now that would depend entirely on your story, Mister . . . Acquillo. Italian is it?'

'Italo-Canuck is the way my father put it.'

'We're Jewish.'

I didn't know where to go from there, but she was patient with me. She put a hand on her hip and leaned on the door jam. I tried not to look at her chest.

'Your interest in Mr Lombard?'

'I'm trying to work out some tricky ownership issues on a piece of property up in North Sea. Your father's name was all over the documents, so I thought maybe he could help clear it up.'

'Real estate matter.'

'That's pretty much what it is, yeah.'

She shrugged and walked away from the door. I took that as an invitation and followed her in. Time inside the house was stalled in mid-century. Glossy white trim paint covered lumpy woodwork. The wallpaper was covered with baronial garden parties and foxhunts. The odour of pipe tobacco and unwashed wool mingled with kitchen grease and sachet.

Arnold was sitting in the living room in an overstuffed easy chair. His hands gripped the armrests like he was preparing for take off. He was much older than I thought he'd be, well over ninety. His clothes were clean, but ancient and threadbare. There were pipes arrayed around a free-standing ashtray, but no ashes. A dusting of white hair covered his long, bone-hard skull. His daughter had come by the nose honestly.

'Daddy?'

He looked up at her.

'This gentleman has a real estate matter to discuss.'

He frowned with the effort to understand.

'A real estate matter,' she repeated. He looked over at me.

'Then what's he doing here?'

'I thought maybe you could answer some questions for me about a property up in North Sea.'

'I'm retired.'

'This was a property you handled back in the seventies.'

He looked down and shook his head.

'I don't know if I can remember all that.'

His daughter massaged his shoulder and smiled sweetly.

'Oh, sure you can, Daddy. You know about every piece of property on the East End.'

He raised his thin eyebrows in a type of smile.

'That's true. Your mother says I'm nothing but a head full of topographicals.'

'That's what she always said,' said his daughter, correcting the tense.

She swung around and dropped into a love seat and patted the space next to her. I sat down and pulled out the file from the Town records. She drew her legs up so the soft soles of the dancing slippers applied a slight pressure to my right thigh.

I handed him a copy of the rental agreement his firm had drawn up for Bay Side Holdings. He took it with one hand and, with some difficulty, dug his glasses out from under his wool cardigan. His daughter let him struggle on his own. Patience hung in the air.

When the tiny silver wire rims were finally perched on that mighty outcropping it made him look like a sorcerer in a Disney movie.

'Oh yes, well, we did a lot of these. Certainly.'

I let him read for a while.

'Hm, hm,' he said, and handed it back to me.

'Yes, we managed all the Bay Side leaseholds. Had the exclusive.'

He sat back, satisfied.

His daughter had her chin cupped in her hand with an index

finger braced against her nose. She closed her eyes, shook her head and smiled that beatific smile.

'That's fine, Daddy, but I think he's looking for a little more detail,' she said.

Arnold thought about it. He leaned back in his chair and looked up at the ceiling.

'Well, as I recall, that outfit owned a fair number of these parcels up there in North Sea, some of which had houses built on them. They were concerned they'd be vandalized if left unoccupied. We were charged with keeping them filled with the best possible people – considering the location, mind you, which was not ideal.'

Class paranoia washed over me.

'That outfit was Bay Side Holdings.'

'Well, certainly, Bay Side were the people who engaged the services of the firm. However, they were the agents for the actual owners. This was made clear to me from the start. I don't recall their names, precisely, but I believe we could discover that in our files.' He looked over at his daughter for confirmation.

'I'm sure we could dig something out, Daddy.'

He swung his gaze back to me as something else occurred to him.

'I do have a theory about Bay Side, however.'

'Do you.'

'Yes. But,' he pointed at me with a bent knuckle the way Regina always did, 'it would likely be a sensitive matter. The firm's standing depends on discretion.'

His daughter looked over at me. I kept my eyes on Arnold.

'You shouldn't tell me anything that would betray a confidence, Mr Lombard.'

'I don't believe in that.'

'I can't promise I won't use information you give me in dealing with this – it's an estate settlement, by the way – but I'll keep your name out of it.'

'You're an attorney?' his daughter asked.

'Estate administrator.'

I didn't think Arnold understood the distinction, but I was more concerned about his daughter. I wanted her to like me.

'Well,' he looked up at the ceiling again as if his thoughts were written out up there. 'I always felt that Bay Side was a captive. You're familiar with the term?'

'You mean the owner of the property was their only client. They were owned by the owners.'

'Yes, something like that. I'm not suggesting there was any impropriety, just that Bay Side was a dummy. You know, a front. Perfectly legal, of course. Commercial interests often structure real estate management as a separate enterprise – a subsidiary.'

'Daddy started in corporate real estate. In the city,' she said, looking at him.

'What gave you this idea, if you don't mind me asking.'

'Well, I've done quite a bit of this sort of thing, sir. You get to know how things are. Patterns and rhythms. A feeling, really. Ask Rosaline.'

She puffed out a little breath.

'He thinks I'm psychic because I predict the weather. Hasn't caught on to the Weather Channel yet.'

Humour lit his eyes to spite his deadpan face.

'I know perfectly well how to locate the Weather Channel. I only mean that we often discuss the mysteries of intuition.'

She shrugged at me again. I think she did a lot of shrugging.

'I'm a big supporter of intuition myself, folks,' I said. 'No need to explain further.'

'Would you like some tea? Caffeinated or Red Zinger,' she said, now that we'd bumped the conversation up a notch.

'Sure. A little Zinger'd be good.'

'Daddy?'

He made an ambiguous gesture with his mottled hands. She seemed to know what it meant.

'I'll help,' I said, and followed her into the kitchen.

All the appliances were stainless steel Hotpoints from the mid-Fifties. The linoleum on the counter was covered with colourful little boomerangs. We had the same thing in our house when I was growing up. The association was oddly appealing.

'Are there files?' I asked her.

She looked surprised.

'Why of course. Why wouldn't there be?'

'Uh.'

'You think I'm just humouring him?'

'Sorry. I guess I was.'

'There's nothing wrong with his mind, Mr Acquillo. He's just old.'

'I can see that.'

She brushed past me and put a full kettle on the stove. 'He was almost fifty when I was born,' she said, apropos of something that wasn't apparent to me.

'Can I take a look at the stuff relating to this property?' I wrote out Regina's address on a memo pad.

She took it out of my hand and studied it.

'Sure, but you'll have to do the digging. We don't have much of a research staff.'

'The files are here?'

'In the basement. My father is loathe to discard such things.'

'I have a feeling he'd know right where to find it.'

'A minute ago you thought he was off his rocker.' It was my turn to shrug.

'And now you'd like him to find what you need.'

I did, of course. She looked at the memo pad again.

'I do have other things to do,' she said, studying the slip of paper as if it held the secret meaning of my mind. She handed it back to me, then opened the old Hotpoint dishwasher and got out mugs for the tea. The way she bent over the dishwasher made it hard to avoid noticing she was female. I kept my eyes on the mug while she poured the tea.

'Do you have any children?' she asked me.

'I have a daughter living in the city.'

'Did she go to school in Southampton?'

'No, Connecticut. Why?'

'I work at the high school. Thought maybe I knew your kids. That's usually how I get a fix on people.'

'She came out sometimes in the summer.'

'With you and your wife.'

'Yeah. Now ex.'

'Oh. But your daughter still comes out.'

'No. She exed herself as well.'

'Sorry. Certainly not forever.'

I had a hard time not looking into those sad, patient eyes.

'Yeah. Hope not forever.'

'I have an ex, too. No kids.' I thought about the old crows back at the coffee place.

'Happens.'

'All too often. Mostly miss all that regular sex. You?'

I laughed. 'Not regular enough to miss.'

'There you go,' she said, resonating again to some private frequency. 'What happened to your face?'

I guess women with big noses and pretty blue eyes get to pry into anything they want.

'A rock-hard Filipino middle heavyweight named Rene Ruiz got me to look over my shoulder for a second. Caught me when I turned back.'

She nodded, 'Boxer.'

'We called ourselves fighters. "Boxer" seems kinda refined. Too removed from the actual endeavour.'

'Which was to beat the hell out of each other?'

'Basically.'

I resisted the urge to touch the right side of my head where my hair covered the stitches. I knew she'd make me explain.

'You only fight Filipinos, or did a few demons creep into the ring?'

'I'm too tough for demons,' I said, showing her I'd learned to duck from Rene Ruiz.

She took a slow sip of her tea, looking up at me over the rim.

'Yes, I'm sure you believe that.'

'What do you teach?'

'I'm the school psychologist. What did you study?'

'Avoidance. Graduate level.'

She toasted me with her mug and drifted back out of the

kitchen. I followed her toward the living room, but she made a right turn before getting there and went down a narrow basement stairway. I followed her. The basement was filled with musty wet air and exhausted clutter. The file storage, about twenty bankers boxes, was in a corner lit by a pair of 100-watt utility lamps.

Everything was organized by date, and then coded by account numbers and some other designation I didn't understand. It was very tidy and clearly labelled, but the scale was daunting.

'Sure your dad isn't looking for something to kill the time?'

'Long as the air down here doesn't kill him first.'

'Not as fast as an easy chair.'

'Leveraging my concern for my father to facilitate your project?'

'Yeah, something like that. A little leverage is good for an old guy – taken in moderation.'

I got her to laugh an honest little laugh. She stuck an index finger into my sternum and gave it a shove.

'What was your name, again?'

'Sam.'

'Rosaline.' She put out her hand.

I gave her mine, then had a little trouble getting it back again.

'When I get a chance I'll look through the files. See what I can find.'

'I appreciate it.'

'I know you do, because you should. Let's go have another cup of tea.'

She flicked off the big lights and we swam back out of the dead time that had settled under the house like a stagnant pool.

SONNY'S GYM was wet with ambition. Lots of tough, mostly stupid young guys and older guys who hadn't wakened to the realities. They strutted or lumbered around scratching their nuts and looking nervous or fierce depending on their confidence. All wanted to prove something, to make their time on earth count, at least within the arc of their circumscribed lives. All I wanted to do was maintain a decent heart rate, hold down the fat and maybe hone whatever reflexes I had left. And at this point, maybe regain some of what I lost since getting my ass kicked.

The soggy sweat smell was worse than usual, in contrast with the scrubbed luminescence outside. I wrinkled my face at the towel guy, but his sense of smell had dimmed long ago. His nose had a big black mole with a hair about the size of a three-penny nail growing out of the middle. He sat on a short stool with his inflated midsection pouring over the top of his shiny polyester pants. He moved in a steady 180-degree swing from counter to hamper, handing out towels the size of cocktail napkins and the delicacy of medium grade sandpaper. I was impressed that Ronny knew to hire an authentic towel guy, just like they had back in the city. Maybe they had to. Maybe towel guys have a union that sets the standard. Maybe I've spent too many years hanging out in boxing gyms.

'Smells like a beer fart in this place,' I told him.

The towel guy ignored me, looking past my shoulder at the fix on reality he'd established out there in middle space.

I went into the locker room and pulled all my stuff out of the old canvas duffel bag that once belonged to my father. That shrink I had to see told me I started boxing because my father was beaten to death. He thought this was a brilliant insight. I said, yeah, I started boxing because my old man was beaten to death. Wouldn't you?

When I was younger, I was mostly afraid my father would be the one doing the beating. Which never happened, that I remember, but he sure threatened a lot, and yelled a lot, and came close a few times. All out of sheer meanness. What I remember mostly was the back of his hand, raised in sudden threat. I think, under those circumstances, you either get some confidence, or you wrap yourself up in fear and let your insides die an early death. I don't know. Maybe I should get another shrink to explain it to me.

Whatever the motivation, I was there at Sonny's trying not to understand how I felt. About anything except my sore ribs. I started with some stretching, did the rope, did the light bag, then did a little on the big bag. I got so absorbed in everything I didn't notice Sullivan standing there again, like he seemed to do whenever I worked the big bag. I stopped and held it still with both gloves.

'Hey.'

'You ready for that?' he asked.

'I'm okay.'

'Memory getting better?'

'About the guy?'

'Yeah. About the guy.'

I shook my head.

'Not yet, but it could improve with time.'

'I'm sure.'

I did a few more patterns, but it's hard to talk and whack a big leather bag full of sand at the same time.

'I got Regina buried,' I said.

'Andre told me. What about the estate stuff?'

'No big deal. Waiting for some information.'

He stood silently with his arms crossed. Irritated.

'I'm waiting, too,' he said.

'For what?'

He uncrossed his arms and gestured with both hands the way you do when guiding a car into a parking space.

'Cough it up. What are you thinking?'

'You think I'm full of crap.'

'I do. I still want you to talk to me.'

I went back to the bag. But it's no easier to think than to talk when thus engaged. So I gave in.

'Joe, you like to drink?'

'Off duty.'

'Let's go get a drink.'

'Long as you're buyin'.'

Sullivan was familiar with the Pequot. Like everybody else around town he'd done some time as a kid crewing on the charter fishing boats that ran out of Pequot Harbor. Mostly the job was to schlep stuff on and off board, clean the catch and kiss the customer's ass. Dotty set us up with beers and menus, then left us alone.

'Ever heard of Bay Side Holdings?' I asked him.

He shook his head.

'Own a lot of property in North Sea. Maybe other places, too. Don't know.'

'What about 'em?'

'Own Regina's house.'

'Really. Shit bad luck for Jimmy.'

'Yeah. But he knew about it. Knew his aunt was a renter. Only I don't think she paid any rent.'

'That I doubt.'

'Doesn't make sense. But there're no bank records. No cancelled cheques.'

'Ask Bay Side Whatever.'

'Bay Side Holdings. I did. I mean, I went to their business address, which turns out to be a house in Sag Harbor, owned by this guy Milton Hornsby, who's the only name I have connected to Bay Side, and he won't talk to me. Sent me to his lawyer.'

'Who said ?'

'Haven't seen her yet. Called her. Left messages. Thinking of going over there.'

'Where?'

'Bridgehampton. It's Jacqueline Swaitkowski.'

'Yikes.'

He looked amused.

'So I heard.'

'Fucking whack job.'

'Why'd a guy like Hornsby hire her?'

'Fucking brilliant whack job. And connected. Husband was Peter Swaitkowski. Potato field money. Political. Master of the Universe till he stuck his Porsche in an oak tree.'

'I remember that.'

'Went to high school with her. Jackie O'Dwyer. Summa Come Loudly.'

'A friend of mine, another lawyer, said I can't compel Hornsby to talk to me. But why wouldn't he? It's his goddam house.'

'He's Bay Side Holdings?'

'I don't know that either. My friend's finding out.'

'Who's your friend?'

'Burton Lewis.'

'Rich fuck. Rich fag fuck.'

'Friend of mine.'

'I didn't know you ran in them circles.'

'My ex-wife's circles. But Burt's okay.'

'He's asshole buddies with Chief Semple,' he said, then caught himself. 'Not literally. Lewis is a sure mark for Semple's fundraising. They'd mixed it up a bunch of years ago over this black kid we busted up in Flanders. He was going down till Lewis stuck his nose in it. Could have been bad for the Town, since apparently the kid'd been tuned up a little, and probably wasn't actually guilty of the crime. But then, you know, everybody gets in a room and backs are gettin' scratched, and dicks are gettin' jerked, and before you know it, the kid's out, the Town's clear, Semple's smilin' and your buddy Burton Lewis is payin' for open bars and fireworks.'

'Doesn't sound like the worst deal.'

'I guess.'

Sullivan wasn't going to press it. He also wasn't going to give up his local allegiance, his bigotry against all things Manhattan.

'So that's where it's at. Besides Burton, I'm gathering up what I can on Bay Side from real estate records. The Surrogate's Court still has to have a hearing on making me administrator, but I can keep going. Should be a slam dunk unless Jimmy Maddox wants to make trouble, which I don't think'll happen.'

Sullivan drank some more of his beer and looked around the inside of the Pequot. The midday regulars were hunkered around the bar trying to hold coherent conversations with Dotty. Hodges was in the back rustling up Fish of the Day for the guys coming off boats that'd been out since four in the morning. Sullivan looked like he wanted to say something.

'What.'

'It bothers me,' he said.

'What bothers you.'

'I'm responsible for the safety and well-being of all the people and property inside about a five square mile chunk of Long Island. You're put in charge of something like that, and everybody has to pretend that it's actually possible to do the job. But it's really not, at least not the way everybody wants you to. It's nobody's fault, it's just you gotta act out this fantasy that we're all some kind of superman. But that's okay. I do the job anyway, my way, as best I can. Only my way makes it hard to buy into the bullshit. I can't help havin' a mind of my own.'

'What's your mind telling you?'

'Nobody gives a shit about dead old ladies. And I don't even blame 'em. There's so much shit going on all the time, there's so little money to ever get it all done. Out here you got homegrown idiots stealing shit and selling drugs, and shootin' each other, you got all kinds of crazy evil shit coming out of the city, especially during the season. You got all these people along the water who act like they own the world, because, basically, some of 'em do. Then there's the people in the court system you have to keep happy. You got County people, State people, fucking Feds if you think about it, all doing nothin' but figurin' out ways to make your job harder. The last thing any of 'em wants you to do for Christ's sake is say, "I *know* this is what you *think* happened, but it ain't that way, it happened like *this*." That'd mean paperwork. Time away from other shit that's already more than they can handle. That'd mean somebody'd have to say, "oh, I guess I fucked up a little bit on that one".'

It was too bad, but Hodges picked that moment to come over and say hi. Sullivan stood up and shook his hand. They ran through a bunch of names looking for connections, which wasn't hard. Sullivan dredged up some nice things to say about Hodges' joint. Hodges pledged admiration and support for all boys and girls in law enforcement. All of which was fine, but I wanted to find out where Sullivan was heading. Which I couldn't do until much later, back out in the parking lot.

As soon as we were outside I said, 'So, Joe, what were you saying in there?'

He dug around inside his jeans' pocket for the keys to his old Bronco.

'Broadhurst might've been a lousy old bitch, but she was my lousy old bitch. My beat, my neighbourhood. I don't care if you're full of crap. Until I can prove to myself one hundred percent that you're full of crap, I'm interested in this. Let me know what you're doing.'

He walked over to his truck, carrying the extra weight around his middle with obstinate dignity. I went home to feed the dog and nurse my wounds.

THERE WERE little clouds of grey-blue mist rising up from the harvested potato fields when I drove out Scuttle Hole Road on the way to Jackie Swaitkowski's place in Bridgehampton. It was midmorning and you could see the clear sky above waiting for the sun to dry out the air. Despite the mist, everything looked sharp and scrubbed clean, even through the Grand Prix's pitted windshield. Ribbons of fresh white fencing separated crop land from pasture, where dressage horses grazed and tried to look indifferent to their status. Huge piles of postmodern architecture and partially submerged potato barns broke up the slow curves of the landscape. To the north were short hills covered by forests of red oak and scruffy pine. Jackie was somewhere up in there, if I'd read my map right. Her answering service said she'd be there all morning. The woman I spoke to said not to bother with an appointment.

'Go ahead up there. I know her, she won't mind.'

'Really.'

'She's bored. She's been stuck on this brief for a bunch of people trying to run this poor guy off his gas station. They say it's a blight on the neighbourhood.'

'Not if you need gas.'

'People are so touchy about property values.'

'Because they're so valuable?'

'That's the thing. Everything's so expensive. Hey, got another call. Say hi to Jackie. Tell her not to work too hard.'

I called for an appointment anyway. The answering service was right. Jackie Swaitkowski longed for distractions.

'Sure, come on over. Ring the bell,' she said before I'd given much of an explanation.

Once in the woods, the atmosphere changed abruptly. Enclosed by tall oaks, the air was cool and the light was splattered pattern-less across the ground and up the sides of thick tree trunks. The iridescent red and orange fall foliage betrayed the deep green of scrub pines and hemlocks and wild mountain laurel. A few more weeks and all the leaves would be on the ground and the forest would give in to the grey gloom of winter.

Jackie's house was the kind of flimsy, unadorned wooden box real estate people called a Contemporary. It was built into the side of a hill at the end of a long dirt drive. Jackie, or whoever owned the place, wasn't much of a landscaper. A rusty Toyota pickup with oversized tyres and welded metal racks was in front of the garage.

Next to the front door were two buttons – one labelled 'Jackie Swaitkowski, attorney-at-law.' The other said 'Jackie Swait-kowski, Private Citizen.' I rang the lawyer.

She had a long, thick crop of strawberry blond hair and a lot of freckles splashed across a reddish tan complexion. Her face was wide open and pretty, and could have been used to promote Irish tourism. She had a nice figure stuffed into a yellow cotton jersey dress and flip-flops on her feet. Maybe thirty-two, maybe more. It was getting harder for me to tell.

'Hi.'

'Attorney Swaitkowski?'

'Jackie.'

'Sam Acquillo.'

'Like the saint?'

'That'd be Aquinas.'

'Right. Missed that catechism.' She walked away from the door and invited me in with an exaggerated wave of her arm. I followed her into a sloppy, cheerful living room furnished with two dirty white couches and a coffee table made from a gigantic slab of cross-cut timber. It was buried under heaps of magazines and catalogues. She walked across the table and dropped down cross-legged into one of the couches. I took the other.

Hardly seated, she bounced up again and asked if I wanted anything, like coffee or tea. I said coffee and she disappeared for a few minutes to rustle some up.

While I waited, I looked around at the overflowing bookcases and poster art plastered on every scrap of wall space. There were probably thousands of books and CDs, but no TV. On a side table was a stack of used dinner plates and a roach in the ashtray.

'I'm actually kind of glad to be getting away from this godawful case,' she said as she came back in with two mismatched mugs.

'So I hear.'

She huffed.

'That's Judy, she's such a pain. We talk all the time, of course. She should be paying me, I'm so entertaining.'

She climbed back into the couch, slumped down and put her feet up on the coffee table. Her legs were pinkie brown and freckled like her face. They'd seen a lot of beach time. She held the mug with two hands and blew the steam off the top.

We talked about Southampton past and present and tried to find common ground. It was the kind of conversation you have on a barstool or at a checkout counter. With a little prompting, she talked enough to hold up both our ends.

'Always practiced out here?' I asked her.

'What, does it show? Yeah, of course. Born, raised, and so on. Except for law school. Even married a Polish potato boy. He's dead,' she said quickly, before I could comment. 'Sold the farm, then bought the farm, so to speak. Stuck that cute little car about halfway up the side of a great big oak tree. Right out here on Brick Kiln Road. Perfect, huh?'

'Sorry.'

She set down the coffee and sat back, throwing her arms across the back of the couch. 'Hey, what am I doing here telling you my life's story.'

'I got you started.'

'That's right, you did.'

She looked me over a little more carefully.

'You gonna tell me what happened?'

'To what?'

'Your head.'

'Oh.'

I reached up to feel the wound. I'd actually forgotten it was there. Maybe those cumulative effects had begun to accumulate.

'I didn't know it still showed.'

'I'm observant. So what happened?'

'I ran into a wrecking ball.'

'Really?'

'Just felt like one.'

'Which means none of your business.'

'Means it's a long story.'

'It sort of suits your face.'

'That's what they said at the hospital.'

Her attention suddenly became unmoored and started to drift away. She looked out the window for a while, then around at the disarray in the living room as if unsure how it got that way.

'Okay,' she said, looking back at me, 'What can I do you out of?'

'I was wondering if you could tell me anything about Bay Side Holdings. Milton Hornsby.'

The air inside the room dropped about ten degrees.

'Who did you say you were with?'

'I didn't. I'm the administrator of an estate. Regina Broadhurst. According to the real estate and tax records, she was living in a house owned by Bay Side Holdings. I went over to Sag Harbor to tell Milton Hornsby and he basically threw me off his property. Your name was on some documents submitted to the Town appeals board. So here I am.'

'Do you have any identification?'

I got out my wallet and tossed her my driving licence. I also tossed her a death certificate and the Surrogate's Court paper naming me administrator.

'Are you an attorney?' she asked, looking up from the court papers.

'Industrial designer. And the old lady's next-door neighbour.'

She got up from the couch to hand back my licence and the Surrogates Court's document. She left the death certificate on the table. She scooped up her coffee mug and took a sip, standing over me.

'You're aware of attorney-client privilege,' she said.

'Yeah, of course. I'm only here because Hornsby won't talk to me. All I want is to give him back his house. After I clear up whatever might be hanging, and get her stuff out of there. That's all.'

'Industrial designer?'

'That's what I did. I'm an engineer.'

'What you did?'

'Don't do it anymore.'

Somebody threw another switch in her head and she tossed herself back into the couch, sprawling out across the entire length. She put her forearm up to her head.

'I was sane until those assholes drove me crazy. Honest, Doc.'

'Define crazy.'

She looked over at me from her swoon.

'You shrinks are all alike. All talk and no cure.'

I drank some of my coffee. It was just a little more viscous than the transmission fluid I used in the Grand Prix. I sat back, therapist style.

'Maybe if we started with your childhood.'

'Nah, too depressing. Anyway, I was fine until I got handed that dumb case.'

'I could use some help on this. If it doesn't violate attorney-asshole privilege.'

Jackie hooted.

'Where'd you get the act?'

'MIT. Comedy's part of the curriculum. Everyone knows that.'

'My dad was an engineer.'

'I knew you'd drag your childhood into this.'

She rolled over on her side and flipped off her flip-flops. She let her hand fall to the coffee table so she could fiddle with a bunch of rose-coloured glass grapes.

'I guess I'm not much of a lawyer,' she said, much in the way people do when they want you to disagree with them.

'You're probably great when you feel like it.'

That was the right tack.

'Hey, affirmation. I like that. Yeah, I'm actually pretty good at the job itself. I'm just really bad at being a person. Really fucks up the career.'

That sounded like me. Maybe Jackie and I should start a club.

'This is getting awfully heavy for people who just met each other,' she said, abruptly launching herself off the couch. 'Let's find another venue. All I gotta do is see a couch and I start baring my soul. You oughta see me in a furniture store. It's like Pavlovian.'

I followed her out to a glassed-in porch that had been converted to office space. There was masonite paneling below the windows and indoor-outdoor carpet on the floor. It smelled like a greenhouse. She dropped into an expensive-looking ergonomic desk chair, spun around once and put her bare feet up on the desk. I cleared a space for myself on a long wooden bench.

'Bay Side Holdings, is that where we're at?' she asked.

'Trying, anyway.'

'Okay,' she said, 'I can tell you I was young and stupid. Stupider, anyway. I was hired by the lead, Milton Hornsby, who's general counsel for Bay Side Holdings, as you know. He wanted me to come in as consulting on a big zoning appeals case. Hornsby paired me up with this city guy named Hunter Johnson, believe it or not. He was like incredibly gorgeous, intelligent, rich, witty and handsome. Did I mention athletic and a good cook?'

'And an asshole?'

'Not at first. No, not ever, really. It's not like they did anything, it's more like what they didn't do. Which was actually try to get the funky job done. When you're going for a variance and you hit a little resistance, you're like supposed to at least *try* to make your case. I mean, that's the way you play the game. The appeals board's not just gonna jump down off their freaking platform and give you a great big hug and say, hey, you want to change a whole bunch of setbacks? Excellent! We've been here sitting around on our asses just *waiting* for something like this to happen. I mean, hel-*lo*. I told them how to play the course. I mean, I do know how to play. I do know how to deal with Southampton zoning issues. My God, I used to babysit for the planning chair's kids. One of the guys on the appeals board has been hitting on me since high school. I know this shit, inside and out.'

'I didn't know Hornsby was a lawyer. He didn't tell me. So I guess he failed to take your counsel.'

'Yeah, I guess. They wanted to completely reconfigure a whole slew of properties over in North Sea. Here, it's in here somewhere. I'll show you. Though I shouldn't.'

She spun around again and pulled open a deep legal-sized drawer. She curled her feet around the base of the chair to keep from falling into the file cabinet.

It was a copy of the aerial map I'd pulled from the Town records. Each lot was outlined with white ink over the black-and-white photographic image. They were all numbered, though several, about a dozen, were marked with a yellow highlighter. Only this one had a transparent overlay, which showed an alternate configuration of the lots. Through various combinations and border adjustments, my neighbourhood had become an entirely different animal. Maybe twelve properties were converted to five, all bordering the bay or the deep harbour inlet that formed the east coast of Oak Point. The largest of these was at the centre of the plan, marked 'common area.' Which put it right in the middle of the WB site. A similar reformation was repeated opposite WB's other shore on Jacob's Neck. The entire development was enclosed by a green line labelled 'privet'. A hedge. The way it was roughed in, the hedge ran down the middle of my side yard. And there was a question mark, also in yellow marker, right on top of my roof.

'This ain't some third-rate pre-existing, non-conforming, switch-a-couple-things-around-all-approved-thank-you-very-much-have-a-nice day kinda shit here. This is big time surveys and wetlands hearings and bulldozers. You'd think a little due diligence mighta been in order.'

While she talked I noticed my heart had contracted down to the size of a cherry tomato. My sore tongue started to throb. Jackie was poking the map with her right index finger and ranting about something or other.

'Due diligence?'

'Well, we hardly got near any actual hearings. Just a lotta backroom chats with all my dear friends on the appeals board, and with the building inspector and some County schlubs. All we ended up with was a list of things we'd have to do if we wanted to pursue. My point being, why go this far and at the first sign of any real tussle, fold up faster'n an origami master on amphetamines? Nobody thought to check this stuff out beforehand?'

She moved away from me and sat back in her desk chair. She slumped down and put her feet up on the desk. Jackie made an art of repose, however briefly maintained.

'Sorry,' she said, 'It just still pisses me off.' She gnawed on the cuticle of her right thumb, stopping occasionally to check the results. 'It was a big project and I coulda used the damn work. Not the damn money so much, but the complexity. And the credentials. And the trips to the city for lunch meetings with Mr Johnson, who, forgive me for saying, was a major piece of ass. We don't get enough of that around here. Not loose anyway.'

'Yeah?'

'Yeah. Though I guess not really loose enough. Not if you count all the floppsies and moppsies draped all over him day and night. Including some other guy's wife, which can irritate the hell out of a person.'

'Especially her husband.'

'He's a drip. She's a babe. Happens all the time out here. Probably not to you.'

She looked me over.

'You don't look the type. Too craggy.' she held up her left hand and wiggled her fingers. 'No ring?'

'Divorced.'

'Kids?'

'A daughter.'

'My age?'

'A little younger.'

'That's how I like my men. Sorry.'

She grabbed a clump of her reddish-blond hair and held it up to the light, looking for split ends.

'That makes me sound so ageist,' she said.

'Huh?'

'Ageist. Like sexist.'

'Oh.'

She was suddenly back up on her feet.

'So, what else can I do for you? Legally.'

'Who's Bay Side Holdings?'

She frowned in thought.

'The guys who own all the land. Investors, I guess. I never met any of them. Hornsby was the man.'

'"All the land." Where'd they get "all the land"?'

'I don't know. Groups of guys are always buying up hunks of land. That's what they do.'

She picked an ashtray off her desk and rooted around until she came up with another half-spent joint. She waved it in the air.

'What do we have here,' she said.

I demurred.

'You go ahead. I'm all set.'

She lurched over to a desk drawer and got out some matches. I waited while she lit the joint and took most of it down with the first drag. She talked as she exhaled.

'What else.'

I had to think about that for a second.

'My dad looked after Regina. She didn't have anybody else. He's dead, she's dead. I'm just trying to wrap it up.'

'A philanthropist.'

'I'm still curious.'

'About what?'

'Why didn't Regina pay rent?'

'She didn't?'

'You didn't know that?'

'No. I mean, why would I? I was focused on revising an original plot plan. We never talked about the people living in the houses.'

Then she switched to a singsong lampoon of sensitivity.

'Not that I didn't care . . .'

I sensed it was time to wrap this up. I tidied up my file and made motions to leave.

'You could give me Hunter Johnson's address and phone number, if it's okay. I might want to talk to him.'

She went back into her file cabinet. She whipped out a letter.

'*Voilà!*' she said. Then, 'This is from Mr Doll-face himself.' She pulled it back against her chest. 'Why would you want to talk to him?'

'Curious, like I said.'

She handed me the letter.

'Keep it. I got more.'

'Thanks.'

'Can I borrow this?' I held up the map of Oak Point.

She wagged her head as if to shake out the right answer.

'Sure. Why the hell not. Can't hurt. Just don't lose it. The case might come back.'

'I'll make a copy and send back the original.'

'No problem.'

'Thanks.'

'Fagetaboutit.'

She was smiling at me through the tumbled mass of strawberry blond hair, but I felt her attention starting to dissipate again.

'I guess I'll let you get back to your case.'

'Thanks a bunch.' she said, and walked out of the room.

I slipped the map and letter into my file and followed her back through the house to the front door. She held it open and leaned her whole body against the jam. We shook hands.

'Good luck with whatever you're doing,' she said, 'which, by the way, is more than you're telling me.'

I smiled at her.

'Says who?'

'I gave you my freaking map, for Pete's sake.'

'You did. I appreciate that.'

'So?'

I pulled out my wallet and gave her a dollar.

'What's this?'

'A retainer. To assure confidentiality. Attorney-client privilege.'

She held up the dollar bill.

'Never hold up in court.'

I left her watching me from the doorway of her house, pausing for a moment's reflection before rocketing back into the chaotic Brownian motion of her life. A vision of my daughter threatened to sneak into the receding picture in my rearview mirror, but I distracted myself with thoughts of an army of bulldozers and backhoes led by the profane Jimmy Maddox, crashing over Oak Point like the blitzkrieg, leveling hedgerows and laying waste to the last refuge on earth.

CHAPTER FIVE

My house in Stamford was in the woods not far from the northern border of town. It sat on the edge of a short cliff formed by glacial boulders. At the bottom of the cliff was a small pond that made a home for Canada geese and bullfrogs. The deck off the rear of the house was shaded by a canopy of oak and maple in the summer, and by hemlocks year round. We had a lot of free-loading birds who worked the half-dozen feeders mounted off the deck and in the surrounding trees. One of the few things I enjoyed doing around the house was inventing ways to keep the squirrels out of the feeders. It was a battle of wits I never entirely won. There was one tough, mangy old squirrel who used to sit on the railing and stare at me. I thought he might be the head of engineering, sizing up the competition.

There was a wall of glass between the deck and the living room. It was so hot that afternoon I couldn't leave the air conditioning, so I just sat there and looked through the windows at the competing fauna. I was on my third tumbler of Absolut when Abby came home from wherever she went during the day. She didn't expect to see me there.

'My God, you frightened me. What are you doing home?'

'Drinking.'

'Obviously.'

She dropped a handful of large plastic bags filled with merchandise on the sofa next to me and poured herself a stiff one from the wet bar in the corner of the room.

'And smoking, too, I see.'

'Yeah. You can't quit these things for too long. It's not good for you.'

'Yes, of course. What's it been, twenty years?'

'About.'

Abby moved very gracefully. She flowed into a chair on the

other side of the room, sat back and crossed her legs, resting her elbow on the armrest so she could hold her drink aloft, shaking it occasionally to dissolve the ice. She wore a silk blouse with large square pockets and an off-white skirt. A gold chain looped around her neck and disappeared down the open front of her blouse. Her legs were deeply tanned, nicely offset by a pair of white high heels. Her hair was still mostly natural blond, formed into elegant waves that made me think of Ethel Kennedy. Maintenance costs for hair, nails and face ran about $500 a month, not including yoga, health club, and massage therapy. And it showed. Abby set an unachievable standard for women her age.

'Well?'

'Well what?'

'Are you going to tell me why you're sitting there getting plastered? Or do I have to guess.'

'Seemed like the best course of action, all things considered.'

The ceiling in our living room was two stories high. There was a balcony above that led to three of the bedrooms. One was my daughter's. She used to sit up there Christmas night and wait for the grownups to go to bed so Santa could make the scene. When I went upstairs, I'd scoop up her limp little body and put her to bed, always wondering if she was faking it.

The house had been designed by an architect who'd been a friend of Abby's father. She told me this guy was the only architect alive who could possibly do the job. I didn't think we needed an architect at all. Or for that matter, a custom-designed house. She said I had no aesthetic sensibilities. I'd never seen Abby open a book, or listen to a piece of music that wasn't on a greatest hits album, or go to a museum that wasn't having a fundraiser or an opening everyone was talking about. In Abby's world you defined things worth caring for by how they were classified by her parent's social set. It was much easier than valuing possessions, vacation spots, friendships and personal beliefs on their intrinsic merits. To this day, I don't think I could tell you what that house actually looked like. I do remember that I didn't like living in it.

'The mall was so crowded I thought I'd scream,' Abby said to me.

'The people here are so rude and pushy. I don't know why it doesn't bother you.'

'The people here' was Abby's secret code for Jews, presumably plentiful in the area because of our proximity to New York. Abby had grown up in a suburb of Boston that fairly bristled with anti-Semitism. It frustrated her that I didn't share her feelings. It forced her to keep her bigotry euphemistic, but after twenty-five years, I could interpret.

'Because I love people,' I said.

'Oh please. You hate people.'

'Not all people. Only some people.'

'Could have fooled me.'

She watched the ice swirl in the glass, then took a sip.

'No, you're right,' she proclaimed, 'You're simply indifferent. You don't even know there *are* people in the world. You have no feelings for anything. Or anybody. I can't believe you are smoking a cigarette.'

The way she was looking at her glass I thought she might be trying to see her own reflection. Checking her lipstick.

'Camels. They come in a filter now.'

'How salubrious.'

I looked around at our living room and wondered why it looked the way it did. I paid for it all, but really didn't understand the significance of the furniture or the decorations. Abby once told me I wouldn't be much at interior design. She said you had to grow up with nice things to know which things were nice.

'What're all those boxes in the backseat of your car?'

'That's the stuff from the office I wanted to keep.'

She cocked her head like a spaniel hearing a high-pitched sound.

'I don't understand.'

'Well, most of the stuff I threw out or just left there. But some of it I couldn't part with. Hard to explain, but something tells you to hold on to certain things.'

She leaned forward in her chair, holding the drink in both hands.

'What on earth are you talking about?'

'If you don't take it with you, they'll just throw it out.'

'Are you completely drunk?'

'No, not yet. It's not that easy to do anymore.'

'You've had enough practice.'

'Drinking, Abby. I've practiced drinking, but not getting drunk. That's a very important distinction.'

'There's a word for people who drink all the time and never get drunk.'

'Unlucky?'

I went over to the bar and filled up my tumbler again. Abby watched me in silence. When I sat down, she asked again.

'So, are you going to tell me what's going on or should I just go take my shower and get on with my day.'

'I quit my job.'

She sat back again, relieved.

'That's amusing. And I got elected pope.'

'No, I actually quit. I don't have a job anymore.'

'What are you saying?'

'I said, "I quit," and they said, "okay". More or less.'

'More or less?'

'It's not entirely official yet. I think I have to write a letter, or sign something. I don't know, it's been a while since I did this kind of thing.' I looked to see how the wildlife was doing out on the deck, but nothing was stirring. Too hot, maybe.

'What the hell . . .'

I waved off the question before she was through with it.

'I got called down to the board meeting. George's got a strategic plan worked out for TSS. Pretty slick, really. Make 'em a lot of money. Short term.'

'Did you do something stupid?'

I was grateful for the fuzzy cushion provided by the Absolut, even if I wasn't entirely drunk. I ignored her question.

'The plan was to push really hard for the next six months to show an increase in productivity, lean out expenses and stop filling jobs lost to attrition. This pumps up profitability, as you know,' I paused, she blanched a little at the obvious condescension, 'which is what you want to do if you're fattening up for a sale.'

'What kind of sale?'

'The division. Technical Service and Support. My division. Spin it off and sell it. The whole thing, lock, stock and barrel. The ultimate unbundling.'

'They're going to sell TSS? You can't sell a division of a major corporation.'

Abby always told people I worked for a *major* corporation. It made me think of the blurbs on paperbacks. 'Now a major motion picture, starring . . .'

'That will be a big surprise to George Donovan.'

'Who could possibly want to buy a *division*?' Like it was a piece of real estate in a crummy neighbourhood.

'Probably one of the oil companies. A *major* oil company. A lot of what we've developed supports hydrocarbon processing. Most of the big refiners are dying to get their hands on a little high-tech. They want it for the same reason I thought we wanted it. To diversify and hedge against the curse of commodity manufacturing.'

'I've never heard of anything so ridiculous.'

'Don't sell yourself short.'

'Even if it's true, why does it have anything to do with your job?'

'Oh, now Abby, anybody who buys us'll have a Technical Service and Support division of their own with a bunch of people who do a lot of the same things we do. That means probably half our guys'll be on the street within a year – after busting their asses for six months running up the value of the spinoff. They'll gut us like a fish, then eat what's left.'

'Including you.'

'A definite possibility.'

Abby noticed with a start that she'd finished off her drink. She rarely had more than one a day – usually a glass of white wine. Everything but vitriol in moderation.

'That's not what they're telling you. You're on the presidential track.'

It irritated her that I was just a lousy divisional VP. I'd once made the mistake of telling her my job was often a step on the way to unit president. Which is what they called the guy who looked after a bunch of divisions. This was a pleasing eventuality for Abby to contemplate, though I always thought it was silly having more than one president at a single company, even a major corporation. Reminded me of Gilbert & Sullivan. Everybody gets to be the perfect picture of a British major general.

'This is why you quit your job? Because you *think* they're going to fire you *anyway*? You were going to be president and now they're *selling* you? I'm just trying to understand.'

'Yeah, I guess that's it. I could fill in the details, but that's the gist.'

Something had begun to tighten up Abby's face – probably the first signal to her brain that her life was about to career off the highway.

'You're serious, aren't you.'

'You bet.'

'What do you think will happen to us if you do this monstrous thing?'

She sank way back into her chair, gripping the arms firmly enough to keep the chair from lifting off the living room floor.

'I'm tired,' I said into my drink.

She didn't hear me.

'You're what?'

'I'm retiring.'

'You're forty-eight years old.'

'I'm retiring early.'

'We'll lose the house.'

'We own the house. If I never earned another penny we could still live a thousand times better than my parents ever dreamed possible.'

'I have no intention of living like your parents.'

'That's not what I said.'

'Why are you doing this to me?'

'I'm not doing anything to you.'

'This is unacceptable. I want you to take back everything you just said.'

I demurred. She pressed on.

'What do you expect me to do with this? What do you expect me to tell people you're doing? What could possibly be in your head to think it would just be peachy keen with me for you to walk away from an important position at a major American corporation, to just walk away from everything we have so you can, what, just sit around the fucking house and drink yourself into fucking oblivion? Is that what you think would be okay with me? You fucking lowlife wop bastard.'

'French.'

She sucked in a rough breath and said, 'French?'

'Fucking lowlife French bastard. Just a quarter Italian. Mostly French. My mom had a little American Indian mixed in there, too, we always thought. Would explain the cheekbones.'

She stood up from her chair, smoothed the wrinkles out of her skirt and picked up her empty glass, I think to provide a prop for the final flourish. She thrust it at me to emphasize each point.

'When you're ready to stop speaking nonsense, when you get your nose out of the fucking vodka bottle, I'll be willing to speak with you about this. In the meantime, I have things to do,' she said, and walked out of the room.

The next time I saw her was about six months later, and I haven't seen her since.

THE SUN was trying like hell to break out of the early morning haze. I was in the Grand Prix heading down North Sea Road toward the Village. WLIU was playing jazz. Early Miles Davis. I had the windows open and the heat on. Eddie had both ears flapping in the wind. I was drinking a vat of straight unflavored coffee from one of the North Sea delis that catered to locals and tradesmen.

I almost had full use of my tongue. I used it to scat sing along with Miles. He didn't seem to mind.

I carried the Styrofoam cup with me when I rang the Lombards' doorbell. I had their *New York Times* stuck under my arm.

'Do you always bring a newspaper when you come to call?' Rosaline asked when she opened the door.

'Once a paperboy . . . '

She was wearing a sleeveless, collarless white shirt, a blue jean skirt over bare legs and moccasin slippers. Her long hair was piled up in the back and held in place with bobby pins, randomly situated. Her nose still filled up half the house.

'Did you bring me coffee, too?'

'Get a mug, we'll split what's left.'

'Very gallant.'

I followed her into the living room. No Arnold. She pointed at the ceiling.

'Still sleeping. Not dead.'

'I assumed.'

Rosaline settled herself comfortably in her father's chair and offered me the couch, gesturing with both hands.

'Take a load off.'

When she crossed her legs her skirt rode to the tops of her thighs. Her legs were a pale version of Abby's – smooth and muscular.

'I feel like an intruder.'

'What do you think you're intruding on?'

'Your life.'

'What life?'

Then she laughed.

'I'm actually having a nice time. We weren't that close when I was growing up. Too much of an age difference. It's funny how you're a better child when you're an adult.'

'Or he's a better parent.'

'Perhaps.'

She put her fingertips together in the prayerful way Burton liked to do. It usually meant he was thinking.

'What are you thinking?' I asked her.

'I wasn't thinking. I was wondering.'

'About what?'

'About you. What happened?'

'What do you mean?'

'Why did you quit?'

'Not following you.'

'Your job.'

'I don't remember talking about my job.'

'You'd be amazed what you can learn on the Internet.'

'I guess I would.'

'You think I'm invading your privacy.'

'Yup.'

'But you're willing to put up with it.'

'To a point.'

'To get what you want.'

'I'd like what you have on Bay Side Holdings. It'd be a good deed.'

She uncrossed her legs and stretched them out in front of her, knees together and toes pointed, like a dancer.

'That's supposed to be adequate incentive?'

I didn't answer her. She kept her legs outstretched, partly supported by her hands gripping her thighs.

'Mr Acquillo.'

'Sam.'

'You have far greater powers of perception than you seem willing to demonstrate.'

'I perceive you're a woman of intelligence with uncertain, probably conflicting, desires.'

She pointed at me.

'There, you see? I knew you could do it.'

She dropped her feet to the floor and re-crossed her legs slowly enough for me to catch a glimpse of the dark triangle and pink folds between her legs. She reassumed Burton's prayer posture.

'I'm having it done after he goes,' she said.

'Done?'

She used a forefinger to trace the impressive arc of her nose.

'I can see why.'

'Honesty. Excellent.'

'Your father thinks nose jobs are an affront to God.'

'Right again. Give the man a cigar.'

'I think you should. Then you can face your shortcomings and insecurities like the rest of us, without an excuse looking out at you from the mirror.'

'My. Brutal honesty. Take back that cigar.'

'In the meantime, who gives a shit? You got a swell body and loads of sex appeal, and a nose that makes a great conversation starter.

Consider it a gift.'

She sat up straight in her chair.

'Can I get you some coffee?' she asked.

'Sure.'

She stood up demurely, took my hand and led me into the kitchen. She poured us both coffee from an ancient percolator and had us clink the mugs in a toast.

'To honesty. Brutal or otherwise.'

I clinked with her. As I sipped the coffee she picked a stuffed number ten envelope off the kitchen table.

'Names, addresses and phone numbers of everyone who leased or rented a house from Bay Side Holdings – up to 1983 when Daddy retired. At that point, it was all passed over to the Sinitars, who bought up Daddy's business – whatever was buyable, any-way. Plus whatever correspondence I could find with Bay Side's office in New York, plus a photocopy of the ledger subaccount that records how Daddy received and distributed rental proceeds. I had it ready the day after you were here. I wondered if you'd be back.'

She handed me the envelope.

'Thanks.'

'Some people thought you lost your mind. Blew up your whole life.'

'Don't believe everything you read.'

'I don't believe anything I can't see with my own eyes.'

'An empiricist.'

I stuffed the envelope into the inside pocket of my jean jacket.

'You're not gonna check it?'

'I trust you.'

She put down her mug and gathered a handful of my jacket,

pulling me toward her. I leaned into the kiss, which was long and warm and filled with promise. As she kissed me she felt around the front of my pants.

'You act so sure of yourself, but you're not,' she said, pulling back far enough to see past the bridge of her nose.

'I'm not.'

Still holding me with one hand, she adjusted a lock of hair that had fallen across my forehead and tidied the area around the big scab on my head.

'Then it's a good act. Maybe you can teach me how you do it.'

She put both hands on my chest and gently pushed herself away. That's when I heard sounds upstairs, and the raspy wet croak of an old man clearing his throat. She gripped my arm, then went upstairs to see her father. I let myself out.

I DROVE directly to a picnic table in the park behind town hall and opened Rosaline's envelope. I put the list of names and addresses she'd prepared on top of the stack of papers. Then I got out Jackie Swaitkowski's map, unrolled it and held down the corners with a mug and three stones I picked off the ground.

Next to the map I put an extended plot plan I'd picked up from Bonny Martinez at the Town Tax Collector's office. It showed the borders and street addresses of every taxable piece of property in North Sea owned by Bay Side Holdings. They were all contiguous. Lombard's records carried the same plot designation as Jackie's map, so I could easily cross-reference between the three documents.

My fourth data point was a telephone directory I'd dug out of the trunk of the Grand Prix.

First I matched up the Oak Point street addresses on the tax map with Lombard's records, which corresponded to the high-lighted sweep of territory that started with Regina, curved around Oak Point following the waterline of the cove, washed across the WB grounds and over to the next peninsula, where it also followed the water about three-quarters of the way up the coast. Regina's house, 18 Oak Point, was labelled number thirty-three. Next was lot thirty-five, Herbert and Louise Radowitz at 16 Oak Point, who'd rented for about ten years, followed by John and Martha Glenheimmer. Then Edward and Sherry Feldman, then Eric Fitzsimmons, and so on. I was a little disturbed to realise that Regina Broadhurst was the only name I recognized on my own street. I checked all the names in the phone book. Only Ed and Sherry were still in their Bay Side house. The others were some-where else in town or gone completely.

At least half the houses in the highlighted area on Oak Point weren't on Lombard's list. I wondered if the same held true on the other side of WB. That section was part of a much bigger area called Jacob's Neck. That neighbourhood was unfamiliar, so it took a little longer for me to get all the paperwork organized.

The first number was lot fifty-two, Gary and Elizabeth Richardson. Then fifty-four, Mary Fletcher. Then John and Judy Eiklestrum. Then Wallace and Dolores Weeds. That stopped me. I knew the name, and the house. I was now oriented with a mental picture of the neighbourhood.

Wally Weeds was known to my father. I hadn't thought of the name in years, but I could hear it now, spoken in my father's voice. I also knew he'd been dead for a long time. I could almost remem-ber the exact day it happened. The day my best friend Billy Weeds woke up somewhere in the woods of Connecticut and found his father shot in the face with his own shotgun.

As with Oak Point, most of the highlighted properties weren't on Lombard's list. There were only two more after the Weeds' place. Number seventy-three, George and Janice Fitzhenry, and at the end of the line, the house opposite Regina's, the last house at the extreme end of the Bay Side sweep.

Lot number seventy-eight. Julia Anselma.

I DECIDED to spend the rest of that day cracking golf balls across the yard so Eddie could shag them out of the flower garden and off the pebble beach. My father's three-quarter Harmon Killibrew bat was ideally suited to the purpose. Eddie probably had a little retriever in him, since he liked to retrieve. But he often got dis-

tracted mid-run, and peeled off to track down heretofore unde-
tected evidence of who-knows-what. This gave me the chance to
sit down in one of my two exhausted redwood lawn chairs and
look at the Little Peconic over an Absolut on the rocks. I didn't
have a strict rule about drinking during the day, just a general
guideline – no hard liquor before noon. I had all the material I'd
gathered up pertaining to Regina's estate organized and waiting
for me on the table on the screened-in porch. The urge to start in
on it again had thus far eluded me. So I drank instead. And
brooded.

Eddie would always complete the cycle, no matter how long
the detour, running back without apology, the golf ball hidden in
his mouth.

I'd just hauled myself out of the lawn chair so I could smack
the ball out toward the bay when I noticed a sailboat coming in
close to shore. Boats of any kind were far less common on the bay
in October, even though it was an ideal month for sailing. The air
was cool, but there was almost always a breeze, either a prevailing
south southwesterly or a seasonal northwesterly, clean and dry,
riding down from Canada. It was a decent-sized sloop, probably
around forty-three feet. I thought it was going to tack when I saw
the sails fluttering in the wind, but then I saw the big headsail disappear into a roll. Though it's hard to judge distances across open
water, I thought his depth might have been about fourteen feet,
judging from the boat's proximity to the green buoy that marked
the entrance to the cove bordering Regina's property. After the
jib was rolled as tight as a joint, the mainsail fell to the boom. The
wind was mostly out of the west, so the boat's beam drew parallel
to the shore. It looked like some type of fast-cruising boat, with
lots of sharp angles, but also a lot of equipment hanging off the
transom and mounted to the mast.

I saw a lone figure dressed in white run out to the bow to drop
an anchor mounted off the base of the bowsprit. The boat swung
gently at the end of the anchor until settling nose to the wind. A
few minutes later an inflatable dinghy busted out of the cockpit
and dropped overboard right off the back of the boat.

The guy in white descended a swim ladder into the dinghy with a small outboard on his shoulder, which he mounted at the transom, and soon after was heading across the bay directly toward shore.

Eddie was also looking out at the dinghy motoring in our direction. I tucked the bat under my arm and went out to the beach to help whoever it was make a dry landing. Eddie stood and waited with me at the edge of the water.

The dinghy slowed as it approached, and you could hear the revs from the outboard rise and fall as the operator tried to calibrate the proper speed for hitting the beach. By now it was close enough that I could see his face.

'Hi, Burt.'

'Grab the bow and give a good pull, would you?' he said as the inflatable nosed into the beach and he killed the outboard, nimbly tipping the prop up out of the water. I dragged it up on shore.

We shook hands.

'Expecting pirates?' he asked, pointing to the bat.

'Just shaggin' balls with Eddie. Though you never know.'

'Well, I'm unarmed. And thirsty.'

I led him up to the cottage and sat him down in a lawn chair. I went in to put together drinks, leaving Eddie to pester him into hitting out another ball.

'I called ahead but no one answered,' said Burton. 'You know they've developed answering machines.'

'I got a phone. That's as far as I go.'

By now it was beginning to cool off. The sky had mostly cleared up and the westerly that Burton had fought all the way from his mooring in Sag Harbor had picked up a few knots. I got us both sweatshirts so we could stay outside and watch the sunset. Burton told me he'd designed his boat mostly himself, with a little help from Sparkman and Stephens, who'd produced designs for several generations of Lewises. I knew just enough about sailing to follow his story, having crewed for friends of Abby she'd acquired during childhood summers in Marblehead. I had to transfer my own childhood experiences on the Peconic in busted up clinker-built dories and catboats to the graceful Herreshoffs and Hinckley the poshes in Massachusetts raced off the coast. I learned a lot, but I didn't like the people. Though I sure loved their boats.

As the red ball of a sun burned its way into the horizon, lighting up the bottoms of the few remaining clouds in electric shades of pink and yellow, I caught Burton up on what I'd learned about Bay Side Holdings.

'Mr Lombard is an astute man,' said Burton, when I was finished.

'A captive.'

'A wholly-owned subsidiary of Willard and Bollard, Incorporated.'

'Willard and Bollard.'

Burton had been holding the Harmon Killebrew bat. He used it to point over my shoulder at the clump of woods across the entrance to the cove next to Regina's house.

'WB,' I said.

'The manufacturing arm. Bay Side was set up to manage the real estate owned by the company. The buildings and the land it sat on. Great tax advantages, then and now, if you do it right.'

As far as I was concerned, the old WB factory was as old as the Peconic itself. It had always been just there, invisible from land or sea, accessible only to the people who used to work there every day, whose numbers steadily dwindled until the gates closed and the rust and sumac took over. I never knew what the initials WB stood for.

'Son of a bitch.'

Burton reached under his sweatshirt and pulled out a folded sheet of paper.

'An e-mail, courtesy of our research department.'

He started to read.

"If you go all the way back to the original owners of the site, you're in the nineteenth century, when they held a sizable chunk of North Sea, including farms and woodlands. Willard Wakeman and Carl Bollard bought the place in 1908, and ran a fairly successful business for the next thirty-four years. They specialized in sporting goods – camping gear, volleyballs, quoits, whatever people played in those days."

He looked at me.

'No roller blades or wind surfing, I'd imagine.'

'Rafts,' I said. 'My father always said they made rafts for the war.'

'Right. Rafts and rubberized tents for the Pacific. If you notice, everything they manufactured was at least partly rubber, or some kind of synthetic material that was tough and waterproof. Perfect for rafts.'

He read the rest of the e-mail, skipping ahead since I'd scooped part of the report.

"From it's peak in about 1896, the WB landhold was reduced through normal attrition, and as an important capitalization tool for the core manufacturing business, leaving the last important segment – the peninsula adjacent to Oak Point – with its access to the Little Peconic, and subsequently, to Greenport and on to the sea. In order to preserve free use of the two inlets on either side, they retained all the shore property. Plus a few large tracts across Noyac Road, which were sold off in the 1960s.

"WB was strictly manufacturing, working to specs from brand marketers, or in the case of the war effort, government contractors. Post war they continued with the same mix of products, but sales apparently declined steadily until 1976 when they closed down the shop permanently. Since private companies have minimal re-porting requirements, this information has been derived from var-ious secondary sources, including Dunn and Bradstreet, and should not be regarded as definitive, but rather directional. We're going deeper into some other databases that take a little longer, but I thought this might give you a start.'

'So Bay Side Holdings is all that's left of WB.'

'Bay Side Holdings is WB, since there's nothing related to the corporate entity *but* real estate. All of it right here, by the way.'

'So who owns Bay Side Holdings?'

'That's the interesting part,' said Burton, handing me the e-mail printout, 'we have no idea.'

'Really.'

'Not that we won't find out, but it won't be automatic.'

'For you guys?' I had a mental image of Burton's big building down there on the Street.

'For anybody. It's in a trust.'

'Really.'

'For which there's no public record. Bay Side is a privately held C corp, chartered under the laws of New York State, all of whose assets are held by the eponymously named Bay Side Trust.'

'And we're not allowed to know who owns what?'

'By "we", if you mean the general public, yes and no. The creators of a trust have no obligation to publish the names of the beneficiaries as a matter of course, but they can be compelled to do so under certain civil actions. Beneficiaries have to be named in the trust document itself, which in certain circumstances will end up in the public record. But there's no legal requirement to do so just because. Ninety-nine percent of the time, these are all tightly controlled, personal things that have little effect on anyone beyond the principals, unless there's a contested estate, or a tax dispute, or legal claim. That's the next place we're going to look.'

Eddie had heard enough and decided to trot off to the beach to check for encroaching sea life. I found myself looking over at WB as if the dense tree cover was about to open up and disclose another stunning revelation. You think you know a place.

'So who's got the trust document?'

'I'm guessing Milton Hornsby.'

'I'm back to him.'

'I'm afraid so. But don't be discouraged. We'll find everything out, eventually.'

He took a sip of his drink.

'One more thing. Regina Broadhurst. No assets we can find, unless you consider Social Security. There's so little on her, she almost doesn't exist. Hasn't filed a tax return to the IRS, or to New York State, since 1976. The last year she received a W-2. There are two points of interest here, in my mind.'

'She worked.'

'That's point one. She did indeed. As a floor supervisor. Essentially a foreman, watching over manufacturing, assembly, or materials handling.'

'In a factory.'

'Yup.' He gestured again with the Harmon Killebrew bat.

'WB?'

'Yup.'

'How 'bout that. Walked to work.'

'Nineteen hundred seventy-six was the year they closed down. Never got another job. At least, nothing she shared with the IRS.'

'I'm trying to remember her husband. What he did.'

'You'll be trying a long time.'

'Meaning?'

'Regina got her Social Security number in 1938, when she was sixteen. Under the name Regina May Broadhurst. Just to be sure, the researcher found her in the Suffolk County birth records. Born at Southampton Hospital, June 5, 1922. Regina May Broadhurst.'

'There was no Mr Broadhurst.'

'We'll keep looking. You never know.'

'You've already done too much.'

'So get me another drink.'

We moved on to other topics while we drank and gazed out at the waning sunset and the steel blue water, now uniformly roughed up by the freshening winds. His boat looked great, now a backlit shape rocking comfortably at anchor and casting a shadow across the water, a formless reflection of the dark blue hull and towering mast.

THE SUN was just starting to light up the oaks and scrub pines of North Sea. I'd started running before dawn, and had already covered about ten miles. I'm not very fast, but I can run a long way when I'm in the mood. I'd been up to Long Beach and back, toured the seafowl refuge on Jessup's Neck and stopped at a deli for coffee. The day was cold and overcast, a sample of the coming November. On the way back I ran along the bay coast up to the

WB peninsula. I cut back inland and ran along the sand road that ran parallel to WB's cyclone fence. At one of the sharp turns in the road, I ran straight for it and leaped. I stuck about half way up, and climbed the rest of the way. I pulled a pair of wire cutters I'd brought along out of the back pocket of my shorts and snipped the barbed wire. Then, very carefully, slipped over the top and dropped into the WB grounds.

The landscape had completely reverted to weedy grass and first growth – pin oak, cedar and sumac. But the asphalt driveway looked almost new. Evidence of teenagers was piled next to rusted machinery that lined the driveway. I trotted up to the main entrance and tried the door. Locked. I circled the building looking for unboarded windows. I found a busted-out basement window half obscured by broken bricks and cinder block. I cleared a space and shimmied through into an icy black depth. I had a miniature Maglite, but it barely cut through the darkness. I felt my way along while my eyes adjusted enough to see glimmers of light above me. I searched, and finally found, a staircase up to the ground floor. The door opened.

I was in a corridor. The walls were a faded pale green and the woodwork clear pine stained to simulate mahogany. Behind the doors, some of which were panelled with translucent glass, were office groupings – a block of four with secretaries in the middle. Little departments. At one time they'd been identified by removable placards that slid into chrome holders mounted to the wall. Most had been removed.

I moved methodically from office to office, opening desk drawers and file cabinets. There was almost nothing there. A few empty hanging folders. Cracked and stained coffee mugs. Empty steno pads and a rusty hole-punch.

I found what looked like a common area. There were two linoleum-topped folding tables with a few chairs, and an area for vending machines. There was a bulletin board with some yellowed safety posters and a few regulatory notices. On the other wall was a glass trophy case, long smashed into particles and stripped of its trophies. Still stuck to the disintegrating corkboard were three curled and yellowing eight-by-ten-inch black and white photographs of bowling teams and softball players. I popped them off and stuck them in the rear waistband of my shorts.

I worked my way through the rest of the offices and out to a shop floor. Attached to the ceiling were long I-beam rails that supported sliding chain hoists used to transport raw materials and assembled parts. Huge incandescent lights were caged overhead at the end of a galvanized conduit. In the centre were a half-dozen benches, each about forty feet long, lined up in neat parallel rows. Around the perimeter were machine tools and pressure vessels of various shapes and sizes. It looked naked without the distributed control equipment – computer automation – that I'd been working with for the last twenty years. No sensors, controllers, activators, big red coil cords, keyboards or CPUs. None of the signposts of late twentieth-century manufacturing.

There were three other interconnected areas where things were made. It looked like WB was ready to make almost anything, and probably tried to in its relentless pursuit of market redemption. I was able to identify compressors, hydraulic lines, conveyors, centrifugal sorters, parts bins, and machines that cut, stitched, folded, wrapped, stacked and packed. There were large empty spaces where equipment was once bolted to the floor. Either salvaged or purloined long ago.

I went back outside, squinting at the hazy sunlight. There was one building left to look in. It was red brick like the others, but unattached. I jogged across the overgrown lawn and looked for a way to get inside. The front door was locked, but there was an open window on the east side. I jumped up and grabbed the sill, and pulled myself over. I dropped into a janitor's closet. It was still stocked with buckets, mops and assorted cleaning utensils. Nothing worth pilfering. The door was locked, but gave in easily with a solid kick. On the other side was a big open warehouse. I waited for my eyes to adjust again to the dim light. As expected, the room was almost empty. There was one rusted-out wreck of a forklift, stacks of splintered skids, a lot of metal shelving racks and a few dozen ten-gallon drums. Plus a lot of seagull shit and the mildewed smell of a dark, damp place.

I'd worked up a sweat during my run, so my body temperature dropped quickly as I walked around the cold rooms. I needed to start running again, so I scaled the main fence and took up my regular route where I'd left off. By now the day was fully underway, though the diffused sunlight did little to warm things up.

I began to picture hot coffee and toasted sesame seed bagels.

And the way Amanda Battiston looked that day walking toward me across the sand, her hair blown off to the side, her back straight and her face filled with thwarted plans and threadbare expectations.

SHE CALLED me when I was in the shower. I stood in the kitchen with my parents' Western Electric handset at my ear watching the water puddle at my feet.

'Roy's in the city and it's my day off,' she said.

'Really.'

'What do you think I should do?'

'Go to the 7-Eleven.'

'That's where it's happening?'

'That's where I'll pick you up.'

'How will I identify you?'

'Grey hair, bent nose.'

'What time?'

'Half an hour.'

'What should I bring?'

'Suspended disbelief.'

I thought I should shave and put on a clean shirt. I worried about the Grand Prix a little. I'd cleaned the blood off the backseat, but it hadn't done much to reduce the dog smell. Eddie liked to lie around in the car even when it was parked in the driveway. Hearing the jingle of car keys always threw him into a frenzy of joyous anticipation.

'Okay, but you got to sit in the back.'

Amanda stood on the sticky sidewalk outside the 7-Eleven in a blue windbreaker, yellow skirt and Reeboks. Her hands were clasped in front and she was looking out into the world as if expecting something wondrous to suddenly appear. All she got was me and my dog. I pulled up and she hopped quickly into the Grand Prix. I noticed for the hundredth time her lovely tanned legs.

'Right on time,' she said.

'Had all morning to practice.'

She reached back and ruffled up Eddie's ears.

'Guard dog?'

'Freeloader.'

She looked very bright and enthusiastic. I felt the need to catch up.

'Coffee?'

I'd brought along a thermos filled at the corner place and two travel mugs.

'Sure,' she said, like I'd offered her a ride on my private jet.

'You're in a good mood, Mrs Battiston.'

'I'm not at the bank. That's enough to put anyone in a good mood.'

'I thought you liked your job.'

'I love my job. It's just Wednesdays are so nice.'

I felt her presence fill up the inside of my car. She poured us coffee.

'Where to?'

'Where thou goest.'

I took her up to North Haven where we caught the South Ferry over to Shelter Island. For a few hours I just let the Grand Prix rumble around the easy hills and shady curves of the island, pausing for a spell at the wildlife preserve so Eddie could flush out endangered species. Then we stopped at Ram's Head to see the last and hardiest cruisers of the season anchored out in Coecles Harbor. Then finally worked our way over to Sunset Beach where we ate lunch at the rooftop place.

When the salads arrived I finally got around to asking her.

'So, where'd you live when you grew up out here?'

'North Sea,' she said, without hesitation. 'I thought you knew that.'

'Maybe I did. Memory's not what it used to be.'

'North North Sea. Almost Noyac. Right near you. Why?'

'Maybe that's why we get along. Shared North Sea sensibilities.'

'More sensible than the rest of Southampton, if you ask me.'

'Did you sell the house?'

She shook her head while she chewed on a mouthful of salad.

'No, Roy thought we should try renting it. He's been good about it, though. He hasn't pushed. I have to clean it all out and I can't face that yet.'

'I shouldn't be reminding you.'

'That's okay.'

We got off on other things over the rest of lunch. But after the cheque came, she had an idea.

'We drove right by there on the way up here,' she said. 'Want to go look?'

'It's not upsetting?'

'I'd like to see it. Someday soon it'll all change forever. Everything does.'

'Entropy.'

'Whatever you say, Mr MIT.'

The ferry loaders were a little challenged by the scale of the Grand Prix, but managed to get it on board. All that sheet metal can intimidate a younger person. I thought they might try to charge me a premium for the effort. The guys in the electricians' vans and pick-ups were more appreciative.

'389?'

'400. Quad, posi, Hurst four-speed. Out of a '67 Goat.'

'Yowza.'

Amanda seemed to enjoy the attention.

'No one ever slobbers over my little Audi.'

'Not until they see the driver.'

I was a little unsure about the right turn off Noyac Road. So was Amanda.

'Yes. No. A little further. Turn. Wait a minute. Okay, go down that way.'

I drifted up to the single-storey white house. There was a short white pebble and grey gravel driveway, but no garage. The siding was the old-style asbestos shingling formed to look like cedar. There were some gangly old yews planted along the foundation, a slate path to the front door, and no mailbox. I braked and crunched up into the drive.

'What do you think?' she asked me.

'A North Sea classic. Could use a little fix up.'

She leaned toward the windshield to get a better look.

'It does. The lawn's been cut, but none of the shrubs have been trimmed in a while. My mother and I planted that dogwood in front.' She put out her hand, 'It was like this tall. Look how big it's gotten.'

Next to the drive was a white gate with a curved top covered with ivy and exhausted strands of clematis. In the backyard were rose vines that looked like tangled netting tossed over a split rail fence.

'Let's go take a look.'

Amanda jumped out of the car and ran up to the front door. There she stood stymied. I called to her from the car.

'Keys?'

'Of course not.'

She followed me as I walked around to the back of the house. Another little stoop led to the back door. It had a window, so you could see into the kitchen. Amanda made a tunnel with her hands and looked through the glass.

'Looks exactly the same,' she said. 'I don't know why it wouldn't.'

On impulse I tried the door knob. Locked, of course.

'My key's at the house,' said Amanda.

Next to the back stoop was a metal Bilco hatch. I tried that and it opened. The door at the foot of the stairs had a lock, but it didn't look like much. Designed more for an interior door. I took out my keys and stuck one of them in the keyhole. The lock mechanism was loose, but wouldn't give it up. So I took out my Swiss Army knife and selected the slot-head screwdriver, bottle opener feature. Amanda wasn't saying anything, but I could hear noises coming from her repressed concerns. The lock quickly surrendered to the Swiss Army.

'Why it's good to bring an engineer.'

'For breaking and entering? '

'This is your house. You're allowed to break in.'

She followed me into the damp basement. It smelled like a compost heap. I found a light switch and snapped it on. It made both of us jump. I had to remind myself, and her, that nobody was home.

I took her hand and led her up the stairs. Her grip was sure and strong, her palm smooth and dry. She let me pull her along without resisting.

We poked around like a pair of home buyers The kitchen was straightened, but oddly lived in. There were dishes and non-perishables in the faux colonial cupboards and drawers. The refrigerator was turned off. The counters were covered in textured, lime green Formica. The kitchen had been thoroughly cleaned, though the house smelled like an empty house. We went out into the living room and I found the thermostat. I put it up to seventy degrees and the boiler came on. I turned it back down to shut it off.

I followed her down a narrow hallway that led to the bedrooms. I had to flick on the hall light to see where I was going. It took me a while to find the switch. Amanda was standing so close to me I'd hurt her if I moved too quickly. From where we stood you could see doors to four tiny bedrooms.

'Which was yours?'

It was painted pale blue and crammed with furniture and dolls and stuffed animals. Some looked almost new.

'You liked a lot of friends around?' I asked her.

'My mother was the doll fanatic. Come see.'

One of the bedrooms had been converted into a small sewing room. In the centre was an ironing board. An iron lay flat on a piece of gingham fabric. There were tables and cabinets lining the walls.

All the horizontal surfaces of the crowded little room were covered with large fabric dolls in various states of finish. The strange quality of all those grinning lifeless faces caught me unprepared.

'Gosh.'

'See what I mean?'

Amanda picked up one of the dolls and looked it over, brushing back its hair and pulling at the tiny outfit.

'She was very talented. Most of these were probably going to charity, but when I was growing up it helped feed us. You'd be surprised how many adults collect dolls.'

'She didn't have another job?'

'WB. Didn't everybody? At least till it shut down.'

'Your father, too?'

'That's what my mother said. I don't remember. I was too little when he died.'

I thought of Jackie's aerial map showing my cottage at the tip of Oak Point, right outside the invisible walls that enclosed the WB domain. Invisible to me, because there was never any reason for me to know it was there. It wasn't my world. 'This is where I found her,' said Amanda. 'Right there on the floor. Not surprising, I guess, since this is where she spent all her time.'

On impulse I picked up the iron and smelled it.

'A heart attack?'

'That's what they thought. We could have done an autopsy, but Roy didn't like the idea. What difference does it make, he said, how she died?'

I took a closer look at the old iron. It was very old and heavy. The cord was covered in black fabric with white hash marks. The plug at the end was of the same vintage, so you could see how it was wired just by looking at the bottom.

'Did you ever see your mother test the iron to see if it was hot?' I asked her.

She pondered for a moment

'Well, I guess she must have.'

'Held it with her right hand, wet her left index finger and tapped the underside of the iron like this. Psst.'

Amanda nodded as she played the visual in her mind.

'Why?'

'My mother always did that. It seemed so reckless. But that's what our parents' generation did. Learned it from their mothers, who heated irons on the stove.'

'I let the cleaners worry about all that. That's what my generation does.'

She led me back out to the living room where she spent a few minutes looking around and picking things up off tables and the bookshelves on either side of the fireplace. I hadn't kept any of my parents' stuff. I thought I would before my mother died, but then when it happened, I just wanted it gone.

'You're right about your mother,' I said to her.

'What do you mean?'

'I would have liked her.'

'You would have. Everybody did.'

'Everybody but Regina.'

'Everybody but her.'

'You ready?'

'I'm ready.'

We went back out the kitchen door.

'You go ahead. I'll lock up.'

I let Eddie inspect the yard for a few minutes while Amanda settled back into the Grand Prix. She slid down in the old leather bucket and let her head fall back against the back rest.

'I was fine until we went outside. Now it's all sort of attacking me.'

'I'm thinking about something clear in a glass. With ice.'

'At least.'

Oriented once again, I quickly found my jogging route behind WB. The Grand Prix tracked along the deep grooves of the sand road like a rail car. We were back at my cottage in about five minutes.

I equipped myself with a vodka on the rocks. Amanda opted for gin and tonic.

'Kinda past season, but who's counting.'

She dug a bottle of tonic out of a kitchen cabinet and promptly dropped it on the floor. Before I could stop her, she'd scooped up the plastic bottle, gripped it under an arm and twisted off the cap, shooting off a foamy spray of tonic that soaked the top half of her body and most of my kitchen.

'Oh shit, oh shit.' She put down the bottle and went to wash her hands. 'Do you have something to clean this up with? I'm so sorry. I'm soaked.'

I handed her a dish towel, and while she dried off her hands I mopped up the devastation with a roll of paper towels.

'I hope this thing's waterproof,' she said, looking down the front of her windbreaker. She unsnapped the snaps and I helped her slide out of it. Her yellow blouse was unscathed. Underneath, her breasts moved freely, unfettered.

'I need to rinse this off.'

'I should make a fire.'

'You stoke, I'll rinse.'

I had the woodstove going by the time Amanda came out to the living room holding her wet windbreaker and hard-won gin and tonic. I hung the jacket over the back of a chair and slid it up close to the fire. Amanda curled up next to the arm of the sofa, I sat on the floor.

'That was a wonderful day,' she said.

'It's still a day for another hour or two.'

'I should go after this.'

'Your windbreaker has to dry.'

'After that.'

She'd rolled up her sleeves and bent up the collar of her yellow blouse. And unbuttoned a button. She noticed me noticing.

'I don't mind,' she said.

'What?'

'If you look.' She unbuttoned another button and spread open the yellow blouse just enough to expose the faded tan lines. 'At least it tells me you're interested.'

'I'm interested.'

'But that's all?'

'More than interested.'

'But.'

'There's Roy . . . '

'That's why?'

'Probably not. Though he doesn't make much sense for you. But, then again, that can't be a good enough reason.'

'Good enough to date?'

'Yeah. Good enough to date.'

I was grateful that she left it alone after that. I didn't want to have to explain myself any more than I had to. Mostly because I didn't really have an explanation. I knew there was one, I just didn't know how to get at it. Or I didn't want to try. Anyway, it had been a long time for me. Maybe I was just afraid. Maybe that's what I didn't want to explain.

I took her back to the 7-Eleven in her dried-out windbreaker. We didn't talk much on the way over there, but it felt nice just to drive along in silence. I smoked a cigarette, she closed her eyes and sat there looking like female perfection. Luckily it was too late to turn around and go back to the cottage.

'I like you, Sam,' she said to me, getting out of the car. 'Anyway you want it.'

'I'm not sure what that is.'

'Then let's play it by ear.'

'I might be tone deaf.'

She laughed, then leaned back into the car across the seat and kissed me.

'That's already well established.'

ON THE way back to the cottage I swung past Amanda's mother's house. I went back through the kitchen door which I'd left open and grabbed a plastic bag out of the broom closet. I made a quick trip to the sewing room. I picked the iron up off the ironing board, curled the cord and dropped it in the bag.

Then I went down to the basement to look for the electrical panel. I found late-vintage circuit breakers mixed in with the original fuses. One circuit breaker was thrown. I switched it back and it held. I got out my Swiss Army knife and unscrewed the face plate from the box. I thought about how badly I needed reading glasses to do close-in work, especially in low light. When I was done picking through the wiring I screwed everything back together again. Then I traced one of the lines from the box, across the ceiling to a location somewhere among the bedrooms. Before I left the basement I unlatched the basement door at the bottom of the hatch. I locked the kitchen door.

I tossed the iron into the trunk. Then I went home and hit tennis balls around for Eddie until it got dark. I was glad to finally have the night to sit inside while I drank and watched the white caps dance across the Little Peconic as the sou'westerlies gave in to the harder, colder winds from the north. I wanted to think things through, but instead I fought off images of wild-eyed dolls and smooth, olivey tanned skin, the touch of silk, and the smell of possibility.

In the morning I retrieved the iron from the Grand Prix's cavernous trunk and took it down along with a cup of coffee to the basement where my father built a small workbench with a big drafting light. I put on my reading glasses.

THE IRON could have been almost forty years old. The handle was made of heavy black plastic, reminiscent of Bakelite. The inset Phillips head screws that held the base to the handle were slightly peened over. It had been opened up at least once, probably recently given the bright metal scratches on the screw heads. I unscrewed them and pulled the handle section up off the chrome base so I could look inside. The smell of burned insulation I'd noticed before was now far stronger. I pulled the drafting light down a little closer and deconstructed the little wiring harness that fed power through the switches and rheostat, and ultimately into the iron base, whose only job was to get real hot and boil some water for release as steam through a row of little vent holes. A fairly heavy piece of Romex copper wire had been neatly introduced into the system, connecting the ground lead from the power cord to a little threaded column soldered to the base that secured an inset Phillips head screw from the plastic handle. The original wiring and the new piece of Romex were partially blackened, but not burned through. The manufacturer's logo and instructions for operating the iron were printed on a heavy metal plate, probably aluminium, screwed to the black plastic directly below the handle itself. I dug around inside with my long screwdriver until I identified where another new piece of wiring was soldered to the threads of a screw holding down the plate.

I reassembled the iron, sat it in the upright position and plugged it into an outlet which had a dedicated fifteen amp circuit to run the bench and the basement lights.

I had two large screwdrivers with plastic handles. I wrapped them with old scraps of inner tube to provide an extra layer of insulation. I held one screwdriver to the logo plate and brought the other to the base of the iron.

Pop.

Even with the insulation, fifteen amps was enough to jolt my arms clear of the iron, and make a noise loud enough to set off Eddie. In the grey diffused light from the basement windows I could see smoke curl out of the vent holes at the base of the iron.

I unplugged the iron, lit a cigarette and drank some of my coffee. My eyes slowly adjusted to the dim light.

I threw the breaker back on and went upstairs. Then I went outside to hit a few more tennis balls around for Eddie. A hurricane somewhere out in the Atlantic was sending twenty to thirty knot winds across the East End. The Little Peconic was a roiling stew pot of grey-black water and off-white foam. The winds were warm and smelled of their tropical origins, all wrong for the autumn light and red-yellow days of October. A windsurfer was out on the bay skimming across the chop like a lunatic water bug. I envied his foolish abandon.

That afternoon I took a long run. I needed the oxygen, and the endorphins. And whatever blessings the windswept Peconic was willing to bestow.

CHAPTER SIX

The company I worked for created wealth out of thin air. We owned giant processing plants that sucked in atmosphere and pumped out freight cars full of pure oxygen, nitrogen and helium. We made hydrogen from water. Fertilizer from natural gas. Converted crude oil into gasoline additives, road surfaces and plastic housings for TV sets and microwave ovens. Though fundamental in our use of natural resources, we needed highly refined technology, research scientists and applications engineers to maintain a competitive advantage over the other monstrous corporations who made the same stuff we did. This technical support was so vast and sophisticated that the managers of the corporation began to view it, correctly, as a valuable product in its own right. We began by licensing proprietary processing and manufacturing technology. Then technical services and on-site support. Eventually we unbundled almost everything we did and peddled it to anyone who didn't directly compete with our core operating divisions. The crosspollination of ideas was an unexpected side benefit. While we were selling them ours, we'd pick up a few of theirs. This further strengthened our ability to develop new technology for the home front and stimulate development of products our operating divisions could never imagine, much less produce. We sold instruments, robotics, software, training programmes and combustion efficiency enhancers like the SAM- 85. And a lot of sheer technical know-how. I kept a small stack of CDs in my right hand desk drawer that held data people paid $100,000 just to look at on my laptop. If they wanted the disc, that was another $900K.

This was my part of the corporation. It wasn't a simple job, but they paid me a lot of money to do it.

Eventually, people began to notice our division had gone from overhead expense to self-funding enterprise, to major profit centre. Even better, we proved that a 100-year-old company living off

God's own air, water and light sweet crude could also be in the vanguard of high technology. Since I'd helped conjure all this, I was one of the few in the company who knew how to do it. This gave me a healthy share of cachet. That was a good thing for people's careers in our company. Many had far more cachet than me, though they'd often caused the company more harm than good. That was because you could acquire cachet through means other than producing profits or good will for the firm. This is often called corporate politics, but the truth is bigger than that. It's something more essential to the chaotic dynamics of large-scale social behavior.

Some people tried to share the success of our division by association. Others undermined us at every opportunity. Most of the people in upper management who weren't threatened found a way to slip under the halo. A sidebar article in *Fortune* gave us a little outside validation and caught the attention of the Board of Directors.

An elderly woman who'd been handling appointments for each successive Chairman of the board since the early fifties wrote to me through interoffice mail. Never e-mail. She said I was on the agenda for the monthly board meeting at 7:30 AM, Tuesday. This stood as an invitation. The boardroom was on the top floor of corporate headquarters on Seventh Avenue. At that altitude, you could literally conduct business among the clouds.

After passing through a metal detector, you took a special elevator run by a man who pushed the floor button for you. He wore a tiny earphone and a blank expression. The inside of the elevator cab was lined in stainless steel so you had to look at a vaguely distorted image of yourself as you took the long ride up. Vivaldi was playing through the speaker overhead. I could feel the acceleration collect around my feet, then lift up through my body as we came to a soft stop. The operator ushered me into a foyer with a dark grey carpet and wine-coloured walls trimmed out in hand rubbed and oiled Honduran mahogany. Somehow they got the Vivaldi up there, too. There were a few recognizable Impressionists on the walls and two gigantic vases decorated with dragons and nicely-dressed Chinese people. A very tall, very white young woman with dark hair cinched up at the back of her head appeared out of nowhere and asked me if I wanted a cup of coffee. I said sure and she disappeared again. The elevator operator was still there waiting with his elevator, one hand on the open button, the other resting comfortably just inside the front of his sport jacket. I wondered if they were playing Vivaldi through that earphone. There was no place to sit, so I paced the foyer until the woman showed up with a crystal mug filled with *café noire*. After I took a sip, she turned on her heel and I followed her down a long hall to the waiting area directly outside the boardroom. I settled into a chair and she took her position at the ornately carved four-by-eight-foot table that served as a reception desk. A field of green inlaid leather covered the surface. She had a charcoal grey phone console and a matching laptop, flipped open. No more Vivaldi. It was so quiet a pin drop would have hurt your ears. I tried to hear her heart beating from across the room, but all I could hear was my own. I unbuttoned my suit jacket and leaned back in my chair so my head could rest on the wall, and closed my eyes. I tried to fill my mind with somniferous images of sports cars, tropical waters and women I wanted to see without their clothes. It worked well enough to put me to sleep. I bathed in the soothing, narcotic effect of sudden REM sleep. My dreams were frantic and incoherent, but not disturbing. I heard someone call my name, 'Sam,' several times, and when I snapped open my eyes I was looking across an acre of Persian rug at the double doors leading into the boardroom. One of the guys was standing there holding the doors open and calling out my name with a calm, amused insistence.

'We keeping you awake?' he asked as I walked past him into the boardroom.

'Seven-thirty is kind of barbaric,' I said to him.

He actually slapped me on the back.

'Always the comeback,' he said in the avuncular way a professor talks to a favourite student, which in a way I was.

The boardroom had floor-to-ceiling glass walls on three sides. If you walked straight into the room you'd be at the end of a long table facing the chairman, George Donovan, who sat a mile or two down at the opposite end. To either side were all the inside directors and the few outside directors who thought they ought to show up for form. In front of each was a maroon leather folder, closed. Inside was the agenda they'd covered before I came into the room. They looked at me with the benign disinterest of recently fed carnivores. I fought the urge to give my name, rank and serial number.

'Hiya, there, Sam,' said George.

'Hi, George.'

'Why don't you find yourself a chair and sit down. They get you coffee?'

'Thanks. All set.' I held up my half-empty cup.

I walked around to the right and sat in the first chair I came to. Louise Silberg, VP, Finance and Administration, was on my right. Jason Fligh, president of the University of Chicago and the only black man on the board, on my left. They both shook my hand and smiled pleasantly. I liked Jason; Louise was very scary. Even split.

'How's Abigail?' George asked.

'She's good. Thanks.'

'Lovely girl.'

'Yeah.'

Big time corporate guys are geniuses at this – remembering the names of your wife and kids. I couldn't remember a damn thing about his wife, assuming he had one. I didn't ask about her. He didn't care.

'We've been reviewing quarterly figures,' he said, and on cue all the board members flipped open their maroon folders and pulled out a single spreadsheet. 'Before the meeting I asked Joe Felder's people to do a look-back of the last twelve quarters, and run comparisons of the performance of Technical Services and Support against the adjusted norms of the other divisions.'

He looked up at me over the top of his plastic-rimmed half-glasses.

'Wanna guess how you did?' he asked, and looked around the room to see if anyone was ready to chance a position. Nobody bit.

I could hear Jason making humming noises to himself, as if struck by a revelation. I didn't think George wanted me to say anything, so I waited him out.

'A helluva lot better,' he said, sitting back to take another look around the room. 'Forget the percentages. Let's just say it's a hell of a lot better.'

A few of the inside directors ran divisions of their own – massive enterprises more like city-states than business ventures. They were the landed gentry of the corporation. Survivors of the big hike up the ladder. Obsolete, but secure for the balance of their working lives. Even so, they'd all made runs at me when it looked like my little division was generating a decent flow of cachet. None successful. Their faces were neutral.

'It helps to be small,' I said to the group at large. I was trying to tell the operating guys that George was doing this all on his own. I wasn't looking to bite any elephants on the ankle.

'Yes, of course,' said the chairman, 'but profitable. Extremely. We like that.'

Assent burbled around the table. I took a sip of my coffee and sat back in my chair. It was late summer and a witches brew of auto exhaust, industrial fumes and sea-borne mist lay like a hot towel over the city. I looked at it through the tall walls of glass. As high as we were there were even higher buildings that broke up what would have been a perfect view of the Hudson. Beyond the river, New Jersey was a distant, hazy lump.

On a day like that, people on the street would be stripped down and crabbier than usual, forcing their way through the dense, malodourous air with stern, unforgiving faces. Along the horizon charcoal grey clouds threatened thunderstorms. Against the dark backdrop a 747 making its approach to Newark stood out like a brilliant white bird.

'Sam, did you hear what I said?' George was asking me.

'About our profitability. Sure. It's been pretty good.'

'No. About the opportunity.'

'Opportunity? No, I guess I didn't hear that part.'

George frowned up at the ceiling.

'How's the hearing there, Sam?'

'I guess not what it used to be.'

George dropped a stack of reports down on the table with a disdainful flourish.

'Well, that's what we're talkin' about here, Sam. An opportunity. For the company. For you.'

'Ah.'

'No better way to impact shareholder value,' said Mason Thigpin, our corporate counsel, who was sitting across the table from me.

I tried to imagine Mason as a teenager, or even a college undergrad. He was about five years younger than me, but looked much older. His hair had retreated from most of his scalp, leaving behind a monkish ring of curly grey fuzz. He was at least thirty pounds overweight, which actually smoothed out some of the lines of his face before adding back a lot of extra years. He wore heavy horn-rimmed glasses. This intrigued me. I imagined him at the optometrist, picking out these glasses from thousands of possibilities, choosing, helplessly, the one pair that would most clearly confirm his allegiance to the soulless aridity of his calling.

I struggled to concentrate on what George Donovan was saying.

He was explaining to me the future of my division. It was expressed as an option, a possible course, as yet undecided, though everyone in the room understood the language well enough to recognize a done deal. Our corporate management was patterned after the early English monarchy. George needed the general support of the nobility, but each individual decision was unilateral and absolute.

They all smiled at me. All but Mason. They were pleased. I had accomplished great things. Recognition had been bestowed. A royal gift was being given. George folded his arms and leaned out over the table to receive my approval *pro forma* so he could move on to the next item on the agenda.

Jason gave my shoulder an affectionate, congratulatory squeeze. Louise smiled with her lips pinched together. The tall woman who'd greeted me at the elevator came in with a tray of fresh coffee, causing a minor disturbance, so George asked me to speak up.

'I'm sorry, Sam,' he said, 'I guess my hearing's going south, too. What'd you say?'

Whatever I said, I said it again, but still not loud enough for Donovan to hear at the other end of the room. I wasn't speaking to him anyway, but to Mason Thigpin on the other side of the conference room table. He said something back, which I don't remember either, though I think it's in the DA's file. I do remember lurching across the table and grabbing Mason by the fat Windsor knot he had cinched up around his throat. I remember pulling back my right fist and hearing Louise Silberg yelping in my ear.

IT WASN'T hard to find Jackie Swaitkowski's place in the oak groves above Bridgehampton. You just had to count the driveways down from the big oak tree with the giant scar halfway up the trunk. I worked my way down the long, dirt and gravel driveway and pulled the Grand Prix next to her pickup truck. I grabbed my coffee, tucked my cigarettes in my pocket and rang her time-off bell.

Marijuana smoke, Nirvana and Jackie Swaitkowski poured out the front door. A firm grip on the doorknob was the only thing that kept her from being propelled into my arms. I spilled some of my coffee getting out of her way. She jerked her head up and tried to focus on my face.

'Oh.'

'Hi, Jackie. Got a minute?'

'Holy shit, that door opens easy.'

'Sorry I didn't call ahead.'

She scooped up a handful of blond mane and tossed it back over her head.

'You didn't?'

'Can I come in?'

She swung back into the room without letting go of the doorknob, almost closing the door in my face.

'Sure.'

I eased through the opening and followed her into the living room. She was wearing an extra large flannel shirt, blue jean shorts and bare feet. She moved with deliberate care over to the stereo stack and stared for a few moments before finding and turning down the volume. Now it was barely audible, though it made the atmosphere in the house a little less demented.

She spun around and got a bead on where I was standing.

'What can I getcha?'

I held up my cup.

'Brought my own.'

'A roadie?'

'Coffee.'

'Cool.'

She took a few steps and launched herself over the big coffee table, clearing the mountains of papers and catalogues, and landing butt down on the couch. It was too difficult a manoeuver to have been unrehearsed. I took the land route and came around to sit next to her. She slapped my thigh.

'So, how you been? Still full of bullshit?'

'I guess. How's your case?'

She slumped deeper into the couch.

'It's going really well, goddammit.'

'That's bad.'

'I'll have to keep working on it. Killed by my own competence.'

She pulled herself back out of the cushions and searched the table top with her eyes.

'Ha.'

She found a slender, tightly rolled joint and stuck it in her mouth. When she spoke it jumped up and down between her lips.

'You want a hit?'

I took out a cigarette and a pack of matches.

'I'm fine with this.'

I lit us both up. Jackie consumed about half the joint on the first pull, her eyes and cheeks squeezed tight. The smoky aromas commingled and billowed around us on the couch. I wondered how much sin the atmosphere of a single room could absorb.

'So's this a social call or you still diggin' around?' she asked me, once again languidly composed within the depths of her fluffy cushions.

'I was wondering about Milton Hornsby.'

'Def'nateley not social.'

'How was he to work with'

She rolled her eyes.

'I told you, man. A stiff.'

'As a lawyer.'

'Aw, Christ, don't make me think.'

I sat back into the overstuffed cushions to give her more breathing space.

'Did you know Bay Side Holdings was a WB subsidiary? The old plant sitting on the property?'

She rolled up on her right side and looked at me over the top of a cushion.

'No.'

'No?'

'No, I won't talk about it.'

'You knew all along.'

'Can't go there.'

'Or at least figured out along the way.'

'You got an imagination,' she said.

'You spin a good story.'

'Works on judges.'

'Not so well on engineers.'

'No imagination?'

'Too analytic.'

'I need a good analyst.'

'So you say.'

'Need my head examined.'

'What'll they find?'

'Conflicted interests.'

'Caught between the Bar and a hard place?'

She sunk deeper into the couch and draped her long bangs over her face the way my daughter would do when she didn't want to talk about something or finish all the peas left on her plate.

'You're not as funny as you used to be.'

'That's why you're so pissed at those guys,' I told her, 'not because they wouldn't press the case. Because you thought they weren't telling everything you needed to know to do your job. They were holding out on you, treating you like a lesser partner. Like a local.'

'You're also not as nice.'

'Quite a conflict. On one side, a great case, lots of interesting law, the kind you could take advantage of out here. Lots of money. And a heartthrob for a co-counsel. On the other side, a feeling you're aiding and abetting the enemy. The City People, with all the money and none of the feeling for the real Southampton. Where you were born and raised and still refuse to leave, even though you're smart enough and capable enough to have a real career anywhere you want.'

'Time for the fifth.'

'I could get you one.'

'The amendment, dummy.'

'Something about this whole scene really bothered you. But you're constrained by attorney-client privilege. Though not enough to stop you from giving me that map.'

'You know, I'm either too stoned, or not stoned enough to listen to all this.'

She gave my leg a squeeze, then used it to haul herself up on her feet. I gripped her forearm and hauled her back down again.

'You don't have to tell me anything. Unless you want to.'

After that she seemed happy enough to stay put. I slurped my coffee and lit another Camel. We sat quietly for a little while.

'I never saw them.'

'The clients?'

She nodded. Then shook her head.

'Client. Only spoke to one guy. Never saw him in person. Just talked to him on the phone. Me, Hornsby and Hunter would sit in Hornsby's office with a speaker phone. Hornsby always made sure he knew we were all in the room. Never even heard his name. When I asked Hunter, "Does this guy have a name?," he'd say

"Mr Client". He was nice enough about it, but you know, Mr Client was a very uptight person. Insistent, or insinuating, or insulting, one of those "in" words. Hunter handled him fine. Whenever the guy handed him some crap, he'd hand it right back. That's what made me think there were other clients behind the client. I know it sounds terrible, but the real giveaway was the way Mr Client talked. You know, a little of the "dees", "dem" and "does". I guess that's snobby of me.'

'A little.'

'And the profanity. Fuck this and fuck that. Like he was trying to sound tough. He did sound tough. And the way he talked about handling the Appeals Board, and the DEP, how to get around this and get around that, and who do you have to take care of, and whose arm do you have to twist and who's got the juice with who and all this stuff that had no regard for due process or the spirit behind all these regulatory hurdles, no matter how stupid they might look to these developers. Jesus Christ Almighty.'

She reached over and took my cup out of my hand, downed a gulp, and handed it back. She wiped her mouth on her sleeve and burped. I wondered how Jackie got to sleep at night with all that noise in her head.

'Of course, they had a lot of hurdles to leap,' she said. 'They probably couldn't believe the regulatory resistance they were getting. All the signs, stated and unstated, that said this project was going to get the full treatment. And that's no idle threat from a town that'll fight like rabid badgers over the slightest variance. If they're in the mood. Mr Client was nervous as a cat. Until the Town told us the next steps and he pulled the plug.'

'Stopped the project?'

'Cold. Just ended it. I got a cheque, cutie pie went home. That was it.'

'What did the Town want?'

'Neighbourhood Notice. Couple different types. For a normal variance, you only need a four-hundred-foot radius around the property. Send the neighbours a postcard, tell 'em there's going to be a zoning hearing, if you want to come and raise a stink, here's your chance. Appeals Board takes these things seriously. Neighbours can make board members miserable.'

'What other kinds of notice?'

'Bay Side pulled the absolute worst kind you can get because of the old factory. It's a DEP thing – they go out like a mile and send everybody this big questionnaire that just about begs you to come up with environmental reasons to oppose the project. It's really punitive, frankly, but that's federal Superfund shit and nobody screws with that.'

'Bummer.'

'So who gets blamed? The co-counsel. The local. Like I'm supposed to anticipate this kind of thing? I felt so bad.'

'Was Hunter mad at you, too?'

She looked thoughtful, 'I guess not. He didn't ask me out afterwards, like I thought he would, despite it all. But, no. He wasn't pissed. He said I'd done my job as well as I could.'

I realised she was crying. I should have seen it earlier. It was the kind of insensitivity I'd honed through years of practice. I hauled myself from out of the white couch and went to the bathroom for tissues. I'd done a lot of that, too. Going to get tissues was one of my specialties.

She looked up at me after she blew her nose.

'Is this some investigation? Are you really from the goddam FBI? Are you going to ruin my life?'

'I'm an industrial designer. No arrest powers.'

She pulled another joint out of the ashtray, then tossed it back.

'Enough of that shit. Makes me all weepy.'

We sat quietly for a little while. Talked out. I tried to listen to the sub rosa soundtrack coming from the stereo while I looked around the heap of a room, wondering how you could maintain all that chaos and your sanity at the same time. Maybe that was part of the point. Maybe sanity wasn't such a great thing to aspire to.

'I'd really like to talk to Milton Hornsby,' I said to her.

'Not a very talkative guy.'

'Tell him I think I know why he won't talk to me. At this point,

I'm keeping it to myself. Which is not going to last forever. If he's interested in getting a little ahead of things, he'll sit down with me. With you present if he wants. It's up to him.'

'Officially I'm fired. What's my interest in this?'

'I got your name from the public record. You're just facilitating communications.'

'I guess you won't tell me what's really going on. After I spill my guts and violate every canon in the book.'

'Probably better if you didn't know beforehand.'

'Because I'm a dumb local?'

'We're all dumb locals. That's the problem.'

RODE DOWN from Bridgehampton and out to the shore. I meandered through the new developments carved out of the potato fields and joined the parade of vans and pickup trucks that constituted most of the traffic between weekends. At Mecox Bay I turned north again and got on Montauk Highway until I cleared the water, then dropped back down Flying Point Road toward the sea.

I stopped off at the Town's beach access. This close to the ocean the sea air dispersed the sunlight, deepening all the colours and setting snares for unsuspecting painters and sentimentalists. The wild roses that lined the parking lot were still enjoying the last cool autumn days before winter; they would stay green and semi-floral well into December. Sand, blown over the dunes, formed a grainy skim-coat over the black asphalt, empty now since early fall. In the spring, maintenance crews would sweep it all up again and renew the illusion that you could halt nature's irresistible advance.

I continued to follow the coast until I was all the way out on Dune Road in Southampton Village, where giant shingle-style mansions and architectural fantasies stood like devotional monuments before the sea. To my right, the sun dropping toward the Shinnecock Bay was airbrushing the underside of the clouds a soft reddish-yellow. In the morning, people who lived on Dune Road could walk to the other side of their houses and watch the sun rise over the ocean. All for an admission price that started around twenty million dollars. When my father first started digging the foundation hole for his cottage, nobody but reclusive eccentrics wanted to live out in the dunes. It was a wilderness where locals like us camped and had family barbecues and risked our lives bodysurfing in storm-swept seas. Now it was the realization of billionaires' dreams.

I recalled what Amanda's friend Robin said as she distractedly searched the Playhouse for someone to break her heart. 'What do you get when there's more demand than supply, and the demanders have more money than God and all His angels put together?'

I added to the list of things I knew one thing I knew so well I'd completely forgotten it. People made huge fortunes somewhere else so they could bring them out here. And there was only so much here to go around.

THIS TIME I didn't have a newspaper to give Rosaline when she answered the door. Her hair was pulled back into a ponytail and her clothing was in the same loose, deconstructed style I'd seen her in before. Comfort designed for the long haul. I held my hands up.

'No offering.'

'I think we're past that,' she said quietly. 'Come on in.'

Arnold was in his seat in the living room, asleep. Rosaline put her finger to her lips and led me into a graceful study across the hall. It was walled with overstuffed bookshelves and furnished in early twentieth century oak. A pair of brown leather chairs was placed side by side in the middle of the room, each with an ottoman and reading lamp.

'My parents' inner sanctum.'

'Readers.'

'Never owned a TV.'

'My kind of people.'

'Good. I share the genes. What can I get you?'

'I'm intruding again.'

'You are,' she checked her watch. 'Close to cocktail hour. Forces me to offer you a drink.'

'Vodka on the rocks. No fruit.'

'Coming up.'

I sat in the chair and rested my manila folder on my lap. It felt better to have a prop, more official.

'Did the information I gave you do any good?' she asked, coming back with my drink and a large red wine.

'Yeah. Helped a lot.'

'But you want more.'

'After I thank you again for what you did. Thanks.'

'You're welcome.'

'Though I'm not sure if you're the one to ask about this other stuff.'

'Ask.'

'I was thinking about what you said about the Internet.'

She looked a little uneasy.

'I was nosy.'

'Not what you said, but the fact of it. You're probably a good surfer.'

'What, with all the time I have on my hands?'

'That's right. You need to tie up that busy brain.'

'Is that what you do?'

'I don't own a computer. I've never seen a web site that wasn't a printout. People did that stuff for me.'

'Mr Big Shot.'

'I had a PC, but I used it to access technical data from the central servers.'

'So what do you want from me?'

I took a sip of the vodka.

'Nosy work.'

'For pay?'

'For the hell of it.'

We were both jarred by the sound of Arnold calling from the other room.

'Who's there?' he yelled.

Rosaline put a calming hand over her heart.

'Can usually sleep through an atom bomb.'

She got up and waved to me to come along. Arnold was trying hard to make out who I was. He wasn't wearing his glasses.

'Sam Acquillo, Daddy. You remember he came to visit last week.'

Arnold put out his hand to shake.

'Sorry to bother you again, sir. I was asking your daughter for a favour.'

'Sure, go ahead,' he said. 'I do it all the time.'

He liked to tease her. She liked it, too, only not as much.

'We're drinking, Daddy. Care to join?'

This sent him into a prolonged deliberation, but he was clearly interested. He looked at the glass in my hand.

'That's vodka. You want rye on the rocks?' she asked, loudly.

He nodded, as if convinced by a superior argument.

Once we were all set with our drinks I explained to Arnold how I needed Rosaline's help looking up some things on the Internet.

'She's the one to ask. Spends a lot of time on that thing,' he said, then he had another thought. 'Maybe you could explain something to me.' Rosaline looked like she knew what was coming. 'I know you can look up anything you want on the computer, but how did all that information get in there in the first place? Who put it in there?'

It took him a while to get out the whole question. But not long enough for me to come up with an answer.

'It's kind of complicated.'

Rosaline was enjoying this.

'Mr Acquillo supervised hundreds of engineers, Daddy. What could he possibly know about computers?'

'You haven't told him about shared databases and search engines?'

'He doesn't know, Daddy. Nobody does. It's a modern mystery.'

'Phoof,' said Arnold, a sentiment I shared.

'I do have something for you, however,' I told him. 'I asked you about Bay Side Holdings and you thought they were a captive. Turns out they were. Part of WB, the old manufacturing plant out there between Oak Point and Jacob's Neck. Bay Side was WB's real estate arm.'

'I suspected as much.'

Rosaline looked proud of him.

'I told you he knew his stuff.'

'How well did you know Carl Bollard and Willard Wakeman?' I asked.

He worked on his drink while he pondered.

'I never met Wakeman, he died many years ago. But I knew Carl Bollard well. And his idiot son.'

'Daddy.'

'Not my cup of tea, Carl Junior. A wasteabout. Most people in town were glad to see the place close down, except for the ones working there. Not the right image people thought Southampton should have, even though it was up there in North Sea. There was a deep harbour there long ago. You could bring a large vessel all the way down from Greenport, which had ships coming in from all over the world.'

'What's that got to do with Carl Junior?' asked Rosaline, gently keeping him on track.

'He shut it down. Everyone thought it was his fault. Though, in truth, a little outfit like that wasn't going to make it out here. That sort of plant belongs in New Jersey, for God's sake, not a resort area like this.'

'You still didn't like him.'

'My father came to this country with nothing. He had to work like a dog, and so did we. This was the way it was. And this boy is handed everything, and what does he do? He drinks it all away.'

He punctuated every sentence with a knuckle pointed at my chest. You'd think he took lessons from Regina.

'He drives expensive cars and lives in night clubs. Dishonours his father. All he cares about are the fancy people at the Meadows. As if they would ever accept a boy like that.'

There it was again. The ultimate betrayal. Consorting with City People.

'Carl Senior must have been disappointed.'

'Broke his heart. Every day I thank God for a daughter like Rosaline.'

Her face looked sceptical, but she was clearly pleased.

'Only because I feed him rye on the rocks.'

'So if your agency was retained to manage the Bay Side rentals, in effect you were hired by Carl Senior. He didn't tell you?'

'Carl Bollard died a few years after the war. His company lasted another twenty years or so. I don't know what happened to his son. I never met the people who retained the firm. It's hard for you to understand, but this happened over a very long period of time.'

I'd probably worn him out. That and the rye on the rocks. We both noticed it, and Rosaline gracefully picked up the conversation so Arnold could rest. I spent another hour with them before Rosaline said she had to fix dinner.

'You're welcome to stay.'

'Nah. I've already taken too much of your time.'

'Time we have in abundance. You spoke about a project.'

'I just got a lot from your dad. Maybe enough for now.'

'Really.'

'Though if you learn anything more about Carl Bollard, Junior, I'm interested.'

Her eyes scanned my face.

'You ask a lot for someone who doesn't give up much in return.'

'I'd tell you more if I knew myself.'

'I don't believe you.'

'I'd tell you more if I knew what was true and what wasn't.'

'Better.'

She kissed me again as she escorted me out the door. It wasn't as serious a kiss as the last time, but more confident. Arnold called for her again and she slipped quietly back into the house, a place where time both advanced and stood still, a paradox that was understood and embraced by the occupants.

THE NEXT day I had to do something I didn't want to do, so I hoped the ride over to Hampton Bays would help me feel better about doing it. It didn't.

The Town police HQ was just north of Sunrise Highway in an area reminding me of the pine barrens that started in earnest a few miles to the west. I'd called Sullivan on his cell phone and he asked me to come there since he was deskbound for the day doing paperwork. I asked for him when the lady desk sergeant slid open the security glass.

'He said you'd be here,' she said, buzzing me in. 'Wait over there.'

I stood in an outer office that had a general purpose feel about it, with safety posters and duty rosters covering the walls and casual debris strewn around the desk tops. A bulletin board displayed a crowded gallery of federal fugitives, artist's sketches and missing children. Also a notice from the Labor Department that gave explicit instructions on how to rat out management for hiring violations. It was partially obscured by one of the cop's kids selling gift wrap to raise money for the school band.

Sullivan was in full uniform, armed and ready.

'You can't wear civvies to fill out forms?' I asked him.

'Professional discipline. Improves performance.'

He took me into the main office area predictably filled with glass-walled cubicles and serious-looking men and women staring at computer screens and talking on the phone. The air was close and composed of gases found only in cheerless administrative offices. Just like the division I ran in White Plains, only more overtly concerned with criminal behavior.

'The chief wanted to say hello when you came in. I'll see if he's there.'

'Semple? How come?'

'He helped me wire in the Broadhurst thing. Just wants to meet the Good Samaritan.'

Sullivan led me to the back of the building where Ross Semple had his office. He wasn't there, but his assistant told us to wait. Sullivan got us both coffee to drink while we waited. Mine was French Vanilla served in a decorative paper cup. Not exactly Dirty Harry. I noticed a full ashtray on Semple's desk, so I asked Sullivan if I could smoke.

'Your lungs.'

While I smoked and drank coffee, I admired the studied lack of adornment Ross had achieved in his office. Only family photos in a single plastic cube on his desk. In one of the photos the chief wore a shirt featuring random-width vertical stripes and a collar that buttoned above his Adam's apple. His wife was an equally bad dresser. The kids looked panic-stricken, as if they'd been trapped with their parents for all eternity in the little plastic box.

Semple busted into his office and dropped a stack of files on his desk. He stuck his hand out to me, looking at Sullivan to confirm he had the right man.

'Ross Semple.'

'Sam Acquillo.'

He sat in his chair and pushed it back against a metal credenza, getting himself settled. He had thin, curly brown hair, a high forehead and a small chin. He wore heavy tortoiseshell-frame glasses that seemed on the verge of sliding off his nose. Like me, the chief smoked Camel filters, though with a lot more flourish, like the cigarettes were little conductor's wands used to orchestrate his life. I saw him as a physically weak man with a strong sense of mission and a cynic's determination.

'How's it going?' he asked. 'County giving you a hard time?'

'Going fine. Haven't had much to do with the County. Have a hearing coming up which Goodfellow said was pro forma. The Town's been good. I appreciate your help.'

He looked over at Sullivan.

'Joe sold you pretty hard. His beat, I thought, his call.'

'I appreciate it.'

Semple rolled the lit end of his cigarette in the ashtray. He was the type who had a large repertoire of mannerisms continually engaged in releasing excess nervous energy.

'So you're thinking everything's routine. About the old girl's estate.'

'Estate's a big word for such a little thing.'

'Still has to get done.'

'I think I've collected all the information. She's buried. I found her nephew, Jimmy Maddox. He's cool with everything. Probably just a few more details. It'll all be done before they hold a hearing on me doing it.'

Semple nodded.

'And the assault. Still the memory lapse?'

I could feel a slight increase in the room's air pressure. Sullivan sat there impassively.

'I wish I could do better there. I got my eyes open.'

'Do that,' he said, stamping out the butt and standing up to let us go. 'We take everything seriously.'

I believed him.

Sullivan took me through his office so he could pick up a pad, and then led me out to a concrete patio where we could sit at a picnic bench and talk in private.

'That was interesting,' I said.

'In case you wonder if I keep my boss informed.'

'Never doubted it.'

'He's all right, Semple. I wouldn't want his job.'

I wasn't sure that was true.

'Don't say that out loud. They'll give it to you out of spite.'

'Not management material, unlike yourself.'

He tried to get more comfortable on the picnic table bench. Probably hard to do with all that leather and hardware around his waist.

He pointed at my manila folder.

'Go ahead. I'm all ears.'

'That's what I want to talk about. What you can hear.'

I really hated the feeling this was giving me. It was making me tense.

'Don't forget,' he said, 'you're the one that was all over me about this.'

'I know,' I took a breath. 'Look, I don't know how things work here, but I bet you're obliged to act on anything you genuinely believe is police business.'

'That's how it works.'

'You also told me once there's a real criminal investigation, you're out of it.'

'Basically.'

Making lists is an engineer's habit. When I moved into the cottage I made up a short list in my head of all the things I never wanted again. Near the top of the list was wanting itself. I never wanted to want, to hope for, to wish, to have anything more than a vague expectation that could ever be thwarted again. I didn't want to care enough to want.

'If you ask me to tell you what I'm thinking, I'll have to tell you, because I promised I would. Once I start talking, there's no going back. And what I have to say will take us both out of it in pretty short order.'

'Then you have to start talking.'

I took another deep breath.

'I'm not ready yet.'

'Not ready.'

'I need a little time. Not a lot. I'm asking you not to push it right now.'

'You called me.'

'I promised I'd talk to you. We're talking.'

'I knew you were trouble.'

'What do you say?'

Sullivan looked really unhappy. I didn't blame him.

'You heard Semple in there. Holding out on him is not an option.'

'What's to hold out? We're just talking here.'

'That's what this is? It feels like fuckin' *Alice in Wonderland*.'

'I'm stuck here. You been square with me all along. I want to be square with you, but that creates other dilemmas which I'm hoping to avoid for a little while. Just a few weeks, max. I'm asking you to trust me. Even if you have no reason to.'

'Jesus Christ,' he said, shaking his head as he leaned back and put his hands on his hips. A little lift in my guts told me he was about to cave.

'I won't let this come back at you,' I said.

'That ain't up to you.'

'I'll keep it on me. I've got nothing to lose.'

'Except your ass, which I promise I'll kick from here to forever if this fucks up in my face. Brain damage or not.'

I'd lied to him about the bear, but I couldn't do it again. Now I didn't have to, at least for a while. I was glad for that. It was another item on my list, maybe holding down the top spot. No more things to feel guilty about. That was a whole separate file, already bulging.

I left Sullivan before he could change his mind and drove back to Oak Point to look after Eddie. He could get in and out of the house through the basement hatch, but I hadn't left out any food. If I didn't get there soon he'd start foraging in the wetlands. I didn't want him developing a taste for cormorant.

I KEPT the phone I found when I moved into the cottage, my mother's old-fashioned black rotary Western Electric, hardwired through a little hole in the switch plate. My sister had badgered her to get touch tone, but she couldn't be bothered. Neither could I. Nowadays there isn't much you can do with a rotary besides call a number and hope you get a human being. So I was glad to hear the disembodied voice that answered the phones at Litski, Goethles and Johnson in New York City say I could wait for a human to emerge.

The phone played Vivaldi while I waited. The corporate standard.

'May I help you?'

'Does he know what this is in reference to?'

'No. Tell him it's about Bay Side Holdings in Sag Harbor.'

I had to wait about five minutes for him to come on the line. I didn't mind. I liked Vivaldi.

'Hunter Johnson.'

'Sam Acquillo. I've got a situation here I thought you might be able to help me with.'

'Before you start, I should tell you I've represented Bay Side Holdings on several occasions.'

'That's why I'm calling. I'm the administrator for an estate of a woman who apparently rented a property from Bay Side.'

'We wouldn't be involved in estate issues. I could give you another name.'

'Milton Hornsby. I know. I've spoken to him.'

'Well, then there's probably not much I can help you with.'

He spoke the words as if to propel me off the phone.

'I understand, but there're some aspects to the estate settlement I need to address with the Bay Side principals, and I'm exploring all available means to do so.'

'Again, I think Mr Hornsby would be the most likely to help you. He's the company's chief counsel.'

'As I said, I've spoken to Mr Hornsby.'

'Our practice is strictly real estate law. Mr Hornsby retained our firm to assist with a zoning variance.'

'How did that work out?'

It was quiet for a while on the other end of the line. I half thought he was about to hang up on me. I tried something else.

'I wonder if you could give me about fifteen minutes of your time so I can share something with you.'

More quiet. That's why I hate phones. You can't see the other guy's face.

'I'm not sure I understand your question,' he said. 'Could you tell me your name again and what this is in reference to?'

I couldn't see him, but I could hear the yellow pad come out of the drawer and imagined the expensive pen pop out of a marble-based holder in front of him on the desk.

'Sam Acquillo. I'm the court-appointed administrator for the estate of Regina Broadhurst, who lived for over forty years in a home owned by Bay Side Holdings. Something's arisen that requires a discussion with the principals of Bay Side, and if you give me fifteen minutes you'll see immediately it's something your firm will take a keen interest in.'

At this point I could actually hear the pen scratching across the legal pad. 'Well, you can send me the information.'

'I think it's sufficiently sensitive to warrant a face-to-face discussion. How's tomorrow look for you?'

'You say you've taken this up with Mr Horsnby?'

'As I've said, I've spoken to him on other matters. This is an issue relating specifically to your firm. If you wish to contact Mr Hornsby, please do so.'

One of the best ways to stop someone from doing something is to tell them to do it. Though I knew it was a risk. My stomach clenched. I felt way out of practice.

'Hold on a moment.'

Vivaldi again. Someone must have thought it made the firm seem sophisticated. Like you were supposed to believe they always had classical music playing around the office. Why not let the folks calling in enjoy it as well? He came back on the line.

'Mr Acquillo. I have time in the morning.'

I interrupted him.

'It'll have to be afternoon.'

'I'm not sure about that, could you hold again?'

Checking with his secretary or his nervous system. I couldn't tell which.

'That's fine. How about two?'

'Sounds fine.'

I wanted to tell him he should've dated Jackie Swaitkowski, but instead I hung up the phone and looked over at Eddie. What was I going to do with him? Then I wondered if the Grand Prix would overheat in traffic. And if I had any clean khakis, much less a decent shirt. I'd been improvising on the phone. Hadn't really thought everything through.

'So, man,' I asked Eddie. 'Ever been to the Apple?'

I FOUND some clean khakis, an ironed shirt, and a fresh thermostat for the Grand Prix, which I installed that morning. Then I showered and shaved and got dressed. I had a tattered plaid tie I'd brought back from an engineering conference in Edinburgh in the early eighties which went okay with a Harris Tweed I wore when I went out to hit tennis balls around for Eddie. The elbows were about to bust through, but I couldn't help that.

I hadn't driven any further west than Hampton Bays for over four years. It felt surprisingly strange to contemplate a drive all the way to Manhattan. What was I thinking?

On the way out of town I stopped at a pet supply store in the Village and bought a leash and harness for Eddie. I put it on and practiced walking him around in the parking lot. When I'd sprung him from animal rescue they told me he was about a year and a half old. The vet confirmed this, and said he looked well cared for. So it was possible that he'd worn a leash once before, though I didn't know that until I tried to put it on him.

He looked a little confused by the harness, but once we started walking around the asphalt he seemed to understand the concept. I can't say he liked it, but he was willing to put up with it. I didn't think I had a choice, given where we were going.

Once I had the window open and we were blasting along Sunrise Highway he didn't seem to care. I'd picked up a large Cinnamon Hazelnut at the gas station, which I hoped would get me through Suffolk County. All the traffic was heading the other way – an endless caravan of tradesmen's vans and pickups and customized Japanese economy cars filled with Hispanic day-workers in sweatshirts and baseball caps. And SUVs and newer cars bringing in the professionals and sales clerks who lived up island where you could still afford to buy a house.

Route 27 was now a four-lane highway all the way to the hookup with the Southern State. The time it saved seemed futuristic. I remember my father driving us back to the Bronx for the weekend, the endless stop and go, the lights and strip development. He'd always remind us that it took four hours when he was a kid.

When there was a lot of traffic he'd often just pull over to the shoulder and pass everybody, occasionally bumping the curb, blasting the horn and yelling at the other drivers like it was all their fault. My mother would sit motionless, my sister and I huddled in silence in the backseat. He seemed to be able to do this without ever being stopped by the police. Just when you thought the tension was about to burst open your skull he'd turn on the radio and start singing along with Paul Anka or the Ronettes. That always put a weird kink in the already psychotic mood inside the car.

I was playing whatever jazz I could get as I moved through successive PBS broadcast territories. Somewhere near the border with Nassau County they petered out and I had to settle for road noise and the basso profundo vibrations coming from the Grand Prix's exhaust system. I stopped once more to resupply coffee and give Eddie a chance to pee. The strange smells of the place got him all worked up. He was a little hard to control, the harness notwithstanding. I had to dig a wad of gum out of his jaws that he pulled off the pavement before I had a chance to stop him.

'Obviously not a city dog.'

I took the Cross Island up to the Long Island Expressway which took me to the Midtown tunnel, and subsequently to the thirty-storey building near Grand Central Station that housed Litski, Goethles and Johnson. There was a little bunch-up at the tunnel, but the Grand Prix's cooling system showed remarkable restraint, and once I was in Manhattan, everything worked right to specs. I congratulated myself for doing the shocks and struts earlier that year. Still, you wouldn't have picked a '67 Pontiac Grand Prix as the ideal city runabout. I was starting to get a little seasick, but Eddie was distracted by Manhattan's assault on the senses. I rolled the window down so he could stick his head out.

'Don't pick any fights. It's a tough town.'

I sampled a half-dozen parking garages until I found one with a wide enough entry to accommodate the Grand Prix.

'Ya can't leave the dog in'na car.'

'I'm not.'

'Twe'ny dollas. Leave the keys.'

The way Eddie erupted from the car terrified a tiny Oriental couple who were waiting at the cashier's office. I tried to reassure them, but Eddie had already moved on to the sidewalk. He raced from pant leg to lamppost to hydrant in a state of olfactory frenzy until I pulled him up short with the leash. I hated to do it, but I had to grab him by the muzzle, and look into his big round brown eyes.

'Knock it off. They'll think you're a tourist.'

That settled him down, and after he peed on a few things, including a stack of the *New York Post* bundled up next to a kiosk, he slowed to a more comfortable pace.

Litski, Goethles and Johnson had only one floor of the building. The guy at the security desk in the lobby was a little unsure about their dog policy.

'They're waiting for him,' I told him. 'Has to do a deposition.'

'Deposition. No shit.'

We took the elevator up to the seventeenth floor. It opened on somebody's den, complete with bookcases, easy chairs and a fireplace. Plus a mahogany desk with a woman working at a black computer terminal. She wore dark blue.

'Well hello, fella. Aren't you cute.'

Women are always telling him that. Probably explains his high self-esteem.

'I'm here to see Hunter Johnson. Two o'clock appointment.'

'He's expecting you. Can I get you anything?'

'A cup of coffee would be great. And a little water for the dog.'

Eddie was panting, but in control of himself. The china bowl she brought was a little small, so half the water slopped on to the carpet. The woman in blue took it all in stride.

Johnson came out at the stroke of two. He was movie star handsome, with a smooth tan complexion, full head of wavy brown hair and clear blue eyes. True to his press. His handshake was firm and dry. His suit expensive. He lit up when he saw Eddie.

'I didn't know you brought co-counsel,' he said, roughing up Eddie's head. 'A mix, right? Setter-lab?'

'Name's Eddie. Origins a mystery.'

'Who's a good boy? Hey, there's a good boy. How 'bout the ears, how 'bout a little scratch . . .'

Eddie ate it up. Their display of mutual admiration lasted so long I started to feel forgotten. I made a little noise.

'So, Sam, let's go find a room. Bring your friend.'

The office area behind reception was built out with raised paneling and thick moulding, all painted a soothing off-white. The carpet was deep forest green and lint free. It was virtually silent.

We settled in a conference room next to his office. More books and high-back chairs, tea sets and original oil paintings. Abby would know if the pieces were authentic or the overall design true to form. You could rate it by how hard she tried to hide the sneer.

Johnson took off his jacket before he sat down, so I did the same. I put a yellow pad, a stack of loose papers from my Regina file and a plain white envelope face down on the table in front of me. He looked down at the envelope then back at me.

'So, what can I help you with?'

I liked him a lot better in person than over the phone. I think I would even without Eddie to break the ice.

'I'm not a lawyer, I'm an engineer. I was appointed administrator by Suffolk County, so sorry if I don't know how this stuff works.'

'I think I explained estate planning isn't within our expertise.'

'That's right. But zoning is.'

'You'd mentioned you had information that might be important to our firm.'

'If you could help me with the protocol.'

'Certainly.'

'I told you this was sensitive. In a moment you'll understand why.'

I tapped the white envelope, then pulled my hand away when he caught me doing it. He still looked relaxed, but caution was forming in the air.

'You have my attention.'

I took a breath.

'Okay, say I accidentally discovered there was a criminal act committed during the course of Bay Side's development efforts, is that something I should talk to you about, or Milton Hornsby, or should I just go to the police?'

I'd spent a lot of time with lawyers when I was running my company's technical services division. We had a complicated array of scary legal threats, like product liability, patent infringement, unfair trade practices, environmental compliance, as well as the usual human resources and regulatory hazards that stalk every operation. I liked our lead corporate guy. Unlike his boss, Mason Thigpen, he had a degree in engineering. And a sense of humour, which meant he had a little perspective and imagination. One thing he taught me was what you say or don't say, when and where, what you do or don't do, how you do it and why, are all perceived in the legal world through a filter that is entirely invisible to the rest of us, and entirely outside normal intuition. What they can't see is a straight ball right up the middle.

'And this involves our firm?' he asked in carefully measured tones.

'I don't think so. But I don't know.'

'This is also likely beyond our purview.'

'You're probably right, but here's my problem. I've tried to speak with Milton Hornsby about this, and he won't do it. So I asked this lawyer friend of mine if I can make Hornsby talk to me, and my friend says no. So, I talk to Hornsby's lawyer, Jackie Swaitkowski, and of course she's bound by attorney-client privilege, so she can't help me. The only guy left, who I know is connected with this thing, is you. If you can't help me, I don't know what's next.'

Johnson was studying me like a shrink. Looking for signs of underlying truth. Something to tell him to either throw me out or keep me talking.

'I'm sorry,' he said, 'but I'm having difficulty connecting our work on a straightforward zoning appeal in Southampton with some sort of criminality, which you haven't specified or revealed in any way.'

'Yeah, I know.'

'And further, why, if you believe there's been illegality, you haven't already contacted the police.'

'That's the other problem. I'm not sure about that part, either.'

Before he could say anything I said, 'As you know, Bay Side Holdings is part of a trust, Bay Side Trust.'

'We were retained by Bay Side Holdings,' said Johnson.

'Right. But as I see it, the only people who really matter in this are the guys who actually own all that property, along with whoever's controlling the trust. Which could be the same, for all I know. The beneficiaries, and those with fiduciary responsibility. Am I seeing this right?'

Johnson brought Eddie into the conversation for the first time. 'I think your master is trying to score a little free legal advice.'

We all grinned at each other.

'Actually, my lawyer friend's already offered. It's just, before I ask him, I'm seeing if you can help me out.'

'Is that what you're doing, Sam?'

'Yeah, he's a big-time guy. It's embarrassing to ask for favours.'

'I still don't see what sort of favour you're asking of me.'

'Who are they?'

'Who?'

'Who runs the trust?' I asked.

'The trustee?'

'Yeah. And for whom?'

Johnson readjusted himself in the big chair, which had a back that went up way past his head. Made it harder to shoot him from behind.

'I can't help you. I don't know.'

'Who besides Milton Hornsby?'

'You still haven't given me a sense of this alleged criminality.'

'He's the only one you know? Him and Jackie?'

He lifted his hands, resigned to his state of ignorance. We sat quietly for a moment, letting a little dead air fill the room. Stalemate.

'Who's your friend?' Johnson asked, finally. 'With the free advice?'

'Burton Lewis. You know him?'

Johnson actually sat up a little in the tall leather chair. It made me feel bad to use Burt's name, but I knew he wouldn't mind. Though my soul didn't feel much improved for it.

'Big time indeed.'

I started to gather up my stuff.

'I appreciate your fitting me in. I'm sure you're busy.'

He watched me stand without getting up himself. His expression, always neutral, gave a little.

'You realise I'm constrained by the same attorney-client privilege as Ms. Swaitkowski,' he said.

I stopped messing with my stuff and sat back down.

'Sure.'

'As is Mr Hornsby. It's an essential ethical principle.'

'I'm getting that.'

'In fact, it's about the highest level of trust imposed on all legal representatives. On par with the fiduciary duty required of a trustee, though that person needn't be a lawyer. The law is very clear on the magnitude of that responsibility.'

'Okay.'

'So, if, for example, Mr Hornsby were both an attorney, and a trustee, you might say he's in a double bind. It would explain perfectly, if that were the case, why he'd be unwilling to discuss anything related to Bay Side Holdings with you. Or anyone else. If that were the situation he faced, which I'm not suggesting it is.'

'It's a hypothetical.'

'Call it a lesson in law, which is free. Actual advice I charge for. My partners insist on it.'

'That's really interesting. I still like learning things, even at my age.'

'If there was any question over Mr Hornsby's competence to do his job, to preserve the body of the trust, there'd be grounds to take some action on the part of the beneficiaries.'

'Whoever they are.'

'Or, civil authorities could intervene on the beneficiaries' behalf, if there was clear evidence the fiduciary duty was being neglected or abused.'

'Hypothetically.'

'In Mr Hornsby's case. We're simply discussing the issue in global terms.'

'As part of the lesson.'

'Exactly. Mr Lewis would tell you the same if you asked.'

'Got it.'

He looked at his watch.

'And that's about all the legal training I can afford to put in today. Unless there was something else.'

'That's up to you.'

'I think I've exhausted my ability to help.'

'I appreciate it.'

I stood up again and went through the routine of gathering my papers. As before, Johnson kept his seat.

'As I recall,' he said, 'you had something to show me.'

He nodded at the papers I was stacking together.

'I did?'

'The envelope?'

On my way out that morning I'd grabbed a handful of un-opened mail off the kitchen table. I hadn't bothered to look at the one I'd picked for a prop. I flipped it over. It was my monthly statement from Harbor Trust.

'Oh, this.'

I dropped it face up on the table. He reached over and picked it up.

'Cute.'

Not really, I was about to say when he said, 'I get the point.'

'Not too subtle?' I asked, hoping the point would come to me as well in the next few seconds.

He looked amused.

'Well, I've never known a financing source who wasn't a ball of nerves over a big development. Could give you some leverage with Mr Hornsby. Not that I'm suggesting that.'

'Another lesson?'

'Not in ethics. Their interest is strictly money. No moral conflicts there.'

'I guess you'd consider the Bay Side plan pretty big.'

'For Harbor Trust. At least for the branch office in Southampton. Huge would be a better word.'

'Impress the hell out of the home office.'

'Oh yeah,' said Johnson, finally getting up to steer me back out of his office and, with any luck, out of his life, 'Roy Battiston would sell his soul to get that thing back on track.'

I WAS tempted to stop at a place I knew in Tribeca that had been there since before the revival, where I knew they'd welcome dogs who had the right introduction; but I also knew I'd get to talking and probably drink too much, and probably insist on driving home, then maybe kill us both or somebody else on the way back to the East End. It didn't seem fair to Eddie to risk it. So instead, I retrieved the Grand Prix and beat it out of there before the really big commute got underway. I followed the same route home, which was fairly unimpeded after dropping down to the Southern State and making a beeline for the Sunrise Highway.

Night fell before we made it to the cottage. Eddie was ecstatic to be back on terra firma. While he ran reconnaissance I filled my big aluminium tumbler with Absolut and parked myself outside on one of the Adirondack chairs. It was cold, but my RISDE sweatshirt, vodka and cigarettes kept me warm.

For some reason, I felt all jammed up around my chest and throat. I was hoping the vodka would loosen things up. It was a prodigal feeling, one I remembered from the past, but hadn't felt for years. I didn't like it. Too close to home, too much like everything I never wanted to feel again.

The wind off the Peconic was sharp on my face. Only eighty miles from Manhattan, but the climate was ten degrees colder and heavy with wet, salty air. The water was black slate, not a trace of colour. The wind blew from the west, but the surf was moving straight into it from the east. The resulting collision clipped the tops off the little bay waves, shooting foamy white water off the crests in little bursts of spray.

'Goddammit,' I said to the Little Peconic, who offered nothing in return.

CHAPTER SEVEN

I'd fallen asleep in the Adirondack chair, so it took me a while to figure out where I was, much less realise there was somebody using a flashlight to poke around Regina's house. Eddie was standing next to the chair, growling.

I put Eddie in the house, closed the basement door and retrieved the Harmon Killebrew bat from next to the side door. Then I opened the trunk of the Grand Prix and took out my big Maglite, a club in itself. I tucked the white collar of my shirt down into the RISDE sweatshirt and strolled over toward Regina's.

The tumbler of Absolut was clogging my brain and weighing on my limbs. I shook my head to clear it out. I stopped for a second to make sure I had my balance. Good enough. I got a firm grip on the bat and walked as quietly as I could toward the house. The lights were out in the neighbourhood, but there was plenty of moonlight. My breath formed little clouds in the damp cold. The miniature waves of the Little Peconic were the only sound. Even the insects had all gone to bed. The light inside Regina's house flashed across a double window. The drapes were drawn, but I paused for a moment behind a big hydrangea in case I'd been seen. Nothing. I went on.

Like most of the houses on Oak Point, Regina's was a single-storey, asbestos-shingled bungalow. There were two ways out, the side and the back. The back of the house faced the driveway, so the choice was a toss up. I looked around for a car and saw something parked between a few of Regina's overgrown arborvitae, about five feet off the driveway. I got a little closer. Pickup truck. No black BMWs.

I took a chance and approached the pickup. It was empty. I stuffed the bat through my belt, took out the flashlight, leaned up against the front fender of the truck, and waited.

The wee hours of an October night on eastern Long Island are dank and quiet. I wondered if standing out there alone made any sense, armed with just a three-quarter baseball bat and a Maglite. I decided it made no sense at all. I thought about calling someone to come over and stand there with me. But I didn't know anyone well enough to bother at this time of night, except Joe Sullivan, and I didn't want to do that. He might not mind, but then I'd have to go all the way back to the house, wake him up, listen to his bullshit and nurture his dignity. It seemed like too much work. Better to just risk my life. Simpler that way.

I heard an occasional car out on Noyack Road. I watched a small plane flying overhead, probably headed for the airport in East Hampton. Probably some overachiever from the city, all tired out from playing hardball with the big boys. Getting ready to curl up in his 20,000 square foot hideaway by the sea.

A cat had a brief encounter with something in the woods a few doors down from Regina's. The sound prickled the hairs on the back of my neck. The light inside Regina's was in the kitchen. I saw a shadow pass in front of the window. Went nicely with the sound of the cat fight. I calmed myself and secured my footing.

The back door opened and a man, medium height and build, stepped out on the back stoop. He wore a short coat, cap and boots and was carrying a large shopping bag. I couldn't see much else in the low light.

I stepped away from the truck, a few feet from the driver's side door. I hoped I was completely hidden in shadow.

The guy stopped at the truck door and dug his left hand in his pocket for his keys. I walked up behind him, grabbed his right hand by the wrist, yanked it up behind his back and shoved him into the truck's left front fender. As I shoved him I twisted him around so his left hand was pinned against the truck body. His breath popped out in a surprised little whoof.

'One wiggle, and I'll break your arm,' I said into his ear.

'Fuck you, you fucking ass-wipe cocksucking motherfucker,' he said, whipping his head around. A tangled bunch of red hair popped out from under his cap.

'Jimmy Maddox, where *did* you get that mouth?'

'Let go and I'll show you.'

I let him go and dropped back a few steps, pulling the bat out of my belt.

'You're a dickhead, mister. You really are. You scared the shit out of me.'

'What's with the sneaking around?'

'I'm not sneaking.'

'Oh, really. Flashlight in the middle of the night.'

'I'm just here pickin' up some stuff.' He looked over at the Harmon Killebrew bat. 'Whattaya gonna do, club me?'

'Not yet.'

'I'm not doing anything wrong.'

I gestured with the stick.

'What's in the bag?'

He just looked at me.

'Who the fuck *are* you, anyway? Who made you such a big fucking deal?'

'Step away from the bag.'

Even in the low light, I could see him bunch his shoulders and lean forward, ready to launch. Indecision formed around him like a cloud.

'Don't do anything dumb, Jimmy. I'm really not in the mood.'

'It's just some shit from the house. She's not usin' it.'

'Why the late hour?'

'I was at my girlfriend's in the Village. I just stopped on the way back. I don't have to ask your fucking permission.'

'Well, actually, you do. I'm like the official guardian of Regina's stuff.'

'You're more like an official pain in my ass.'

I tapped him with the bat to move him out of the way. He moved a half-step, enough to let me pick up the bag. It was a doubled-up grocery store bag with handles. It was heavy.

'What do you got in here, Regina's barbells?'

'Fuck you.'

'You should work on the invective, Jimmy. It's tiresome.'

As I talked I went through the bag. There were two folded towels on top. Underneath was a collection of kitchen utensils – knives, ladles, big spoons – and a pair of cast-iron frying pans, which explained all the weight.

'What's for dinner?'

He stuck his hands in his pockets and leaned up against the truck. He'd decided he was finished talking. But I hadn't.

'You know, I'll give you all this stuff, and more, if you just ask. You don't have to sneak around.'

'I wasn't sneaking.'

'What's this? A sentimental journey?'

'Just stuff I need. I didn't know you could hand it over.'

'You just had to ask.'

'Well, I don't know about that kind of shit.'

I curled the top of the bag over and stuffed it under my arm.

'It's all yours, Jimmy, but I'm not gonna give it to you now.'

'Why the fuck not?'

I used the bat to point to my cottage.

'Say, Jimmy, come over to my place and have a drink with me.'

I walked away and left him standing there by his truck. I could hear him snorting and shuffling his feet around in the grass.

'I want my stuff,' he called after me.

I kept walking.

'You'll get it. Come on and get a pop. Do you good.'

I walked the rest of the way without looking back. The night hadn't changed much in the last half-hour, but I was a lot more tired out. There's only so much adrenaline your body can soak up over a normal twenty-four hour period. I was starting to feel fuzzy with exhaustion. I unlocked the door and was about to push it in when Jimmy came up behind me.

'That's all you got? Soda pop?'

'Not soda pop. A pop. A drink. I got anything you want. Beer?'

I parked the Harmon Killebrew bat next to the side door and let the scruffy jerk into my house. Eddie greeted him like a long lost friend. Big deal watchdog.

I got Jimmy a beer and showed him out to the porch. I sat him down, then went back to the bedroom to stow the bag. I tossed it on the floor of my closet and dumped my laundry on top. Guys don't like to touch other guy's dirty socks. I went back out to the porch, partly refilling the tumbler on the way, like I needed it.

'I didn't know you could see the water from this place,' Jimmy said when I came out on the porch.

'Sure. The sacred Peconic.'

'I thought it was the Little Peconic.'

'Yeah. That's right. The little one.'

'I don't know about religious stuff.'

'How's the beer?'

'It's all right.' He took a sip. 'Why're you driving that old Pontiac?

Can't afford a new car?'

'Came with the house.'

'Can't see driving some old piece of shit like that.'

'That's 'cause you never drove one. Try it once,' I snapped my fingers, 'you never go back.'

'Yeah, bullshit.'

It was clear over the Peconic, and colourless under the brilliant moon. Night was locked in solid. I started to fantasize about pillows and blankets. Jimmy looked all settled in with his beer.

'You're not gonna give me my shit, are you?'

'Not now. Later. I promise.'

'You're some kind of strange fucker.'

'Glad you noticed, Jimmy. It usually takes people longer to figure that out.'

He was content to drink his beer and pet Eddie's head. Every asshole in the world seemed to be a dog lover. I wondered what that said about me.

'Jimmy, do you remember your Aunt Regina's husband?'

He looked at me blankly.

'What're you trying to do now?'

'Nothing. I'm just curious about her husband. I'm having trouble remembering him.'

'I can never tell whether you're bullshitting me or not.' He finished his beer and set it down on the table with more force than necessary. 'She didn't have no husband. Now, tell me you didn't know that.'

'I didn't know that.'

'What *do* you know, anyway?'

'Less than I should, I guess. When I was growing up my parents always acted like there was a Mr Broadhurst.'

'Jesus. You don't know shit.'

'So, okay, you got me again. Enlighten me.'

'Why should I tell you anything?'

'Aw Christ, Jimmy, give it a break. I gave you a beer. And I'm gonna give you all kinds of stuff from Regina's house.' I took a sip of the Absolut. 'Eventually.'

Jimmy thought about it for a few moments. Anger and defiance are tough habits to break.

'My mom told me she called herself Mrs Broadhurst because she didn't want guys hittin' on her, if you can believe that. A million years ago she had a guy, but it wasn't her husband. Carl something.'

'Carl? You sure?'

'Yeah. Fuckin' Carl. I never seen him, but my mother'd talk about him.'

'Carl Bollard?'

'Yeah, that's it. Carl Bollard. Owned that piece of shit factory over there, was what my mom told me. She was wicked pissed about the whole thing, my mom. I don't know why. Fuckin' women always pissed about everything. You can't ever figure out why. She was a lot younger than Aunt Regina, even though she died a lot sooner.'

His voice fell away at the end of the sentence. He picked up his empty beer to cover the moment.

''Nother one?'

'Sure.'

I got it for him. I sat at the table and slid over his beer.

'Carl Junior or Carl Senior?' I asked him.

'Shit, I don't know. Carl Bollard's all I know. He didn't have a wife, just a bunch of girlfriends all over. If he'd been married my mom would've disowned Regina, if you can do that to your sister. My mom was into religion. Fuckin' Presbyterian, you'd think she was Catholic the way she went on.'

It did the kid a lot of good to see me surprised, so I saw no harm in digging in deeper.

'Jimmy, you told me Regina didn't own her house, that it went back to some fucker after she died. Were you talking about Carl Bollard?'

'Yeah, of course. That's why my mom was so rip-shit.'

'Let me get this straight. Are you telling me that wiry old broad was Carl Bollard's kept woman?'

'That's not the way my mom would've put it. Religious or not.'

I laughed. That ornery, flinty old harpy was Carl Bollard's honey bee. His mistress – wanton and alluring. And in return, a house of her own? Maybe. Complete with the dubious gift of the Acquillos to look after her, put up with her crap, pull her busted body out of the bathtub and plant her in the ground. For the first time I truly missed my mother. I finally had some news worth telling her.

Jimmy was laughing, too.

'Aunt Regina fuckin' some old guy for a free house.'

We just sat there and laughed for a long time. It felt good.

When we were done laughing, Maddox left and I fell back on the bed and crawled under the covers, still dressed, tapped out and supine before life's hallowed irregularities.

THE NEXT day I drove over to Sagaponack to look at the ocean. Normally, staring at the Little Peconic helped me think. I needed something bigger this morning to stare at. Something with a horizon that curved off into infinity.

The Atlantic Ocean was looking big and moody, and unconcerned with my fears and compulsions. There was an offshore breeze, so the waves were neatly formed and evenly spaced. The surf was taller than normal, probably from a storm out at sea. I looked for surfers, but saw none. The beach was empty in all directions except for seagulls, sandpipers, and dead horseshoe crabs.

The sky was big and the wind hard. We were almost past hurricane season, but this time of year almost anything could piss off the Atlantic. It was vast and dangerous and unknowable. I got out of the car and went and sat on the beach to watch the early hour sun warm the colour of the sand and turn the saltwater an inky blue.

Billy Weeds and I once went bodysurfing right after a big storm. The day was dry and washed clean by the Canadian air that often swept down to push tropical storms out to sea before they could crash into Long Island. The full weight of the storm missed us, but its energy had thrust up gigantic waves that broke over sandbars a quarter mile off the coast. It took us a half-hour to fight through the messy chop close to shore to reach the real action.

We eventually met mountainous swells coated in foam that broke in twenty feet of water, creating impossibly enormous waves which we rode for an hour, heedless and awestruck, oblivious to the risk. We were young, strong and stupid, and I will always remember Billy laughing hysterically at the craziness of it all, and the angry power of the ocean that was too involved with its own majesty to bother drowning us like it should have. When we decided we'd had enough, we tried to swim to shore, but we couldn't get past the undertow. We kept getting knocked back into the surf. It took another hour to get all the way in, and only because we'd ridden the current all the way to the Shinnecock inlet where the undertow let go.

After that, I knew it was possible to die. The lesson didn't stick as well with Billy Weeds.

I WAS only a few blocks away from Burton's house, so I could honestly say I was in the neighbourhood. I pulled up to the gate and pushed the call button on the intercom. Isabella was her regular welcoming self.

'He's working in his study.'

'Can you tell him I'm here?'

'If you want.'

'Yeah, why not? Since I'm out here at the gate.'

'Okay. Up to you.'

The giant blue hydrangeas that lined the long driveway had turned brown from the frost. A crew of landscapers were cleaning things up, trimming bushes and raking out the white pebble road surface. They admired the Grand Prix as I passed by, I could tell.

Burton met me at the door.

'Sam, excellent timing. Saved me from my work.'

'So Isabella said.'

'Let's go sit.'

He led me down a long corridor, through a sitting room and out to a screened-in porch. A porch like mine only ten times bigger and furnished to look like the British Raj. Lots of teak lounge chairs with built-in cupholders and magazine racks, woven foot stools and grass mat carpets.

There was always some place new at Burton's house to sit. I wondered how he kept track.

It was only about ten-thirty in the morning, too early even for Burton and me. So he called Isabella on his cell phone and asked for someone to bring us alcohol-free mimosas.

'Provide the illusion.'

While waiting we quickly covered the baseball situation, which meant a general agreement over the appalling inferiority of every team that's ever competed with the Yankees, including those guys who also played somewhere on Long Island. Apparently they were both in the World Series.

'Their stadium is in Queens, I think,' said Burton. 'I really don't know.'

'The boys lost last night. So it's two-one.'

'Piffle.'

We also reviewed prospects for the NBA season, in which Burton took a far greater interest. He had a box at the Garden, away from the celebrities to avoid TV exposure. I used to join him every once in a while.

'We should do that again,' he said. 'I've refurbished the box.'

I looked around the screened-in porch.

'Teak?'

'Something more appropriate to the setting.'

Isabella showed up leading another woman holding a tray with the drinks, a basket of croissants and some fresh fruit. She hung around to convey her general disapproval of me until Burton managed to shoo her away.

'So, Sam. I have some information. Not a lot.'

'Me, too. A fair amount.'

'I received a message from an attorney named Hunter Johnson. Inquiring about you.'

'Checking my story.'

'I let it be known we were closely associated and left it at that. An assistant handled the communication.'

'I dropped your name so hard it busted the floor.'

'Hope it helped.'

'It did. I appreciate it.'

'Tell me what you've learned and I'll see if I can fill in the holes.'

So I went through everything I'd learned since he'd sailed over to the cottage. About Carl Bollard, Jr. and his girlfriend Regina. Julia Anselma's Bay Side house and tricked-out iron. Jimmy Maddox and his midnight raid. Jackie Swaitkowski's confessional. Harbor Trust and the Battistons. Even my encounter with the trained bear, which I'd left out of our last conversation.

'I'm not happy about that,' said Burton.

'No permanent damage. Nothing that shows, anyway.'

I told him about my meeting with Ross Semple and conversation with Joe Sullivan. And finally about the trip to New York to see Hunter Johnson in his opulent offices.

'Place is really plush, Burt. You should check it out.'

'I'm sure. Real estate practice,' he said, by way of explanation.

'So what do you think of all this?'

'You've been busy,' he said. 'I haven't much to add, except something on the trust.'

'You wouldn't happen to know the beneficiary?' I asked.

'Carl Bollard, of course.'

'Of course. Who's got to be pretty old at this point.'

'Would be, but he's dead.'

'Dead.'

'Died some time ago. 1977 to be exact. Alcoholism. Had a room at the Institute of Living in Hartford. Was there for one last try at sobriety.'

'So that's it for the trust. What happened to the assets? Who owns them now?'

'That's a very interesting question, Sam. We have no idea, and as far as my associates can tell, neither does anyone else. As it is, everything we have comes from a retired loan officer who reviewed the trust as part of a WB capitalization programme. This was back in the early fifties. Luckily, he still had his notes. You're going to find that most people involved in this are either long dead, or past the point of clear recollection.'

'What about Bollard's will? His heirs?'

'No heirs we know of. The trust was established by his father, Carl Senior, the year his mother died, leaving Carl Junior the sole heir. Within the trust were all the assets of Bay Side Holdings, which included WB Manufacturing, the real estate it sat on, plus contiguous properties around Oak Point and Jacob's Neck, corporate equity – basically the cash in the business, and a substantial investment account with a portfolio of bonds and securities. Carl Junior, who was an only child by the way, was the beneficiary, along with his father, until his father's death, which happened in 1950. Carl Junior also worked at WB in a succession of jobs typical of a young scion being groomed for succession. The trust at first glance looked like a typical tax vehicle used for estate management and the fluid transfer of corporate authority from one generation to the next. But it was clear to me, having some experience with these things, that it was also meant to keep young Carl in control while the father lived, and out of trouble once he died.'

'Meaning?'

'Meaning the trust was revocable during the old man's life, then unmodifiable for five years after that. Carl Junior got the benefit of the income, but he couldn't touch the business itself until 1955, when he was forty-six years old.'

'Arnold Lombard said he was a wasteabout.'

'That would follow. His father made the calculation that after five years on his own his son should be ready to accept responsibility. If not, then to hell with it. This is a very common practice in family situations.'

'So you're saying that since, what, 1977, all that stuff's just been sitting there, nobody owning it but a piece of paper? That's nuts.'

'Yes, nuts and illegal, and entirely out of the question.'

'Okay. Keep explaining.'

'The trust was formed in 1948 in conjunction with the wills written for both Carls. Also very common. These I have. Carl Senior's we already know. Carl Junior's says when he dies, the assets of the trust flow to his heirs and assigns, as designated in the trust. It doesn't say anything about what would happen if he had no heirs or assigns beyond his father, who would get everything back if he died young. In which case Carl Senior could nullify the trust and move on with his life, all of which is purely academic at this point since that didn't happen.'

'But Carl Junior had no heirs.'

'I said heirs, not assigns.'

'I presume an assign is just that. Somebody you say is an heir.'

'Exactly. That's what we don't know, because we don't have the trust document itself. Wills have to be registered on the death of the signer. Not trusts. Once Carl Junior was free of the restrictions, he could modify the trust any way he wanted. It became his trust, just like it was his father's before him.'

'We got to have a chat with Mr Hornsby.'

'We do indeed.'

I stood up and walked over to the screen to look at the outside. The lawn stretched away for a few hundred yards, terminating at a tall privet hedge. The ocean was one estate away. Burton's great-grandfather determined it was better to have twenty acres of developed real estate and landscaping between you and a big storm surge than a flimsy dune, and he was proved right in '38 when the next-door neighbour washed out to sea with his whole family and fourteen friends who'd driven out from the city to watch the spectacle.

'You got a theory here, Burt?' I asked him as I finished off my second emasculated mimosa. Burton was still in his chair, pensive and removed. I sat back down next to him.

'I do. But it's full of holes.'

'Me, too.'

'You know what might be happening here.'

'I do. It's just hard to believe.'

'One of my law professors had a maxim. Just because you think it's true, doesn't mean it isn't.'

'Must have shaved with Occam's razor.'

'Sharpest blade in the drawer.'

We went back to the NBA after that, which was a big relief to me. I knew and Burton knew that the best thing to do at this point was to hand it all over to him, so he could hand it all over to the people officially responsible for this stuff. He knew and I knew I didn't want that. I had my teeth in it now and I didn't want to let go till I had it worked out. I just didn't. Can't explain it.

'I hate to owe people, you know that. But I'm glad for the help,' I told him before I got up to leave.

'Piffle,' he said, and took me on the long walk to my car.

I headed back to the cottage with both windows open to help fuel my brain. The cool, soggy October air was uncomfortable, but extra oxygen helped me focus. It was a practice I learned young. To get in a car, open all the windows and drive fast enough to fill the passenger compartment with a private hurricane. I could think better when other things overwhelmed my senses. Sometimes I'd drive home from work like this, even in the dead of winter, and when I reached my driveway I'd keep driving, and use up an hour or two buffeting my brain into submission.

Abby never asked where I'd been. She was never concerned when I failed to show up, or when I worked through evenings and weekends. Her indifference to my presence was one of the things I most appreciated. It gave me the freedom to distract myself with aimless open-air driving, or raging, drunken road trips across Greater New York with my sparring partners from the gym, or obsessive attempts at mastering some arcane scientific principle, or months of near catatonia, in which I'd descend into my own customized well of despair. Through it all Abby tended the house, maintained the proper social connections, shopped and calmly raised our daughter.

I skated across the years of my marriage like an ice sled – moving at blurred speed, barely touching the surface. The weeks were filled with boiling tension and anxiety, the weekends lost on fatuous conversations and alcohol. Through it all I never once felt like my wife knew who she was married to. As she surrounded us with a gaggle of nitwit acquaintances, I was condemned to an ugly loneliness of the mind.

I stopped at the cottage to check on Eddie. He was sleeping on the landing at the top of the side door steps. He wagged his tail without bothering to get up.

'Calm down there, boy, you're gonna hurt something.'

I made a pot of coffee, gathered up my Regina file and spread it out on the porch table. The air was cool, but the coffee kept my fingers warm as I leafed through the papers.

I was looking at all the words and notes, the real estate documents and other stuff I'd collected, but it wasn't registering. I wasn't really reading, just scanning with my eyes. What I wanted to know wasn't there, so it felt pointless to look. But I looked anyway, out of habit, an engineer's obsession with data gathering.

Eddie made himself comfortable on the bed. I tried to talk it out with him, but he wanted to sleep. All I got was an occasional raised head and a wagging tail. No analysis or conclusions.

At the bottom of the file were the old photographs I swiped out of the display case at the old WB. One was an eight-by-ten-inch black and white print. The setting was ambiguous, maybe a conference room at the plant, or a meeting room at a local restaurant or hotel. There were about ten men standing shoulder to shoulder. The shot was a little overexposed, and sepia tinted with age, but you could easily make out everyone's face. I was intrigued by the conformity of their clothes and haircuts, the homogeneity of their skin, the sureness in their eyes.

On the floor was a banner, mounted on rigid backing so it could stand supported at their feet. It read 'WB Bomb Squad.' Then underneath, in much smaller type, 'Management Defence Team.'

The word management caused me to flip it over and look at the back. Neatly penned along the bottom were the names and titles of all the men in the photo. Beginning with Carl Bollard, Jr., President and CEO. To his left was Milton Hornsby, Exec. V.P., Chief Financial Officer. All the way at the other end was Robert Sobol, Q.C. Director. A red stamp from the photo processor showed the date to be 1970.

I looked at the back of the bowling photo, but it was unmarked except for the processor's stamp with the date, 1972.

'Attorney Swaitkowski's office.'

'You must be Judy.'

'The same.'

'Is Jackie around?'

'She is. You want to talk to her?'

'I do.'

'Okay, so give me your number, I'll have her call you back.'

'Interesting.'

'It's how she likes to do it. She's got her quirks, but she's cute, don't you think?'

'Cuter than me.'

'Send me your pictcha. I'll decide for myself.'

I gave her my name and number, then hung up and waited for Jackie to call me back, which she did, about ten minutes later.

'He won't talk to me,' she said as she came on the line.

'Who?'

'Milton Hornsby. I called him a few times, sent over a registered letter, even went and rang his bell. Nothing.'

'But he was there?'

'He was there, he just told me to go away. I think it was something like, go away or I'll have you prosecuted for harassment, or something like that. So I thought, what am I doing here? I was going to call you, but you didn't give me a number.'

'What are you doing right now?'

'Talking to you.'

'Want to take a ride?'

'Where we going?'

'I'm going to Hornsby's house. I can't wait anymore. I think it's better if you were there. For his sake and mine.'

'You going to tell me why? "No",' she answered for me.

'He might have fired you, but he'll want you there when I talk to him, which I'm doing even if I have to yell through the door.'

'I was actually heading to the courthouse. Can it wait an hour?'

'I'm going now.'

'You could use a little more give.'

'I'm sorry, you're right. I'll be at Hornsby's house in about forty-five minutes. Hope to see you there.'

'Man.'

Eddie heard the jingle of keys and ran to the door. I felt like a heel leaving him, but I needed my concentration and Jackie Swait-kowski was distraction enough. I closed the basement door so he couldn't use the hatch. I needed to know someone in this world was safe, at least for a few hours.

Forty-five minutes was more than I needed to get to Sag Harbor, but it gave Jackie a little leeway. I took my time heading north on Noyac Road and chose the long way to town, following Long Beach as it curved gracefully around the east side of Noyac Bay.

The signs of late afternoon were already in the sky. A cluster of thick clouds along the western horizon were lit from below in a soft gold that reminded me of Maxfield Parrish. The water was roughed up by a steady westerly breeze, the air cold and wet coming off the bay, contrasting with the deep colour saturation from the lowering sun. Time was running out on the season.

Construction was underway on the Sag Harbor bridge, so I had to wait in a line of cars before I could cross. That ate up more time than I allotted, so when I finally got to Hornsby's Jackie was already there. She was standing next to her Toyota pickup, talking on a cell phone. She wore a loose, deconstructed silk jacket, white cotton sweater, a knit wool skirt that stopped well above her knees, and heels that extended her legs by a few hundred miles. Her thick blond hair, brushed into large waves, was pulled back from her face with a flowered headband. She wore lipstick that matched her sunglasses, the kind you only find in places like Venice, California. She looked like a million bucks.

She clicked the cell phone closed as I approached, and said, 'Don't start.'

'What.'

'Whatever you were going to say.'

'About what?'

She put a hand on her hip and did a little bump.

'You know, the girly clothes.'

'I know better. I got sensitivity training.'

She snorted.

'There's money well spent.'

'Is he here?'

'Haven't checked. I honestly just got here. Can you give me something to work with?'

'Hornsby has something I need to see. I can't ask for it, because he won't talk to me. Which makes me want to see it even more.'

'What?'

'Hornsby's the trustee of a trust that owns Bay Side Holdings. That makes the beneficiary the developer. Your ex-client. I need to talk to him. Or them.'

'I'm not big on trusts, or estates, but I don't see a connection between rental property and a dead woman.'

'That's exactly the point.'

'What is?'

'She's dead.'

I walked away from her to avoid more questions. I hoped she'd follow.

Hornsby's car was still in the driveway. Jackie joined me as I walked up the path and rang the bell.

'Did he answer the door last time?' I asked her.

'He yelled at me to go away. From the inside.'

I rang it again and called his name. Nothing.

'Let's check the back.'

'Huh?'

'Last I saw him he was working in his backyard,' I told her as I led her through the arborvitaes.

I yelled his name again as I walked around clusters of crowded shrubbery, through pachysandra and over balls of flowering mums. Jackie followed as best she could in her spiked heels.

'If I'd known we were on safari – '

We stood on the small patch of grass at the centre of the garden and looked around. She gripped my right bicep with both hands to keep from sinking into the moist soil.

'Must have flown the coop,' she said.

'Or he's hiding inside.'

I noticed there was a little footpath partially obscured by the draping branches of a big Norway maple, now mostly denuded of its bright yellow-orange leaves. I remembered Hornsby heading that way with his wheelbarrow after he told me to get lost.

'Let's look back there before I start yelling,' I said.

'If the cops show, you get your own counsel.'

The lot was much deeper than it looked, obscured by the dense foliage. The path threaded around bunches of overgrown forsythia, holly and bamboo. Mingled with the pungent odour of rotting leaves was the shoreline smell of Sag Harbor Bay, only a hundred feet away. Low tide.

The path opened into a clearing. Milton Hornsby was lying in the centre on another patch of grass. He was on his back with his legs stuck straight out. He was wearing the same clothes I'd seen him in before, but his face was less recognizable under all the blood. A Smith & Wesson .38 revolver, not unlike Sullivan's, was in his right hand. The top of his head was mostly gone. It looked like he must have done it lying down, through the mouth. Neater that way. Attached to his chest with a big safety pin was a blood-splattered five-by-seven-inch index card.

'Don't touch him,' said Jackie, through a clenched fist held to her mouth. 'What's the note say?'

'Go to hell.'

'Pardon me?'

'The note. That's what it says. "Go to hell."'

'Famous last words.'

'Or shipping instructions.'

'I called to say we were on our way. You and me together. I got his answering machine. Oh, man.'

The blood was bright red. Fresh.

'You have your cell phone?' I asked her, but she was already dialing. 'Wait,' I said.

She looked at me wide-eyed.

'I can't wait,' she yelled. 'I have to call right now.'

'I want to look in the house.'

'No.'

'It's probably in there.'

'No can do. That's an illegal act. Disbarment just for starters.'

She started dialing.

'You're his lawyer.'

'He fired me. Wouldn't do it anyway. I like you, Sam, but not that much.'

'Goddammit.'

'I can do it later if you give me a chance. Legally. I'll get permission to examine. To make sure everything's secure. Right now, we got much bigger fish to fry. Jesus, I can't believe this.'

I looked down at Hornsby. And his note.

'Same to you, you miserable, old . . .'

'Hey, hey, hey,' said Jackie, interrupting me, and taking my arm again, 'don't knock the dead. Crazy bad luck. Come on, walk me back to the house. I'm gonna get sick.'

As we walked I listened to her call the police.

'Sag Harbor have their own cops?' I asked.

'Of course.'

'What about the Town?'

'Depends on the case.'

When we reached the area behind the house, I checked the back door. Jackie shoved herself between me and the door handle.

'I swear to God, Sam,' she yelled, pushing on my chest.

'Take it easy. I'm not going in.'

She was breathing hard, looking frantic and furious. Seemed like the ideal time to ask for another favour.

'Could you call the Town cops? Have them relay a message to Officer Joe Sullivan. Tell him what happened – that I'm here with you.'

'What the hell for?'

'He'll want to know.'

'Friend of yours?'

'In a manner of speaking.'

'God knows you could use a few.'

Ten minutes later the street was full of cops stringing yellow tape and paramedics and investigators snapping on plastic gloves. Blue and white lights flashed from the rooftops of emergency vehicles, causing a strobe effect that made everyone's movements look stiff and artificial. The distorted blare of cranked-up two-way radios and small clumps of startled and curious neighbours completed the familiar scene.

Jackie and I sat on the tailgate of her pickup truck while a young lady cop took our statements. Jackie went first so she could essentially frame my story for me. Everything she said was true, and plausible, without saying anything we wouldn't want on the record. It was an impressive performance.

We were almost finished when Sullivan pulled up in his cruiser.

'Hi, Joe,' said the lady cop.

'Hi, Liz. Just dropping by. I know this guy,' he pointed at me.

'Hi, Joe,' I said. 'This is Attorney Jackie Swaitkowski.'

'Already got a lawyer?'

Jackie almost leaped off the tailgate in her haste to clarify.

'No, no, no. We came together on another matter. Officer Grady has all the information.'

Liz Grady jotted down a few more items then handed her casebook to Sullivan. He read it carefully while we sat there and waited. When he was done he tapped the palm of his hand with the book.

'So, Sam, you think it was suicide?'

'Doesn't look like anything else to me, but I'm no expert.'

'I mean, you might have a reason to know it's suicide.'

'Not for sure, but it's a pretty safe bet.'

'Good. Thanks.'

He put his hand on my shoulder.

'Hey, Sam, did I tell you I got that thing you were asking about?'

'No, you didn't.'

'I do. It's in my cruiser. Wanna take a look? Don't go anywhere,' he said to Jackie. 'We'll be right back.'

Jackie looked at me as if to say, which turnip truck do you think I just fell out of. Officer Grady went off to handle more official business.

'What the fuck,' said Sullivan when we got to his car.

'It's bad,' I said.

'So it's not a suicide.'

'It's definitely a suicide. That's what's bad.'

'We should investigate.'

'Absolutely.'

'So you're not sure.'

'I'm sure, but you want confirmation from the medical examiner.'

'So what's so bad?'

'Hornsby'd rather kill himself than talk to me.'

Sullivan spun half around on his heel.

'Jesus Christ, what are you saying?'

'You said you'd give me a couple weeks. It's only been a couple days.'

'That was before the dead body.'

I had trouble arguing with that.

'I called you right away.'

He jerked his head at Jackie Swaitkowski.

'What's with the mouthpiece?' he asked.

'She used to work for Hornsby. I thought if she was with me he might open up. That's all.'

'I got to know what's going on.'

'Okay, forget the two weeks. A couple more days is all I need.'

'To do what?'

'I don't know. I'm working on it.'

'What's "it"?' he almost shouted at me.

'Two more days.'

Sullivan nervously tucked in his shirt and ran both hands through his hair. Trying to get at least something in his life in proper order.

'I'm out of my fuckin' mind.'

Jackie was a little frosty when we got back to her.

'He didn't want to talk in front of Liz.'

'Right.'

She was mad at me, but she looked impossibly great sitting there on the tailgate of her beat-up old truck. In the midst of all the tensed-up cops and radio noise and otherworldly flashing lights, I had a clear vision of Jackie Swaitkowski, perennially in a state of man trouble. Dead husbands, bad boyfriends, married guys, an endless trail of disappointments, betrayals and thwarted expectations. The good guys will be inadequate, the bad boys destructive, the right ones taken. It won't be her fault. She'll just always be too good-looking, or not good-looking enough, too smart, too lazy or too strange.

'Listen, Joe. It seems to me you ought to take a look in that house before anything's disturbed. Especially since the back door is unlocked.'

'I can't believe it,' said Jackie.

'If you're concerned about it, Hornsby's lawyer here can go with you. Tag along.'

'I don't need that,' said Sullivan.

'No, I think you do. I think you want to ask her to come with you. And while you're checking around, Jackie can make sure all his files and office stuff is where it ought to be. In case there's a question later on.'

'You have *got* to be kidding me,' said Jackie again.

'You need to do it pretty soon.'

Jackie stuck her nose right up to my face. So close I could see she was turning red. She still looked good.

'Are you going to tell me what the hell is going on?'

'Then you can tell me,' Sullivan said to Jackie.

'I could tell you, but then you couldn't do it,' I said to Jackie. 'You know what I need.'

The two of them just stood there and looked at me for a painfully long time. Painful for me, anyway. I could feel all the muscles in my neck and back tighten up and that familiar sensation of a knife being thrust into my right eye. Just like being back at work. The ravages of wanting.

'Please,' I said to both of them.

They still didn't budge.

'Well, shit,' said Sullivan, finally, 'if you're gonna use the magic word,' and walked off toward the house.

Jackie started to follow him, shaking her head.

'Be careful,' I said.

She turned around and walked backwards as she spoke.

'You should get out of here. We'll meet later.'

'I'll call in a few hours.'

She walked a few more steps, then turned around again, pointing her finger at me.

'You're gonna owe me for the rest of your life.'

I knew she'd do it, though I felt bad about messing with her principles. When I was her age I always let principle overpower common sense. It's what you do when you're young and dumb. Before all the consequences of bitter experience pile up. And you become like Milton Hornsby, unable to outpace the hurts, sins and miscalculations you've let loose on the world, until they literally hound you to death – calling, writing, leaving messages on your answering machine.

THERE WAS some sort of big celebration going on at the Polish Church, so the parking lot at the Senior Centre was almost full. It was about four PM. I wondered what kind of hours Barbara Filmore kept.

The million-year-old woman was at her post at the front desk.

'Welcome.'

'Thank you. Is Barbara Filmore here?'

'The director?'

'That's the one.'

'No, she's not.'

'Not the director?'

'Not here.'

She tapped the counter above her desk a few times to cement the point.

'Who fills in for her on when she's gone?'

'She fills in for herself. She's just not here now.'

I let the logic of that one just float on by.

'Barbara has a friend, a guy named Bob Sobol. You see him around much?'

'Oh sure. He comes and takes her to lunch. He's sweet on her.'

'Does Bob hang around the place much, talk to everybody?'

She motioned me to come closer.

'Likes the cards,' she whispered. 'Handles 'em real slick.'

'How 'bout you? You play with him?'

She got coy.

'I just might. Been to the casinos. Know my way around a poker game.'

'I'll remember that.'

She waved that off, but liked it.

'How long's Barbara been seeing Bob?'

'You're a nosy newt.'

'Just curious. How long do you think?'

'I don't know. A long time. Two or three years, maybe more.'

Time had lost continuity for her. Too much had gone by unexamined.

'Been here playing cards ever since.'

'Every once in a while, that's right. Helps out with activities. Have I told you about the Oktoberfest? Lots of beer.'

'Maybe I'll check it out.'

'Lots of beer.'

'You remember Regina Broadhurst?'

'Oh sure. She's a great old gal.'

'You know she passed away.'

She looked confused for a moment.

'I suppose I did.'

'She ever play cards with Bob?'

She looked back toward the main room of the Centre where they served food and held activities. Looking for the answer.

'Oh, sure. Everybody plays with Bob. He's a kidder.'

'You like him, too.'

'Oh sure. Everybody loves a kidder. Of course, everybody's so nice here. There're always nice to me, all the people.'

'That makes you a great old gal yourself.'

She stared up at me for a moment, working her jaw side-to-side like a cow with her cud.

'Bullshit'll work on almost anybody, mister.'

We parted happy.

I STILL had a little time left in the day and was too keyed up to go back to the cottage. I thought about heading directly to the Pequot, but I wanted to keep my head clear for Jackie later on. I thought of one more stop I could make.

The Village municipal offices on Main Street were set to close in ten minutes. I ran down the stairs and got to the double glass doors just as the Records Department battleaxe was about to shut down. Keys were poised before the lock. I tapped my wrist where a watch would have been if I wore one, then pointed at the hours painted on the glass door.

'I'm really sorry,' I said to her as she opened the door a crack, 'I just need one little thing. Take you two seconds.'

She opened the door the rest of the way and trudged back to her post behind the counter.

'Computer's logged off for the night,' she said to me, to kick things off.

'Here's what I need,' I said, as I dashed off the address on a slip of scratch paper and slid it across the counter, 'This file. Specifically the purchase history. Before the '57 re-zoning.'

'That's in the dated stacks.'

'That's right, that's why I'm here. Just bring me the whole file. I'll dig out what I need.'

She probably wanted to put up more of a fight, but it was late, she was tired, and I'm sure I had a determined look about me. She capitulated with token resistance.

'No time to make copies.'

'I just need to take a look.'

As she walked away she said, 'At four-thirty the door's locked.'

As it turned out it took her a lot longer than that to locate the file. When she got back to the counter her battering ram hairdo had come a little loose and dust smudges were all over her dress. I was making a lot of friends today.

'Here,' she dropped the file in front of me, 'I already put the purchase history on top. Pull out what you need, I can make copies tomorrow.'

She'd chosen a new tack. Grace in defeat.

I read the top pages while she dusted herself off. I wrote a few notes on the scratch paper that was out on the counter, but I didn't need to. I'd remember the details. I was done in a few minutes. I shut the folder and slid it back across the counter.

'Thanks for taking the trouble. No need for copies.'

'I hope it was important,' she said, somewhat heartfelt.

'Life and death,' I said.

'Aren't they all.'

After leaving the Records Department I drove out to Dune Road so I could watch the magic-hour light warm up the sand and blacken the sea. The air was already a lot cooler for this time of the evening and the leaves were falling in a steady cascade, littering the world with red, orange, yellow and brown.

I was at the stop sign at the bottom of Halsey Neck and was about to turn right on Dune when the trained bear drove by in his black BMW.

He was talking on a cell phone. I turned left instead to follow, but let him get well ahead of me before following in earnest. He was moving fast, but I could easily keep the shiny black mass in view. He was heading down Meadow Lane toward the south part of the Village. A pickup truck pulled out ahead of me and got between us. That provided some cover so I could snug up the gap.

I lit a cigarette and wondered how inconspicuous I could be in a 1967 Pontiac Grand Prix.

The bear drove parallel to the ocean until he entered the southernmost reaches of the estate district. The pickup had the good manners to follow the same route all the way to Gin Lane before pulling into a driveway. I slipped back until a vintage Mercedes convertible took the pickup's place. We turned left and caravanned up South Main Street, and into the centre of the Village.

I lost the Mercedes at Job's Lane, but kept a bead on the BMW till it turned off Main Street into the big Village parking area behind the storefronts. I passed by the entrance and sped around to another one off Nugent Street. There was a real chance I'd lose him in the big lot, but I didn't want to rush in blind. I drove in slowly, scanning for the black 7 series sedan.

It was already parked and the bear was climbing out. He still had the cell phone stuck in his ear. He wore the same black leather duster and motorcycle boots I'd recently seen up close.

He leaned on the open driver's side door while he talked on the phone. I parked a few rows over and shut off the engine. As he talked he looked steadily at the back side of the shops and offices that fronted on Main St. I got out of the Grand Prix to get a better view. I moved a little closer and stood behind a tall Range Rover. The bear was still looking up at the back of the buildings. My eyes left him when I tried to follow his line of sight. When I looked back, he was out of the BMW, holding the cell phone with one hand and waving with the other.

I came around the Range Rover to clear my view of the buildings and searched for movement. That's when I saw Amanda Battiston standing with Bob Sobol on a rear balcony off the second storey of the Southampton branch of Harbor Trust, waving back at the bear, holding a cell phone of her own up to her ear.

CHAPTER EIGHT

Embarrassment is a complicated human emotion. Probably because it's an aggregate of other emotions – shame, guilt, anger, regret – that assemble in temporary alliances to suit the particulars of the moment.

It's also one of the few emotions truly scalable to large organizations. Like fanaticism, or hubris, embarrassment's progenitor.

Most corporate leaders would rather be boiled in oil than embarrassed. For them, it's an exposure of weakness, an admission of fallibility. To themselves and to the world at large.

Mason Thigpen's staffer and two outside counsel joined me in the conference room with the two security guys who'd escorted me from the board meeting. The lawyers entering the room were fully focused on the company's desperate desire to avoid embarrassment. This was complicated by another emotion, belonging to Mason himself, best described as vengeful wrath. Which is why the task was consigned to surrogates.

Mason's staffer, Barry Mildrew, was young and bright, and a former middle linebacker at Boston College. I didn't know him well, but he seemed all right. I can't remember much about the other two lawyers, except they were uncomfortable with humour and sweated even in the climate-controlled atmosphere.

'How're you feeling?' asked Barry as he sat across from me.

'Not bad. Yourself?'

'I'm fine, Sam.'

He waited for me to say something. When I didn't, he said, 'So, what do you think?'

'I think you're here to work something out.'

'I'm here to talk about you, Sam. You're my concern at the moment.'

'That's good of you, Barry.'

'I want to do what's best for you. And the company, of course.'

'Of course.'

He put a manila folder on the table, but kept it closed.

'We have a couple options.'

'But before we share our thinking with you,' said one of the other lawyers, 'we'd like to hear your thoughts.'

'My thoughts? I have lots of thoughts every day. You want general or specific?'

'Anything you want,' said Barry, interrupting whatever the outside counsel was about to say.

'Anybody want coffee?' I asked the group. 'I can go get some.'

Their discomfort was palpable.

'Maybe Lou could bring us some,' I said, pointing to one of the security guys. Everyone looked relieved.

'Sure,' said Lou. 'Place your orders.'

After Lou had a chance to write down what we wanted and go off to get the coffee, Barry tried again.

'So, your thoughts.'

'I'm thinking I should have asked for double cream.'

'Tell Mr Acquillo what we're thinking,' said one of the outside guys. That annoyed Barry, but he pressed on.

'Our choices are limited here, but as I said, we do have them.'

'Pending a medical report,' said an outside counsel.

Barry kept his eyes on me. I knew then the other two guys were there to bird-dog Barry, not me.

'Actually, Ben,' said Barry, 'that's not a stipulation. Mason is willing to drop the entire matter. As is Mr Donovan and the rest of the board.'

'If,' I said.

Barry smiled again.

'Come on, Sam, you and I wouldn't be in business if we didn't horse trade. There's always an if.'

'That's what we're in? Business?'

'Don't you want to hear the if?' he asked. 'I think you'll find it interesting.'

'Sure.'

Ben and his sidekick were eager to get my reaction. The security guys looked implacable. They were good at that.

'We want you to stay on as president of TSS.'

'I'm not a president. I'm a divisional VP.'

'See? Interesting, huh? That's your new title. To see us through the sale.'

I think I laughed at that point. I couldn't help it.

'I'm getting promoted for punching our chief counsel in the nose? Now there's a company worth working for.'

Barry was the only one who enjoyed the thought.

'In front of the whole board of directors,' he added. 'But that's not why. The president of TSS will lead the transition team, and his prime role will be selling the living hell out of the idea to the buyers, our shareholders and your people.'

'Chief cheerleader.'

'After George Donovan.'

'I guess he's more willing to overlook Mason's nose than Mason is.'

'Mason is a team player.'

The words conjured up an image of Mason Thigpen that would never survive outside the imagination.

'So, what's option two?' I asked.

Barry sat back in his chair and tapped the working end of his ballpoint pen on the table.

'You take a sabbatical during the sale period and refrain from commenting on the division, the buyers, the deal or anything relating to the corporation as a whole. To anyone at anytime.'

'Keeping Mason in a forgetful mood.'

'You'll retain your full salary and benefits. After the sale, your role will be up to the buyers.'

'Is their chief counsel bigger than ours?'

Barry let that one pass. Being much bigger than me, he could afford to.

'I've got a third option,' I said. 'Tell Donovan to go fuck himself. Mason can do what he wants.'

Ben didn't seem to like this option, though his partner probably did. Appealed to his blood lust. Barry stayed neutral.

'Then you go to jail,' said Barry.

'One punch? No priors? I don't think so. Be a juicy court case, though. Press'd eat it up. Meanwhile, I'd have plenty of time to work on my memoirs. All about my life running the division you're trying to sell. Should interest the buyers.'

Barry listened without giving up anything. He had plenty of poise, I'll give him that.

'So,' he said, 'I guess we got our horses out of the barn where we can see 'em.'

He kept smiling and tapping the pen on the table, which got to be so annoying I finally reached over and held his wrist. When I let go he stuck the pen in his pocket and folded his arms over his chest.

'Sorry. Nervous habit.'

'Understandable. But calm down. I know what we're doing.'

That cheered him.

'Good. Let's hear it.'

'It's simple. I quit. I'm quitting because I'm against the sale. Why I'm against the sale is nobody's business but mine. Not another word from me on the subject. Unless Mason puts up a stink, then all bets are off. You writing this down?' I asked Ben. He reflexively grabbed a pen and started writing.

'Put it in proper language,' I said, 'but nothing fuzzy. We're only doing this once.'

'I'll have to go back and see how this flies,' said Barry.

'Do what you want. I really don't care. I don't care what happens to me. I don't care what happens to your company. I cared about my division, but that's gone. Everything's pretty much gone. I've got nothing to lose.'

Ben had stopped writing while I talked.

'Hurry up with that. I want to get the hell out of here.'

He looked at Barry who nodded his head. Ben drafted something and slid it over to Barry, but I caught it halfway. The wording was close. I borrowed a pen from one of the security guys and made a few edits. Then I gave it to Barry.

'I just simplified a little,' I told him.

Barry read it over several times.

'It's clear, I just don't know if they'll agree.'

I swiped Ben's pad and wrote out a fresh version without all the scratch outs. Then I wrote out a copy. I signed both.

'Here's yours, I'll keep this. I'll pick up my stuff on the way home. Unless you don't want me to, in which case, you keep it.'

I looked at my watch.

'This time of day I should get there in about forty minutes.'

Then I stood up to leave. The two security guys stood up like a shot and looked over at the lawyers.

'You guys should see me out,' I said to them, then left. They followed a few seconds later. The elevator played Haydn on the way down. I tried to talk to them about baseball, but they maintained their implacability. They stayed with me all the way to my car, then watched me leave the parking garage. When I reached the street I dropped all the windows and let the steamy, malodourous air of the city bust into the car. I stopped at a bodega and bought my first pack of cigarettes in twenty years, a six-pack of beer and a fifth of vodka.

I sang along with the radio on the way up to White Plains until the vodka kicked in. Then I wept like a baby. It was strange to be in a company car driving eighty miles an hour, in the middle of the day, with the windows down, smoking cigarettes and drinking warm vodka out of the bottle. Wiping tears and snot off my face with the shirtsleeve of my pima cotton dress shirt.

All those bridge abutments along the Saw Mill River Parkway looked so alluring, but for some reason I didn't have the courage to accept their embrace.

SINCE I was already in the big parking lot in the Village, it was quicker to go to a bar I knew that fronted on Nugent Street than schlep all the way to the Pequot in Sag Harbor. I got there quick – it was only about a hundred feet away – and ordered a double Absolut on the rocks, no fruit.

'Want to run a tab?'

'Sure.'

Some bartenders are especially prescient – I had two more singles after that. As a result my mind wasn't as clear as I'd planned, but at least my heart had stopped thumping in my ears. I ordered some bar food to slow the effects.

'Tough day?' the bartender asked.

'Had tougher.'

The place was warm, dark and full of varnished walnut. The waiters and waitresses wore white shirts and black pants. They were all young and slender with the feel of Manhattan in the way they styled their hair and the look in their eyes. Only doing this till the real thing turns up. Grey-haired regulars lined the bar. Mostly overweight and vaguely desperate, just like the guys at the Pequot only better financed. I always got myself in trouble in places like that. I resolved to be polite and keep my opinions to myself.

I had my Regina file with me. I pulled out the yellow pad, and as I munched on some calamari and salad, wrote everything up with boxes and arrows.

I was happiest in my working life when I was troubleshooting big process systems. I liked laying out the process as a whole, then climbing into the complexities, searching out those points in the design that weren't behaving as predicted, or hoped for. I often divined the presence of a system failure the way astronomers discover celestial bodies, not by direct observation but by studying their effects on local energy and mass.

Though I always started a project with well-organized and precise documentation, I'd get swept up as the chase quickened, and become lost in the pursuit, my mind continually reviewing the data and cycling through the possibilities until the answer leapt out of the chaos. Then I had to back-document so I could present a coherent diagnosis to the other engineers.

Starts here, moves this way. First this, then that. When this happens, this follows. Interconnecting data points, process dynamics. A flow scheme, just like I'd do before turning a final design over to the applications people, the engineers and draftsmen who'd input the CAD/CAM servers and render it all in beautiful graphic formats and 3-D models.

Then it went to bench-testing, but I never doubted the outcome. In the secret life of my mind I was flushed with arrogant pride. Let them have their algorithms, diagrams and data organized in endless columns and spreadsheets. I had something better.

When I looked at what I'd drawn up on the yellow legal pad I knew it was time to call Jackie Swaitkowski.

'Attorney Swaitkowski's office.'

'Is she there?'

'Who may I say is calling?'

'Sam Acquillo.'

'Of course it is. She's been expecting you.'

'I'm at a pay phone.'

'Does it have a number?'

'Yeah.'

I gave her the number.

'Hold your ground. She'll call in a second.'

I hung up. Thirty seconds later the phone rang. It startled the bartender and hostess who were standing only a few feet away.

'Holy shit.'

'Sorry,' I said. 'It's for me.'

Jackie burst on the line.

'It wasn't there.'

I looked out into the restaurant like the whole place was sitting there waiting for me to break the bad news. But they were all concentrating on their endive salads and baked pork tenderloin.

'Goddammit.'

'Hornsby was pretty organized, which doesn't surprise me. Your cop friend said to call him when I was done and left me there for like twenty minutes. I went through everything.'

'Maybe I'm chasing a ghost.'

'I didn't say it doesn't exist. I said it wasn't there. Where are you anyway?'

I told her.

'Getting smashed?'

'Trying.'

'Order a cosmopolitan in about ten minutes. I'll be there in fifteen. The bartender's an artist.'

'He pours a mean Absolut on the rocks.'

'Make sure you can still read when I get there.'

I went back to the bar to wait. I told the bartender about the cosmopolitan right away. Better his memory than mine. Then I worked on my flow scheme, adding a few details. It seemed time for a cigarette. I asked for an ashtray. The bartender directed me to the front stoop.

'Or, you can go to the patio out back. Bring your drink. Has a nice view of the parking lot.'

I chose the stoop in case Jackie showed up on time. I was half way through the smoke when her Toyota pickup careened up to the curb.

'Gimme one of those,' she said, pointing to my cigarette.

She was back in civilian clothing – cotton shirt, blue jeans and leather jacket. With a manila envelope stuck under her arm. She handed me the envelope. I handed her a Camel.

'Well?'

'Let's go sit on the patio. We can drink and smoke and who knows what else,' I said.

I got Jackie situated and went in to retrieve her cosmopolitan and a fresh vodka for myself. When I saw what a cosmo actually was, I recruited one of the waitresses to handle transport.

'Be a lot easier to carry that thing in a milk glass,' I told her.

'Sure, and so romantic, too.'

I waited until we were alone before pulling out the envelope. There was a piece of paper torn from a notepad Scotch-taped to the cover. It said, 'This is the Living Trust of Carl Bollard, Sr., and Carl Bollard, Jr., dated March 18, 1948. Addendum November 4, 1960, prepared by Milton Hornsby, Attorney at Law, Trustee. Addendum October 24, 1961, prepared by Milton Hornsby, Attorney at Law, Trustee.'

Inside the envelope was a printed pamphlet from the New York Bar Association on the general subject of trusts and trust preparation, a few inconsequential notes to Hornsby from 'CB, Sr.,' and a tissue carbon copy of a cover letter that must have accompanied the trust when it was first presented. But no trust.

'Somebody took it out of here,' I said.

'I searched all his files. It wasn't there.'

I looked across the parking lot at the back of Harbor Trust. It was built in a colonial style, though clearly from another time, probably the nineteen twenties or thirties. It was big for Main Street, but not too big. The architects probably thought the bank's customers would feel more secure putting their money in a place that looked like it belonged to Thomas Jefferson. Four square and filled with enlightenment.

And as solid as Fort Knox.

'Of course it's not there,' I said. 'What a dope.'

'Who's a dope?'

'I'm a dope.'

'Okay, I'll go with that. How come?' she asked.

'If I told you that – '

'You'd stop pissing me off.'

'It's better I just buy you another cosmopolitan.'

Night had completely fallen. With the darkness I could see that all the lights on the second floor of the bank, the offices and conference rooms, were lit. Working late.

Jackie said something, but I didn't hear her.

'Hey,' she said, 'are you listening? Hello in there.' She turned around. 'What are you looking at?'

She said something else, but I didn't hear it, because I was watching Amanda go down the backstairs of the Harbor Trust building and walk up to her silver Audi A4.

'Give me your keys,' I said to Jackie, digging mine out of my pocket.

'What?'

'Quick.'

She gave them to me. I gave her mine.

'What the hell?'

'I'll call you. I already paid for the cosmo. My car's right over there. Hope you can drive a stick.'

'A stick? In that fucking thing?'

Jackie was still yelling to me as I ran around to Nugent Street where she parked her little truck. Amanda was already at the light on Main Street. I pulled up behind her as it turned green. The Toyota had a notchy five-speed with a long throw, but it was tight and easy to manoeuver, despite its age and hard duty. It smelled like Jackie. I checked the ashtray and found a half-burnt roach. I lit it up.

'What the hell,' I said to the inside of the Toyota, 'been a rough day.'

Despite my success following the trained bear, I really didn't know how to tail a car without giving myself away. I wished I'd read more crime fiction or watched more TV.

She took Hampton Road out of the Village and headed east on Montauk. Even in October there was plenty of traffic. I let one car get between us and prayed it would keep pace. The three of us were in solid formation all the way through Water Mill, and most of the way to Bridgehampton. Right after the big shopping centre outside Bridgehampton Village she took a hard left and zinged into the night. I followed as aggressively as I dared, losing sight of her taillights until I got to the next decent straightaway. I realised Jackie's pickup would have trouble keeping up with a rocket sled like Amanda's A4.

She flew past a long row of white horse-farm fencing, but had to stop before turning right on Scuttle Hole Road. I took a chance and ate up all the slack as she waited to turn. When she turned right, I followed close behind.

She hit sixty-five mph on Scuttle Hole, forcing me to back off again. At the Bridgehampton-Sag Harbor Turnpike she hung a hard left.

I fell in behind and followed her into Sag Harbor.

She turned right at a light a few blocks from the centre of town. I let her get some distance, then followed. The street ended in a T. You could go left or right, or straight through a private entranceway. It was framed by a grand wrought-iron gate, capped with a large metal cross. Maybe it was the gates of heaven. Amanda shot straight across the intersection and disappeared through the hole.

'Okay,' I said, and after waiting a decent interval, followed her into paradise.

Just inside the gate was a small sign.

'Conscience Manor Retreat. Private.'

The grounds were deep and dark, filled with huge old shade trees. There was no general lighting, but you could see evidence of several buildings from lit windows peeking through the thinning foliage. I killed my lights, and looked for Audis. Nothing.

I followed the crushed seashell drive up to a large stucco Victorian house that looked like the main building. Most of the windows were lit. There were two main stories plus a third built into an elaborate roof structure. A deep porch, partially obscured by sculpted yews, wrapped around the entire first storey.

Amanda's car was stopped at a small structure adjacent to the parking lot. I dodged around a row of cars and parked at the other end of the lot.

Her lights went out and she left her car and went into the little building. As my eyes adjusted to the ambient light the building took shape as a small chapel, with a high-pitched, slate roof and a cross moulded into the gable end. The door had an arched top and the windows were leaded glass through which a low light suddenly sprung.

The big mediaeval door opened more easily than I expected. The inside was dimly but uniformly lit, so I could easily see the interior detail. It was a rectangular room with an oval, moulded wood bench in the middle. The outside walls, which you faced when sitting on the bench, were lined with square, raised-panel drawer fronts, most of which had a small brass plaque, engraved with a name, date and simple message. Amanda sat on the bench, which up close looked more like a pew, or the curved oaken seating you see in old train stations, with her hands clasped in her lap and her head bowed.

I walked over and sat down next to her. She was directly across from the drawer labelled 'Monica May Anselma. 1991–1996. My light, my dream, my hope.'

Amanda looked at me with swollen eyes. Then she looked back at the wall.

'I should have known you'd figure it out,' she said, quietly.

I didn't answer. I didn't know what to say.

'You're such a good figure-outer.'

We sat silently for a very long time. Amanda had her head lowered and seemed to be having trouble breathing.

'How did you know I was here?' she asked.

'You drove by and sucked me into your tailwind.'

She nodded as if that was a fair explanation.

'I tried to tell you,' she said.

'I guess you did.'

'You didn't let me.'

'I didn't know.'

'You didn't want to know. That's what you told me. You didn't want any old baggage. Well, there's mine, right there. My little baggage.'

'I don't mean to intrude,' I said. 'I just wanted to talk to you.'

'I bet you do.'

We sat quietly for a while.

'Do you want to know?' she asked.

'About your daughter?'

'Yes.'

'Only if you want to tell me.'

'What else is there to tell?'

'Other stuff. It can wait.'

I looked up at the exposed rafters. They were mortised and tenoned and shaped into pseudo-Gothic arches. Tiny low-voltage quartz fixtures cast a clean, but pale incandescent light. Torchières mounted on the wall drew shadows across the orderly drawer fronts. Small bouquets were placed randomly along the floor. A larger arrangement anchored the far end of the room.

'You didn't know. About Monica.'

'No.'

She looked at me.

'So why are you here?'

'Bay Side.'

'Oh that. You figured that out, too.'

'Maybe. Not sure.'

She took a deep breath to force the quaver out of her voice.

'You ever live in the city?'

'For over ten years,' I said. 'We left when my daughter was born. Abby wanted her to have a yard.'

'I really couldn't afford to be there, but I was determined to make it work. My mother was so mad at me for leaving home. She didn't understand you can't be born, live and die in just one place. Even a place like Southampton. Especially a place like Southampton – it's so unreal in so many ways. Kids have to get out in the world and live a little. I was only a few hours away, but she rarely came to see me. To her, I might as well have moved to Calcutta. It was a matter of pride that she'd never been in the Empire State Building, or rode the boat out to the Statue of Liberty. She surely never set foot in Times Square. My God, she'd have a coronary.'

'My mother didn't like it, either. I think my dad built the cottage so he had a place to keep her outside the city.' I noticed tears falling as she talked. She stopped occasionally to wipe her nose.

'I was the secretary for the editor of this semi-scholarly technical magazine. I worked my way up to editorial assistant. I was a biology major at Southampton College, but I was also good with grammar and spelling. I proofread the articles and worked with all the authors. There were only a few of us in the office. It was nice and friendly. And the work felt like it meant something. Didn't pay much, but enough to live on, to pay rent on my apartment. I had to move a few times till I scored a semi-permanent sublet in the West Seventies from this young guy who'd been transferred to Japan. I even published a few of my own articles. My boss encouraged me to write. It would take me months to research and compose. I'd agonize over it like you wouldn't believe. But they were patient with me, him and the other editors. Like those guys in *My Fair Lady*, you know? Help the ignorant girl make something of herself.

'If they only knew what I did after work, which was mostly go out and fuck myself all up. You're young, you're pretty, you get a lot of attention. You go to the disco.'

She said it with a feigned French accent.

'You dance like a crazy person and feel like a beauty queen. You snort a lot of coke and bring home handsome young assholes in flowered suspenders who tell you about possessions you never even heard of, and want to fuck you before you're even up the stairs to the apartment. One of these guys left me with a little present, but unlike every other girl I knew, I didn't want to go to the clinic and zip-zip, "take care of it". I wanted to keep it, whatever it was. So I did, and the guys at the magazine were totally cool and never asked me anything or made me feel weird in any way. Instead of hassling me, they gave me two months maternity and an apartment full of kid stuff. I think they loved me, in a really nice way.'

The tears were now rolling out in full flow. She didn't bother to wipe them off her face.

'It's not very easy to raise a kid in the city, especially when you're a single mom without a lot of money. But, I loved my little baby with every particle of my being. She was my light and my dream and my hope.'

She stopped to wipe her face and take a breath.

'You don't have to . . .' I started to say.

'Yes I do,' she said, through her teeth. 'And you have to listen.'

'Okay.'

'She was so smart – her dad was this really sharp professional guy, I think. Cute as hell, and destined for great things. I never tried to find out for sure, or pull any paternity stuff. I didn't want that kind of thing to spoil what I had with Monica. It's hard to explain, but some people understand. We had our own little universe, and I didn't know if I could let anyone else in. But oh man, the cost of a nanny in New York. There were plenty of nights when I'd lay in bed and daydream about money and apartments with lots of rooms and Monica's daddy bringing her toys and sending her to private school. I didn't have a daddy of my own, but mom did what she could. Whenever she had a spare twenty or something she'd slip it into some ridiculous Hallmark card and send it to me. I showed her pictures when we came home. She even forced herself to come to the city a few times. She'd fuss over Monica like you wouldn't believe. And I was doing it, by God.

'Monica was just starting first grade. I was cutting back my hours so I could be there when she got home, and make up for the lower pay by writing articles at night. My nanny already had her next thing lined up. Getting rid of that expense more than compensated. She was a sweet woman, really. She knew what raising a kid on your own was like. She had a son. I didn't see him much – he was in fourth or fifth grade at the time. She had him with her that day when she went out for a second to buy some milk and cereal. I'd forgotten to get any, and Monica needed breakfast. I didn't know this, until later.

'They called me at my office. Monica was in the hospital. The nanny was too hysterical to talk to me, so I didn't know anything till I got there. Apparently, Monica was hungry and fussy and threw a little tantrum. The nanny's kid was alone with her, and thought he'd get her to stop crying by hitting her on the head. And then, after she was unconscious, he thought he'd hit her some more, which he did until she suffered massive, irreversible brain damage.

'I was seriously thinking about swallowing a bottle of sleeping pills, but I was afraid to leave Monica alone. What I really couldn't do was support myself now that I had this crazy huge expense. I came home to Southampton hoping my poor mother, bless her, could look after both of us. But look, you can't expect a person to care for somebody in a state like that. Especially an elderly woman. I might have been young and healthy and crazy with grief, but I couldn't do it all either. Monica couldn't do anything on her own. *There was nothing there.*'

She pulled some more tissues out of a box on the side table and wiped her face.

'I had to keep her in the city to stay on Medicaid. They all made it clear I should pull the plug. All the doctors and Medicaid people. I can understand why. The rest of the world shouldn't have to pay for one little vegetable. But she was my *daughter*. I loved her with all my heart. How could I do that, Sam?'

She was crying now in a solid, steady kind of way. I took her hand and she squeezed hard. With her other hand she pulled out a few tissues and blew her nose. She looked at me.

'Then she made it easy for her mommy. She just left.'

It took a long time for her to catch her breath.

'I'm so sorry, Sam.'

'Nothing to be sorry for.'

'Oh yes there is.'

She shook her head and a long sweep of auburn hair fell in front of her face.

'It's about Roy. I knew him in high school. We dated a little. He was nice enough, but, you know, not very interesting. Not for a girl like me who was burning to get outta town. Roy had no such desire, though he had a real thing for money. His father died when he was little and his grandparents basically raised him with his mother. They never had anything. I bet you always wondered who lived in those houses along the dump road. One of them was Roy's grandparents. You wouldn't believe how they lived, so close to so much.

'But Roy was going to change all that. He was going to make money, goddammit, and he did. He did really well for himself. Paid for his own college, went to business school, joined the bank, worked his way up. I was very impressed with him, really I was. Proud of him for actually doing something he said he was going to do. It's hard, you know it is Sam, to be around all this money out here and not have any of your own. It can twist you all up, if you let it. But Roy was never like that. He just did it the hard way, working his ass off and doing what he had to. For years he supported his whole family. Now he's got me, and… '

She looked at the mute wall of ashes, lowering her voice to a near whisper. 'I could have never afforded this place. Even this tiny little place for my baby girl. Roy paid for it all.'

She looked over at me for the first time. Beseeching, or questioning, I couldn't tell.

'He tried to ask me out from the get-go, when I came back from the city, but I couldn't face anybody. Finally, I went to dinner with him a few times. Invited him over. He was very sweet to my mother. He's not a bad man, he's just who he is. And he loved me. He told me he always had, and that when I left for the city it was the saddest thing that ever happened to him. I didn't even know he felt that way. He was so shy and self-conscious.

'But then he made some pretty good money – you know, he started a whole commercial lending operation out here for Harbor, and did great – it gave him some confidence. It was nice. And easy, and I was so tired and lost. When he offered to marry me I felt like an angel had come along and plucked me off the tracks. He saved me, he really did.

'I knew this wasn't what I wanted, but it was far better than killing myself, which I strongly considered, oh, maybe a thousand times. But then I thought about my mom, and what I was going through over Monica. So we got married and it all happened like he said it would. I didn't love him, but I appreciated what he'd done. I tried to hold up my end, and I think I did pretty well. He was always patient with me. He liked to control things, and I was so sick inside, I liked letting him do it.

'And then you. You. You. You.'

She swatted me on the shoulder.

'All busted up yourself. Big sad eyes and crunched-up nose. Flirting with you wasn't a huge deal in the grand scheme of things, but it was the only pleasant thing happening to me. I prayed I wasn't being too obvious, so I wouldn't scare you away. But you kept coming in every once in a while, and I'd look forward to it. I could tell you liked me. I wasn't that far gone. And I knew I would *really* like you if you'd only let me in a little. Then you starting asking me about Regina and that made me think of my mother, and before I knew it we were spending time together. It made my heart just leap right out of my body.

'But you know what the problem was?' she asked.

'Roy knew.'

'No, worse than that. Oh, God.'

She'd stopped crying when the story moved off her daughter, but then she started again.

'It was his idea,' she said, ripping out the words through her tears, 'Roy's.'

I waited till she was ready to get back on track.

'Soon after we were married, Roy came home from work more excited than I'd ever seen him. He said we had the opportunity of a lifetime. A big real estate deal, the biggest in the Hamptons, he said, our ticket to the ball. You should have seen him. Roy's a very positive person on the outside, but he worries, and broods a lot when nobody else is around. Nobody but me. This was so different. He was like a little boy. He went on and on about it, though I had a hard time following everything. I love science and technology, but all this financial stuff, it bores me.'

'Not a good thing for a personal banker.'

'The bank would handle financing, and Roy was going to take a position personally, which was the main thing, but we'd also make out because my mother's house would be part of the plan. That upset me a little, which I know is silly. But, what the heck, he was so happy, and it seemed like a long way off. I don't know.

'The next year was wonderful. Roy was crazy busy at the bank, especially with this big project. He worked late a lot and went into the city at least once a week, which was very nice for me. It gave me a little break. People also came out from the city to talk to him, to help with the Town, I guess, and other things. I admit I didn't pay much attention to it all.

'Then something happened. It wasn't all at once, but slowly Roy got more and more nervous. Distracted. Something was going wrong with the project, but he didn't want to talk about it. Not at first. Then he told me there was a snag with Environmental Protection. Nothing real, just a bunch of regulations that could stall progress and endanger the deal.

'"The neighbours", is what he kept saying. "Amanda, the neighbours could ruin the whole thing." He always insisted we keep everything hush hush. He said if one word of this got out, other players could elbow their way in. Investors would come out from the city and he'd say, "don't even act like you know them. People will put two and two together".'

'Bob Sobol,' I said.

She looked impressed.

'That's right. The creep. Always trying to knock me off-balance. I wouldn't give him the pleasure.'

'He brought the deal to Roy.'

'No, it was Roy's deal, all the way. Bob Sobol and this guy in Sag Harbor are investors. Or front the real investors, I can never figure out which, though frankly, I don't care. I don't like either one of them.'

'Milton Hornsby.'

She swiveled over on the bench so she could get a clear look at me.

'You know him?' she asked.

'A little.'

'What an unpleasant person. He always looks like he's swallowed a frog or something. No sense of humour. How did you know he was involved?'

'It's a long story, too.'

'So, I guess you know they're old friends, Bob Sobol and Milt Hornsby. Or something. Can't honestly say Hornsby was friendly with anybody. Bitter old bastard.'

'So Roy was worried about the neighbours.'

'He said there'd be public hearings and that some people with adjoining properties might put up a fight. He was mostly concerned about you.'

'No kidding.'

'Oh, you were a big topic at the dinner table for a while there. He said you were a retired executive with a reputation as a first-rate SOB, his words not mine.'

She smiled for the first time

'Though you can be difficult,' she said.

'So I'm told.'

'It was obvious you liked me. Roy told me to pal around with you.

Find out what you were thinking.'

'Mata Hari.'

'Hardly. All I wanted was to kid around and have a nice time. Who cares about Roy's dumb project? And you made it easy. Even when I tried to tell you the truth.'

'What did you report?'

'I told him you were upset about Regina Broadhurst, which wasn't big news. You're the executor of her estate.'

'Administrator.'

Her eyes shifted away from me and she looked at the floor. Quiet suddenly. I thought she might be about to cry again, but then I realised her face had hardened into a mask.

'I didn't know about Buddy until that night at the Playhouse,' she said, almost through her teeth. 'I didn't know Roy was capable of such a thing.'

'Bodyguard.'

'Thug. Friend of Sobol's. Fucking gumba. Pardon the language. But I'm allowed to say that, I'm Italian.'

'Me, too. About a quarter.'

'I told Roy if that bastard laid another hand on you I'd leave him. I can't have a person's death on my conscience.'

'But he's still around?'

'He and Sobol come out a lot. They're meeting Roy at the bank tonight. Another big to-do. I don't know what it's about this time. Roy was all worked up. I thought it was a good time to slip away and visit Monica.'

She looked over at the wall, as if saying her daughter's name broke some sort of spell.

'My precious baby.'

I thought about my own daughter, beautiful and accomplished and living like a princess in New York City. I knew what she did for work, and where, but I didn't know if she liked it or not. I knew her address and phone number by heart, but I hadn't ever called her because she told me not to. I knew she was a huge social success, but I didn't know any of her boyfriends. What kind of guys they were, or what kind of life they would make for my only daughter, my only child. I knew almost nothing except I loved her as much as Amanda loved Monica, and that I constantly asked

God, a God I didn't want to believe in, to please keep my daughter safe. Take whatever you want from me, but please keep her safe.

'I'm so sorry I lied to you,' she said. 'You have a right to hate me.'

She was rubbing her hands together, the way I saw her do at the cottage. Warming the climate of her mind.

'You never knew your father,' I asked her.

'No. He died when I was too little to remember.'

I was really tired. The combination of everything – the shock of Hornsby lying in his garden, the stress of working on Jackie and Sullivan, all the vodka, the chase across Bridgehampton, and the lingering effects of the concussion courtesy of some asshole named Buddy, as it turned out – had begun to take its toll.

I wanted to go to sleep.

'I'm sorry to bother you here,' I said. 'Not the right place to talk about these things.'

She shrugged and looked around.

'They can't hear us.'

'I'm still sorry.'

'How much sorry do we have to have, and for how long?' she asked.

'People die.' I said. 'You can't do anything about it. It's not your fault.'

Amanda crossed her arms over her chest and squeezed, as if trying to keep her heart contained within her body.

'Is that what you tell yourself?'

I sat with her until all the tears were exhausted. Then I left her alone in the little mausoleum. There wasn't anything else I could do, and there were people I had to call. And a dog to let out.

As I drove the bouncy little Toyota pickup around the hairpin curves of Noyac Road, I wondered how long it would take to pay all my debts to Jackie Swaitkowski, mounting by the minute.

When I emerged from the tree cover I could see the moon, almost full, high above the Little Peconic. The air was clear, but the water was being churned up by a stiff northeasterly. An unusual wind for that time of year. Unless there was a storm on the way, or passing off the coast.

I stopped at the mailbox and pulled out a stack of envelopes and junk mail. The moon was so bright you could clearly see the cottage, my yard and Regina's place, lit only by the porch light I kept on since my night with Jimmy Maddox. Probably the only reason I saw the car parked in her driveway. It was backlit by the porch light, but as my night vision improved I could make out the contours. A 7-Series BMW.

I saw a black shape explode out from behind a stand of trees just in time to throw my arms up over my head and duck. The blow landed on my right shoulder with enough force to knock me off my feet, but it wasn't very damaging. It gave me an opportunity to roll away and get back on my feet and face him head on. For a change.

I set my stance and danced to the right. Buddy just walked toward me, his long coat open to the breeze, the chains around his neck reflecting the bright moonlight. He used both meaty hands to point to his stomach.

'Hey, fucker,' he said, 'check it out.'

There was the butt of a big automatic sticking out of his belt.

'You going to shoot me?'

His mouth was a wide, humourless grin.

'Fuck no, I'm gonna beat you to death.'

He made a quick little move inside my reach, then backed out again. It caused me to dance back to my left, which I never liked. He tried to meet me with his right, but I leaned out of the way and he missed. Not a good tactical fighter, but fast for his size. And very big.

He came straight in, trying to catch me on a turn. I closed and tried out a combination left jab and right undercut to the body, but it didn't do much against the mass of fat and muscle around his waist. It also left my own less protected gut exposed.

Buddy caught me on the right side at the bottom of my rib cage. I felt the air phoof out of my lungs. I had to roll back sharply and drop my arms so I could catch my breath. Buddy just kept moving forward, steadily, deliberately, eager for a chance to close again.

I rotated to the left as I moved backwards to keep my right side protected. I was afraid of his longer reach, and I couldn't risk clinching – he outweighed me by half a guy and I'd never win a wrestling match. My only hope was to get in and out fast enough to hurt him before he could get those gorilla arms into play. But I didn't know how. The moon was so bright I could easily see his face. He was really enjoying himself.

I heard Eddie in the house, barking his head off. That gave me an idea. I turned around and ran as fast as I could toward the Peconic.

'Run if you want, asshole,' he called to me in his dumb trained-bear voice. 'You're a dead motherfucker.'

I ran straight up to the front of the cottage. Then I turned and stood at the front door. Buddy loped up behind with his fists clenched and the tails of his leather coat flapping back behind his arms. Before he could reach me I cut left and ran around to the side of the house.

'Stand and fight, pussy,' said Buddy, almost cheerfully as he fol-lowed me around the shrubs and into the side yard. I leaped on the landing and stood facing the side door, listening for him to get closer. I made a rough guess at timing, took a deep breath, wrapped my right hand around the handle of the Harmon Kille-brew bat, and swung around backhand with everything I had.

I misjudged the distance by a few inches. The tip of the bat caught him in the front teeth. They snapped off, spraying my hand with spit, blood and little white splinters. His hands flew to his face and I swung again, this time like a baseball player, with both hands.

The bat cracked across his temple, but his fingers were in the way and took some of the edge off the blow. He spun away and bent down, covering as much of his head as he could with his hands. I stepped into the breach, and taking careful aim, put my whole body into the swing. This one connected well. His hands flew away and his head snapped back. He staggered as he tried to regain his balance, arms flapping. Blood gushed from his forehead, blinding him. I held the bat with my left hand and plucked the automatic out of his waistband with my right. I tossed the gun into the bushes, then stuck a right jab into the red pulp that used to be his mouth. He fell back further, swatting openhanded at the air.

'Motherfucker!'

I dropped the bat and hit him again with my right. I didn't measure out the punches the way the trainers always told me to do. I didn't care if I kept my balance, stayed up on my toes, or exposed my right kidney. I didn't have to care. The bear was through. I hit him with a combination. His knees began to bend and he had to spread his feet to stay upright. He was mumbling something, but I couldn't hear him through the roar in my ears. I brought my foot up between his legs and felt the splash of soft tissue. He doubled up and fell headfirst into the grass. I kicked him in his bloody face and went back to get the bat.

I scooped it up off the ground and walked over with it held slightly off my right shoulder. I stood over him, picking a spot. He wasn't moving. The last kick had rolled him over on his back. The mass of crushed tomatoes that now composed his face stared up at the moonlit sky. He was still breathing, rasping wetly through the blood in his mouth. I let the bat down slowly. I nudged him with my toe. Still didn't move.

I pulled the automatic out of the bushes, found the release and dumped out the clip. I put the gun in the big inside pocket of my jean jacket and the clip in my pants pocket.

Then I went inside to call Joe Sullivan.

CHAPTER NINE

The weeks after leaving Abby and my job have always been a bit of a blur. Mainly because I was drinking a lot and disregarding common conventions like mealtime and *Monday Night Football*. I stayed in my room at the hotel, or drove my car, the company car I was supposed to return, around western Connecticut and up into the Berkshires and southern Vermont. Not because I wanted to visit those places, they were just where the roads I knew tended to go. I daydreamed a lot while I drove, and tried to remember moments in my past that weren't freighted with impossibly painful associations.

I kept clear of thinking about the immediate past. I pretended I didn't have one, as if I'd awakened from a five-year coma, slightly brain damaged. Not a hard act to sustain, given my condition at the time.

My hotel was off the Merritt Parkway not far from the house in Stamford. It was the kind frequented by middle and upper level executives passing through the economic distortion field of Fairfield County. Big comfortable double beds, disinterested employees and a vapid overpriced bar and restaurant filled with forced theme entertainment and lonely distracted guys trying to look comfortable in conformist casual clothes. A dozen or so TVs disturbed the utter silence and saved the tired blond woman working the bar from having to indulge people from other parts of the country in desultory conversation.

I'd left all my belongings at the house in Stamford, so I had to go into town to provision. I'd never been to a store in the middle of a working day to buy a can of shaving cream. I felt impossibly alien walking down the crammed retail aisles surrounded by stay-at-home mothers and retired guys in Jeff caps and polyester stretch pants. The woman behind the checkout counter wore a red smock uniform and a distant disorganized expression. I bought enough shaving cream to keep me out of places like that for at least as long as I thought I'd survive.

I bought a few pairs of jeans and some T-shirts, but held on to the suit, thinking I might need it some day. Abby had paid a lot of money for it at Brooks Brothers. It was a Christmas gift one year. I remember it fit perfectly and that she was disappointed when I didn't fuss over the label. I wondered why just liking the suit for its fine intrinsic qualities wasn't enough.

I used to watch television when there was a game on, but now avoided it completely. I lay on the bed in the quiet of the room and drank Jack Daniels until I fell asleep. I paid my bill a month in advance, so everyone left me alone.

Two weeks into that month a private investigator showed up with a letter from Barry Mildrew in Mason Thigpen's office. It was my copy of the signed agreement. Also a letter outlining my severance package, if I agreed. I signed that, too, and sent it back with the PI after getting him to buy me a round of drinks. He was an ex-fighter, and a night school student at Central Connecticut, so by definition my kind of thug. The salesmen at the hotel bar kept their distance. Survival instincts.

Abby's lawyers sent their own guys a few days later. I entertained them in the same venue. These were more like paralegals than knuckle busters so we had less to talk about. But at least they knew to buy the drinks.

Their paperwork was a little more troubling, which resulted in my field trip to the Meadowlands with the interior of Abby's house, but that came later, after I'd sobered up enough to actually make out the text.

My daughter was the last visitor to my hotel. She found me in the bar, at one of the heavy oak cocktail tables surrounded by an overabundance of padded rolling chairs. It was about four in the afternoon, so I was already ramping up nicely to the first real drunk of the day. She wore faded blue jeans decorated with runic symbols drawn with indelible ink, a wool sweater and silver wire-rim glasses. Her dirty blond hair was pulled back with a cotton scarf rolled into a headband. She carried her jacket hugged tightly with both hands against her midsection, as if trying to contain her entrails. Her face was pale, her eyes braced.

'Hi, sweetheart.'

She sat in one of the chairs and rolled back from the table to give herself ample running room. I had to greet her again before she'd say anything.

'I can't believe this.'

'That's okay,' I said. 'Your choice.'

'I really can't believe this.'

'You look great.'

'How can you say that?'

'It's great to look at you.'

'You should see yourself. That wouldn't be so great.'

'No argument there.'

'Mommy's beside herself.'

'And behind herself. All the way.'

'Everything's always a joke.'

'And not very funny, either. How's school?'

'I can't think about school right now.'

'Now's the best time. Throw yourself into your work.'

'That's your deal. Throw yourself in and never come out.'

'I'm out now.'

'Too late.'

'You forgot the "too little".'

'The what?'

'Too little, too late. Those things usually go together.'

'With you too little's assumed.'

'That's my girl. Sharp as a dart.'

'When are you going to stop this?'

'Stop what?'

'What you're doing. It's crazy.'

'You got your tenses goofed up. I'm not doing anything. I've done something.'

'You and your word games. Mommy's just as bad.'

'The heart of the relationship.'

'No relationship I can see. And certainly no heart.'

'Then why all the fuss?'

'You're not supposed to give up.'

'Says who?'

'Says me. Your daughter, remember? "I'll never let anything bad happen to you, honey?" What do you call this?'

'You turned out great. You're beautiful, intelligent, artistic. You're self-reliant and resourceful. You're actually a nice person, most of the time, which is a real blow against genetic determinism.'

'You're changing the subject.'

'No I'm not. You're all grown up. You're who you are. Go be it.'

'Like, this is none of my business?'

'It's completely your business, it's just not your life.'

'You won't admit you're wrong.'

'Is that all this is? Okay, I'm wrong. I admit it.'

'Then come home.'

'First off, sweetie, it's not your home anymore. You live in Rhode Island. Secondly, it's not mine either, it's your mother's.' I held up my empty glass. 'Can I get you anything? Drink?'

'You can't be serious.'

'I'm buying.'

'With what? You quit your job.'

'They give you a drinking stipend. It's part of the severance.'

I waived to the woman at the bar. She caught me out of the corner of her eye and nodded.

'Mommy said you're in wicked bad trouble, but she wouldn't tell me what, or why.'

'Not really in trouble, but the night's still young.'

'Did you hurt anybody?'

'Nobody that matters.'

'Everyone matters.'

'No. You matter. The rest is up for grabs.'

'If I really mattered, we'd be having a different conversation.'

'I never fell for that "if you really loved me" stuff.'

'Too much of a hard-ass.'

'Too realistic.'

'Hard-assed engineer.'

'Worst kind.'

'Think scaring people is some kind of triumph.'

'Only your boyfriends.'

'You don't scare me.'

'Then I did something right.'

'You should scare me, but you don't.'

'Because you've got nothing to fear. You could tear my throat out with your bare hands and I'd kiss your wrists while you did it.'

She clutched her jacket even tighter to her chest.

'I don't get it.'

'You're not supposed to. Later on, you will. Maybe.'

A pallid young waitress dropped another Jack Daniels on the table and looked at my daughter to get her order.

'I'm fine. Thank you.'

The waitress kept her face in neutral and walked off.

'So this is it,' she said to me. 'You're going to sit here for the rest of your life and drink that shit.'

'I'm very proud of you.'

'Stop doing that.'

'I am. Sometimes I can't believe it. What a gift.'

'No help from you.'

'Exactly.'

She seemed to be a little lost for words, an unaccustomed state of affairs. I used the silence to drain off a little of the Jack.

'So this is it,' she said, finally.

'It's great to see you. Even when you're mad at me.'

She stood straight up out of her chair.

'Then take it all in. It's the last time.'

'Aw, geez.'

She pointed her finger at me.

'I know what you're doing. I know exactly what you're doing. But I won't be a witness to it. I'll just wait for the official notice. Bye, Daddy. Thanks for whatever.'

And she turned on her heel and walked away with her head up, briskly, but self-assured, like she was about to catch a train the conductor was holding for her at the platform. I told her I'd always love her, no matter what, but she was way out of earshot by then and wouldn't have heard me anyway.

After that I lost track of time, about two weeks' worth. I know things started with a trip down to a neighbourhood in Stamford where I met up with a bunch of kids I knew from the gym. They had a good time touring me around the local action and unsettling their families by feeding me and letting me sleep on their sofas. My colour got us into a lot of fights, which broke up the monotony of stuffy apartments and ratty neighbourhood hangouts. On one of the nights I left my car, the company car, next to a curb with the engine running. According to the Stamford prosecutor it never turned up again, though I doubt anyone actually looked for it. A few other things happened that I only dimly remember, but it was all pretty thoroughly detailed in the charges they filed against me.

True to her word, my daughter never talked to me again. I knew she wouldn't. She always had a stubborn streak and never would let go once she got a good grip on something.

Joe Sullivan was big enough to take up half the couch in my living room, leaving just enough room for Eddie to scrunch up next to his butt. Sullivan made up for it by rubbing him behind the ears, a treatment Eddie found tirelessly engaging.

By now the ambulance had hauled Buddy off to Southampton Hospital and all of Sullivan's colleagues had drifted away. Ross Semple had threatened to make a personal appearance, but Sullivan had gently discouraged him.

'He still wants you to show up tomorrow for a little chat,' Sullivan told me.

'Not a problem.'

'Not yet.'

Sullivan was still officially on duty, so I felt a little bad about drinking in front of him, though not bad enough to stop. He took it in stride.

He waited till I'd dropped down on the floor with my back

against the fireplace before asking me again if I'd left anything out of my statement.

'I was getting my mail when he cold cocked me, only this time it didn't land straight on and I was able to get away. He chased me up to the house where I got my little bat, which I used to successfully fight him off.'

'I'll say.'

'You writing all this down?'

'Already did. No witnesses?'

'I don't know. You can ask around.'

'Nothing to add?'

'Only, I guess, I know who he is.'

Sullivan arched his eyebrows and let his hands fall into his lap, a gesture I'd seen my mother use on more than one occasion. Usually under similar circumstances.

'Memory coming back? All of a sudden?'

'I didn't see him at the Playhouse. Just his boots. But I saw him before that, down at the ocean. I was running on the beach. When I got back to the lot this guy was nosing around my car. I was probably a little less than polite about it. A few words. I ended up backin' into his Beemer. Gave it a little bump with the Grand Prix. You know, meatball like that, easily offended.'

'Easier when it's you.'

'Come on, Joe, I'm not interested in any more of that shit. Honest to God,' I said, like I really meant it, because I really did. 'Though I guess I provoked him somehow. Anyway, he'd've killed me if he could. I know that.'

Sullivan flipped ahead in his casebook.

'You wouldn't be the first.'

'What do you mean?'

'Buddy Florin. From upstate. Ten years for manslaughter. Two other charges, later dropped. Freelancer from out of the city. He's a punk. Old-fashioned kind. That tell you anything?'

'Bad luck.'

'Nothing else, huh? No other bells going off? Nothing else you want to tell me about?'

I thought about it for a minute.

'I'm glad I fucked him up,' I admitted.

'Oh, you fucked him up all right.'

'Better me than Eddie. If I'd've let him out, there's no telling.'

Eddie picked his head up at the mention of his name. The fur on the left side of his face was pushed up from sleeping on it, imparting a look of lunatic disequilibrium. Sullivan looked down at him and brushed the hair back into place.

'Yeah. I'm nervous just sittin' here.'

'You sure you can't have a beer or something?'

'I can have a beer. Actually, it's encouraged. Fraternizing with the public.'

I got it for him and we spent the next hour or so talking about the Knicks, a subject I felt more comfortable discussing, whether with honest Irish cops or earnest gay tycoons.

For some stupid reason I walked Eddie on a leash before we went to bed. It was either the smell of evil out on my lawn or the adrenalin still itching at my nerves. Whatever it was, it kept me awake, so even after Eddie was zonked out on the bed I was up pacing around. On an impulse I got Buddy's gun out of my sock drawer where I'd stashed it before Sullivan showed up. It was a Glock 23, .40 calibre. Fashionable gun for an old-fashioned punk. Probably liked the look of it. Matt black, polymer and steel. Lots of kick.

Too wired to sleep, and nothing else to do, I took the gun down to my father's workbench so I could look at its innards. Typical hard-assed engineer. Always curious about instruments of death.

EDDIE STUCK me in the ribs with his back feet when he jumped off the bed, barking like mad. It was daylight, but I hadn't been sleeping very long, so it took a little while to get my bearings. I could hear the sound of someone banging on the front door even through all the frantic yelping.

'Goddammit, Eddie.'

I pulled on a pair of jeans and a sweatshirt and answered the door.

'Hi, Jackie.'

'That has got to be the stupidest car on the whole planet.'

'The standard shift throws a lot of people.'

'Did I wake you? I hope so. What happened to your hand?'

Eddie had regained control of himself and was out on the lawn, buzzing around with his nose an inch off the grass.

'Coffee?' I asked her.

'No. Pickup truck.'

My automatic coffeepot had done its duty a half-hour earlier and the results were wafting around the house.

'Come on, it's already brewed.'

'You got a lot of nerve.'

'You don't want to know what happened?'

'Jesus Christ.'

After I had her hands filled with my biggest ceramic mug, I was able to talk her into waiting for me out on the porch while I took a shower. She was still thoroughly pissed, but her curiosity, as always, held her on the line. I told Eddie to keep her company.

'Just don't give him any dope. He's loopy enough as it is.'

I poured myself a cup and took it with me to the outdoor shower, which I used until the pipes threatened to freeze, usually after the first of the year. Even in the early morning light, the day was clear and full of colour, the sky the deepest blue.

I squandered gallons of hot water, creating clouds of steam that billowed from the shower and upset the local climatic balance. The floor of the shower was filled with red, yellow and orange leaves from the oaks and maples overhead. I cleared the drain with my feet and watched the water swirl away in a tiny vortex. I turned the hot water up another notch to massage my shoulders and the back of my neck. I took a sip of the coffee. I tried to picture Regina seducing Carl Bollard, but it wouldn't work. I wondered what she looked like as a young woman, and that was easier. Tall and straight-shouldered, firm handshake, and wary eyes. A hard outer shell that was tough to crack, but once you did, it was all soft and tractable inside. Hopeful, but afraid of hurt. In need, despite her better judgement.

And always braced for the worst kind of disappointment.

I was able to stay clear of Jackie's questions until I was in my clothes. I could feel the frustration penetrate the walls between my bedroom and the screened-in porch. She was pacing when I got there.

'I owe you big time,' I told her, before she had a chance to speak.

'I know that.'

She was wearing a short wool coat in a giant red and black plaid. Her thick strawberry hair was tied up in a ponytail that spewed like a fountain almost from the top of her head. On her feet were a pair of beat-to-hell cowboy boots. Ready to start kicking.

'Don't tell me you're going to apologise,' she said.

'Actually, I need another favour.'

'Now who's smoking dope?'

'Just drive to the Village with me. I'll tell you everything on the way.'

She squinted at me as if contemplating a right hook. Probably pack a more effective punch than Jimmy Maddox.

'You think I have nothing else to do?'

'Okay. You're hired.'

'What?'

'You're hired. For real this time. Where do I sign?'

'I can't do that.'

'Your last client just shot himself. You got an opening.'

'Jesus Christ.'

'Come on. We gotta move. I'm not paying you to just stand around.'

Eddie was unhappy in the backseat of the Grand Prix. I rolled the windows down so he could stick out his head. The wind made it hard to talk, but I felt I owed him, after leaving him inside for so long the day before. I was still able to tell Jackie the gist of what I wanted to tell her before we got to the big parking lot behind Main Street. I gave it to her in a disorganized, disconnected jumble, without a lot of detail, but that was fine. If I'd told her more she'd have bailed out of the car.

'What's my role here again?' she asked as I parked the Grand Prix behind the bank.

'Bodyguard.'

'Great.'

'Just stay alert and watch my back.'

'Speaking metaphorically.'

'Right.'

You could get to the main floor of Harbor Trust through a rear entrance off the parking lot. It was a simple glass door with the bank's name stenciled in bright gold leaf. Inside was a long corridor that opened up into a big room with all the tellers, loan officers and personal bankers at their stations. I never came in this way, so it took a few moments to locate Amanda. She was at her desk, staring at her computer. She almost missed us walking by, but at the last moment her eyes left the screen and locked on to mine. She looked startled.

'We're here to see Roy,' I said, without stopping, though I tried to look breezy and offhand. Her eyes shot to Jackie Swaitkowski. I smiled and waved as we walked by the other personal bankers and up to the guy who manned the desk right outside Roy Battiston's office. I didn't know what his official job was, but I thought he'd suit the purpose.

'I'm Sam Acquillo. This is Attorney Jacqueline Swaitkowski. We're here to see Mr Battiston.'

The guy automatically looked over his shoulder at Roy's door.

'I'm not sure he's in. Can I say what it's about?'

'Just tell him who's here. He'll see us,' I said. Then to Jackie, 'His car's in the lot.'

The guy went back to Roy's office and disappeared through the door. Jackie and I stood there and waited. Amanda was frozen in her seat, her hands motionless on the keyboard, her face taut. And alert. The other bank employees ignored us, going about their silent tasks with an air of placid resolve. There were customers in line at the teller windows and a few at the desks of personal bankers, or waiting, seated on woodframe benches upholstered in synthetic suede. No canned music, I noticed, gratefully.

The guy came out and closed the door behind him, but not before I saw Roy at his desk, in shirtsleeves, writing something on a pad.

'Just give him a few minutes,' the guy said, then sat back down at his desk.

We went back to standing there in the dead calm of the bank. Jackie was doing a good job looking neutral and disinterested. As if she had complete command of the situation. Poised and prepared for any eventuality.

I began to wonder if there was another way out of Roy's office when the door opened and he waved us in. He still had his assertive, can-do handshake, but his palm was hot and wet.

'Sam. Jackie.'

'Hi, Roy,' I said.

'You know each other,' he said, in a way that was part question, part revelation.

'Jackie's my lawyer,' I said to him as I sank into one of his two herculean guest chairs. Jackie took the other. She manifested a fine lawyerly posture, even though dressed like she'd just come from mucking out a stall.

'I've worked with Jackie,' said Roy, dropping into his own chair behind the desk, 'right?'

She nodded. He waited for her to say something, but she didn't. He quickly gave up waiting.

Roy didn't look too good. His skin was moist, adding a slight sheen to his bloodless complexion. He had the type of head that was more narrow at the top than the bottom. It expanded at the jawline, causing a jowly bulge he'd probably never lose even if he starved to death.

'So, folks, what can I do for you?'

His office was panelled in a light walnut ply, the carpet was deep green, his desk was chrome and covered in a laminate reminiscent of the masonite found in basement remodeling projects. No photos or trophies or insipid executive games you get for Christmas from your family, or as a token of appreciation for speaking to the Kiwanis. There were two tables flanking the desk like outriggers. They were covered with files and stacks of loose paper.

'I'm here to pick up a document.'

I thought Roy looked relieved.

'Okay. Maybe Amanda could help you.'

'You know I'm the administrator of Regina Broadhurst's estate.'

'Of course. We had her account as well. Amanda can pull the records, make copies.'

'That's not what I mean.'

He still had the look of helpful curiosity.

'Okay, I'm sorry. Why don't you tell me.'

It was never easy being Roy Battiston. He must have realised at an early age he was the only one in his family who could think. As he moved through school and got to know other kids and other families, as he read and looked around at people in Town, he must have been appalled at what fate had allotted him. Taunted, probably, like all chubby kids with glasses and intelligence, but worse for him, with his bad clothes and embarrassing relatives. The awakening must have dawned slowly, but then steadily strengthened, driving him deeper into his own mind. Forming a bedrock of worry and resentment.

And eventually hunger took hold. Desire. Inflamed by the secret knowledge that he could do things nobody ever suspected he could do. Propelled by determination and conviction. Maybe a promise to himself to soothe away the pain with achievement. To cleanse shame with success, the kind that mattered to people who mattered to him.

I never knew Roy very well, but I understood what happened to him.

'The trust. Carl's trust. I need to see it.'

He started to fall back into his chair, thought better of it, and sat back up again. He put both hands palm down on the desk and took a deep breath.

'I really don't know what you mean,' he said.

'As administrator of Regina's estate,' said Jackie, 'Sam has the obligation to identify and adjudicate all surviving assets and liabilities. Even those Regina may have been unaware of.'

Roy's face had moistened even more while we talked, though his voice was still evenly modulated. The real story was in his eyes. Even behind his glasses I could see they were lit with alarm.

'You might have an opinion on this,' I said to Roy. 'You think Hornsby planned it all along, or just let it happen?'

'Let what happen? Milton Hornsby was a business partner of mine. I have no other opinion of him.'

'Really. So you didn't know Bay Side Holdings was owned by a trust created to manage the assets of a guy who'd been dead for over twenty years.'

'Of course not.'

'Personally, I think he just let it happen. Things just sort of flowed along and there was nobody there to do anything about it. After Carl and WB crapped out, Hornsby just kept right on going, paying bills, filing tax returns, complying with every statute and regulation, and generally keeping his head down. Meanwhile siphoning off a nice income for himself.

'Oh, and keeping the monthly allowances going to Regina and your mother-in-law. Barely enough to live on, especially when you think about what was there, but on time, every month.'

Roy's face finally took on a little colour. A bright dab of red on each cheek.

'I have no idea what you're talking about,' he said.

'We know everything, Roy,' said Jackie. 'The only question is what we're going to do about it.'

'No, I disagree. You have no idea what you're talking about.' He surprised me by half standing up from his chair. I stood up all the way.

'Sit down, Roy. You need to listen carefully. Concentrate on what we're saying. This is the only chance you're going to get.'

He slowly sank back down in his chair. So did I, trying to get comfortable in that scratchy upholstery.

Roy knew that Hornsby was a lawyer and the CFO of WB manufacturing, but I told him again anyway. It was partly for Jackie's benefit. I went on to tell them about Carl Bollard, Sr., who had set up a trust after his wife died, realizing his wayward son was next in line. Anticipating his own demise, he wanted a way to keep a leash on Carl Junior, preserve the assets of the estate and keep the plant in operation. It gave Carl Junior five years to grow up. After that, he got everything no matter what. At some point, Carl Senior. named his young CFO, Milton Hornsby, the trustee, probably to tie his son more tightly to the family business.

This was prescient, because the next thing Carl Senior did was die, leaving Hornsby in control of the company, all its property and assets, and Carl Junior's personal fortune. And consequently, Carl Junior himself. As it turned out, both guys were fine with the deal, given the tidy *quid pro quo*. Carl got to live like a king, or rather a legitimate CEO, while Hornsby basically ran the show. Carl was probably more than happy to let him. Hornsby was a lot younger than Carl, but he was Carl's fairy godfather.

And the trust his magic wand. No better way to plaster over Carl's indiscretions. Carl was rich, spoiled and wild, and plugged into the Hamptons' social scene. Regina worked at WB, in the plant. Handsome girl and hard as nails. But not too smart about men. He scoops her up, a few drinks, a few laughs, the usual ensues. He's not about to marry her, but he takes care of her, financially, anyway. Out of conscience or fear, who knows. Regina was never anybody you'd want to cross, at least not out where she could see you.

By 1960, Carl Junior has full control of the trust. He simply orders Hornsby to write Regina into the deal as a full beneficiary and instals her in a house on company property. The only hitch is now that Regina's an equal beneficiary of the trust, she's also an equal partner in the whole enterprise. Technically. But it really doesn't matter because she doesn't know it. Why should she? Carl's not entirely stupid. And Hornsby sure as hell wasn't going to tell her. He figures in a few years Carl will come to his senses, Hornsby can just scratch her off the list and WB can go on its merry way.

Roy was listening to me, but not happily. He kept trying to get comfortable in his chair, as if they'd just bought it for him and it wasn't yet broken in.

'I really don't know what all this has to do with me or Harbor Trust,' he said.

I ignored him.

'Trouble is, guys like Carl Bollard make a habit of fucking up. New chick shows up in the office, probably in the typing pool, sexy little Italian named Julia Anselma. Boppin' around the office in those hot fifties fashions. Before you know it, Carl's at it again.'

'Carl Bollard was Julia's boss,' said Roy, as if disputing the notion.

'Right. Only this time, there's another wrinkle. The chickie on the side produces a chicklet. Your wife, as it turns out.'

Roy's face went slack as he saw the rest of his life board a train and leave the station.

'By the time Amanda was born, Carl had moved on to another girl. But Julia got the same deal as Regina. A lifetime of security in exchange for a zipped lip. Say what you will, I think Julia did a brave thing. She gave Amanda a safe, comfortable upbringing, with a minimum of turmoil. All she had to do was keep a secret.'

I hadn't told Jackie about Julia or Amanda. But she still maintained her professional reserve. The girl had good game.

'Of course, Julia doesn't know about the trust either. Though you can just hear Milton Hornsby excoriating Carl, 'No more! This one is the last!' He wasn't a nice guy, Hornsby, but you can't blame him for being a little frustrated. Here he is busting ass for the company, building it up and keeping it running through all kinds of tough times, only to find himself babysitting the spoiled, screwed-up son of the founder, who winds up owning everything, while Hornsby is left to play loyal family retainer. Must have really eaten him up.

'Lucky for him, though, Carl's go-go lifestyle also featured oceans of alcohol, so right after the company folds, so does Carl. That's when Hornsby decides it's payback time. Carl's will left all his assets to the trust. Since Regina and Julia are listed as surviving beneficiaries, the trust is technically still in force, controlling all the assets, the girls just don't know it.'

'You have to register wills on the death of the signer,' said Jackie, interrupting, 'but not trusts. It's up to the trustee to come forward with that kind of information.'

'Hornsby does everything but. He closes down the plant, pays debts and corporate taxes, fills out forms, satisfies employee claims, sells off viable equipment. Zip zip, the estate is now pretty clean. Just the real estate and investment portfolio, which covers the estate tax, and still throws off enough revenue to keep the whole thing going. And that's where it sits for about twenty years.

'Until you came along, huh Roy?' I said.

By now he had his head in his hands, finally unable to support the weight of his fear.

'You finally score the prettiest girl in the class. She's a bit of a basket case, but what the hell. She's willing to be looked after, and who knows, over time, maybe she'll really dig you. You like her mother, like to chat it up over Thanksgiving dinner. You're a local Southampton guy, obsessed with money, and a banker to boot, a guy who knows real estate. Wouldn't be surprising for you to ask, "So, Julia, your mortgage all paid off"? "Oh, no, Roy, we don't own the house, it belongs to my old company, WB Manufacturing. It's an arrangement." "It is"? thinks Roy, "How could that be?" Easy enough to check your mother-in-law's account at Harbor Trust and see the monthly direct deposits, then trace the ownership of her house through the tax rolls to Bay Side Holdings, which leads directly to pay dirt. Milton Hornsby. Carl Bollard's loyal CFO, livin' large in Sag Harbor.'

'You caught Hornsby violating his fiduciary duty. A very serious matter,' said Jackie, swept up in the moment, or maybe just offended by Hornsby's professional lapse.

'Must have been quite a conversation,' I said. 'You're married to Amanda, after all. What's hers is yours. The simple, easy thing would be to expose Hornsby and just take control of the assets. But you're an ambitious boy who lusts after the Big Play. Why settle for a bunch of millions when you can have gobs of millions? Better yet, be the power behind a huge development scheme. Have the same people who've ignored you or treated you like white trash kissing your ass. And why wait for the ponderous legal system to sort it out when you can have it all now. I mean, if Milton Hornsby could keep it secret, why couldn't Roy?'

'You make Hornsby an offer,' said Jackie. 'Total ruin or help you develop the property. As far as anyone knows, Bay Side Holdings is a legitimate entity, with Milton Hornsby the controlling party. No need to messy up the deal with the actual facts.'

I'd been staring hard at Roy while I talked, but now I snuck a peek over at Jackie. I could feel her flair for outrage about to ignite.

'So now you got Hornsby playing property owner, but you need a developer,' I said. 'Hornsby suggests another WB alum, Bob Sobol, whom Hornsby knows will keep his mouth shut, and make useful connections, inside and outside the legal lines.

'The three of you put a plan together. You handle financing, of course, which gives you a reason to visit the home office on a regular basis. Which also makes it easy to stay in touch with architects and planners in the city, people avoiding locals so the plan won't leak prematurely.'

I heard Jackie give a tiny, barely audible snort.

'Everything's cookin' right along until you're ready to subdivide the property to suit modern development. Bay Side might own everything, but property lines are regulated by the Town. You need variances. Which means you have to go before the zoning appeals board.'

'Not a problem,' said Jackie. 'Sobol brings in Hunter Johnson, a hotshot from the city, and teams him up with me, who I must say commands the local scene, and we put together an excellent case. Big, and complicated, but nothing the Town hasn't seen before. Except for the ratty old plant sitting in the middle of the concept. It's an obstacle. But not insurmountable. It just means a wider than normal scope for a variance request. Everyone on Jacob's Neck and Oak Point has to be notified. And invited to a public hearing.'

'Including Regina,' I shot in before she could get there. 'It suddenly dawns on you – when notice goes out to Regina, who knows what'll happen? Who knows what she's going to say, and to whom? Everything's legally half hers – what if she finds out? Julia Anselma didn't know anything, but who knows about Regina? She's a crazy old broad, with a big mouth. Can you afford to take the chance?

'You panic. Shut it all down. And wait. Hoping something will come to you. Away out. Away to get everything back in gear. The pause is great for Hornsby – takes the heat off. But not so great for Sobol. He's still young enough to enjoy a big windfall. And he's not happy that the only thing standing in his way is a few old ladies.'

Roy was still holding his head, with his eyes closed, but as we talked he started to shake it back and forth.

'Are you listening, Roy?' I asked.

He nodded.

'Good, I'm not done yet.'

He stayed still.

'I don't know how it worked. If you talked about it, if you were actively involved, or if Sobol took care of everything himself and kept you and Hornsby in the clear. Sobol got to know both the old girls by hanging around the Senior Centre. He could have worked it out all by himself. He used to be in quality control. I could see an engineer's touch in how it was handled. I don't think it was Buddy. He's just muscle.'

Roy looked up.

'What are you saying?' he asked.

I thought about Sullivan telling me Regina might have been a lousy old bitch, but she was his lousy old bitch. That's how I thought about my father. He was a lousy father, but he was my lousy father. And he gave me my lousy life. People like Regina and my father, living side by side on the tip of Oak Point at the feet of the holy Peconic, never really figured out why they were here on earth, never really had a chance to know much more than hope, hard work and disappointment. And all they got in the end was the privilege of being beaten to death by people who thought they had a greater purpose, thought they could just sweep those shabby crippled lives away from their feet like so much useless trash.

'You killed her. And you killed Julia Anselma.'

I realised Roy was weeping. He'd been sweating so hard the tears had just blended in.

'Lock the door,' he was saying. 'Please lock the door. I don't want anyone coming in.'

He waited until Jackie got back in her chair. She tossed him a crumpled napkin dug out of her wool jacket. He ignored it.

'Those bastards,' he said. 'They'd say things about wasting the old ladies. That nobody'd even blink an eye. I couldn't tell if they were just provoking me, or if they meant it. But I swear, I never ever would have done such a thing.'

'Doesn't matter. They're in it, you're in it,' I told him.

I looked over at Jackie. She nodded.

'Oh, God.'

He dropped his head to the desk.

'Roy, listen to me. Look at me.'

He looked up again.

'Let's take this one step at a time. You have the original trust document. I want it.'

He started to deny it, but I cut him off.

'That was your leverage with Hornsby. As long as you had the document, you had him by the balls.'

I leaned forward and said, between my teeth, 'Give it to me.'

It was on the bottom of a stack of papers on one of the tables. All he had to do was roll his desk chair over a few feet and pull it out. The paper was yellowy brown along the edges. On the cover was the same label Hornsby had taped to the envelope. It was typewritten and you could feel the impressions on the back of the individual sheets. There was a table of contents. I flipped to the article describing beneficiaries, titled, 'Distribution of Trust Property.' The first section said, 'Upon the death of any beneficiary, as described in Article Six, the trust property shall be divided into as many shares as shall be necessary to create one equal share for each of the living beneficiaries, and one equal share for each deceased beneficiary who has living descendents.'

I flipped to Article Six. Regina and Julia each had their own sections. Other sections described how the entire principal and net income of the trust belonged to the beneficiaries. The trustee had full powers of administration, though the beneficiaries had the right to appoint or excuse the trustee. At least Hornsby had the good manners to finally excuse himself.

I handed it to Jackie.

'I was going to tell her,' said Roy.

'Who?' Jackie asked, looking down as she leafed through the document.

'Amanda,' I answered for him, 'who you knew would be gone like a shot the second she learned how rich she really was. On her own, without you. To say nothing of the betrayal. So, you were going to tell her like Hornsby was going to confess on the front page of the *New York Times*.'

'I was only trying to care for her.'

'By killing her mother?'

He winced. Then started to whine.

'I told you,' he started.

I stopped him.

'Roy, shut up. If you say one more word I'm liable to change my mind.'

By this point he was way too desperate and terrified to think clearly.

'What are you talking about?'

Jackie looked up again from the trust, curious herself.

There was so much about the world I didn't understand. And never would. Like why my parents had married each other in the first place. It was never explained. It never even came up, but my sister and I would have cut off our own limbs rather than ask.

It was as if some external event had brought them together involuntarily, but irrevocably, and they were resigned to their fate. It was unclear whether they loved or despised each other. They simply existed as an official pairing, charged with the responsibility of feeding and housing two children, keeping the house clean and the lawn cut, and the apartment in the Bronx free of dishes in the sink or dirty laundry on the floor. My father was in a near state of rage most of the time, much of which he directed toward my mother, but only because of her proximity. My sister and I were expert at making ourselves scarce, otherwise we'd have attracted a greater share of his wrath. Maybe as much as the guy who pumped his gas, or the check-out girls at the grocery store, or local, state and federal government officials, or the IRS, or any professional athlete who ever won or lost anything. Fury was his natural state of being, unlike my mother, for whom the situation involved a greater degree of happenstance. She bore it silently, at least as far as I knew. Yet I imagined her seeking rescue, in whatever form it offered itself. She never said it, but I always thought it. As I passed through adolescence, and my perceptions matured, I began to feel responsible for allowing her circumstances to persist. I developed an unrelenting compulsion to do something. I just didn't know what it was supposed to be. So I did nothing, beyond wishing things would change. That something would happen to end the dreadful state of despair and indecision.

And then it did. Two anonymous thugs, agents of a secret power, came into the world and flicked my father into oblivion.

My mother was rescued. But she didn't want to be. She was utterly grief-stricken and furious, suddenly at odds with the entire world, as if taking up my father's blind rage as her just inheritance.

I wasn't much comfort. All I could think of was my own dismal calculation. That I'd wished it all into existence, thereby denying my parents their lives and me any hope of reprieve from my remorse, for the rest of mine.

So it seemed inevitable that I would marry someone I'd never want to know and help create a child who didn't want to know me. That I'd destroy my working life and burn my future to the ground. I couldn't save any of it.

Just like I couldn't save Regina, even though she was the only thing left for me to save.

'Here's the deal,' I said. 'You tell the cops and Amanda about the whole scam, including your thing with Hornsby and the development project. In return I let the old ladies stay dead of natural causes.'

Jackie's mouth actually dropped open.

'What are you saying?'

'It's how I want it.'

'I don't think it's up to you,' she said. 'There's the matter of the truth.'

'I'm in charge of the truth. I got all the evidence, all the information. It's not going anywhere without me. Anyway, this is in the best interest of your client, Mr Battiston.'

'Hold on a minute,' she started to say.

'You're the only one who can make this come out right. Roy goes down for colluding with Hornsby to defraud Amanda and her mother. Nobody, especially Amanda, ever learns about Julia. Or Regina, for that matter. That's the deal.'

It took a few more minutes to get Jackie all the way on board. I really didn't have a good reason for her to do it, which is probably what ultimately appealed to her. That and the possibility of being shut out of the whole thing, whatever it was. That was Jackie's Achilles' heel. Fear of being the oddball left sitting alone while all the other girls were out on the dance floor.

As Roy listened to us talk his face didn't know whether to look hopeful or horrified. When I pointed my finger at him he almost jumped out of his chair.

'But if you try to test me, or weasel on any of this, it's all yours. I don't care how much you actually had to do with it. I don't care what it does to Amanda. I'll make sure she thinks you were in it up to your neck. You might talk your way out of ripping her off. Killing her mother, probably not.'

Before he had time to think it all through Jackie had him on his feet, his face wiped off and his suit jacket on. We marched him through the big banking room, past Amanda, who didn't say a word to any of us, and out to the parking lot. He got to ride in the back of the Grand Prix with Eddie, who was indifferent to his sins and avarice, all the way to the Town police headquarters in Hampton Bays where we called ahead to have Joe Sullivan and Ross Semple waiting for us.

I left him there with Jackie. She seemed to be warming to the whole idea, and Roy was so afraid of me he had to take her. Sullivan said he'd give her a lift back to my house to pick up her truck. I was glad to leave it all with them. I didn't know how it was going to work out for Roy in the end, but I was sore all over from my little dance with Buddy, and tired from staying up most of the night cajoling and dodging questions from Sullivan. I just had to make another stop.

THE SENIOR Centre was in its usual state of glacial clamour. My friend at the counter greeted me like it was our first meeting.

'Is Ms. Filmore in?' I asked her.

'You from Mississippi?'

'No Ma'am.'

'My grandmother was from Mississippi. She wanted us to call her Miz Clarke.'

'A feminist.'

'All us Clarke girls were feminine, Mister.'

'I bet I can just go in and find Barbara for myself.'

She gave an expansive wave toward the door.

'Après vous, Senior.'

'Grazie.'

It was easy to spot that big mane of ersatz hair standing out from the prevailing white and grey. Her right hand was on her hip and her left was wagging an index finger at a frightened little gnome of a guy holding a cafeteria tray piled high with creamers and sugar bowls. She clammed up when she saw me approach.

'Mr Acquillo.'

'Hi, Barbara.'

'I don't think Mr Hodges is here today.'

'Too bad. Looks like you could use the help.'

Her victim had already slipped quietly out of range. She pretended to ignore him.

'Not at all, Mr Acquillo. Everything's quite under control.'

'Actually, I was looking for Bob. Your Bob. Sobol.'

If her back had straightened any further she'd have snapped her spine.

'My Bob? Really.'

'Okay. Bob's his own man. Know where he is? I got a tip for him. Real estate.'

She softened a little.

'Really. He's quite in the market.'

'Well, gotta find him to tell him. *Carpe diem* and all that.'

She pondered a second or two.

'You know Moses Lane?'

'I do. Down near the Red Sea.'

'Funny. Here's the address.'

She wrote it down on a piece of paper, then watched me walk all the way out of the building. So did most of the old folks manning the card tables and conversation pits. I thought if I suddenly whirled around and yelled boo half of them would go into cardiac arrest.

I had to drive through the Village shopping area to get to Moses Lane. It was full of Summer People who'd learned you could stretch the summer out to Thanksgiving. They mostly looked nicely dressed and well-fed, but not entirely sure of themselves, as if fearing discovery. I liked it better when they all went home after Labor Day, but you have to be realistic. It wasn't their fault that God put a place like this only two hours from midtown Manhattan. On a good traffic day.

I noticed pumpkins everywhere, and tied-up cornstalks and cardboard cutouts of witches and ghosts hung up in store windows. Not many kids ever came to the cottage on Halloween. I always made them say please and thank you, which used to mortify my daughter. The other parents in Stamford said she was the most polite kid in the neighbourhood. She'd probably grown out of that living in the city with all the other overachievers.

Moses Lane was off Hill Street just west of the Village. It was typical of the areas once lived in by Southampton locals – modest, well-kept houses, neat lawns and gravel driveways. Now you could see the encroachment of postmodernism and German cars, seeping out of the estate district and spreading out like the brown tide across the neighbourhood.

Barbara Filmore's place was a nice pre-restoration bungalow with a tiny mother-in-law building in the back. You got to the front door through an arched gate covered in wisteria. I left Eddie locked in the car and went up to ring the bell, but no answer. So I knocked loudly enough to be heard next door, which brought a muffled yell from the backyard. Shades of Milton Hornsby. When I went back there Sobol was sitting at a picnic table in the middle of the yard, just to the left of the mother-in-law shack. He was smoking a cigarette, dumping the ashes in a big bowl full of butts on the seat next to him.

'House rules,' he said to me as I approached.

'Which house?'

'Both of 'em. I got this little one here,' he jerked his thumb back to the mother-in-law place, 'but I got bigger ambitions.'

'Apparently.'

I sat across from him and dug out a Camel. He offered up his lighter.

'Barbara told me you were coming over with a tip.'

'Good lookout.'

'She wanted to make sure I was around.'

'So, are you two,' I made the universal New York gesture for, you know, what we often gesture about. He didn't like it.

'I think that's somethin' of a private nature.'

'You're right. None of my business.'

He nodded.

'So, this tip.'

'Big development up in North Sea. Right next to me, as it turns out.'

Sobol's head was just a little too small for his body, which was a solid round ball. His lack of hair and grubby little moustache did little to aid the overall effect. He'd tried to help things out by dyeing what was left of his hair an unnatural black, which contrasted poorly with the white stubble on his unshaven face. The only part of him that didn't look like it belonged to a natural schlub were his eyes. They were hard black and fixed on my face.

'I might already know about that one,' he said, slowly.

'Yeah, I know. That's why I thought you'd be interested.'

'Interested. Yeah. I'm interested in what your deal is in this.'

'It affects my neighbourhood. I'm captain of the neighbourhood watch.'

'That'd be news to the neighbours.'

'I like to keep it on a need-to-know basis.'

'Self-appointed, huh?'

'No. Hereditary.'

'Yeah, whatever.'

'Plus all the professional training.'

'Must be a tough part of town.'

'Mostly quiet. Occasionally get a rat passing through.'

'Really. Seen any lately?'

'Last night, as it turns out.'

Sobol finally stopped trying to stare my eyeballs out of their sockets and looked down at his pack of Marlboros. I thought it was safe to blink. He flicked out a cigarette and lit it.

'That's what exterminators are for,' he said, puffing the smoke out with the words.

'You must know our rat. I think he's done a little exterminating himself.'

I pulled a cloth bag holding Buddy's Glock out from under my jacket and dumped the gun on the table. It hit the wood with a loud noise – loud enough for me to realise we'd been speaking very softly to each other. Sobol didn't flinch. He just shook his head and went back to the big stare.

'Don't know anybody like that,' he said, 'but I've heard there's an unlimited supply of 'em back in the city.'

'More the reason for restrictive zoning.'

'That's right,' he said, waving his Marlboro at me, 'you're into real estate.'

'Only a spectator.'

'I figured that. Like some of the old ladies when I was growing up. Watchin' everything going on in the street from behind their Venetian blinds. Nothin' better to do.'

'Piss you off, did it? The old ladies?'

Sobol leaned back from the table and pulled back his shoulders, grimacing.

'It's hard sitting on these benches with no backs,' he said. 'I think Filmore put 'em here on purpose.'

'Another reason to quit smoking.'

He settled himself back into his original uncomfortable position.

'Didn't you come over here to give me a tip?' he asked. 'Like, where's the tip?'

'The project in North Sea. Looks like Roy's going to have to turn the whole thing over to his wife, now that he's in jail for defrauding her. Actually, at the moment he's spending some quality time with Chief Semple. You know, unloading everything. Clearing his conscience, I guess. I'll bet it's a pretty interesting story. But I thought you should know Amanda's in the driver's seat now. I remember you asked her to help you find a place.'

'Good-looking girl, Amanda. You say Roy was trying to screw her?'

'Yeah, imagine trying to screw your own wife.'

'Why I never got married.'

'Don't touch it.'

'What?'

Sobol's hand had somehow moved to within a foot of Buddy's gun. I placed my hand on the table at approximately the same distance.

'I'm an ex-fighter, Bob. I got reflexes like a mongoose.'

Sobol pulled his hand back a few inches.

'I hate weird fuckers like you, Acquillo.'

'There's gratitude.'

'Screwball fuckers. You think I don't know all about you? About what you been up to? I knew you'd stick your fucking nose into my shit. Fucking whack job.'

'Too much time on my hands.'

Sobol still hadn't raised his voice, but his ugly little face finally had some colour in it. Suited him better.

'I still don't know your deal,' he said to me, patiently.

'I'm the administrator.'

'What the fuck is that?'

'When my neighbour Regina died, she didn't have much of a family, so the County named me administrator to clean up her worldly affairs. That's all. I'm just trying to clean things up.'

He thought about that for a few moments. Sizing up the situation. 'I don't know what you think you know, but if you think that bag of shit Battiston's a problem for me, you're a bigger whack job than I thought.'

I snorted out a little laugh. I couldn't help myself.

'Roy's not your problem, Bob. I'm your problem.'

Sobol had something else to think about, so he stalled for time by looking around Barbara Filmore's backyard.

'It's not bad livin' here,' he said, 'but I'd like a little more property. I need elbow room.'

'Not me. I've been scaling back.'

'You know what this little joint's worth? Like, two million bucks. What's with that? I lived in this town twenty years ago. Back then you could buy any of these places for about 50K. Now it's like all the rich fucks decided nobody like me's allowed in. Everything's jacked up to the stratosphere. It's unnatural.'

'The coffee's gotten better.'

'Oh, yeah, that's right. What am I thinkin'.'

'You might just have to look somewhere else, Bob. Set your sights on another horizon.'

'Not goddammed likely.'

'Just trying to help.'

'You keep saying that, but I'm not hearing anything that sounds like it.'

'Fair enough, Bob,' I told him. 'You're right about sticking my nose in your shit. Trust me, I know your shit inside and out. Everything, every step of the way. So, the tip I've got for you, if you will, is more like a proposition.'

The word 'proposition' seemed to register with him.

'You don't talk to Amanda Battiston. In fact, you don't talk to anybody. You clean out that little hole you're living in and scurry back to wherever you came from. Whatever Roy gives up on you can't be helped. Otherwise, I keep your shit to myself.'

Bob wasn't immediately receptive to the idea. In fact, it caused him to crack a little bit of a smile.

'Unless I'm imagining things, I think I just heard a threat,' he said.

'More of a once-in-a-lifetime opportunity.'

'Yeah. A threat.'

'Okay, a threat. Have it your way.'

'Nobody threatens me.'

'I just want you gone. When you consider the alternative, not a bad deal.'

'You don't have anything,' he said.

'I got everything. Hell, Roy'll get me most of the way there, all I got to do is push it over the edge.'

He was back to his staring thing. I broke away from the deadly gaze long enough to light my second smoke of the conversation. Nothing like a cigarette to give your hands something to do. Only, it's a good idea not to forget they're supposed to be guarding a Glock automatic.

Sobol snatched it up, checked the clip, slammed it back in and had a round racked in front of the hammer before I had a match fully ignited.

'Some fucking mongoose,' he said, pointing the barrel directly at my chest. The gun had so much of my attention I almost burned my fingers, but I finally got the cigarette lit. Another way smoking can get you killed.

'That's not going to solve your problem,' I told him.

'Yeah, well, what the fuck. Just say it'll make me feel better.'

I hadn't seen the barrel of a gun from that vantage point since those carefree days after leaving Abby. The experience hadn't gained any allure. It was a strange feeling, other worldly. You think you'd imagine the impending impact of a .40 calibre round ripping into your body, but you mostly think about all the dumb stuff you did that led you to the situation you're in. It must be some sort of denial, otherwise, you couldn't think at all.

This time, though, mostly what I thought about was my daughter. After the divorce the only asset I had that was worth anything, beyond the cottage, was a gigantic, paid-up life insurance policy. I'd been able to drop Abby as a beneficiary, so it would all go to my daughter. It had some symmetry. She'd be done with me and set for life in one fell swoop.

'I don't care,' I said to Bob Sobol.

'About what?'

'If you shoot.'

'Everybody cares.'

'No, I really don't. Haven't for years. Actually, I'm glad you thought of this. You'll be solving both our problems.'

'More head game shit. It doesn't work with me.'

'Typical engineer.'

'Fuckin' right. Villanova. Three-point-eight average.'

'At least you put it to good use.'

'What, like you? Pathetic, burned-out whack job.'

I couldn't think of much to add to that. I wondered what my father said when he fully realised his big mouth would finally get him killed. I wanted to think he kept it up anyway, right to the end.

'You're actually going to do this,' I said to Sobol.

'I actually am.'

'So whatever I say really doesn't matter.'

'No, I guess it doesn't.'

'Okay, then let's just say, fuck you, Sobol. You're a dick.'

'Last words?'

'Last words.'

'Okay.'

And he pulled the trigger.

The sound was really loud. The air filled with an acid grey smoke, blood spray and tiny pieces of Bob Sobol. Not much of which reached me, miraculously. The concussion made my brain bang around inside my skull and my ears ring for days afterward, but all the destructive force went in Bob's direction. It seemed to kick him up and back, till he was clear of the table and splashed out across the grass. Somehow the bowl of cigarette butts got in the act, so when I bent over him lying there on the lawn I was more struck by the ugliness of all that tobacco ash than the sight of the shattered slide from the top of the automatic sticking out of his forehead. Those murky little eyes were still open, staring up through bright red blood at the clean blue October sky.

'Thing about a mongoose, Bob,' I told him, 'is they never come at a rat straight on.' But he was past listening.

I PROMISED Sullivan I'd go to see Ross Semple that day, so I just left Sobol there on the ground and drove over to Hampton Bays. I figured it was better for Barbara Filmore to call it in after she got home, but as it turned out, she didn't find him until the next morning. That got me tied up again with Sullivan and Ross for the better part of the next day, but I spent that evening productively, drinking Absolut cut with a little orange soda and tossing tennis balls across the lawn without getting out of the Adirondack chair. Eddie liked me to show a little more effort, but did his part anyway, retrieving the yellow balls from off the beach and dropping them at my feet.

The Peconic was all worked up over something, even though the sky was moonlit and clear and the prevailing winds out of the south southwest only slightly more gusty than usual. White caps were springing up all over the bay and a herringbone pattern was etched across the surface of the water. The bay turned out to be a harbinger, as it often does, as bigger, northerly winds swept in on the heels of roiling dark grey clouds and colder air, filled with a frigid mist. The evening slowly darkened into night, so we were finally forced to give it up and head into the house.

The fresh wind from out of the north was icy, but I thought it also had the faint hint of redemption mixed in with the salty spray and bitter brine from off the sacred Little Peconic Bay.

CHAPTER TEN

In February, the Little Peconic is painted in subdued shades of silvery grey. The sun struggles to clear the horizon before retreating again just a few hours later behind the green hills of the North Fork. The soft south-westerlies that soothe the summer months turn into brutish, sodden gales that rush down from the north to beat furiously against the wood-frame storm windows my father installed as winter protection for the screened-in porch.

The woodstove keeps the living room livable as long as it's fully stoked, and if I put a little window fan on the floor facing out the connecting door, I can almost warm the porch enough to hold a book or light a cigarette. This allows me to stay out there through the winter. If I don't monitor the Peconic at all times I might miss something important. Like a passing ocean liner, or the sudden appearance of a plesiosaur.

Eddie seems indifferent to the cold, especially when outside touring the grounds, but once inside he's drawn to the braided rug in front of the woodstove.

'You look like an L.L. Bean catalogue,' I tell him, but he's unfazed. It's all in the breeding.

That afternoon in February he jumped up and barked when he heard a knock at the door, but you could tell it was mostly for show. Looking after his franchise.

'Christ, Sam, I thought this place had central heat,' said Burton, reaching down to pat Eddie's head after stripping the tan kid-leather gloves from his hands.

'Not as long as there's North Sea scrub oak. God's own fuel source.'

'And to warm the inner man?'

'Vodka or bourbon, though God's role in either is debatable.'

'Pour it anyway, for heaven's sake.'

His coat was camel hair and his scarf a grade of cashmere so fluid you could pour it into a bottle. Both were smudged and slightly threadbare, as if he wore them to chop wood or haul stuff to the dump, which he probably did.

I poured us both Maker's Mark on the rocks in my best jelly jar mugs. He pointedly sat in the easy chair next to the woodstove in the living room, so I took a spot on the sofa where I could make polite conversation while keeping an eye on the bay. It was still a sombre battleship grey, though the waning sunlight put a faint gloss on each of the little bay waves. A stalwart seabird swung in loose circles over the water, seeking prey numbed to distraction by the cold.

'I just came from a nice long chat with Ross Semple,' said Burton, after an appreciative slurp of the single malt.

'How's he feeling?'

'Sceptical, I'd think you'd say.'

'Important quality in a police chief.'

'Indeed. He wanted to talk to me about Bob Sobol.'

'Too bad about Bob. But nothing to do with you.'

'Never met the man. Though we had a mutual acquaintance.'

'Last to see him alive.'

'Ross made the same observation.'

'How's that bourbon?'

'Delightfully smooth. And subtle, like the company.'

'Not me. I'm an open book.'

Eddie tried to reclaim the braided rug, but Burton's feet were in the way, so he jumped on the sofa and made a spot for himself by shoving me out of the way. I gave up as much territory as my dignity would allow.

'Ross wanted to know if I thought he should declare the death accidental. The County is badgering him to close out the case.'

'He asked me the same thing.'

'I said no other interpretation was plausible, given the facts at hand.'

'Me, too. Or something like that. But you're the expert. Mean more coming from you.'

'The presence of solder in the barrel of the gun is the only aspect left unexplained. I'd call that a question of engineering, more your bailiwick.'

'Yeah, I can't explain that either. Sobol was an engineer himself, maybe he tinkered where he shouldn't have.'

'That's my sense,' he said, looking at me with eyebrows arched in that way only guys with Burton's pedigree could get away with.

'Indeed,' I said, one of Burt's favourite words.

I lifted my jelly jar to the light. 'Well, I'm ready. What do you say?'

I went back out to the kitchen to get us each a refill. When I came back Eddie had staked out a dominant spot on the sofa, but I fought back a share.

'Pain in the ass.'

'And it looks like Roy Battiston is pleading out,' said Burton.

'That's what Jackie told me,' I said, after getting resettled.

'Rather forthcoming of her.'

'She'll tell you anything if you catch her at the right moment.'

'He'll only do a little jail time, but that's irrelevant,' said Burton. 'His life is over. At least the life he wanted to live.'

I didn't know exactly what to say about that, so I didn't say anything at all. I sat there and sipped the bourbon, scratched Eddie's head and pretended to be contemplative. Burton finally saved us all by filling in the dead air.

'You'll never guess who I've taken on as a client.'

'I didn't think you did that anymore. Unless you're talking about Spielberg, or General Motors.'

'Mrs Battiston.'

'Really. Interesting.'

'I thought so. She came to me. Apparently because of you.'

'Not my idea.'

'Indirectly. She said you only had nice things to say about me.'

'Yeah, but I didn't say you took clients. Like, what the hell for?'

'She's filing for divorce,' said Burton. 'Apparently sufficient grounds.'

'I guess.'

'She asks about you every time I see her. Tells me to tell you to call her. She won't call you, I suppose. Can't imagine why. You have a phone, or at least you did at one point.'

He looked around the room inquisitively.

'It's in the kitchen,' I told him. 'Good old Western Electric.'

'So, what should I tell her?'

I really do like Burton Lewis. I'm always happy to see him. Though sometimes I wish he had a better instinct for things I like to talk about and things I don't.

'That she's got the world's best lawyer.'

'One skilled in pursuing evasion.'

Not knowing exactly how to respond to that, I got off the sofa and went out to the porch to get a better angle on the bay. All clear. Cloud cover was still a uniform, low altitude grey, but you could see some clearing along the western horizon. A harbinger. I went back to my guest, hoping he hadn't noticed I'd been gone for a few minutes.

'So how's everything else, Burt? Isabella keeping you in line?'

'I suppose since Mrs Battiston owns Regina's property, that makes you, technically, next-door neighbours.'

'Amanda. Soon to be Amanda Anselma. Owns almost everything around here, which means she could be a neighbour of yours before you know it.'

'Do you know what she plans?'

'No idea. Haven't talked to her in four months. And I don't want to know. She could own the whole fucking world and it's not going to interfere with my nine-tenths of an acre.'

'Just curious.'

'Indeed.'

'About your social inclinations. Planning to hole up again?' He took another sip from the bourbon and looked at me in anticipation. 'Do you want to go out on the porch again before answering?'

Whenever I did a mental accounting of friendships past and present I tended to draw a line between pre- and post-Billy Weeds, demarcated by the day I learned he'd died in Vietnam. I'd always thought of him as my best friend, though in retrospect, I guess he was the only friend I had. So after he died I had trouble attaching that label to any subsequent relationship. Even to people I liked, like Burton Lewis or Jason Fligh. Or Paul Hodges. That made it easier, maybe, to ignore them. To invest almost nothing in sustaining connections with other human beings, so I could devote all my attention to doing what I thought I was supposed to be doing as an adult. Achieving, producing things, solving puzzles and developing octane-enhancement technologies. And avoiding deadly threats, like human kindness and affection. The deadliest of all.

'Geez, Burt, and here I am buyin' you a drink.'

'Just asking.'

'Jesus.'

'So you're in the mood to be sociable.'

'What the hell do you think I'm doing? You know, we are sittin' here talking, for Chrissakes.'

'So I can ask her in. Probably getting cold in the car.'

'You got somebody out in the car? What the hell for?'

I started to stand up, but he waved me down. Eddie jumped up and looked around, on alert.

'I promised her I'd check the temperature in here first. Soften you up.'

I sat back down on the sofa.

'What are you doing, Burt? You know I hate that shit.'

'I know. That's why I had to talk her into coming. But now that she's here, try to act like a civil human being. She is your only daughter, after all.'

When he left with Eddie to go out to the car I made a full retreat to the farthest end of the sun porch, where I had a miserable old oak drop-leaf kitchen table, brass pole lamp and assorted ashtrays. I sat down and looked out at the water. That rise in the cloud cover to the west had already made its way to about twelve o'clock high, opening a band of pale blue sky.

So I sat there and waited, fortified by bourbon on the rocks and the pallid white glare of the winter sun as it lit up the wave tips dashing across the sacred Little Peconic Bay.

Published in Great Britain by:

Ashgrove Publishing

an imprint of:
Hollydata Publishers Ltd
27 John Street
London WC1N 2BX

Originally published in the UK by Robert Hale Ltd.

Published in the USA by The Permanant Press.

ISBN 978 185398 176 0

First Edition

Book design by Brad Thompson

Printed and bound in England